THE BLOOD OF GODS AND MONSTERS

MORTAL GODS
BOOK THREE

LUCINDA DARK

MORTAL GODS 3

THE BLOOD OF GODS AND MONSTERS

USAT BESTSELLING AUTHOR LUCY SMOKE WRITING AS

LUCINDA DARK

When did a dragon ever die from the poison of a snake?

— FRIEDRICH NIETZSCHE

Copyright © 2024 by Lucy Smoke LLC

All rights reserved.

No part of this book may be reproduced in any form or by any electronic or mechanical means, including information storage and retrieval systems, without written permission from the author, except for the use of brief quotations in a book review.

Developmental Editing by Heather Long

Line Editing by Kristen Brianne at Your Editing Lounge

Proofreads by Alexa Reads

OG Cover Design by Simply Defined Art

CONTENTS

Glossary/List of Gods	xi
1. Kiera	1
2. Kalix	9
3. Kiera	15
4. Kiera	22
5. Ruen	33
6. Kiera	40
7. Kiera	55
8. Kiera	72
9. Theos	84
10. Kiera	89
11. Kiera	98
12. Kiera	106
13. Kiera	124
14. Ruen	132
15. Kiera	149
16. Kiera	158
17. Kiera	169
18. Kalix	184
19. Kiera	192
20. Kiera	201
21. Ruen	209
22. Kiera	221
23. Theos	230
24. Kiera	234
25. Kiera	243
26. Ruen	251
27. Kiera	255
28. Ruen	267
29. Kiera	279

30. Kiera	286
31. Kiera	294
32. Kiera	304
33. Kiera	312
34. Kalix	322
35. Kiera	328
36. Kiera	335
37. Kiera	345
38. Kiera	353
39. Kiera	362
40. Kiera	382
41. Ruen	389
42. Kiera	394
43. Theos	399
44. Kiera	406
About the Author	413
Also by Lucinda Dark	415

GLOSSARY/LIST OF GODS

Ariadne: (Upper God) Goddess of Darkness
Axlan: (Lower God) God of Victory
Azai: (Upper God) God of Strength
Caedmon: (Upper God) God of Prophecy
Day of Descendance : a national Anatol holiday to celebrate the day that the Gods descended upon the mortal realm.
Danai: (Upper God) God Queen, Goddess of Beauty and Pain
Dea: (ancient language) endearment meaning either "goddess" or "fortune/treasure"
Demia: (Lower God) Goddess of Birds
Denza: money, currency
Divinity: magic or otherworldly abilities possessed only by those who are Gods or descended from Gods.
Dolos: (Lower God) God of Imprisonment
God City: A city chosen as tribute to the Gods, usually more opulent and wealthy than smaller cities that are ruled by God Lords.
God Lord: A God/Goddess that has been granted rights to rule over a specific town, city, or territory as its governing head.

Gygaea: (Upper God) Goddess of Strategy
Hatzi: (Lower God) God of Travel
Hinterlands: unsettled lands outside of mortal and immortal civilization inhabited by monsters and Nezeracians. The only piece of land upon the Anatol Continent that is not ruled or inhabited by Divine Beings.
Makeda: (Upper God) Goddess of Knowledge
Maladesia: (Lower God) Goddess of Praise
Mortal God: A mortal with God/Divine ancestry
Narelle: (Lower God) Goddess of Scribes
Nezeracians: Nomadic mortal tribes or individuals that usually live in the hinterlands.
Pachis: (Lower God) God of Study
Sigyn: (Upper God) Goddess of Strife
Talmatia: (Lower God) Goddess of Vanity
Terra: term used for the human/mortal servants that dwell and serve the Gods and God children within the Mortal Gods Academies.
Tryphone: (Upper God) King of the Gods

CHAPTER 1
KIERA

11 years old...

My feet drag along a stone floor. The smell of something wet and rotten enters my nose, but I have no energy left to flinch from it. My eyes are swollen and my limbs don't react as the two men hauling me through the hall cut a corner too close and my foot catches on a crack in the ground. The toe of my boot gets lodged and nearly rips my foot off before the crack releases me.

Breath saws in and out of my chest. I've never felt so weak in my life. When was the last time I saw the sun? I miss it. I never thought I'd miss being outside. I never even contemplated a time when it wouldn't be readily available to me.

The harsh burn of tears threatens to fill my eyes. I don't even try to hold them back, but instead, I let them flow free and down my dirt smeared cheeks. I want to go home. The craving is so sharp and desperate that I choke back another sob as more tears fall.

"Here," one of the men snaps. One side of my body sags as the man who had been holding me up there disappears. The creaking *of metal fills the silence as the faint scent of urine burns my nostrils.*

Lifting my head slightly—as much as I can manage in my current state—I spot the opening of a dark room. A cell. A shiver chases up my spine. There's no window. No light. I bite down on the urge to beg these men to free me, to not hurt me. They're going to, whether I ask them or not. I'm starting to learn that it's better to just keep my requests to myself. Adults can't be trusted. Not anymore.

The man who is still holding me drags me forward and then tosses me inside. My side hits the ground hard, and I let out a soft cry of pain as it rattles through my body. The brimstone cuffs on my wrists dig into the skin there, and somehow, it makes me feel even more tired than I know I should be.

I've always been sturdy. A strong girl, my dad had often praised me. His strong girl. I close my eyes once more, ignoring the physical pain as the emotional agony takes over all thought.

"Daddy..." My lips form the word, but it's barely more than a gasping whisper. The last of my strength is sapped from me and disappears as the door to my cell is shut once more and I hear a lock click.

I don't know how long I lie here like this, unmoving, uncaring, wishing for someone to come and take me away from this horrible place. I don't care if that means I'll go to the bad place Dad always talked about. The place where villains in stories go. So long as I'm not here without him, anywhere would be better.

My mouth grows dry, tasting of dust and air. My head swims away from itself. I recognize that my body remains in place, but my mind ... my mind goes to distant places. Far, far away.

By the time I come back to myself, there are clinking footsteps echoing up the stone walls, reverberating all around me. Too loud. Too much. I cannot figure out where they're coming from. Then they stop and silence descends once more.

I sink deeper into the mind that has become my safe haven. The place that makes me forget ... everything.

"Have you given up?"

The sound of another's voice shoots through me like an arrow spearing into flesh and bone. I jolt and my eyes flicker open. I find that I'm lying on my side, facing the cell door where a woman now stands. She's beautiful, or at least, I think so. Dad never really spoke about beauty much but to tell me that I was always beautiful, just like my mom. Whoever she is.

The woman stands there, head canted to the side and arms crossed. At her side, a boy with a bored face watches me. His face is of an olive complexion with a cleft in his chin. His hair is dark and shorn close to his head. Equally dark eyes glance up at the woman before looking back at me. His expression doesn't change. Something vile reaches into my chest and grabs ahold of my heart. How can he not feel ... anything as he looks at me?

The anger rears its ugly head in a way it hasn't since the cuffs had been locked onto my wrists that horrible night and I had been forced to watch as my father was beaten and killed. Had this woman been the mastermind? Had she sent them? My upper lip curls back from my teeth.

I'll kill her.

"Mother, do I have to be here?" *the boy asks.*

The woman scowls. "What have I told you about calling me Mother, Carcel?" *she snaps. The boy ducks his head, but his face blanches in clear irritation and hurt. A selfish piece of me enjoys his pain.*

"Sorry, Guild Master," *the boy, Carcel, replies.*

The woman jerks her head towards the end of the corridor that lies outside of this cell. "Go back to training," *she orders.*

Carcel doesn't waste any time following the command. Without a second glance back at me—the girl in the dirty cell—he scampers off, and after a few moments, the woman and I are alone. She turns her attention back to me.

"Are you going to answer me?" she demands.

I blink slowly, confused by her words. "What?" I croak.

"Have you given up?" she repeats her earlier question.

That depends, I decide. Pressing my bound hands flat on the icy stone, my elbows shake back and forth with the effort it takes for me to sit up. I glare at her. "Did you send those men after me and my dad?" I ask instead of answering.

She tilts her head to the other side and continues to stare at me. "No," she finally says. "I didn't send them. They sold you to me when they found out that you were a Divine Child."

My limbs nearly collapse. If she's not the one responsible then it doesn't matter anymore. I sink back to the floor and close my eyes again. A few moments pass.

"So, that's it then, girl?"

My eyes reopen and I fix her with a dead look. "What do you want?"

"I want an answer to my question. Are you going to lay there and die in my dungeons or ... are you going to survive?"

What would be the point? I want to ask her. Nothing matters anymore. My dad is dead. My only family. Unless she's willing to let me go home, to let me return to the Hinterlands—the only place I've ever known—then I don't want to survive. I want to die with my dad.

The woman, tall and straight backed in her leather trousers and cream-colored tunic tucked into the high waistband, clucks her tongue as if she's disappointed by my lack of response. "I had hoped that you and I could have a good working relationship, girl, but if you're so pathetic that one little bad day will leave you to give up this easily, I suppose..."

One bad day? I sit up again and the room spins. I ignore it. "My dad is dead!" I yell. "And you bought me like cattle. What do you want me to do?" I'm a freaking kid. This isn't fair. None of this is fair. Fresh tears prick at my eyes. I want my daddy.

The woman steps closer to the bars and turns those cold brown and gold flecked eyes of hers down on me. "I want you to fight your way back to the surface, girl," she states. "I want you to make a deal with me."

I glare at her, untrusting. "A deal? What kind of deal?"

Her arms unfold and fall to her sides. "Do you know what you are?" she asks me.

Of course I do. I'm special. My dad told me that I was a girl made of two different worlds, born of a love for both.

As if she senses my thoughts, the woman nods. "You are a Mortal God, child, young and so powerful," she tells me. "If you agree to my deal, then you can be free."

Free? Why can't she just free me now? "Let me out," I snap in response, struggling to drag myself closer to the bars. I'm not far, merely a few feet, but it feels like miles until my fingertips brush the edge of the cold metal.

The woman's chuckle might be close to laughter, yet it is anything but amused. She bends down, crouching low on her feet as our eyes meet closer this time. "That's not how the world works, little girl," she says. "It's give and take."

"You took me!" I yell at her, the fingers of one hand wrapping around the bar in front of me as my other hand hangs next to it, trapped in the cuffs still. "So give me back!"

She shakes her head, the dark swath of brown hair held in a ponytail at the back of her head swishing with the movement. "I bought you," she reminds me. "I didn't take you. If you want your freedom, you'll have to pay me back."

"I..." I don't have any money.

The woman nods, understanding what I don't say in that uncanny way of hers. "So, a deal is the only way you can get out of here," she tells me again. "Will you agree?"

I bite down on my lower lip as it trembles. When listening to the fairytales Daddy had told me, there had always been a hero, always someone who comes in at the last moment to save the damsels in distress. Now, there is no one. This isn't a fairytale or a story. This is real life, and no one is coming to save me. I have to get up and do it myself.

"What do you want me to do?" *I lower my head as I ask the question.*

When the woman replies, I can hear the triumph in her voice. "Work for me," *she says.* "Become one of my assassins—I will train you, feed you, and ensure your protection—in return, all you have to do is survive."

I lift my head again and fix her with a suspicious glare. "That sounds too easy."

She throws her head back. This time, when she laughs, it's a full-bodied sound. Her throat moves and her shoulders twitch as she laughs. It goes on and on until finally the sound drifts away and she glances back to me, lifting one hand to wipe away a stray tear of mirth from beneath her eye.

"It won't be easy," *she replies.* "It'll likely be the hardest thing you'll ever have to do. Being an assassin is no simple task. To be what you need to be in order to survive, you need to become everything that you fear. I can't promise that you won't suffer loss from this moment onward. I can't promise that you'll get that vengeance that I can see so clearly reflected in your eyes, child."

My head ducks again, hiding the truth she's already seen. The woman reaches through the bars and tucks two fingers beneath my chin. She lifts my head so that my eyes are level with hers once more.

"I will teach you everything you need to know to endure this world. I will teach you to be colder than ice. To walk through fire without flinching. To seduce and destroy with a mere glance." *My breath catches in my throat, but she continues. "I will teach you to rip this world apart with your bare hands and teeth."*

"Why?"

She pauses at that, as if surprised by my question. The closer she is now, the more I realize that her eyes aren't just green. They are flecked with spots of gold and brown. They remind me of quiet mornings in the forest of the Hinterlands.

"Because," she finally says, "someone did the same for me once." She pulls her hand away from my face. "And because I can use you. Remember that, girl. Nothing in life is free. If you want to live, grab on to any reason. Death cannot be taken back, but life has a way of changing a soul. Altering you in different phases to fit everything that it throws at you."

I stare at the woman, my eyes aching from so much crying that it hurts to keep them so fixated without blinking. Still, I stare. In the fairytales, girls are soft and sweet. Girls are saved. This woman doesn't look like she needs anyone to save her, and I want that too.

She moves to the cell door as if she already knows my answer. Maybe she does. She seems to know my thoughts better than I know them myself. The lock clicks open and the bars swing outward. The woman stands in the entryway and holds out her hand to me.

"My name is Ophelia," she says, introducing herself at last. "Will you make a deal with me, young God Child?"

Using my hold on the bar to my cell, I drag one foot up and stomp it into the dirt and stone floor beneath me. Then I do the same with the other until I'm standing on shaking legs. I stumble, catching myself on the side of the cell as she just stands there. Ophelia doesn't reach out to stop me from falling and she doesn't move any further into the small cramped space.

Ophelia waits for me because this needs to be on my own power. I need to make the decision. Inhaling sharply, I lean away from the bars, my bound hands grazing her fingers until she closes her hand around one of mine.

"Yes," I answer. "I'll make a deal with you."

Her lips curve into a smile that sends tendrils of fear skittering down my spine. I mentally stomp on that fear.

Become what I fear, she'd said, and I wonder if she knew that meant I'd become someone like her. Will I become someone like her?

"Good girl." Ophelia tugs me forward and out of the dank cell. It's not freedom. I know that. But it's a start and a start is all I need.

CHAPTER 2
KALIX

Present Day...

I *don't like this.* In the dimness that lies beyond the window, two shadowy figures—one with hair of silver moonlight and the other with hair of white dawn—slip deeper into the darkness below the window of the great room. The fire in the hearth at my back cracks as the logs break and the scent of pine and ember fills the room. My eyes remain locked on the glass, but now that Theos and Kiera are out of my sight, I switch my attention to the reflection the window presents.

Ruen paces the length of the space behind me, back and forth, back and forth. His booted feet echo up the walls with each passing step he takes. One step. Three. Five. Ten. He pauses for a moment, the soft swish of his clothes shifting through the air as he turns, and then the process starts all over again.

A seed of displeasure uncurls in my gut. *When have I ever felt so much wrongness in a decision?*

Never, I acknowledge. No. I do not feel wrongness. I do *what* I want and I do it *when* I want. *Why, then, am I now allowing someone else to dictate my actions?*

The answer comes to me as clear as any opening for attack. The beautiful creature that I've become obsessed with known as Kiera Nezerac confuses me.

I turn away from the window and stride across the room. In a blink, I'm past where Ruen paces and I rip up my cloak, slinging it around my shoulders and clipping it into place. The thudding sound of steps at my back ceases.

"Where are you going?" Ruen demands.

I pivot back slightly to glance at him over my shoulder. "I am following them," I state the answer, not a question of my own, and certainly not a request.

His hands fist at his sides and he shakes his head. "You can't. We decided to—"

"*You* decided," I say, cutting him off. "I did no such thing. I will follow them. You may stay if you wish."

I turn to go.

"*Kalix*." Ruen's angry growl does nothing to slow my pace as I stride towards the door. His feet stomp against the floors. "Gods damn it, Kalix. Just—" My hand settles on the knob. "Wait a damn minute! I'm coming with you."

Only at his last words do I finally pause, arching a brow as I cast a look over at him. Ruen glares at me even as he grabs his own cloak and tosses it over his shoulders. "Why are you so intent on this?" he demands as he fastens the clip to hold the thing on to his body.

I shrug. "Let the Terra go with no more than Theos?" I give a half laugh as a response. "It was a stupid idea to begin with."

Midnight blue eyes rove over my face as if looking for any

sign of deceit. I let him. I have no reason to hide my desires. "She's just a girl," Ruen grits out, the words squeezing forth through clenched teeth. My lips twitch in amusement. It sounds as if he's trying to convince himself of that more so than me. "You've never been interested in anything this long. What's so different about her?"

I shake my head and twist the doorknob. "I suppose we'll find out, won't we?"

Ruen doesn't dignify my words with a response as we leave the chambers and descend the North Tower stairs. As we hit the outside area around our residence, the soft scent of Kiera drifts back to meet my senses. It's something sweet—floral—but then there's an underlying touch of musk, a spice that cannot be placed.

As Ruen takes the lead, striding ahead of me, my head pivots slowly back to the Academy. Within these walls, all I smell are decay and rot. Something is festering here. I don't have to have the ability of prophecy to know that much. It permeates every stone, every granule of dirt. Perhaps it has for a long time now. I don't know and I don't really care.

Even Olivia was beautiful in death, perhaps more so because she finally stopped whining. A bolt of unease whips through me as an image of Kiera in the same place as my mother slips into my mind. Eyes open and unseeing, body cold and blue with the lack of air. Hanging and lifeless. My upper lip curls back as the bite of rage throbs in my veins.

Kiera Nezerac will not die. I'm not done exploring her yet.

"Kalix." Ruen's sharp whispered bark pierces my thoughts and brings me back to the present. Already at the wall of dead foliage we use to slip in and out undetected, he gestures me forward with a furrowed brow. "Come on," he snaps. "If you want to catch up with them then we need to hurry."

I don't speak as I follow him through the opening he's created, a real thing to the illusion that hides it. Together, we come out along the other side and the tingle of Ruen's power spills over me as one of his illusions clings to my cloak and hides me from view just as I assume it is for him. With it in place, we don't look back or worry that the sentries will spot us as we head into the city of Riviere.

Only once I glance back, spying the fires along the Academy walls. At any point, we could have left this place. We could have disappeared into the world and never again had to bow to the whims of our Sire and the Gods he belongs to. There is something powerful, though, something sinister and pleasing about staying when you can leave. They think they can control us, but nothing ever can.

Well, perhaps not nothing…

The image of a Terra, a lying little thief and secret that should not exist emerges once more in my mind's eye. This time, however, the taint of death isn't upon her. She is life itself. Blood and madness and a storm so brilliant that I cannot recall a moment where I did not desire her, where I did not crave to take her and break her open just to see if her blood runs as red as the rest of ours.

Minutes pass into an hour as Ruen and I speed into the city. We hit the streets, deserted after dark save for the few who still linger on the cobblestones in darkened corners—whores fucking in alleyways and drunks stumbling home from the taverns.

"Up." That one word is all I need and together, Ruen and I leap for the rooftops. It's far easier to make our way across the layout of Riviere this way. I lift my eyes to the night sky even as my hood cloaks my face. The moon hangs with an illuminating glow above our heads, reminding me of Kiera. The color like her hair, and the soft shiny smoothness, her face.

My brother's scent hits me. "We're close," I announce.

Ruen nods his agreement. A moment later, I spy the shadow of Kiera—her long hair glowing brightly under the moonlight—as she dashes across the street and into one of the several rows of dilapidated townhouses across from an open alley.

Theos' scent is stronger here. Ruen and I dive off the rooftops and head towards the alley. Just as I knew he would be, Theos steps in front of us a moment later, his face twisted with irritation.

"What the fuck are you doing here?" he demands, arms crossed.

Ruen nods to me. "Kalix wouldn't stay back and I had to ensure he didn't cause any trouble."

My smile is vicious and full of teeth when Theos turns his accusing eyes on me. "Sure, Ruen," I say around my grin, "blame me, but we both know you wanted to see this through as well."

He doesn't reply, not that I expect him to. Theos uncrosses his arms and shoves a hand into his hair. The hood of his cloak falls back. His eyes span over our shoulders towards the townhouse. "She went inside a moment ago," he says, not even bothering to chastise either of us further—almost as if he expected that we would follow. Perhaps he did.

As one, the three of us turn to face the building across the street. Though the front is dark, I sense light further inside and know if I close my eyes and focus my senses hard enough, I'll be able to pinpoint how many await us.

"She wanted me to wait here." Theos' words are ripe with amusement. Yes, maybe he did know that we would be along behind them because otherwise, he would already be where I know we'll end up—at her side.

I step from the shadows of the alley and stare upward. Ruen sighs and follows as does Theos. Little minds twist out of the darkness, reaching for me—curious and nervous. My smile turns wicked.

Until my interest wanes, there is nowhere Kiera Nezerac can go that I will not follow, nowhere that I cannot find her.

CHAPTER 3
KIERA

Fate is a fickle creature. Men say Fate is a woman and women say it is a man. It is neither. That much I do know. Fate is its own gender, neither one nor the other, but it is fickle regardless of which sex receives the blame.

If my father taught me anything, it is that fate will choose if you do not. It is both clean and dirty, bloodied and innocent. It is all things and we are its servants.

My father's words echo in the back of my mind as I stare across the room at the man—the God—who stands there. All of the actions I've chosen, the survival I've clawed from the world, have led me here. No amount of obligation or duty would have changed this outcome, I think.

In the end, we are but Gods and monsters in the face of Fate's ultimate choice, and that cruel beast has tricked me. I thought I was making my own choices. Now, reality is punching me in the face. Nothing that I've done was of my own choice. I was bound to this path all along.

At least, that is what Caedmon's eyes say.

I stare at the God of Prophecy for several long seconds

despite the fact that I didn't come here for him. In fact, I hadn't expected that he would be here at all. Why would I? He should be back at the Academy, none the wiser that I had slipped out from behind its prison-like walls.

The fact that he's standing across from me in the poorly lit secret room beyond the quarters I'd thought Madam Brione kept for herself is more than a little unsettling; it's confusing. And if he's here, then that means he knows. He knows who—*what*—I am, and that makes all of us well and truly fucked. Or at least, we should be.

I look to the lone woman in the room other than myself—completely ignoring Carcel's irritated and narrow-eyed expression as he stands on Caedmon's other side. Ophelia's gaze is enigmatic with no hint of what the fuck is going on, no explanation for the reason behind the God's presence.

Caedmon clears his throat, a decidedly human sound that has my eyes flashing back to him. Just like that, Ophelia's presence becomes little more than a blight in the back of my mind as I fix my attention solely on the most dangerous presence in the entire room. My skin tingles with awareness and without thinking, I reach for the lone blade strapped to the small of my back.

Caedmon shakes his head. "I wouldn't do that if I were you, Kiera."

My movements still and my gaze narrows on him. The Gods I've killed have always been lesser ones. Gods who wouldn't be missed and who had no connection to the God Council or even the Mortal Gods Academies meant for their Divine Children. I do not doubt that if I tried to attack Caedmon right now, I would lose. No amount of training or years of service to the Underworld can prepare one to go up against a being who can see the various pathways that no doubt exist in the future.

As my hand slowly edges away from my dagger, my eyes flash back to Ophelia. Her expression remains shrouded. *Of course, it does.* She's harder than even Ruen to understand and always has been. It's been months since I last saw the woman who's raised and trained me for the last decade, but the time apart hasn't changed a single thing about her.

Her thick hair is braided and coiled tight, fixed to the top of her head by invisible pins. Streams of silver weave in and out of the dark strands, perhaps one of the few features that indicate her age. Her face is clean and devoid of makeup, but she's never needed it. No. Ophelia is a beautiful woman with or without makeup even if she's not Divine. With her high cheekbones, angular jawline, and glittering brown eyes with flecks of gold in them, she's everything I'd expect a Guild leader to be.

Cold, professional, and above all, calculating.

"What's going on?" As much as I want the question to sound like a demand, it comes out a bit more breathless than I intend and I inwardly curse myself.

Ophelia straightens away from the table she and Caedmon stand behind. Her son shifts on his feet, gaze passing from her to Caedmon and then back to me. My attention doesn't stay on Carcel but on Ophelia and Caedmon. The position of their bodies—close, but not touching—tells me that while they might be familiar with each other, neither truly trusts the other. My attention flicks from their bodies to their faces once more.

"Come in, Kiera." Ophelia's command is spoken with a cool, but succinct tone, brooking no argument.

I release a breath. She sounds like an irritated Mistress ordering the loyal dog that doesn't quite know anymore if it should trust her. That's exactly what I am—a loyal dog on the precipice of going against the one person I've trusted for the last ten years. Though Ophelia has always kept her emotions close to her chest, she's always been one of the few people I thought I understood.

Now, I don't know what to think of her. I am adrift in an ocean of confusion, and a violent storm is coming. I don't know if I'll survive it.

The sound of Regis' footsteps at my back has me turning as he approaches and stops a few feet away. The betrayal in my heart tightens briefly only to ease when he catches a glimpse of the God standing beside our Guild leader. He's a good actor—he's had to be to cover up the few misgivings he's always had being an assassin—but the shock and confusion in his expression are so sudden that I know it's not faked. He had no clue that Caedmon was here. Despite my current feelings towards him, that alleviates at least a small amount of turmoil currently roiling inside me.

I clear my throat and turn back to those standing across the room. "What," I repeat, "is going on?"

Dark eyebrows lower and curve inward as Ophelia's placid expression morphs into one of irritation. Her lips part, but before she can speak, Caedmon holds his hand out, stopping her. I half expect the woman I've never known to let herself be commanded by anyone to slap his hand aside. So, it shocks me when she doesn't. Her expression isn't mitigated, but she closes her mouth.

A sneaking suspicion creeps into my mind and with a jolt, a swarm of little minds call out to me. *Fuck.* It's only for a brief moment, but I close my eyes and reach back. The spiders that I'd used to watch my surroundings while I'd been staying here in the early days of my mission are there and they are nervous. Melding my mind with one of them, I spot not one, but *three* dark figures diving across the rooftop of the building. I could groan with annoyance. They're here. *Not just Theos but all of them.* Of course, they are. I should have known better than to expect that Kalix would stay behind, and if Kalix came, Ruen would follow—just to make sure he didn't slaughter anyone on his way.

Any hope I might have had that Theos would convince them to wait where I told him to dies a swift death. Even now, they're hovering just above our heads, waiting for what, I don't know. What I do know is that I want to strangle the lot of them.

Men never fucking listen.

I reopen my eyes just as Caedmon tilts his head to the side and sighs.

"You may as well tell them to come in," he says drily.

I stiffen. "I don't know what—" The denial evaporates as he sends me an exasperated look.

"Please don't insult me, Kiera," Caedmon says, cutting me off before I can finish the denial. "I may look unassuming"—he doesn't and never has, but I don't say as much—"but I know those boys very well. They would not have let you come alone. Go and tell them to come inside."

Ophelia's gaze snaps to my face and her lips curl down as a sure sign of her disapproval. I don't say anything. Instead, I simply turn away from the room, pushing past Regis as he continues to stare at the God with a pale face, and head for the door.

Moving through the first room, I enter the kitchen beyond and move for the back door rather than the front. The night is cool and it washes over my skin as I step outside. Air enters my lungs and then more as I suck in breath after breath. Now that I'm away from the prying eyes of Ophelia, Carcel, and Caedmon, true panic sets in.

"*Dea?*" As if he senses my impending meltdown, Theos' voice comes from the darkness above my head. The light brush of footsteps over roof slats echo back to me a moment before I hear the dull thud of a body dropping from the top of Madam Brione's shop and boarding house.

A flash of white and gold appears in front of me a second later. My eyes burn and no matter how much I breathe, I can't seem to catch enough air. Theos' brows lower over those shimmering eyes of his as he reaches up and cups both sides of my face.

"What's wrong?" he demands as the sounds of two more bodies dropping from the roof reverberate to the side of where we stand. "What's happened?"

I bite down on my lips hard enough that I taste blood. How did this happen? I ask myself. How did I fall so far? Ten years of training. Ten years of hiding. All of it down the drain in a single day. It's happening too fast and I am freefalling with nothing to break my descent.

"*Fuck*." Theos' dark curse ricochets off my ears a split second before he's leaning forward and pressing a kiss to my cheek. I blink and squeeze my eyes shut as his lips press into the skin beneath my eye and when he pulls away and I open them again, his lips are wet with my tears. "Don't—" Theos cuts himself off. "Fuck, please don't cry, *Dea*."

"What's happened?" Ruen's deep baritone lingers nearby but I can't reply as Theos closes his arms around me and pulls me into his chest. "Why is she crying?"

I am crumbling under the pressure inside me. They know. The Gods know—at the very least, Caedmon knows. What does that mean for me? What does that mean for the Underworld? Are they going to die? Am I?

"I'm not crying," I lie. *Fuck, I* am, and I can't stand it. Why am I crying?

Theos' palm touches the back of my head, moving down my skull, weaving fingers against the strands, gently petting in a way that shouldn't calm me but somehow does. Gods, some fucking assassin I turned out to be.

I allow myself the respite for a moment more, but that's all. Pressing my hands flat against his chest, I push away and am relieved not to feel the burning of tears in the back of my eyes anymore. "Caedmon is here," I say.

Three sets of dangerous eyes fall on me, and one by one, every single Darkhaven turns towards the back door leading into Madam Brione's. Kalix takes a step towards it, placing himself between me and the man now standing in the doorway.

I turn and level my gaze on Caedmon's earthen eyes. He stares over me at Theos and then swaps his attention to Kalix and Ruen who flank us. With a resigned sigh that doesn't appear all that perturbed by what he sees, he turns into the room and motions for us to follow.

Ruen and Theos exchange a look, but Kalix keeps his gaze fixed on Caedmon's back, and from where I'm standing I can't see his face. With nothing else to do, I pull myself from the pleasant circle of Theos' arms and follow Caedmon.

The only way to get the truth is to follow the God of Prophecy and, hopefully, he'll lead all of us to a logical conclusion that won't mean the end of my life or the Underworld.

CHAPTER 4
KIERA

When I return to the chambers, shadowed by three dark hulking figures, Regis is standing there along with Carcel and Ophelia. Ophelia's upper lip curls back. For a moment her scolding gaze lands on me and her eyes narrow, probably annoyed at how close they stand to me. Displeasure fills her expression. I bite back whatever angry words I wish to hurl at her. It's not my place. I turn my gaze to the floor.

The burn of someone's attention sears into my cheek and I glance up once to see Ruen frowning at me, flicking his eyes between me and Ophelia and back again. A dull, aching throb begins in the back of my head and spreads outward.

"Regis told me of your ... *relationship* with a trio of Mortal Gods, Kiera," Ophelia finally says, her voice crisp and tight. I don't flinch. "But I didn't think you would be so stupid as to bring them with you for our meeting."

Sucking in a breath, I lift my head to meet her gaze. "They know the truth now, so it only makes sense that I would bring them." I don't bother to mention that the three of them didn't give me much of a choice.

Her scowl deepens and she pivots to face Caedmon. "Did you know about this?" she demands, accusingly. "About *them?*" The way she says the word 'them' sounds as if she's uttering something as distasteful as the name of a soul-sucking puss-inflicted disease.

I glance at them. They're a bit prettier than a disease, but they're still definitely infectious. I can't seem to escape them. Still, I would also like to know if Caedmon foresaw this.

Caedmon sighs as he takes a seat in one of the lounges, and though Ophelia remains standing, Carcel curses quietly and shoots me a seething glare. If I wasn't still reeling from Caedmon's presence, I'd punch that look off his face. I've always detested the prick.

Carefully, though, I keep my eyes averted away from Regis —it hurts too much to look at him right now—and move toward the center of the room where Caedmon sits. "How long have you known the truth?" I ask him.

Caedmon leans back and casually lifts one arm to perch along the back of the lounge he's seated upon as if he doesn't have a care in the world. Yet with that same movement, his other hand drags down his face, making him appear frustrated as much as he is haggard. He's a dichotomy, this God. Powerful, feared, and yet ... he is the one God within the Academy that has never made it difficult to respect him.

"I've known who you were from the beginning, Kiera," Caedmon states clearly. "Since I'm the one that requested your services."

A frozen wave of shock descends upon me and I stop where I stand. Everyone else, too, it seems, pauses in surprise, save for Ophelia who simply blows out a breath and then moves to a bar cart across from where Caedmon sits.

"*You* are the client?" I clarify after a beat as the clinking of glasses grows too loud for my ears—the only sound in the room aside from our collective breaths. It hadn't been a test?

Caedmon nods.

"Then who is the intended target?" I demand, rage starting to swell low in my stomach and cast warmth outward like long fiery branches because despite how much I pride myself on being so fucking elite, I never saw this coming. It's hard to admit that I'm not as good as I thought I was; perhaps it'd all been my own pride in the first place. "You never sent a name. I've been at the Academy for *months*—"

"There is no intended target," Caedmon says, dropping his arm from the back of the couch as Ophelia approaches and hands him a glass. "Well, not for the contract at least."

My eyebrows shoot up towards my hairline. Not just because of his statement, but because Ophelia never caters to others. The way she'd simply handed him a drink without him even asking makes it clear that even if the two don't trust each other, they're more familiar than I'd originally believed. She's not even attempting to hide it as she drops down at the far end of the couch and throws back her own glass of amber liquid.

I shake my head and fix my attention back on Caedmon. "You're the client that contracted me to kill someone in the Academy, but you never intended to send me a target?" For a moment, I want to look at Regis. I want to at least confirm that I'm not the only one who feels insane at the moment, but I can't. I don't. "What was the point? And how do you know Ophelia?"

"For fuck's sake," Carcel mutters, turning and kicking the toe of his boot against the wall. The picture frames hung against the wallpaper tremble with the action and a plume of dust falls from it. "This is ridiculous." He turns once more and glowers at his mother. "When we traveled here, you told me it was for your damned mutt—"

At my side, Theos tenses, but he isn't the one to interrupt Carcel. It's Ruen. "Now, I'm sure you're not referring to Kiera, are you?" The question is spoken casually—or at least, it would be were it not for the flash of red in his normally deep indigo eyes.

Carcel throws Ruen a dark look that doesn't surprise me in the slightest. Even if he can tell by simple context clues who the three men now standing in the room alongside me are, Carcel's never exactly been the subtle type.

"Forget him," I snap. "He's not the reason we're here. Caedmon," I refocus my attention—and hopefully the others'—back on the lone God in the room. "Why did you hire me if you didn't want me to kill anyone?"

Caedmon twists the glass in his hand, his expression turning contemplative. I've never been one for drama, but I swear, even if Caedmon isn't Dolos, he has the same penchant for production. I despise the fact that I must now sit here and wait for his response when it seems that he isn't quite sure if he wants to tell me. The muscles under my skin bunch and contract even as I try to force them to relax. Anger does not suit a situation such as this. Yet I can't deny that it is rising, stronger and faster with each passing silent beat.

As if sensing my impending outburst, the backs of Theos' knuckles brush against mine. He grabs ahold of my hand. My fingers feel cold in his grip, but I don't pull away as he threads his fingers through mine. I shouldn't let myself take comfort in the touch, but I can't find the energy to pull away either.

I can feel eyes on me, familiar eyes—Regis' eyes. Still, I refuse to look at him. He is *not* my friend. Still, a part of me wonders if he also told Ophelia about what happened with the Mortal God he killed. My eyes flash to her before returning to Caedmon. That's something they'll have to address later. First, I need to know why Caedmon is here and how he knew about me.

"Send your other assassins away, Ophelia," Caedmon says, turning the glass and watching the liquid slosh about. "I would like to reveal this information only to a select few."

"What?" Carcel's shrill cry of anger rebounds through the room. I close my eyes and resist the urge to roll my eyes. "Why should I have to leave?" he demands. "As the next head of the Underworld, I have a right—"

"You have a right to *nothing*," Ophelia snaps, cutting him off. "You are not yet titled my heir, Carcel. Disobeying orders and showing your emotions too readily make me think you're not at all suited for the position. Perhaps if you can prove to me that you can handle yourself adequately, I will change my mind. For now, I will have you and Regis leave."

My lips press firmly together. Though it amuses me greatly to see Carcel snap his lips shut and purse them in a sour expression like that of a child who's just eaten a lemon, there is nothing humorous about the current situation we all find ourselves in. Caedmon is part of the God Council. It's his duty to report my existence. Yet, why hasn't he?

Carcel growls his anger, but does little more than kick at the wall once more, sending more dust falling from the pictures, and then turns and stomps towards the exit. After a moment, Regis follows. His body slides through the room and I feel my muscles tighten, coiling as he grows nearer. Theos quietly nudges me further into the room and turns his back as Regis pauses alongside us. I wait, but Regis never says anything. Instead, the soft whoosh of air escaping his lips is all I hear before he strides from the room and the door closes behind him.

I release a breath I hadn't realized I was holding and pull my hand from Theos'. When he reaches for me again, I step out of reach and round the lounge to sit down in one of the few chairs stationed around the center of the larger room. I level a look at the God sitting there with a still-full glass of amber liquid.

"Well?" I prompt him with a gesture of my hand. "You said you would reveal all once they were gone. They're gone. It's your turn."

The side of Caedmon's full mouth twitches and curls upward. Then he says something completely unexpected. "You are so like your mother," he murmurs, voice full of amusement. "Same eyes and same attitude."

"My ... mother?" My God parent? My breaths grow shallow and the drumming beat of my heart is all that fills my head. "You know her?"

"*Knew* her," he corrects lightly, the humor fading as his lips thin into a dispassionate line. "I have not seen her since before you were conceived."

"Is she..." I hesitate to ask if the woman—the Goddess—who gave birth to me is actually dead. Though it isn't necessarily easy to kill a God, they *can* die. Somehow, I'd always assumed that she was out there somewhere, living her life and completely unconcerned with the fact that she'd left my father and me behind. Perhaps if she's dead, though, then it wasn't her fault that she'd left.

As much as I don't want her to be dead, another part of me almost wishes for it since that would mean that she truly had no choice in abandoning us. In the next instant, however, Caedmon dashes that kernel of hope.

"I don't believe her to be dead," he says, almost picking the thoughts out of my mind as he understands my unfinished question. "I do not know where she is, but I do know that she hasn't attended a God Council in twenty years and no one has seen her. Were she dead, however, I would feel it."

"You would *feel* it?" Panic swells in my breast. Did the Gods know when any other God died? No, that can't be true. If that were the case, then they would feel the deaths of each God I'd caused and they would've ... what? Found me? Even Gods do not have the instant ability to transport themselves through space and time.

"In a way," he says absently, his dark eyes going to the amber liquid in his glass as it sloshes back and forth with the movements of his hand. "Upper Gods, as you know them, as *I* am considered, all have ties to each other. There are many connections and even if some are cut—those ties dying off and removed completely—we can't always keep track of them. Your mother, however, is—was—once a very close friend of mine. I often check to see if she's still there, and as far as I can tell, she is."

"Can you ... would you be able to know where she is? How to find her?"

Caedmon shakes his head, lifting his gaze away from the glass clutched in his fist as he fixes his attention back on me. "No, I'm afraid not. All I can tell you is that I believe she still lives."

Slowly, I nod. It was ridiculous to get my hopes up. She's been gone for twenty years. Why would I ever expect that she'd return now?

"Fine," I say, sitting back. "Then tell me why you put in a request for my services and why you never intended to send a target."

Finally, Caedmon moves his glass closer to his face, places

the rim to his lips, and downs the fiery liquid. I almost wish I was the one drinking it. His throat bobs as he swallows with a gasp and then sets the glass down on the table before him before focusing on me.

"Do you still have the book I gave you?" he asks, surprising me. The question reminds me, though, of the strange text that had changed—altered from the original title to a new one that I hadn't understood.

I nod solemnly, biting down on my lower lip.

The corner of Caedmon's lips lifts. "And did you notice anything different about it?"

I swallow and nod again. "It ... wasn't the same book the second time I read it," I say.

"What book?" Ruen asks.

Caedmon ignores the interruption, never taking his eyes off me as he responds. "That book is special. It's not from the library of the Academy but from my own personal collection. It informs the reader of something they *need* to know versus what they *want* to know. I spelled it myself."

"It..." I glance away from Caedmon to Ophelia who watches on with a calm face. I know it's a facade. She's hard to read, but there's no chance she's as composed as she seems. "It said that the Gods aren't Gods at all."

Dark eyes flare. Caedmon sits forward. "Yes."

"I don't understand," I say when he doesn't elaborate. "The Gods are—"

"Liars," he says, cutting me off. "They—*we*—always have been. What else did the book tell you?"

"It said that the Gods came from a mountain of brimstone —I think it meant the original Mortal Gods Academy. The first one."

All those years ago, my father and I had traveled to Ortus, and from the seaside cliffs, I'd seen the great beast that was the very first Mortal Gods Academy. It had jutted up from a small island set in the crashing waves of the water, a dark crown of jagged black rock. It had been an intimidating thing, a monstrous creature of ancient stories. Sunlight had glittered off the black stone, shining back at where my father and I had stood on the shore, a beacon of warning.

"That's correct," Caedmon states, drawing me back to the present and away from my memories of the place in question.

I shake my head. "That still doesn't explain why you did what you did," I say, confused.

Caedmon inhales and releases his breath, the wide chest beneath his dark tunic expanding and deflating with the action. "What am I called, Kiera?" he asks instead of answering my unspoken demand.

I blink. "The God of..." *Prophecy,* I finish silently as my words trail off. "You ... had a prophecy then? But you just said that the Gods aren't—"

Full, masculine lips turn into a deep frown. "What makes a God?" Caedmon asks. "Is it the ability to control the weather? To alter time and space? No. A God is simply a being of worship that maintains total authority over life and creation. When the Gods as you know them came to this world that is what they wanted to become so that is what they became."

"I still don't understand." Why is he talking in circles? Why can't he just come out and say what he means? What is the point?

As if he feels the same, Ruen steps up to the side of my seat and frowns down at Caedmon. "You're saying that the Gods are not actual Gods at all?" he demands in that gruff baritone of his. Behind him, Theos and Kalix remain silent.

Caedmon shifts his gaze up to Ruen's. "What you know as Divinity is simply magic, Ruen," Caedmon says. "It is something we brought with us from our world and when we came to this place and found it devoid of magic, our ruler decided that we would become Gods in this new world."

"Your ruler ... Tryphone?" Ruen asks.

Caedmon nods. "Yes."

"But what about your prophecy?" I demand. "You still haven't explained why you brought me here, why you contracted the Underworld for my services if you never meant to use them."

"Oftentimes, my visions do not come clearly. They show me moments in the future that are murky—unsure as to whether they will happen or not. Then there are other times where my visions are so clear there can be no doubt as to whether or not they will come to pass. My ability is powerful, but it is not all seeing as one might think. I see all that will happen, but the choices made between when I see the future and when the future becomes the present may threaten to change the outcome."

I wait and this time, Caedmon doesn't stop.

"Twenty years ago, I had a vision such as that. A prophecy that is set within the fabric of time. They are rare visions, ones that cannot be changed and from what I have experienced, they only ever happen when the balance of the world has been altered too far. I fear that my people—Gods to this world—have taken their greed too far."

My gaze skitters to Ophelia, now holding her empty glass as she watches Caedmon with a cold look that tells me nothing of her inner thoughts. I frown as I notice the strings of silver in her naturally dark hair have grown wider since the last time I saw her. The lines around her lips and at the edges of her eyes are deeper too. It hasn't been that long ... has it?

"What does your prophecy have to do with Kiera?" Ruen's

voice drags my focus back to the conversation before me. "Answer her question—why did you bring her here?"

A beat of silence passes through the room. My muscles tense as Caedmon and Ruen stare at each other, then Caedmon's lips part and he speaks.

"Because she's the answer to all of our salvation."

CHAPTER 5
RUEN

*S*alvation. The last word that leaves Caedmon's mouth is the spark that lights the room aflame with activity. Theos stomps forward, the sound of his boots pounding against the dust laden floorboards.

"What the fuck does that mean?" he demands, sliding up to Kiera's other side as he stands above the God of Prophecy. His eyes are glittering, the gold flaring brighter before darkening. Black spreads out from his pupil, consuming all but a thin ring of the burnt amber at the edges of his irises.

Kiera remains silent, her brow puckered in confusion. A look at her face tells me she's as much in the dark about the meaning behind Caedmon's words as the rest of us.

Caedmon doesn't spare Theos a glance even though my brother is radiating aggressive energy. He merely continues to look at me as if waiting for something.

"Explain," I finally say. "No more stories, Caedmon. No more metaphors or talk of books. Tell us the prophecy you wish to see through and what it means for Kiera."

The edges of his eyes crinkle a little and his lips twitch as if he's amused. I bury my irritation at his expression. I fail to see the humor in our situation and already I am repressing my desire to rip into the woman at his side—the woman that had placed the brimstone in Kiera's neck as a way to control her. Before this night is through, I intend to have her remove it, and if she refuses ... well, Kalix isn't the only Darkhaven capable of murder, and Kiera's blood contract with the woman will be null and void if the woman known as Ophelia is dead.

I will release her from the shackles that bind her to the Underworld and I will slaughter anyone who stands in my way.

Caedmon sits back, reclining against the cushions of the lounge as he veers his gaze from me to Kiera and Theos and then over our shoulders, no doubt, to our final brother. Kalix, to my surprise, remains silent as he stands like a shadow against the wall. He hasn't made a sound since this conversation started, and I expect he's watching both Caedmon and Ophelia with more than his eyes. Of the three of us, he sees just as much beyond the realm one can perceive with their eyes. I hope he sees something we can use.

"The Gods are not Gods at all," Caedmon says, repeating what Kiera had said earlier. "We came here from another world, one in which we were not the most powerful."

"Why?" Theos bites out. "Why did you come here?"

I remain silent, curious about the answer.

"There was a war," Caedmon says quietly. "Our Kingdom ... it was falling. Different beings far greater than us, that could control more than we could—more than the weather, but the very structure of the world itself, ripped through the ocean in which our people built our society. Our cities collapsed. Our people drowned, burned, died."

The more he speaks, the more faraway his eyes grow, the life in them fading as if he's looking deep into his past and finding only darkness and horror. I'd seen that kind of look before—recognized it in myself the first time I looked into a mirror after Azai had slaughtered my mother. I cut that thought off before it can bloom into the memory.

"That still doesn't explain how you came to be here, in this world," Kiera says quietly.

"I could not say how or why the two worlds were connected, but as the last of our people gathered upon the final city—survivors pouring in and our own magic burning bright with the fear and hope of thousands—the fabric of our original world split open and a rift opened between the two spaces. Back then, Tryphone was a new King. His father had been killed amidst the battles with the other creatures. He led us—those who had survived into the tear. He assumed that any place would be better than where we were, pushed to the brink of extinction."

Tryphone had been right then. Because now they were here in this world and they were no longer a species being slaughtered, but the predators at the top of the food chain, ruling over everyone else. I keep my thoughts to myself, though, waiting for Caedmon to finish even as my blood heats with rage. The Gods had come into this world and overtaken it, lied to the populace of their greatness, and for what? The answer, I suspect, is obvious.

Why would a people persecuted and driven to the edge by beings more powerful than they come to a new world and overtake it? Because they feared repeating the past, and what better way to prevent themselves from becoming oppressed than by becoming the oppressors themselves.

"The stone that you know as brimstone—the original

mountain of it—was shattered open and from it, we crawled into this new place," Caedmon continues. "The first days were ... horrific. The people here were far less advanced and they feared us. Their language was different from our own and communication between our two peoples was a struggle at best. As a whole, we were traumatized. We feared that our pursuers would chase us here and when they didn't, we were too scared to hope. The brimstone mountain could not be destroyed, and for some reason—that which I do not know, perhaps something to do with the rift that was created within the stone—our magic was rejected by the stone and it became something that could harm us.

"As our days grew longer here and we acclimated to the society of this world, we came to understand that this land was devoid of magic. It had life, but the humans living in this world had no concept of controlling elements or the like. The first people who came across us labeled us as Gods, and after a while, we saw no reason to correct them."

"What's changed?" I ask. "If the ... Gods," I hesitate on the word, but as I have no other title for them, I simply settle on what I know, "have acclimated to this world, what has altered? *What* have they taken too far?"

Caedmon closes his eyes and shakes his head as if ridding himself of the memories he shared with us. When they reopen and settle on me, they are shadowed. I squash the sympathy I feel rising. Liars and deceivers don't deserve my sympathy. A sudden reminder that I am also both stabs at the back of my mind, but I ignore it.

"Our people were never meant to be immortal," he admits. "We are long-lived, yes. Hundreds of years long, but we are not infallible. Because of that and because we are Gods to the people of Anatol, Tryphone feared what would happen if it was found out that our people died naturally. Therefore, he has..." Caedmon swallows roughly and looks to the tabletop before him before continuing. "There is a way for our kind to extend our lifespans and to remain youthful."

A wave of ice washes over me. Palpable and familiar. *Fear*. To my utter surprise, Kiera leans forward as if she doesn't feel it. "What is it?" she demands. "What do they do to extend their lifespans?"

Caedmon's voice drops low and the room fills with a tension so thick that it wraps ugly tendrils around my throat, squeezing the breath from my lungs. I wait, my gaze burning into the being before me—the man that I once trusted more than any other God. No, false Gods.

"Magic," Caedmon answers so quietly that I must strain my ears to hear him clearly despite the choking of air in my throat. "Divinity as you know it."

"That doesn't tell me anything," Kiera snaps, her voice almost hoarse with frustration.

Caedmon's face pinches tight, his brows creasing together and his lips curling down to form lines bracketing either corner. He opens his mouth and then closes it again, grinding his jaw. I watch him carefully, confused by what I see. It's as if some geas, a vow of silence, is keeping him from revealing too much no matter how much he wishes to speak.

With long drawn-out breath, Caedmon unclenches his jaw and then lifts his gaze—first to hers and then to mine, where he holds. His stillness is unnatural. Disturbing. "Tryphone refuses to lose any more of his own people. The decisions he has made to protect the Upper Gods and the God Council are immoral. They are cruel and they are ... wrong."

When Caedmon closes his eyes after that statement, he looks years—decades—older than he's ever seemed before.

He reopens them and fixes them on Kiera. "A sacred taboo has been broken by us—the Gods as you know us—and the time has long since passed for it to be stopped. It should have never begun in the first place." Shadows dance beneath the God of Prophecy's eyes. They whisper of horrors and dread and death and carnage. Still, he doesn't tell us what it is that they do or what taboo they have broken.

"What is it that you've done?" Kiera's question, I'm sure, echoes all of our thoughts.

Silence is her only answer.

She curses under her breath and then shoots a glare at the man. "How can we do anything if you don't *tell* us?"

"Regardless of whether I reveal the act that must not be performed," Caedmon says, lifting a hand to his brow as if his temples are aching. His fingers tremble with the effort. A sick feeling rises in my gut. "You will be the one to stop it."

My head reels from what he's already said and as Kiera curses again, her voice an angry wave of annoyance and, yes, a little bit of fear, I consider the questions that permeate my mind. The Gods are not Gods? Their immortality is a façade? Does that mean that we, as their children, are no different? No, perhaps they are still Gods—after all, the definition is of a worshipped icon, and in this world, that is what they are. They may call themselves whatever they wish, but in this world where we were all birthed, they are the cruel Divine Beings that have ruled for centuries.

Tension builds as Caedmon slowly lowers his hand and when his gaze connects with mine once more, over Kiera's shoulder. Words fail me. My mind empties of all thought. My muscles sag and I have to reach out, clasping my hand over the top of Kiera's chair as I meet his eyes with understanding.

I'm right. I don't know how I know it, but I do. It is not

that Caedmon won't say the truth, it's that he cannot. *Dear ... realm of the Divine.* What *is* the taboo?

"How," Kiera finally asks, "am I the salvation?"

Caedmon's gaze slowly returns to her. The skin around his eyes squeezes, forming wrinkles on either side. His lips twist into a grimace. "You, Kiera, are of Tryphone's blood," he says, "and you are going to kill him."

CHAPTER 6
KIERA

"Kill Tryphone?" I repeat the words as if I heard him wrong. I know I must have, but then Caedmon simply nods, confirming the correctness of the statement. I sit back in shock. A beat of silence passes and then two and three. They continue to pass until I can't take it anymore. "Are you insane?" It's a legitimate question. If he thinks I'm somehow capable of killing the King of the Gods—never mind what he's revealed about the fact that they're not Gods at all but some sort of 'magical' species from another world—he has to be insane.

It's at that moment that Ophelia sits forward and sets her glass next to Caedmon's on the table set before them. "I have to agree with Kiera," she states. "She is well trained, but even she isn't capable of killing Tryphone. Even if what you say is true, he has several hundred years of experience on her. She's more accustomed to catching targets unaware."

"She will be able to catch him unaware," Caedmon states, gaze settled on my face as if he can somehow delve into my mind with simply a will of his own.

I frown as something more penetrates my realization.

"You said that I was of his blood, what did you mean by that? My father was mortal."

Caedmon is shaking his head before I've finished my statement. "Your father was not mortal, Kiera. Not completely."

"He was," I insist. "He never had any abilities and—"

"I know this, Kiera," Caedmon says, interrupting me. "Because I knew your father as well as your mother. Your father was a Mortal God and he was one of the first to—" His words cut off and he closes his eyes, raising a hand to his temple yet again as if he's in pain. Then he shakes himself and his lashes flutter upward once more.

Tension spreads through my limbs. I picture my father, the strong, barrel-chested man who had raised me, who had taught me right from wrong, who had carried me in his arms as he showed me the Hinterlands where I'd been born. He had been a Mortal God? Then ... what did that make me? More God than mortal? No, the Gods weren't Gods.

I shake my head. "You said that the Gods aren't actually Gods," I say, fixing my gaze on Caedmon again. "What are they? What are *you*?"

Caedmon's lips spread into a mockery of a smile. "You would not know of it here, but in our world, we were known as Atlanteans. Our Kingdom was massive and great and we stemmed from a city of prosperity called Atlantis." His pseudo smile falls in an instant. "Unfortunately, when we crossed over into this world, our great city fell and with it, the remains of our legacy."

"Atlantean." The word sounds strange, like something that doesn't belong on my tongue. My eyes squint. "Atlanteans are not Gods?" I clarify.

He shakes his head. "No. Atlanteans are simply long-lived humans," Caedmon answers. "In our world, Atlanteans are simply descendants of what are known as Fae and human races. Our magic and longevity come from our Fae ancestors and everything else, our human ancestry."

They weren't Gods but Atlanteans. Humans. *Mortal*. His earlier words make all the more sense. No wonder Tryphone had needed to find a way to lengthen their lives. They'd come into this world masquerading as Gods and Gods didn't die except under special circumstances.

Then the memory of what I'd discussed with Regis that very morning comes slamming into my head. "Does that mean that anyone can kill the Gods—the Atlanteans?" Is that why Regis had been able to kill that Mortal God? But then, why had the man disintegrated? If he, like any normal person, was just able to be killed then he wouldn't have turned to dust. Could Regis be wrong? Could he have been drugged when it happened?

Caedmon's lips pinch tight into a mulish line. "You're correct," he says, his words stilted, and for a moment I think he's read my mind, but then he continues. "There are many things that Tryphone spread to keep the people of this world from attacking our kind. The belief that mortals of this world are unable to kill us is one of them."

"Regis—" I stand abruptly and turn towards the door as it flies open. All eyes shoot to the figure standing there. It's not Regis though. Nor is it Carcel. Instead, the plump harried figure of Madam Brione stands in the doorway, her bosom heaving with great effort.

Her eyes fly wildly over the three figures of the Dark-havens—each of whom steps closer to me—and then skitter over Caedmon before focusing on Ophelia. "There is trouble, Ma'am," Madam Brione huffs out, her ruddy cheeks flushed with color.

Ophelia stands. "What's happened?"

"The Academy is alight with the flames of welcome," she hurries out, her words stumbling over one another. "Fires are being lit throughout the streets and," she swallows, an edge of fear and concern filling her voice, "carriages are entering."

Caedmon, too, stands. A hard hand lands on my shoulder and grips me tight. I look up as Ruen's face blanches. His normally tanned skin seems to leach of color in front of my eyes. Unthinking, I reach up and cup my fingers over the ones settled on my shoulder. Midnight eyes flick down to meet mine. I frown at him, but he merely shakes his head and removes his hand from me. I let him go even as confusion pours into me.

"What do the carriages have to—" Before I can finish my sentence, Caedmon curses low.

"The God Council," he snaps. "They weren't supposed to arrive for several more days."

I push up from the chair. "We have to get back," I say. "We can't be caught out."

Caedmon waves a hand in my direction. "Worry not about that," he says absently even as he drags a palm over his face, suddenly appearing far older than he looks, especially when his fingers tremble ever so slightly.

"Azai will be there," Theos says quietly on my other side.

As I turn to look at him, Caedmon responds. "Yes, he will, and I have no doubt that he will wish to see the three of you."

Azai, the Darkhaven's God parent—Atlantean parent, I mentally correct. It will be a struggle to remember that all that I have known for the past twenty years of my life is not the truth. Yet, harder still, I believe it will be for me to pretend to know nothing.

Before the conversation can be derailed completely, I direct my attention to Caedmon and Ophelia. "Regis went on a mission and he claims to have killed a Mortal God—he said that they disintegrated when he killed them, that he didn't know until it was too late."

Ophelia's expression tightens but that's all the reaction I get from her. I'm not surprised.

Caedmon sighs. "That is another thing we will have to discuss later."

"But you know why it happened?" I press, frowning.

Caedmon's soil-rich gaze meets mine. "There is plenty more that you do not know, Kiera. More still I cannot tell you or risk changing the future that I foresee."

Frustration pours through me. I've never been good at riddles and that's all he seems to be able to speak in. "What *can* you tell me?" I demand, my fingers clenching into fists.

Caedmon heaves a great breath, but before he can speak, Ruen's hand closes around my upper arm and tugs me back. Caedmon strides around the lounge and heads for the doorway where Madam Brione still stands, her wild array of frayed curls flying in every direction.

"We need to leave."

I ignore Ruen, pulling out of his hold despite his tone. "I have more questions," I call out to Caedmon as he gently nudges Madam Brione to the side and peers down the hallway past the kitchen.

"When did the carriages start to arrive?" Caedmon asks her.

A flurry of movement catches my attention and I turn to watch as Ophelia moves away from the lounges and heads back into the room where I'd first arrived to find her, Carcel, and Caedmon.

"Not but an hour ago," Madam Brione answers.

Caedmon's features darken. "I see." He clears his thunderous expression a moment later as he pastes a small smile on his face before looking back to Madam Brione. "I must thank you for allowing us the use of your home."

Madam Brione blinks up at him. No doubt she's shocked that a God would be so kind to her. "I-it is not a problem," she sputters out a moment later.

"Then we must hurry to be on our way." He looks back at the woman and nods. "Thank you again, darling."

My head spins and I can't tell where to set my eyes. Ophelia is in the smaller room, her hands scattering over the table, rifling through pages. Theos and Ruen squeeze ever closer, but Kalix's presence is practically a shadow still against the wall. The answers I've received tonight have only left me with more questions. My heart pounds in my chest.

"Caedmon, we haven't finished—" My voice is cut off as Ruen sharply pulls on me yet again, turning and twisting me behind him as Carcel reappears in the doorway leading out of the rooms. A low growl erupts from his chest as he practically pushes me against the wall.

No, not a wall, I realize as two familiar hands creep up and grab ahold of my upper arms. *Kalix.* I pull and tug against him. "Stop it," I hiss. "Damn it."

"Carcel," Ophelia calls from the back room. "Come help me."

Carcel shoves past Madam Brione and shoulders around Caedmon—not caring that he's a being far more powerful than himself—as he heads towards Ophelia. A dull pounding takes up residence in the back of my swirling mind. I can't leave like this without talking to Caedmon one on one.

"We have to go," Theos says, echoing Ruen's earlier words as the two look once at each other and then back at where Kalix and I stand.

Ruen's eyes slide over me and narrow on where Kalix's hands hold me in place before he shakes his head and turns back to Caedmon. "We'll return to the Academy," he announces. "If the God Council is arriving earlier than planned, we should be where they expect us to be."

Caedmon turns away from Regis and Madam Brione, his eyes finding Ruen's. Before Caedmon can agree or disagree, however, Kalix's hands tighten hard enough to hurt and I flinch under the grip on my arms.

"There is something else we must do before we leave," Kalix says, speaking for the first time since he entered.

All eyes are suddenly on the man at my back, even my own as I twist to glance at him over my shoulder. The green of his irises is nearly swallowed by the black of his pupils. *Is he ... angry?* I don't believe I've ever actually seen him angry before. Annoyed, yes. Thrilled by potential murder, absolutely. The expression on his face now is not one I've ever experienced and as I stare at the sharp lines of his features, the way his skin tightens over his high cheekbones, turning his face almost skeletal, I decide I never want to see him this way again. I go still, warning bells sounding in my head.

Ruen seems to understand what Kalix means though, and in a flash, he nods and is suddenly across the room in front of the doorway that leads into the smaller section at the back of the chambers where Carcel and Ophelia are.

"You," Ruen snaps, his cold midnight blue eyes glowering at Ophelia. "You will undo the blood contract with Kiera Nezerac."

The sound of blood rushing through my ears becomes louder than wind. Undo the contract with Ophelia? I tamp down the hope that blossoms in my chest. Shaking my head, I speak, "That's not—" What? Possible? Important right now? I don't get an opportunity to finish before Kalix clamps a hand over my mouth, silencing me.

"Quiet," he commands.

Rage replaces nervousness. My teeth sink into the pad of his palm in a split second and blood fills my mouth. Dragging me back further against his chest, Kalix drags a tongue up the back of my ear. "Bite harder, *little Thief*," he whisper-hisses into the shell. "I like it when you cause me pain. Makes my cock want to repay the favor."

I release him immediately with a growl of frustration. The taste of his blood remains on my tongue, a reminder. As if I need that right now with Kalix practically wrapped around me.

My attention fixates on Caedmon, who's watching all of us with a strange sort of contemplative look that I can't quite figure out. He's just as hard to read as Ruen is—or rather, was. I don't know when Ruen became easier to understand, but it's not something I currently have time to ponder.

As much as I want—*crave*—the removal of the brimstone and the end of my blood contract with Ophelia, I know it isn't that simple. "Caedmon," I say again, harder this time. When his eyes fall back to mine, I level him with a meaningful look. "I need a word—*alone*," I add the last word before any of the Darkhavens can protest, and yes, I know they want to.

Kalix's hands squeeze my upper arms in response. Gritting my teeth to keep from yanking myself from his grip and knowing that doing so would only serve to piss him off, I wait for Caedmon's response with little patience. A moment passes and then, finally—blessedly—Caedmon nods his agreement.

I'm out of Kalix's arms in a heartbeat, using my Divine speed—or Atlantean speed—unreservedly to make it across the room to Caedmon's side in an instant. "This way," I say, grabbing ahold of the God's arm and pulling him from the room.

Caedmon comes quietly, easily. I keep going until the two

of us are well away from the group of them. Even though I want to have the conversation sooner—I debate on stopping in the front of the shop, but then decide against it since we're still too close to prying ears for my peace of mind—I lead Caedmon up the stairs to the second floor and into the bedroom that was once mine.

The door shuts behind us and I'm suddenly alone with a man I thought was my enemy. A man who knows more about my past and who I am than I ever thought possible. For several long-winded seconds, we just stare at each other. One gaze seeking and the other ... enigmatic. Damn him.

Caedmon holds his arms out. "Well, you've got me alone, Kiera," he says with a slight smile. Is he amused? At *this* situation? His arms drop back to his sides. "What is it that you wish to ask?"

So much. I have so much left to ask, questions percolating and collecting in the back of my mind. They collide against one another like falling stars, crashing in giant, hulking waves of stardust and rocky uncertainty.

"You're not telling us everything," I finally decide on.

Caedmon arches a brow, but he doesn't deny it.

"Why do you think I can kill Tryphone?" I demand and as his lips part, I hold up a hand with a sigh. "And don't feed me that bullshit about being of his bloodline." A fact that I'm not entirely sure about, but that I'm certain he believes, and ... I don't know, maybe he's right. If he truly knew my parents, then maybe I am. That's something to be considered later though.

Caedmon closes his mouth and turns away from me. He strides across the small length of the room to the lone slit of a window on the far side away from the door next to the twin bed. He settles himself there, a shoulder pressed into the window pane as he gazes out into the night.

I take a step towards him. "How am I supposed to do anything if I don't know what's happening?" I ask him. "I need to know everything that you know."

"No." Caedmon shakes his head as the denial leaves his lips.

"Caedmon—" Frustration pours through me. What is the point of all of this? Why give me scraps of information that only serve to confuse me further?

"It's not because I don't want to," he says, surprising me into silence. "Believe me, were the decision mine and mine alone, I would tell you everything."

"Then why—" My words cut off again as his head turns, the gold of his jewelry glinting in the moonlight that comes in through the window at his side. I didn't realize how dark the room was until now. I should've lit a candle or something.

"The future is not always set in stone." Caedmon's voice is low as he speaks, and the sound of it sends chills dancing along my arms. "There are some things as ever-changing as the wind—one small detail may throw the events off course —and there are other things that will happen no matter what anyone does." When he turns towards me and meets my gaze, a glitter of gold slithers through his dark irises. My blood turns to ice in my veins as a fresh wave of something I've always tried to repress moves through me.

Fear. It's a heady and unwelcome presence but there nonetheless.

"Telling you everything would put the future I wish to see at risk," Caedmon explains. "So, yes, you're right. I haven't told you everything and I have no intentions to tell you. If you know, your actions may change, and therefore, the salvation I desire—that this world *needs*—may be in jeopardy."

I think about that for a moment. "The book you gave me," I start again, frowning as something niggles at the back of my mind. A question I can't quite reach. "You said it's spelled to tell me what I need to know."

Caedmon continues to stare at me, the flecks of gold mixing with the dark brown of his gaze. Gold like Theos' eyes. "That's not a question," he states.

I frown. "Do I have to ask a question for you to tell me something that's not a riddle?" I snap.

His lips twitch, the corners curling up into an almost caustic smile. "Yes."

"Yes?" I stare at him.

"Yes," he repeats.

"I have to ask a question?" I clarify. When he merely stares back at me without a word, I guess again. "I have to ask the *right* question?"

He nods. "Now, she gets it."

I don't get anything. In fact, I'm more confused than before I dragged him up here. I shake my head. "How am I supposed to know what questions to ask to get the answers I need?" I demand. "I don't have time to unravel your ridiculous word puzzles to get to the truth. The longer I remain at the Academy, the more danger I pose—" I cut myself off, remembering what Kalix and Ruen had insinuated and even demanded before I'd come away to speak with Caedmon alone.

"The brimstone..." My words drift as my hand reaches up and touches the back of my neck. "If it's removed, my Divinity—"

"Magic," Caedmon corrects quietly.

I shoot him a look. "No offense," I tell him, "but it's a little difficult to spend twenty years calling it one thing only to be told that it's something else entirely and change my terminology in a single night. So, I think I'll continue to call it Divinity."

His smirk turns more genuine. "Fair enough," he says with a head tilt. "Continue. What about the brimstone?"

I lick my lips nervously as the brimstone beneath my skin seems to heat at my touch and remembrance of it. It's been there for so long now that it's easy to forget it exists for long periods of time.

"If I remove it, my abilities—my Divinity—it won't be hidden anymore," I guess.

"If you're asking," Caedmon starts, "then yes, that is correct. Removing the brimstone that binds you to Ophelia is akin to removing the mask you've worn for the past ten years. It will become obvious to all that you are not mortal—if you prefer the terms of this world."

I bite down on my lip hard enough to taste blood. Rarely have I ever let myself hope, but now, disappointment wells within me—a testament to how much hope I've held out for having it removed. I close my eyes as they begin to burn.

"I see." My shoulders sag. "Then I suppose I should keep it."

Caedmon clicks his tongue and my eyes open again, surprised by the noise. His brow puckers and his smile is gone as he looks at me. "I will take care of the consequences of your Divinity, Kiera," he says quietly. "If you want the stone removed, then remove it."

I straighten. "Can I? Is that the right question? Can I remove the brimstone without being killed for defying the Gods and hiding my existence?"

Caedmon's smile returns and spreads over the lower half of his face. "That," he tells me, "is the right question, and my answer is yes. Do you want it removed?"

As much as I want my next breath, I think to myself, but as my lips part to say as much, the sound of pounding footsteps up the staircase stops me and I turn as a hard hand raps upon the closed door.

"Kiera." Ruen's dark voice comes through the wood. "Enough. Come out here. I'm getting that fucking thing removed if I have to hold you down and cut it out myself."

Caedmon is across the room in the blink of an eye, startling me. I recoil from him, my hand snapping to my hidden blade in an instinctive response. Caedmon holds a hand out to me, though, staying my movements as he turns and opens the door.

"I think that's quite enough, Ruen," he chastises. "It's not like you to interrupt a private conversation."

"It is when the one in that conversation is a liar and a traitor."

My eyes widen at Ruen's cold response.

Caedmon opens the door wider until both Ruen and I can see each other. "That is quite ironic coming from you," Caedmon replies just as coolly before he gestures to me. "There. As you can see, she's quite alright and our conversation is over. You may take her downstairs to get the brimstone removed."

Ruen glares at Caedmon before reaching through the now open doorway. His fingers close around my wrist and he pulls me, quickly but firmly, out into the hallway. Neither of the men says another word as Ruen turns and leads me back the way we came. Distantly, I'm aware that Caedmon follows us, and as we near the doorway that leads into the back rooms, I note that Madam Brione is gone.

Regis stares at me as we pass him. I stay quiet as Ruen gently nudges me back into the rooms and then locks his attention on Ophelia. With her arms crossed over her chest, she doesn't wilt under his scrutiny. Instead, she straightens away from the table and steps towards the Darkhaven facing her down. The blood in my veins chills at the look she gives him back.

It would have had me shrinking away in memory of all the times I'd been tied to a chair and forced to endure her brand of *education* if it weren't for Ruen holding me in place.

Ruen breaks the silence. "The brimstone," he growls before tightening his hold on my wrist and pulling me in front of him. "Remove it," he orders. "*Now.*"

Now that Caedmon has said that doing so won't ruin all of us, I decide that I'm willing to do whatever it takes to make it happen. "And why do you think I'll do something like that?" Ophelia finally asks.

Ruen releases me to step around me, his massive frame larger than hers, his stance menacing. "Because if you don't, I will sever your head from your shoulders and it will become a moot point," he states calmly as if he's saying nothing of importance instead of threatening the woman who's kept me tied to her as a blood contracted servant for a decade. My breath catches in my throat.

"We don't have time for this," Theos snaps. "Do it, woman, or my brother won't be the only one to force your hand."

My head turns and my gaze meets a familiar set of green irises. Kalix is staring at me with all the subtlety of a hungry lion.

Ruen doesn't turn around or acknowledge Theos' statement. Neither does Ophelia for that matter. The two remain standing before each other, eyes narrowed. Finally, Kalix breaks our connection and moves further into the room, drawing all three of their attention. As if they were all aware of him but quietly ignoring his dark shadowy presence until it became more of a threat.

"You will remove that *abominable* stone in her neck or I

will remove yours from your body," Kalix tells her with a cold, almost deranged smile. "It is your choice, but you should know—I hope you fight. It will make killing you all the more pleasurable for me."

Ruen, for a change, doesn't tell Kalix to back off. Instead, he nods in agreement and then flips his eyes back to Ophelia. His hand appears at his back and I blink as he delves behind his cloak and under his tunic and, with careful fingers, he removes a dagger I hadn't known he'd been carrying in the same place where I so often kept my own. "I will give you three seconds to decide," Ruen states before tossing the dagger in Kalix's direction.

My eyes follow the blade as Kalix plucks it from the air and then turns it over his knuckles, catching it again and tapping his chin with the sharp end, smiling a bit wider.

"Starting now," Kalix says.

CHAPTER 7
KIERA

"**G**et. Out."

Three seconds is an eternity when you anticipate bloodshed and dread it. They end with those two words, hissed between Ophelia's pearl white teeth as she glowers at Ruen. I have to give her my respect for those words and her stance. Ruen is not a normal man. He's not mortal and, I suspect, he could potentially end Ophelia—no matter how well trained she is—in an instant.

Kalix's fingers on my upper arms ease ever so slightly. The scent of smoke permeates my nostrils causing my nose to twitch with discomfort. I glance down, seeking out the origins of that smell. A perfunctory once over of Kalix tells me it's not him. I turn my attention to the scene before me. Ruen's cold, dark gaze is still locked on Ophelia and despite her ordered words, he hasn't moved a muscle. Finally, my gaze falls to Theos and what I see sends tendrils of shock through my core. His eyes are blazing, the black completely gone as the golden irises glow with unnatural power and his hands are sparking. Golden flashes erupt from his fingertips, searing up to his palm, and then disappear before starting all over again. The edges of his tunic sleeves are singed. My lips part and I take a step towards him, both confused and wanting to … what? Stop the strange flares of minuscule lightning? I don't know. Yes. Maybe.

I'm drawn up short by Kalix's hold.

"You will unleash her from your contract," Ruen states, the only sound apart from the breaths that fill the room.

My head swivels back to the two of them.

Ophelia's full lips curl up into the facsimile of a smile. It's more of a baring of teeth than a true smile. "I will discuss this with Kiera," she says by way of answer. "Not you."

Ruen's head is shaking before she's even finished. His cool gaze turns into ice chips that threaten to form a sword and stab through her jugular.

"You will remove that stone from her neck or I will kill you here and now and do it myself."

Those words should not soften me towards him. *They don't,* I tell myself even knowing it's a lie. When was the last time someone demanded freedom for me? When was the last time someone fought for me? My chest tightens. I know the answer.

Ten years ago.

"I wish a word with my ward, Darkhaven *child*," Ophelia sneers with insult. "You will leave or you will get nothing from me."

I take another step forward, wishing to ease the storm brewing between them before it gets worse because, yes, it has already begun. Kalix doesn't let me go but he does allow the movement as he, too, steps forward. I can see the truth of rage in the darkened night sky of Ruen's gaze as he turns and glances over at me.

I know what he wants. My response. My decision. I could fucking forgive him for everything he's done to wound me for that one seemingly insignificant little action. "I want to talk with her too," I tell him.

To my utter surprise, he nods his understanding. He does so with no small amount of displeasure on his face, but then he takes a step back from Ophelia and I return my attention to the woman who raised me.

"We will be outside," he says before casting a seething glare at Ophelia even as he continues to speak to me. "Don't be long, and if you do not come out with that stone removed, I shall remove it myself and then cut this woman down."

I don't know if he'll actually follow through on that threat, but I'm not sure I want to find out so I simply tilt my head in acknowledgment of his words and then stride forward, out of Kalix's grip. Ophelia doesn't move from her position in the doorway of the smaller room, but she does cant her head and jerk her chin.

"Out," she snaps to Carcel and the man obeys, though he doesn't look happy about it. Then again, Carcel has always been a shit to me and his mouth is little more than a constant pinched asshole so there's nothing new in his expression.

Ophelia finally steps into the quiet, smaller room. Carcel shoulders past me, shoving into me so fast that it takes all of my self-control not to snatch him back by the collar and plant my fist in his gut. His childishness has long since lost its necessity considering that neither he nor I are children any longer. If he wants to continue to hold a grudge against the time his mother spends with me, that's his prerogative.

Just before the door closes behind me, I see Kalix take two strides forward, and as if he saw right into my mind, he grabs Carcel by his tunic and throws him into the wall with little effort before slamming his fist into his face. If Ophelia sees or hears Carcel's grunt of pain, she says nothing. She doesn't even return to the doorway as Carcel begins to curse.

I quickly enter the room and the door swings shut behind me, leaving the two of us alone for the first time in ... months. Since long before I ever came to Riviere.

My heartbeat doubles as I stand, silent and still, watching Ophelia round the table that takes up the majority of the small room's space. The walls, covered in the same ornate, but dusty, wallpaper as the larger room make the space feel more confined somehow and the skin at the back of my neck begins to burn and itch. I refuse to reach up or acknowledge it in any way so I simply stare at the woman that I've seen as both a jailer and ... a parent for the last ten years.

Once she's on the other side of the table and has placed it between us, Ophelia braces her hands, palms down on the edges, and lets her shoulders sink down.

"I did not wish to see you again like this, Kiera." Her voice is quiet, tight.

My skin draws tighter against my skull as I clench my jaw. "Like what?"

Her head lifts, and the lines of her face, the wrinkles that truly reveal her age seem to deepen. Before she can speak, I move across the floor towards her, not stopping until I'm standing in front of her and the only thing separating our bodies is the table before us.

She doesn't answer my question, so I ask a different one. "How long have you been working with Caedmon?"

Ophelia lifts up and thrusts her shoulders back. "I've known him for quite some time," she tells me. The words are both an answer and a non-answer. Her green eyes, flecked with bits and pieces of gold, linger on my face. Her expression is unreadable and I hate it. I want so badly to know what she's thinking, to know what her plans are for me, and if she'll actually cave to Ruen's demands to remove the brimstone from my neck.

She doesn't seem all that afraid of what he might do to her if she doesn't do as he commands, but then again, Ophelia is a master at hiding what she truly feels. I've known her for ten years and even I have never been certain of her feelings on most subjects. She could be terrified of Ruen, but even if she is, I doubt she'd ever show it.

That's the fate of an assassin. Emotions are a weakness so they remove them. It's a miracle Regis and I have done so well, but I suspect it's more so the fact that we both had little choice. We both had goals that were more important than the lives of others and now we're cursed to live with the blood we've shed staining our hands.

Such is the fate of killers and survivors.

Silence stretches between us, filling the hollow empty places in the room. I shake my head. "Did you send me here knowing that Caedmon was the client? Did you know this whole mission was a fucking lie? Did you know that I would —" I cut my words off, unsure how to finish the question. What should I even say? Did she know that I would meet the Darkhavens? Was that, too, planned?

"No one can know all things, Kiera," Ophelia says, her tone quiet, almost tired. "Not even the God of Prophecy."

I laugh, but the sound is anything but amused. Instead, it hovers over the two of us, caustic and too sharp. "You heard him," I say. "Caedmon is no God." He is Atlantean, a being from another world. A liar like the rest of them. "He's just as mortal as the rest of us."

Just as killable, I realize, though the thought of taking such an action had never entered my mind until this moment.

"Do you want me to remove the brimstone in your neck?" Ophelia asks, returning me to the reason we're locked in this room alone in the first place.

I jerk my head up and stare at her. "Of course I do."

It's what I've wanted since the moment she inserted it. The stone feels wrong under my skin. Though the pain has lessened over the years—no, that's not right. The pain hasn't lessened, I've just grown accustomed to it. I've dealt with it every moment of every day for ten years. I've just fought through it. Spent nights sobbing into my pillows and hands until the rivers of tears had dried.

No one ever thought to help me out of the agony. They just expected me to act as if it wasn't there. So I did what was expected.

The stone, itself, is like a low lying ache—an old wound that will never fully heal—that I've learned to live with not because I want to but because I have to. I tried to ignore the existence of it and even on occasion managed to forget it entirely, but that never lasted. When you're constantly in pain, enduring becomes the only constant. You fight not to relieve that pain, but to survive it. It's only when you become good at enduring the pain that people forget it exists.

Ophelia tilts her head to the side, watching me. Her eyes sharpen, pupils shrinking until all I really see in her gaze are green and gold. "And what do you plan to do once I remove it? Do you plan to leave the Underworld—your debt unpaid?"

A scowl overtakes me. I slam a fist down on the table. "How much denza have you made off my labor, Ophelia?" I snap. "As much as I've taken from my jobs, you've taken more. Each kill. Each mission. You take and you take."

"I trained you," she states simply. "I spared your life. I am owed what I am due."

"I was a child."

Rage burns hot coals in the back of my eyes. I fight back the tears that wish to unleash torrents over my cheeks. "Do not act like you spared me out of the goodness of your heart," I hiss. "You wished to use me and you did. I'm sure you made

Caedmon give over half of this farce of a job's fee. That, combined with what I have made you over the last decade, should suffice for my debt."

End this, I want to beg her. *Set me free.* I want it, crave it. The desire for my freedom is like a living, breathing entity in my breast. It curls around my heart and squeezes in long, drugging pulls as if it can keep the organ beating for as long as it needs to in order to attain its desire.

For a moment, Ophelia doesn't speak. Her hands curl around the lip of the table, fingers digging into the wood as if they can burrow past the planks and break them free. She's angry, but I don't see why. Because she's losing a blood servant? Tough. Fucking. Luck. I've suffered enough, haven't I?

Children aren't meant to be killers.

Wisps of shadows fall from my fingertips, curling up my wrist and circling like shackles. They do no more than that, but I can feel the power of them singing in my blood, moving through me and wanting more. My head pounds, the ache of the stone as it represses my powers as much as it can vibrating up the back of my skull. I bite down against the pain and glare at the woman standing across from me. All around us, in the walls and beyond, there are hundreds of little creatures responding to the call of my blood.

Whether I am half God or half monster, I don't care anymore. All I desire is my freedom. The right to make my own choices, but I will not beg for what I have earned.

"You talk about what is owed." My words come stilted, slowly, as I grit through the pain. "But what about what *I* am owed." I lift my eyes and stare at her through my dark lowered lashes. "I have been nothing but loyal," I remind her. "I took your education, I took your jobs. I did everything you asked."

Please. I silently plead. *No.* I bite down on my tongue. *I. Will. Not. Beg.*

The shadows shiver against my skin, melding tighter. They are liquid darkness, unyielding, and yet, I do not find them restrictive. Instead, they feel like bands of strength, propping me up, urging me to face the woman I have both admired and feared for so long.

Ophelia's nails retract from the tabletop and she straightens, pulling her hands away. "What will you do if I release you from your contract?"

"I won't betray you," I say, assuring her. "I have no intention of revealing the Underworld."

"Will you continue to work for me?"

My lips part, but I have no words, only shock. Continue to work for her? I stare past her, over her shoulder, my eyes sinking into the frayed edges of the wallpaper, crinkling and pealing in the upper corner where the wall meets the ceiling. Beneath my booted feet, the floorboards creak. Particles of dirt float through the air, thickening the stale smell in the room that is both rotted wood and old ink.

Ophelia's attention sears into my cheek, but still, I don't look at her. If I thought she had massive balls to face Ruen and act unafraid, she has even larger ones to ask me that. I never wanted to be an assassin. I never wanted to be wrapped up in Anatol's hierarchy of power struggles.

It had been my dream to return to the Hinterlands, to rebuild the cabin that had been burned down all those years ago. A part of me still wants that. Yet, the thought of staying out in the darkness of the forest, with no one around for miles, no lights, no streets, no taverns or coffeehouses, no sounds save for the creatures that inhabit the woods—it leaves me feeling somewhat hollow. As if someone has scooped out my insides, organs and all, and deposited them on the ground before me.

What would be the point of living a solitary life now?

I turn back and glance over my shoulder at the door where, beyond it, three great men wait for me. How many minutes has it been? How many more will they allow? I'm half worried that if we spend much longer in here Ruen will break down the door and demand to know what's taking so long. Then again, he's already surprised me so much today—they all have—maybe they'll allow me this freedom too.

"Those boys," Ophelia starts, the sound of her footsteps nearing as she rounds the table. I turn to look at her, watching, unmoving, as she strides closer. "They might be kinder than some, more trustworthy than others, but do not forget, Kiera, a sword can cut more than flesh, but death is always its original purpose."

I stare back at her. "You don't want me to trust them." It's not a question.

Ophelia's mouth curves, though the smile doesn't reach her eyes. "You have sought peace your entire life." She withdraws a blade from a pocket in her breaches. With a flick, the sharp silver edge unsheathes from the handle, snapping out with a deft twist of her wrist. I don't flinch as I continue to hold her gaze. "But now, you will need to go to war before you ever find that peace."

"Did you know that this would happen?"

With firm fingers, Ophelia grabs ahold of my arm and turns me to face the wall and the door. Her fingers are cold as they gather the strands of my hair and hold them out of the way to reveal the back of my neck. The muscles in my shoulders pull taut.

The first bite of the blade's sharp edge in my skin doesn't

hurt, but it does make all of the muscles in my back tense further. The well of warm blood bubbles up and I feel a bead slide from the opening Ophelia creates as she draws the knife down further. I close my eyes, falling back into that safe place I've grown accustomed to—the place she forced me to create for myself.

"No one knows how the future will turn out," she answers my question as her fingers make swift work of her task. The blade withdraws from my flesh and I hear it clatter onto the table a moment before her fingers—cooler than most—peel the cut open wider. I bite down on my lower lip to keep silent. "No mother knows how her children will turn out either."

Now, I speak. "You're *not* my mother." The words spew from my lips despite my earlier thoughts. Yes, once, I had thought of her that way. She is, after all, the only adult woman who'd ever remained a constant in my life, but no mother forces her children into the dark for coin. No mother tortures them to keep others safe.

Her fingers dig beneath my flesh. "I won't apologize for ensuring that you would survive a world intent on killing you."

"Is that what you would call it?" I demand, hissing out a breath as her fingers brush against the stone in my neck and more blood flows down my back, soaking into the back collar of my tunic.

"Everyone has an evil side, Kiera. You might think that all of my sides are evil, but it was never my wish to hurt you."

"Yet you did." The words slice out from between my teeth as I clamp my hands into fists, digging the edges of my dulled nails into my palms until they feel as sharp as any sword.

Ophelia's lips twist into a scowl. Damn her. Harder and harder still, my heart solidifies. Fear. I feared this woman. Some part of me still does. Another part, however, freed somehow by the last few months I've experienced within the Academy no longer does. I see her for who she truly is.

A woman. *Just* a woman.

"It takes a great amount of violence to become gentle," she whispers even as her fingers push into my neck, pinching that sliver of brimstone. My spine catches on fire and blood fills my mouth, spilling over my tongue and down the back of my throat before I realize I've bitten the inside of my cheek hard enough to tear it open.

Those scorching tears return. The very air in my lungs evaporates, disappearing completely as I become breathless. My body shakes. My legs weaken. The pain ... it's more than I remember. I'm suddenly so viscerally aware of that tiny piece of brimstone inside me that it feels fused to my very skeleton and she is prying it out.

Black dots dance in front of my vision. Colliding into one another, they shake and tremble and waver in and out of sight as the breath held deep within me releases all at once with a great big whoosh. Suddenly, I can't breathe anymore. Suddenly, the thin light of the sconces on the walls is completely gone, all that lies before me is darkness.

My knees crack as they bow inward, the only thing keeping me from collapsing on the floor. The soft whisper of Ophelia's voice, talking ... talking ... what is she saying? I can't hear her well as the pain overwhelms my other senses. Molten agony spreads from the place in my neck where the brimstone is slowly being pulled free. Vomit threatens to tear a path up my throat. I clench my teeth and hold it at bay with nothing but my desire not to show how fucking much this hurts.

After what feels like an eternity, Ophelia's voice comes to me once more, halfway through whatever she'd been saying.

"—wished for someone to come for me, always did, and

feared that I always would. I never had a daughter, and no, I understand that you don't wish to consider yourself mine."

Bile thickens my throat. My tongue swells. Is it over? No. Her fingers are still against the back of my neck, slipping in the blood there. More coats my flesh and the wet feeling of my tunic sticks to my upper back.

"The more time we spend on this land, the more we realize that few things are in our control," Ophelia continues.

My body sways slightly and I feel more blood drip from my hands where my nails have finally dug past the layers of skin there. *I can't pass out here,* I tell myself. Yet, I don't quite remember how this thing had been put inside me to begin with. I know I hadn't been standing but lying down.

"Peace is not for ones such as you, Kiera. Caedmon knows this. I know this. With what you can do, with the hand that the world has dealt you, you were always meant to do more than run from responsibility."

Responsibility? The urge to turn and slap her rises like a tidal wave. Unfortunately, even as the desire swells, it crashes against cliffs that stop it from doing any damage and I remain right where I am. Sight darkened and unchanged, my body completely ramrod straight as pain darts through me.

As if she finally—blessedly senses my spasming torment—Ophelia's fingers are gentle as she slips a nail under the brimstone and the damn thing comes free. All her prying and wiggling has paid off. The stone slips from my neck, from beneath my skin, and the wash of warmth that encompasses me a second after it's gone spreads from the wound in my neck and down my limbs.

The image of the room flares back to life and I can see—truly see—once more. I blink and frown. In fact, my eyesight is far better than it's ever been. The peeling wallpaper that was once a flat, grotesque design becomes thousands of tiny little fibers woven into one another and stretched into the material that covers the wall. I can pinpoint each individual tear and the wood beyond, scarred by deep grooves.

Slowly, confused by the strange sensations coursing through me and aware of my own skin knitting back together and healing far faster than ever before, I turn to face the woman at my back. Her fingers are coated in blood, but she doesn't move to wipe them.

Whereas before I never noticed, now I can see the soft marks of makeup dotting her skin—covering ... more lines I realize. Far more than I've ever detected previously. The dust is a light coating but still there, and it no longer masks the shadows beneath Ophelia's eyes or her sunken sockets. Her lips, once full, I now recognize are dry and cracked beneath the gleam of some sort of glossy lipstick.

For the first time, I see. See it all in a way that I hadn't in a decade, in a way that I had forgotten was possible. It makes my head throb with all of the information being thrown at my sight at once.

"I will do whatever it takes to not become you," I find myself saying.

"You don't mean that," she says on a sigh as if the words are so obvious that she's annoyed she has to say them at all.

I look at her, and when my eyes meet hers, I repeat myself. "Whatever. It. Takes."

Her lips part and her eyes narrow. "Kiera." She says my name like a mother ready to castigate a recalcitrant child, but I am no child, and I have not been one for a very long time.

"I mean it," I say, my tone quiet. I feel no need to shout or scream. Making the words louder won't make them any truer. "I am done."

Ophelia's brows crease and her lips curl down into a frown. "What do you—"

"I am done letting everyone else make decisions for me," I say. A cold sort of chill comes over me. It starts at my fingertips and slowly crawls up my hand, over my knuckles to my wrists.

"I think it took me this long to realize that I've never made a choice for myself, not really," I continue. "I didn't choose to be born—"

Ophelia scoffs, a sharp sardonic chuckle rising from her throat as she cuts me off. She rolls her eyes and then waves her hand, the frown and confusion easing slightly. One look at her face. That's all it takes and I know she doesn't understand what I mean. Then she speaks, and my assumption is confirmed.

"You didn't choose to be born?" She shakes her head again. "You still have benefited from it. You were given opportunities others would have killed for."

I tilt my head to the side and stare at her for a moment. She won't understand. It doesn't matter what I say or do. Perhaps I'm just now realizing it, but there are some people you cannot convince of anything. They will go their entire lives believing the sky is purple and fuck anyone who says otherwise. I know that ... yet somehow my next words come out anyway.

"If you were told you could either lose your right hand or your left hand, which would you choose?" I ask suddenly.

Ophelia blinks. "Excuse me?" Her tone suggests that she thinks I've gone crazy.

"There's an accident and you must give up one hand. Which do you choose, right or left?" I ask.

She pauses but after a beat, answers. "Left."

I nod, unsurprised. She's right-handed. Therefore, her choice makes sense. "Alright, then, by your own choice, you lose your left hand. Do you agree?"

Ophelia scowls. "This is ridiculous," she snaps.

"You lose your left hand," I repeat. "Do you agree?"

"Yes, damn it," she seethes.

I take a breath. "What if, then, the Gods decide that no one is allowed to use their right hand? They make the law that everyone must use their left hand as it's more Divine. Should anyone be caught using their right hand they will have it cut off. What do you do?"

More frowns from her. "I would go back and choose to cut off my right hand then."

I shake my head. "You can't go back," I say. "It's gone. The decision is made. You only have your right hand."

"If the Gods decree that I cannot use it, though, then it's useless. How was I supposed to know that they would make such a preposterous decree?"

"It doesn't matter if you could tell the future or not. You made a decision in the moment, assuming one thing. Now, you cannot use either of your hands or, if you try to use the one you have left, you run the risk of losing it completely as well."

Her frown turns into a scowl. "What is this?" she demands.

"Choices," I tell her. "These are your choices. If you use your right hand, the only one you have left, you'll have it cut off now. What do you do? Will you use it or not?"

"It doesn't matter what I would decide," she snaps. "It's lost either way whether I use it or not."

"Exactly," I tell her. "Every choice I've 'made' for myself has somehow been controlled by others. First by my mother, then my father, then the bandits, then you, and now ... as it always does, it comes down to the Gods. All I have had has been the illusion of choice and I'm telling you that I'm done with that."

No more.

"The only thing I have left to wonder is, if all I was good for was destruction and death then why?" The question refers to our conversation, but I'm not entirely sure what I want to know. "Why me and not someone else?"

Why did she keep me? Train me? Hurt me? If she wanted a daughter, why did she treat me as she did? Why the servitude? Why the choices she made?

Ophelia's expression—once so difficult to understand—twitches and all of the minute little changes from the dart of her eyes to the muscle that bunches and jumps in the side of her nose or beneath her right eye reveals all. She doesn't like being questioned, but I won't retract it. Whatever she wants to answer, I'll let her. I want her to. I'm curious to see which question she'll take and which she'll respond to.

So, I wait.

Silence stretches between us, seemingly unending until it does, in fact, come to an end with a deep breath from her and the gaze she breaks by looking away. She picks up the switchblade, wipes it on her pants' leg, and then folds it down, closing the sharp edge into the handle before slipping it back into her pocket.

"I will not pretend to be altruistic," she says with a shrug. "You were a good investment and I'm a businesswoman." I wait a beat and she continues, arms at her sides. "With that said, all that I did, I did it to prepare you for the world. When I was a child, no one fought for me, and so easily I could see you killed. I did not wish to do that. Your existence was a danger, but children deserve chances. I had to protect the Underworld, but that didn't mean I had to kill you to do so."

My fisted hands release and blood drips free from wounds that have already healed. The cuts made by my nails are gone, but the remains of them flow over my skin, and ping against the floor one after another. It's ironic.

This woman saved me. Damaged me. I am alive because of her. I resent her kindness as much as her cruelty. Is that fair? Perhaps not, but if there's anything she's taught me, it's that life is not fair.

Without a word, I turn away from her and face the door. I reach for the knob—the sounds of voices on the other side louder than they were minutes prior.

"You are a better woman because of what I did," Ophelia says. "Better equipped to handle the next task set before you. You are stronger for what I did."

I bite down on my tongue even as the words break free a moment later. "Children do not ask to be strong or better, but I guess, in this life, I have no other choice." I don't look back. "It's conquer or die."

CHAPTER 8
KIERA

I leave the small room on my own two feet with blood still soaking my collar, making it stick to my skin. The moment I step out of the door, three unnatural sets of eyes fall on me. Ruen's head snaps to the side and he glares over my shoulder, most likely at the woman who remains behind.

"Let's go," I say, moving towards him. One foot in front of the other. No matter how lightheaded I feel, I won't let myself collapse in front of Ophelia. I don't want her to think removing the brimstone in my neck affected me.

The absence of the pain there has opened a void to something else. A strange sort of sucking of energy as it depletes me faster with every passing breath. As I near the other side of the room, my foot nearly catches on the side of one of the chairs. I stop just as Theos steps forward, reaching me in less than a second. His hand curls around my bicep and I pretend that I allow the action when really, I don't have the energy to stop him. My gaze lifts to the doorway. The only ones who remain behind now are Regis and Caedmon. The former eyes me with concern even if I won't meet his gaze. I'm still too raw from his betrayal, angry even if I can understand where he's coming from.

"We'll be in touch," Ruen states, his tone sullen and his muscles tensed beneath the shoulders of his tunic and cloak. He holds out his hand for me. "Kiera."

I shake my head and finally drag my arm from Theos' grip, grateful when he lets me go easily. Once more, I walk towards the exit with my head held high. I stride into the hallway, bypassing both Regis and Caedmon. Theos follows, his presence somehow a relief. I pause once to glance back; Theos and Kalix are closer to me than anyone else, their bodies nearly blocking the entire narrow hallway. Over their heads, I see Ruen at the doorway. He says something to Caedmon, so quietly that I can't hear it even with my newfound heightened senses.

Perhaps I could have were it not for all of the new sensations coursing through my body. I'm overstimulated. Each creak of the floorboards underfoot screams through my head until it throbs incessantly.

Theos frowns at me. "Kiera, are you okay?" He glances to the back of my neck where my fall of hair now covers what I'm sure is a healed wound.

I shake my head in a non-answer. No. I'm not okay, but I don't want anyone here to know it. Not Ophelia. Not Regis. And certainly not Caedmon. It doesn't matter to me that he's somehow been trying to feed me information about the truth. He was Ophelia's client. He knew everything this whole time. He let me be whipped and he, like the rest of the Gods—Atlanteans, whatever the fuck they are now—cannot be trusted.

I make it to the front door of Madam Brione's shop without seeing her again, and though I am curious as to her whereabouts, the drilling of constant pain in my skull is overwhelming everything else. Kalix appears at my side, making me jolt back even as one firm hand lands on the small of my back. He doesn't speak and he doesn't look at me as he lifts the curtain away from the single tiny slit of a window in the door and peers out.

A moment passes and then another and another until finally, he nods and reaches for the door handle. Kalix slides open the door and his hand leaves my back to find my wrist as he tugs me along with him. Footsteps sound at my back, but it's now taking all of my concentration to remain upright and walking.

The shop door shutting ricochets up the exterior building walls and over the cobblestones of the street. Farther and farther, I walk. Until my vision narrows down to one pinprick of light and I can no longer feel Kalix's firm fingers on my wrist. I'm not sure if that means he's released me or if all of my senses are finally crashing from the overload.

"Something's wrong—" Theos' quiet voice is suddenly cut off as a pair of arms pluck me off my feet and I find myself landing against a broad chest. My head lolls back against a strong shoulder and I peer up, finding the underside of a rough, unshaven jaw. Little dots of black hair line the square cut line and halfway down the throat of the man carrying me.

"Of course there is something wrong with her," Ruen mutters, his voice vibrating against my side, letting me know that he's the one carrying me. My fingers curl into limp fists. I bite down on my tongue, tasting bile. I'm going to be sick. I don't know how to tell him, how to warn him. "She just had brimstone removed from her—a piece that she had inside her body for *years*." The last word hisses from his throat, and in my own mind, fogged over with confusion and pain, I can't guess why he sounds so angry.

"The redhead is a healer," I dimly hear Kalix say. "As soon as we return, I'll send for her."

Ruen doesn't reply for the longest time and I sway back and forth in his arms, growing more and more content with the gentle rocking than I ever thought possible with a man I regarded, once, as my enemy. Is he my enemy now, though? Are any of them?

Before my addled mind can supply an answer, Ruen's low timbre reverberates through me once more. "Fetch her yourself." His voice is low as air wafts over us, sliding past my cheeks and over the bridge of my nose. We're moving fast, I realize. Faster than human speeds. "I want her in the North Tower within the hour we arrive."

My lashes flicker and I glance up. If I still had control of my body's responses, I would gasp in surprise as the glittering night sky is replaced by a different one—just as dark, but far less speckled with white dots.

Ruen's gaze bores into me and his lips curl down at the edges. "We'll have Maeryn check you over, Kiera." I know he's aware that I'm still somewhat conscious even if I'm struggling to stay that way. "Don't worry, you'll be fine."

He sounds sure, but I can't tell if that's hope in his voice or determination. I'm starting to wonder if the two aren't somehow irrevocably linked. One who is determined to hope is usually the one who sees the fruit of his labor, after all.

I don't say as much though. I don't even manage a response at all before the dark midnight of Ruen's eyes swirl into nothingness and I fall into the depths of oblivion.

~

WHEN NEXT I WAKE, my back is pressed into a comfortable mattress and not the rickety and squeaky cot I've become accustomed to. I blink my eyes open and spy a mass of circular etchings in the ceiling of a canopy above me. My gaze flickers over the wooden ceiling of the large four poster bed I recognize from the many times I'd cleaned Ruen's bedroom. Despite how often I've been in this room, however, I've never lain on his bed. Therefore, I never knew that there were so many images carved above the mattress. Scenes of blossoming flowers and filigree dot the outside edges, but the closer I get to the center, the more the swirls of circles darken and take on more deadly imagery. Skulls and swords. Monsters shaped like hungry wolves with fangs that drip with what I can only think is blood since between their massive jaws, they carry hearts and arms and even a few heads.

It's wicked and ugly and yet, at the same time, beautiful. The cycle of life and death, of kill or be killed, of survival. The vision of it is so clear, too, that I'm reminded of the events that took place before I passed out.

Slowly, I shift and sit up in the giant bed, turning my head to scan the room and finding it empty. The curtains on either side of the floor to ceiling window several feet away in the corner furthest from the fireplace reveal that day has broken once more and sunlight pours in across the dark wooden floors and wine-red rugs.

The scent of ink and parchment permeates the space. I close my eyes and inhale. Beyond that studious scent is something else, and I reopen my eyes, turning my head back to the window and up when I spot a hanging basket. Inside is a pot, and from it, long thin strands of greenery flow. I inhale again, and the mint is stronger now with this new awareness.

I suppose that explains why there was always a hint of mint mixed in with his natural ink and parchment smell. How had I never noticed the plant hanging there in all the times I'd been in his room? No, maybe I had but had dismissed it.

The brimstone must have been muffling all of my natural senses and now with it gone, everything seems brighter, stronger. Scents. Sights. Everything from the light coming in from the window to the natural scent that I've smelled on Ruen Darkhaven crushes against me. A moment later, the click of the door opening has me up and out of bed.

Heart pounding against my ribcage, I shoot to the nightstand where I spy a dagger waiting there. I don't know if it was left by Ruen or if it's my own. A cursory glance down reveals that I've been stripped of my earlier clothes and redressed in a nightgown. The dagger and holster I usually have on me are gone as well. I bite my tongue. If Ruen or one of the other Darkhavens stripped me, they'll regret that.

My anxiety eases a split second later as a familiar head of fiery red hair appears around the side of the door. Maeryn's face lifts as she carries a bowl of what looks like water and a satchel in her arms. Pink lips part and her cheeks fill as she inhales. "You're awake," she says. "Oh, thank goodness."

I nod and slowly set the dagger back down on the nightstand. "How long have I been asleep?" I demand.

Maeryn's face twists from relief to a slight grimace. Her skirts, a mass of cream-colored fabric, swish around her legs as she moves. The black vest over the peasant-style blouse of the dress cinches tight at her waist, giving her a similar figure to the one I've seen when she wears trousers and tunics during her battle training.

"It's..." She begins, a v forming between her brows. With a sigh, she shakes her head and nods to the bed. "You should probably sit down. I want to check your Divinity."

I frown at her even as I turn and place my butt against the side of the mattress. Maeryn finishes walking the length of the room and sets the bowl and satchel down on the nightstand next to the dagger. She doesn't comment about the weapon, doesn't even seem to notice as she turns to me, and now that her hands are free, lifts them to my face.

"So, how long have I been asleep?" I repeat my earlier question as her light fingers smooth down my forehead, pushing the rat's nest that is my hair back. Her skin is cool, colder than I expected, but her movements are soothing and calm.

With how close she is, it's not hard to see the finer details of her expression. Her lashes twitch with my words and beneath the smattering of light freckles over her pale skin, her face blanches before smoothing out.

"Three days," is her only answer before she hushes me. Her hands fall over my eyes and I'm forced to close them. "The Darkhavens requested that I come and see to you and Ruen informed me that they'd removed a, er, a piece of brimstone that had been in your body."

"Yes." I keep my own response light as she moves the pads of her index fingers to my temples and then presses down. A muscle jumps between my brows.

"I've never known a Mortal God who has ever had something like that inserted in them, much less for a long period of time," Maeryn informs me. "There might be some lingering effects. How do you feel?"

"Everything is too bright," I admit. "Sounds are too loud. Smells are too strong."

She hums in the back of her throat, not an ugly sound, but instead unintentionally lyrical. As her hands pull back, my lashes lift once more. Maeryn turns towards the satchel she brought.

"What happened while I was asleep?" I ask. "Why am I in here and not in my own room?"

Flipping open the top of the bag, Maeryn rifles inside until she withdraws a glass vial with some sort of dark brown liquid and another with what looks to be crushed spices. Uncapping the first and pouring it into the bowl of water, the smell hits me a moment later and I gag, turning away.

"Fuck, what is that?" I cough out, my eyes already watering. "It smells foul."

"It's probably better that you don't know exactly what it is." Maeryn's voice is full of sympathy.

"Wait." I whip around as she dumps the second container of spices into the congealed mess of quickly muddying water in the bowl. "You're not bringing that anywhere near me."

"It'll help you," she says. "I know it's not going to be fun, but if your senses can overcome *this.*" She pauses and gestures to the bowl before she withdraws a long metal spoon and starts stirring it. I swear to the Gods, I think I see a face forming in the mess, one screaming for help. "Then all of your sensitivity problems will cease."

"Maeryn, I'm not saying this to scare you, but to warn you," I say slowly rising from the bed. "If you put that thing near me, I'm going to stab you in the throat."

She glances at me and bites down on twitching lips. The bitch is amused. This is so not funny. I take a step back and she finishes stirring the bowl of disgusting liquid that's growing firmer by the second. I don't know what it is and I don't care to. What I do know, however, is that the scent wafting towards me is worse than anything I've ever encountered.

"You shouldn't fight it," Maeryn tells me simply. "You have a bathing chamber upstairs that you won't have to share with anyone, so if you just get this over with, you can—no, don't!"

I bolt for the door before she's finished speaking. My hand

latches on to the handle and jerks it open, and I run, head first into a tunic covered chest.

Blinking in confusion, Theos' face gapes down at me as I hear Maeryn yell for him. "Hold her still!"

Fuck. I try to dive around him, but before I can, Theos' arms band around me. He lifts me off the floor, my feet dangling helplessly as I kick and thrash, before striding back into the room and kicking the door closed behind him, effectively ruining my attempt to escape.

"No!" I shout as Theos releases me and without hesitation, I rear back and punch him in the face.

My fist collides with his cheek as his golden eyes widen with shock. My knuckles skip over his cheekbone, narrowly missing his eye socket before slamming into the side of his nose, and his head snaps left. Blood spurts. A grunt follows the movement but then a cold semi-liquid is poured down my spine and I shriek, whirling around as a glob of the putrid stuff that Maeryn had put together slaps me on the chin and drips down towards my breasts.

Mouth hanging open, I stare at her for a moment and the fact that her hands are coated in the stuff. "Did you just ... throw it at me?" I ask, gasping as the acidic scent wafts upward and burns through my nostrils.

A groan sounds behind me. Theos' hand latches on to my shoulder before I feel it recoil, and the sound of disgust in his voice when he speaks leaves no question as to the reason. "Fucking Gods, what is that *smell?*"

Maeryn blinks as if she, too, is surprised by her actions, but still, she doesn't back away as I feel a wet glob of something sticky and grotesque slide towards my ass over the thin material of the nightgown. She takes a step back as I take one forward. Holding up her brown sludge covered hands even as she drops the now empty bowl to the floor.

"Trust me," she says quickly, holding those hands of hers up. "It's better to get it over with than to suffer the new sensations—"

"How did you know what I needed?" I ask, cutting her off even as I narrow my eyes on her and toe the bowl out of my way.

Maeryn, as if sensing my intentions, dives towards the bed and scrambles across the sheets and blankets. With a curse, I reach out, nearly snagging the hem of her skirts as she leaps toward the opposite end. Grinding my teeth, I widen my stance as she reaches the opposite half of the bed and turns, offering me a pitiable apologetic shrug.

"It happens to a lot of younger Mortal Gods," she answers. "Sometimes Divinity takes a few years to form and when it does a bit too suddenly, it overwhelms the senses until you experience something that dampens them once more, makes them easier to handle. Theos knows. He's experienced the same thing."

Turning my head, I scan a scowling Theos as he thumbs away a streak of blood beneath his already healing nose. "Yes, and I was happy to forget about that disgusting concoction."

The pattering of footsteps sounds a split second before a streak of cream, brown, and red shoots past the end of the bed. I don't hesitate. I dive for Maeryn's retreating body and take her down to the floor in a tackle of limbs and shrieks. A piece of muddy sludge slips off my ass and plops onto the floor behind me.

"Theos!" Maeryn shouts. "Get her off me!"

Distantly, I hear the bedroom door creak open, but my focus is completely on pinning the girl's wrist beneath me to the floor rather than seeing who's entered. "I could, but I also don't want to get punched again," Theos replies.

Maeryn grits her teeth and bucks up into my hips. My

grasp slips against the goop covering her palms. From where my hands hold hers down, sparks of pain shoot through my limbs and muscles. A gasp leaves my lips and I drop down on top of her as a hiss escapes my throat.

"Fucking ... bitch," I breathe out.

With a smirk, Maeryn lifts her chin at me. "Healers can do more than just mend wounds, *bitch*," she shoots back.

Maybe any other time, I'd respect her attitude—Gods, were I not the one she just flung shit that smells worse than any horse manure I've ever encountered at—I'd be on the sidelines laughing my ass off.

"W-what's going on?" Niall's timid tone penetrates my skull and with a groan as Maeryn sends another shot of whatever kind of energy-Divinity-magic she possesses through my body, I rear back and snap my skull down, slamming it into hers in a last-ditch effort to get her to stop.

The cry she unleashes is half outrage and half pain, but the bolts of fire and lightning stop slamming into me. Maeryn kicks against my hold. "Come. On!" she yells. "You needed it!"

"Catfight," Theos tells Niall.

"*That's enough.*" Both Maeryn and I fall still as the new, booming voice of none other than Ruen Darkhaven spears into the room.

Our heads twist to the side where Niall is half tucked behind Theos, curiosity, confusion, and worry etched into his slender features. Just beyond them, Ruen stands in the doorway, his tree trunk sized arms folded over his chest and a scowl curling his lips. I roll my eyes. That scowl is always there. It's practically branded onto his features at this point, but instead of arguing with the hard glint in his eyes, I release Maeryn's hands and sit back, holding mine up in a sign of surrender. Maeryn, too, sits up, though a bit slower.

Not by a single blink of his eyes does Ruen reveal if he

even notices the Gods awful odor that now lingers in his bedroom and more specifically over both Maeryn and me. That, more than anything he's shown before, is impressive. The repugnant foul stench clings to both of us while Niall and Theos stand with their hands clasped over their mouths and noses.

"You two," Ruen barks, nodding out into the main room. "Bathe and change."

"I-I'll go get them some new clothes," Niall chokes out, obviously trying to stifle his own breaths so he doesn't inhale more of the stench coating the air. He turns and practically sprints from the room without waiting to see if Ruen will agree.

With a glare at the two Darkhavens, I lumber to my feet, and after a moment, reach down to offer Maeryn a hand. She takes it and climbs to her feet as well. "You don't have two bathing chambers," I remind them, dropping her hand. "So who's to decide who goes first?"

Ruen arches one scarred brow at me. "I didn't think you were a prude, Kiera," he replies, cocking his head.

"You were supposed to be the only one bathing," Maeryn mutters.

I cast a look her way. "You're not that bad off," I tell her, scanning her form. Her hands and arms are the worst and that's not even from me taking her down. Had it been up to me, I would've smeared the disgusting stuff on her face and in her hair.

Maeryn curls her upper lip back and flashes me her middle finger before lifting her skirts in gross goop covered hands and stomping towards the door. Without unfolding his arms, Ruen steps to the side and lets her pass. I roll my eyes and follow her out.

CHAPTER 9
THEOS

Once Maeryn and Kiera are sequestered away in the bathing chamber, I call for another Terra to clean up the mess they made of Ruen's bedroom. Though I have no qualms about leaving him to take care of the filth himself, Kiera's been sleeping in there for the last several nights, and knowing what will happen now that she's awake ... well, none of us want her to be far away. The room beneath ours is too much distance now.

Silence reigns between Ruen and me as the frightened little Terra tasked with the cleaning duties comes in, moving like a wraith as he flitters back and forth between the room and out of it to retrieve more supplies. Each time the door opens, the stench wafts out, and my upper lip curls back. I do not miss that smell—the scent of dirt and other things I'd rather not mention. It reminds me too much of my time in the facilities where the Gods—or rather, Atlanteans as Caedmon had revealed—stick the children that don't immediately portray abilities.

The second the Terra has finished his task, the door

snicking shut behind him, Ruen breaks the quiet. "We'll need to tell her what to expect when she comes out."

Casting a look over at him, I let my gaze trail down the hollows of his cheekbones—deeper than they were three days ago—as well as the shallow bruises beneath his eyes. Three days she'd been asleep. Three days we'd made excuses to the God Council. Had she not woken up today, I fear we wouldn't have been able to hold them off much longer.

"She'll feel betrayed." By the Gods, *I* feel betrayed. When Caedmon had sent us a note after our return saying that he would take care of the consequences of Kiera's brimstone removal, I hadn't expected that he would tell the God Council about her. None of us had.

Ruen reclines in the chair and stretches his neck back as he props his legs up on the edge of his reading table. "I know." He exhales the words.

I turn my head as the sound of something upstairs greets my ears. Watery splashes? The dull murmur of voices on the other side of the door trickles down to me, but I can't pick out what the two women are saying. A thought occurs to me and I scowl, realizing that I'll likely have to call the Terra back to clean the bathing chamber once the two of them are done. After the women are done washing themselves, it will likely smell of the vile concoction I'd thought I'd forgotten from my childhood.

I inhale sharply, trying to drag calm into my lungs, but all I get is the reminder of sickening mud and shit scent of that stuff. Shaking my head, I stomp towards the fireplace, ripping an iron poker from its holder alongside it and jabbing it into the logs with vengeance. The wood cracks under my powerful thrust and breaks in half, embers filtering up the chimney as the crack rebounds around the room.

"We need to be careful while the Gods are in session," Ruen says slowly.

Jab. Jab. Jab. "I know," I snap. I break the large remains of the log in the fireplace into several more pieces before reaching down and snatching another from the nearby pile—stacked neatly against the stones. I toss two into the mess. More ash and red embers emerge, fading quickly after a moment before flames erupt over the new dried wood.

That's just what life is, isn't it—you think you can overpower it with help, and then, eventually, the pain eats away at them too. With disgust, I slam the poker back into its holder and reach up, cupping my hands over the mantle as I force myself to stare into the crackling flames that roar to life.

"Where the fuck is Kalix?" I ask.

Silence greets my question and then the telltale sound of boots hitting the floor hits my ears as Ruen drags them off the table. I glance back once as he bends and snuffs out the half-burned candle with two fingers. The single trickle of smoke flitters up as he takes his hand away and then blows to the side, smacking into the pile of books he's been poring over during the nights we've waited for our—well, I don't exactly know what the girl is to us, but I do know that Kiera means more than any other woman has before. Not just to me, but to Kalix and Ruen as well.

Kalix isn't bothering to deny it. He knows he's obsessed. I've seen the way he looks at her—a mixture of curiosity and excitement thrumming in his gaze. A shiver chases down my spine. That look from him is rarely a good thing. Ruen is different though. I don't even know if he realizes that he follows her with his eyes whenever she enters a room. He tries not to, but I've known him long enough to know when he's truly not interested and when he's forcing himself not to be.

With Kiera, Ruen is always forcing himself to look away. That, more than anything else, is telling.

"He sent me a note this morning," Ruen finally says, responding to my question.

I straighten away from the fireplace, turning, but not stepping away as I face him. "And?"

Ruen's brows pucker as he frowns down at the open book on the table before lifting his blue gaze to mine. "His serpents have confirmed that the Gods are in the Academy—Tryphone as well as Azai."

"We knew that already," I grit out. "Caedmon said as much."

More and more, I am quicker to anger. That's what happens when everything you've ever known is turned on its head. Cursing silently, I drag a hand up my face and shove back the longer locks of my hair, pulling them away from my face as I stalk forward.

"What about the notice we got this morning?" I demand. "The summons?"

Ruen's lips curl down at the corners. "The summons is still in place, once she's—" He pauses and looks up as the door opens above our heads. Long silver hair, wet from the bath, flitters over the railing as Maeryn leads Kiera into Kalix's room. A moment later, the two of them are in the bedroom and the door shuts behind them. Ruen blows out a breath. "Once she's done with Maeryn, we'll tell her, and then ... we'll go before the Gods."

I curse aloud this time, the word ripping free from my throat. "What was Caedmon thinking?" I don't know who I'm asking. Ruen is just as likely to know as I am and I know nothing.

"I don't know," Ruen says regardless.

I close my eyes, blocking out the sight of him and the

room. Even still, I can hear the sounds of the women above, and the lingering scent of the sweet herbs and soap from our bathing chambers filters down to erase the last of the mud scent from the concoction Maeryn insisted on. I inhale it deeply, letting it calm my frayed nerves.

Deeper and deeper we go into this rabbit hole. No weapons. No choices. Just three blind mice following after a fluffy tailed assassin who's done nothing but lie to us for months. I can't even help it anymore. Knowing that she lied, knowing the real reason why she came to the Academy makes no difference. Still, I want her. I crave her.

"Caedmon won't let her die," Ruen says a moment later, but even he doesn't sound convinced.

After a breath, I open my eyes and settle my gaze on his. "No," I agree. "He won't. He wants to use her still." To kill Tryphone, the King of the Gods.

I don't know all that Kiera has been through, but it feels cruel to ask that of her. *Why her?* Caedmon said she was of Tryphone's bloodline. That means that Tryphone has a child out there somewhere.

My hand drops away from the top of my head and I stride forward until I'm standing next to Ruen's reading table. My hands land on the table before him. The white blond strands of my hair fall back into place, partially obstructing my view.

"Whatever happens," I say quietly, distantly aware of Maeryn and Kiera moving about in the rooms upstairs, "she stays with us."

Ruen doesn't even hesitate. He jerks his head in a nod.

"We'll tell her about the summons, but she won't go alone. We are with her," I continue, "all the way."

Beneath the dark wash of fabric he wears, Ruen's shoulders tense. "Yes," he agrees, despite the shift. "We are with her."

CHAPTER 10
KIERA

The bathing chamber is nearly silent as Maeryn and I sit back-to-back in the giant tub I'd cleaned a time or two since coming to the Academy. I'd been in it once—but that memory is tainted by what had happened after. Theos and his ... questions.

Back then, I'd been a bit too concerned with Rahela's death—partially caused by me, but finished by Kalix—to really think about how big the tub I'm in now is. I shouldn't be surprised that it's big enough for both Maeryn and me considering it's large enough to cater to one of the Darkhavens. Yet, I'd never thought to find myself in this thing again, and most certainly not with Maeryn.

The sound of water droplets dripping onto the surface of the water echoes back to my ears as the woman behind me shifts forward slightly. "Here," she says and a bar of soap and a washcloth is shoved over my shoulder.

I'd already managed to scrub off the worst of the brown sludge she'd dumped on me before filling the tub and getting in. Now, my hair hangs in limp, wet clumps down my spine. I take the cloth and soap and start on my front.

"You never answered my question," I say as I slide the cloth up one arm and down the other. My eyes catch on the little white bubbles of soap that cling to my skin, frothing up more with each pass.

Maeryn's spine goes rigid against mine and she shifts once more, causing a wave of water to ripple around us. "What question is that?" she asks, though she doesn't sound like she truly wants to know.

My hands slow to a stop and I turn to glance at her. She keeps her face turned away, as if trying to give me some semblance of privacy. I know better than that now. It doesn't take a genius to know that she was likely the one to change my clothes for me. The Darkhavens are bastards, but Ruen is the most like other men—concerned with some misplaced sense of modesty. He would have ensured someone other than him or one of his brothers took care of the task.

"What happened in the last three days to make you so nervous about telling me?"

A heartbeat passes. Silence fills the chamber, save for the sounds of our bodies shifting ever so slightly in the water and our breaths into the cool air of the room. Finally, Maeryn sighs and her head dips toward her chest.

I drop the washcloth into the water with a resounding *plop*, giving up the pretense as I cup water into my hands and rinse away the suds. "That bad?" I ask lightly when I feel anything but light.

No, I've never felt heavier. Like the weight of some unseen force is pressing against me, crushing me into the world and there's no fighting what I cannot see.

"The Gods have called for you."

I don't know what I expected Maeryn to say, but it certainly wasn't that. Turning fully, I bend my knees and bring them up towards my chest, wrapping my arms around them. "What do you mean the Gods have called for me?"

Long corkscrew curls of amber and copper fall off her shoulder as Maeryn turns and mirrors my pose. She, too, presses her back against the other side of the tub, dragging her legs up to cover her nakedness. Moss green eyes gaze back at me with worry shredding their normal composure. Her lashes, the same copper and normally painted darker with makeup slowly lower as she drifts one hand through the surface of the bath water.

"Kalix came for me three nights ago and said that you had the brimstone removed from your neck by the one who put it there," she answers. "He said that you weren't well and the others wanted me to check you out."

I remain silent, letting her get out the events that have taken place since I fell unconscious. The mention of the brimstone makes me want to reach up and touch the place behind my neck. Strangely, it no longer burns or tingles each time I remember it. Had that truly been the brimstone and not just a pain made up in my head?

"Brimstone is a mystery to many of us, but one thing we do know is that it suppresses Divinity—almost as if it has a natural barrier against our abilities."

Watching her fingers create figure 8s in the water, I think back to what Caedmon had said about how the Gods came to be in this world. The Brimstone Mountain had cracked open when the world tore open for them to enter ours from theirs. Was it something about the magic that had created that fissure that made the brimstone the natural weapon against their kind, that made it reject Divinity—magic?

"The brimstone suppressed your natural abilities for a long time," Maeryn continues. "When that brimstone was removed, all of your abilities—the ones you didn't even know you were missing—came back at once. It overwhelmed your senses and as a result, your body shut down."

"If I hadn't woken up, would you have put that stuff on me while I slept?" I ask, curious, even though my original question has yet to be answered.

Her lips twitch at the reminder. She nods. "Yes, I know it's awful, but it does work. It works with younger Mortal Gods who are either struggling to awaken their abilities or who are afraid of their abilities and unintentionally suppress them mentally. When something happens and their abilities come out, the foul smell of the concoction has the distinct effect of helping them to liberate themselves. After two days of you not waking, I figured it was the only thing that could help."

I nod slowly. I still don't like it. That horrible odor is going to haunt my nightmares and I still feel like there are clumps of the stuff glued to my back even though I rinsed and washed it thoroughly.

I wave my hand in her direction. "Alright," I concede, "but that doesn't explain why the Gods are asking for me."

Copper lashes lift and those green eyes of hers meet mine once more. "I don't know how else to tell you this but to just come right out and say it," she says, her throat bobbing and her brows pinching down. "They know, Kiera."

They know.

I don't have to ask her what they know. Only one thing could lead her to act so concerned and, yes, I'll admit I see it now, scared. Her composure isn't just shredded, it's obliterated. Fear lines her perfect features. My lungs seize as the air in my chest escapes in one long rush. My heartbeat thrums in my ears. Black and white spots dance in front of my vision as horror descends.

The Gods know what I am.

I can't breathe.

I don't realize that the room has turned pitch black until a muffled gasp from Maeryn alerts me and I blink open my eyes only to see ... nothing. Absolutely nothing. There is not a single spec of light. I reach out, feeling water at my fingertips, and then smack my knuckles into the side of the standing tub. Wincing, my pain causes my panic to ease back slightly and a fluttering of curtains above our heads draws my attention.

No. Not curtains. Shadows.

With a gasp, I hold out my hand and call them back to me. What once felt so difficult, like I wasn't even controlling them so much as the shadows were following me, has suddenly become as easy as breathing. The shadows encompassing the room fall immediately, cascading in long strings onto the floor and slithering across the floor until they reach the tub.

Then, one by one, they slide up and into the water before melding to my skin and sinking inside, disappearing. Across from me, Maeryn's face is paler than usual, her eyes wide and her hands are locked over either side of the tub's rim.

"K-Kiera?" She stutters out my name, confused and horrified.

"I'm sorry," I say and mean the words. I hadn't meant to scare the living shit out of her. I hadn't ever lost control like that. It was more work to use my powers than to keep them under wraps.

The pale rounds of her freckled breasts heave up and down with each sharp inhalation. "Y-you just ... the whole room. Those weren't spiders."

I grimace and shake my head. "No, they weren't. I'm sorry. I've never done that before."

My skin feels colder now than before and I realize that the warmth of the water is now drained. I cross my arms over my chest as a shiver moves through me. Maeryn blinks and stands, reaching for a drying sheet. She quickly steps out and wraps herself before nodding to me.

"You need to get out," she says, unfolding the sheet and holding it up.

I stare at the smooth skin of my palms for the longest time before responding. The shadows are gone, visibly, but I can still feel something under the surface, sizzling beneath my flesh. After a few more beats of no response, I shake my head and lift myself out of the tub. I take the offered sheet from Maeryn, and as I wrap myself, I return my attention to the words she'd said before.

"You said the Gods know about me." She tenses but nods her confirmation. "Why haven't they come to take me away for lying and betraying them?"

"Caedmon is the one who revealed your heritage," Maeryn answers, and somehow, it doesn't shock me. He said he would figure out a way to make sure that things would be fine. I don't exactly know how this helps, but with the brimstone removed, my abilities were bound to resurface anyway. The Gods would have found out eventually.

"He said that you were unaware and as an orphan had no knowledge of your parentage. He told the Gods that you never exhibited signs of any abilities, but perhaps being around others with Divinity somehow ... unleashed your own. They wish to see you and determine who your God parent is."

I frown, feeling the skin above my brows puckering at the revelation. "They can do that?"

Maeryn just shrugs and casts me an apologetic look as she moves across the bathing chamber to the clothes that had been left for us by Niall earlier. "I don't know," she admits. "But if he says that's what they want, then that's what they will demand. Caedmon has managed to hold them off. No one knows that you've been in the North Tower this whole time."

"Where do they think I've been then?" I ask, curious.

"I assume they suspect Caedmon is keeping you hidden for now, but even his word can only last for so long. They want to see you, have demanded your presence, and each day, they grow angrier. Everyone in the Academy can feel it." Her eyes turn to the window and even I note that the winter sky outside appears darker, as if a storm is hovering around the entire Academy. "Caedmon has sent many notes to update the Darkhavens, and they've thankfully given me some insight, but they'll want to tell you themselves too."

I remain near the tub as I watch her lift a new gown, just as long as the last one she'd worn—the one I'd dirtied in our fight. Pressing her biceps close to her sides to keep the drying sheet pinned, she holds it up slightly. It's a sword gray color with black beading around the middle to form a faux belt. The neckline is square with a small trim of lace that matches the trim at the hem and on the ends of both sleeves.

"Another reason why I went with that concoction was because we assumed it would also wake you up and you needed to be awake by today because Caedmon cannot hold the Gods off any longer with whatever excuses he's made. He's been telling them that he's keeping an eye on you and that you're under his personal control. Last night, though, someone stole into his chambers here at the Academy and the Gods are angry that they found no sign of you."

"They sent someone." That's not shocking. The Gods are rarely patient. What is a surprise is that they've managed to wait three days before making their demands.

"Yes," Maeryn says, not realizing that my words hadn't been meant as a question but as a confirmation to myself. She sighs and shakes her head at the dress before picking up the second one. Of course, Niall would bring both of us dresses. Like the first, this dress has a floor length skirt, but that's where the similarities stop.

"The gray one won't do if you're meeting the God Council," Maeryn comments with a nod before setting the second dress down and picking up the first. "I'll wear it."

Moving away from the tub, I trail behind her as she takes the first gown and ambles away to a partition that had been set up in the corner. Disappearing behind the three-sided wall, a moment later, Maeryn tosses her drying sheet over the top. I stop in front of the remaining gown and lift the fabric.

It's soft to the touch, and a blue so rich and deep that it almost looks black. There are no embellishments save for the glittering gems that litter the lower half and string over the square neckline. The sleeves are two-inch strands of the same satin fabric as the dress and then a long translucent fabric that when I place my hand beneath, makes it clear that it's just for fashion rather than for any sort of true usefulness.

"Can you lace me up?" Maeryn calls out as she steps from around the partition.

Blinking, I drop the dress and face her fully. I tuck the ends of my drying sheet between my breasts to keep it up and then motion for her to come closer. The gray is beautiful with her pale skin and the smattering of freckles, but I remember her in trousers and tunics, holding a sword. She might look beautiful and fragile like this, but I know more than most that looks can be deceiving. After all, that's how I made it this far.

Maeryn strides towards me, and the skirts swish around her ankles but stop just above the floor so that I can see her bare feet peek out from beneath them. Flipping around to face away, she gathers the length of her wet curls and reveals the sewn-in corset style back that needs lacing. I grip the top string and start to work.

"I suppose the guys told you how Caedmon knew about me?" I ask casually, my fingers moving in increments as I weave the strands through their appropriate holes and then tighten the last section before moving on to the next.

"Yes," she says, blowing out a breath. "It was a shock for me."

"Did they tell you everything else?" I make it to the halfway point and tighten the upper sections all over again to be safe. The fabric grows tighter and tighter to her frame, molding around her as if it were tailored. Who knows, maybe it was.

Maeryn glances back at me once, her eyes unreadable, before she turns back around. "No." That's all she gives me. I want to ask if that means they told her nothing more than that Caedmon knew about me or if there's more she knows. I don't, though, because I'm done and our time is up.

CHAPTER II
KIERA

Maeryn steals me into Kalix's room to finish getting ready once we're out of the bathing chamber. I can tell she hates it, her lips curled down into a perpetual frown even as I sit still and stare at the weapons on the walls. Daggers. Swords. Crossbows. His collection is extensive.

Slender, deft hands lift and twist the strands of my hair back, plaiting it into a long fishtail braid tied at the end with a thin leather band. Once she's done with that, Maeryn calls for Niall to bring her a wooden box that flips open. There's no mirror in here, so I can't see what she's doing, but once the box is in her possession, her attentions get worse.

Forced to close my eyes and sit perfectly still, I grind my jaw as Maeryn dusts makeup across my face. It feels pointless since now that my Divinity is fully unleashed, there's nothing to keep my perfection from showing through. I tell her as much, but she merely snorts and continues her task.

"The Gods don't just want perfection," she tells me. "They want something interesting. Even if they are beautiful, the Gods themselves wear makeup simply because they grow tired of the way they look. Humans use makeup to look more like Gods, but Gods paint their eyelids and cheeks and lips to look different from themselves."

At that, I snap my mouth shut and let her finish. Once she's declared me complete, Niall brings her a small handheld mirror and she holds it out to me. "There," Maeryn says, shoving it into my hand. "You may thank me later."

I hold up the gilded mirror, so stunning that it looks like it came from a God's prized collection, and stare at the reflection that's just big enough to show my face and nothing lower or higher. Somehow, Maeryn didn't take her skills with makeup too far as I'd seen many a whore on a street corner do. My eyes aren't some outrageous purple or blue that goes too far up or side to side. Instead, she merely dusted a light coating of pink over my upper cheeks and streaked my lashes with the same liquid she uses on her own to make them appear darker and longer. I don't look much different at all, simply ... *more*.

"Thank you," I say and am surprised to mean the words. I set the mirror back in her hand before I look at Niall.

He takes the mirror from her and gives me a sad smile. "Thank you, too, Niall," I say.

He tilts his head to the side, one lone lock of mousy brown hair falling over the side of his forehead with the movement. "For what?" he asks.

"For being my friend." Might as well say as much now when I'm not entirely sure if I'll live until tomorrow—no matter what Caedmon promises.

Big brown eyes glisten and his nostrils flare. After a beat, Niall manages to respond with a nod.

Maeryn tips her head to the side as if she can hear something beyond the door. Her lips curl down and a moment later she speaks. "Kalix is back," she says, "and they're waiting for you now." She turns to help Niall gather up the things she had him retrieve for her. The waves of her copper hair fall over her face as she bends to shut the wooden box and gather up a few of the brushes that had fallen to the floor. "I'll return to my dorm, and with any hope and luck, I suspect I'll see you later."

"You're not coming?"

Maeryn pauses and lifts her head even as she passes the brushes over to Niall. A pink tongue peeks out to slide across her lower lip in a nervous tick as she fists her hands in her skirts and lifts them. "Niall, why don't you head back after you drop those off in my room," she suggests.

Guilt eats at me when Niall glances between us, his lips thinning into a mutinous line that clearly shows he doesn't want to agree, but even if I'm a Mortal God, he's not. At the end of this, Niall is still just a Terra and he has no right to refuse his mistress. Cold silence follows Maeryn's kindly worded but no less potent demand. A minute passes as Niall finishes collecting the last of their things and then disappears out the door, letting it snick shut behind him.

"I know it makes me a coward," she starts, "and as much as I wish things were different..." Seafoam eyes lift to meet mine. "I can't be implicated in the discovery of you, Kiera. I can't be attached to that. In private, I can be your friend, but in public ... I'm not the only one I have to look out for. Niall has already had issues with the other Terra and if I were to get in trouble, he might—"

I cut her off with a lifted hand. "He will never have those issues again," I say. "But you don't need to explain yourself to me. I appreciate it, I do. I understand. You want to protect him." And as much as it hurts to learn that she can't acknowledge me in public as a friend, at least not right away, I *do* understand.

Her teeth sink into her bottom lip as her shoulders shrink, curling inward. "Why don't I help you dress before you head out?" she offers and I suspect it's how she wants to apologize.

Despite that, I shake my head and wave her off. "No, I'll be okay," I say. "I think I want some time to myself to prepare."

She presses her lips together, and though I can tell she wants to insist, she doesn't. Instead, she nods and turns towards the door. I frown, though, as she pauses and then—before I can blink—she whirls back and wraps her arms around me. "It'll be okay," she says, whispering into my hair as she holds me tight. "I may not have the power of prophecy, but I believe it. You're strong and you're going to be okay."

Stunned, and a little uncomfortable with the sudden burst of physical affection, I stand there for a moment, unresponsive to the hug. When she merely squeezes me tighter, though, I finally lift my arms and return the sentiment of care.

Sniffing hard as she withdraws her arms, Maeryn absently flicks a lock of my hair that fell out of the braid off my shoulder and nods. Then, without any further interruptions or embraces, she leaves the bedroom.

I stand there for a few more seconds, just breathing in through my nose and out through my mouth as I try to keep the panic at bay. *In and out. In and out.* I think back to that place I created in the back of my mind, the place that made everything better, that could always protect me from Ophelia's lessons or my own rage and fear.

My soul seems to settle more deeply into my bones with each passing breath. *In and out. In and out.*

I want to believe Maeryn. I want to live. I also can't put this off for any longer.

Opening my eyes, I look at the dress that she'd laid out for me to change into on Kalix's rumpled sheets. Stripping out of the robe I'd donned after I'd finished with the drying sheet, I grab ahold of the gown and lift it for my perusal. The delicate lace and chiffon fabric wouldn't be my first choice when meeting the God Council for the first time, but I know there's a reason behind it. Shaking my head, I stop stalling and pull it on, twisting slightly as I grip the laces that come around the front to line up directly beneath my breasts and finish tightening and tying them off. The long midnight colored skirts are a blend of blue and purple that make my skin seem brighter and whiter than ever before. The silver laces around my middle, at the ends of my sleeves, and decorating the square neckline match my hair.

To the side of the bed, I spot a pair of matching silver slippers. The top of each shoe looks like crushed diamonds as I hold them up to the light from the window. Each of them is adorned with more silver laces and when I slip my feet into the soles, I realize they're meant to tie up the length of my calves.

Once I'm done, I feel as though I've taken both a lifetime and not enough time at all to get ready. There's nothing left to do though except meet my fate—whatever it may be.

So, instead of stalling any further, I stand from the edge of the bed and head for the door. It creaks open, and what little conversation I'd dimly heard below cuts off immediately. I step out closer to the railing and look down into the Darkhavens' main room.

Kalix, Theos, and Ruen all stand there in their own suits—each looking like they belong in the window of some famous seamstress's shop. I don't know where Kalix got his, since he didn't have access to his room, but considering that the color is a deep purple, I suspect it might have come from Ruen.

Three sets of eyes land on me, one midnight, one gold,

and one a deep green. My stomach drops out from beneath me. Fear and some other emotion I'm not quite ready to name yet.

"Kiera?" Theos is the first to speak and to move. He nears the end of the staircase. "Are you alright?"

"Are you feeling lightheaded?" Ruen asks, his brow furrowing.

I shake my head and move towards the top of the stairs. "No," I lie, not wanting them to know how I'm feeling because the reason isn't one I want to examine. "I'm fine."

"Maeryn said she told you that—"

"The Gods are waiting," I say, cutting Ruen off as he frowns.

Though it wasn't a question, he nods. "They know you're awake," he says. "They expect to see you."

"And they're not willing to wait anymore," I guess.

Theos scowls. "We can send a note to Caedmon if you're not ready," he says quickly. "We didn't even get to tell you ourselves. We planned to, it just—"

Not ready? When would I ever be ready to face the Gods as ... not a Terra but as myself. My real self. Divinity—or magic—and all.

Whatever Theos means to say, however, is cut off by a low, dry chuckle. At once, all of our attentions turn to the source of the caustic amusement. Green and flecks of red glitter in Kalix's gaze as he shifts his gaze up to me. My hand wraps around the railing, practically strangling it as the skin over my knuckles whitens.

"Our *little liar* isn't so cowardly as to run from the Gods, not when she's trod upon their territory, right under their noses for so long." Kalix's words aren't a compliment, but a challenge. He tips his head back, continuing to stare at me down the bridge of his long aristocratic nose. "Is she?"

I grit my teeth and take the first step down the stairs. Ruen and Theos' heads whip towards me as I scowl at Kalix. "No, she isn't," I snap.

Damn him.

I descend the length of the staircase with my skirts swishing around my thighs, calves, and ankles. When Theos reaches out to offer his hand, I shake my head and bypass both him and Ruen until I'm standing before Kalix. His lips twitch. My heart pounds an irregular beat in my breast. I glare at him. He doesn't look perturbed. In fact, whatever he sees on my face has him bending, his fingers come up and capture my hand as he lifts it. Up and up some more until his mouth presses a close-mouthed kiss to my cold knuckles.

"The Gods are waiting," he murmurs, his lips still pressed to my skin. "What will you do now? Face them? Run? Make them pay?"

I scoff and yank my fingers away from his. "Must you always suggest killing and violence?" I demand, unwilling to look deeper into the way his mouth on me reminds me of other parts of him. Parts that hadn't just been on me, but *in* me as well. Beneath my dress, my stomach muscles contract.

"There are a thousand reasons to kill. I don't need any of them. I just want to," Kalix responds, his voice cold despite the fire burning in the depths of his eyes. "If any of them attempt to steal you from me—take you away from my brothers and me—then I will simply add another name to my list of kills."

"You can't—" I stop talking. I'd just been about to tell him that he couldn't kill a God, but that's not true. By the lies of Tryphone, Mortal Gods can kill Gods. By the supposed truths of Caedmon, it wouldn't matter Kalix's background or blood, he could still kill a God. Staring at him now, with his muscles tensed beneath his borrowed suit, I suspect he wants to.

His hand comes up and a lone finger strokes over my lower lip. I jolt at the sudden electrifying sensation that pours into me from that single touch. "I can do many things, little liar," he says, completely ignoring the fact that we aren't alone in this room. Either he's forgetting or, I suspect, he simply doesn't care that his brothers are also here. "And regardless of how I've held myself back for my brothers these last several years, if they try to take you from us, I will kill them. *All* of them."

In that terrifying moment, I believe him. If the Gods try to take me from the Darkhavens, Kalix will keep his promise. He will kill them even if it means his own death.

CHAPTER 12
KIERA

It's neither dawn nor dusk as the Darkhavens and I leave the North Tower, but perhaps somewhere in the late afternoon. I try to recall what day it'd been when we'd left the Academy to go to Madam Brione's, counting backward from the three days Maeryn had told me it'd been. Still, I don't know what day that makes today, but what I do know is that classes most certainly are not in session.

No one lingers in the corridors or the courtyards. I can't exactly blame them since one look up to the skies is enough to assume that rain will soon fall and no one enjoys getting wet in a thunderstorm. But why not the inner corridors?

I glance up one way and down another as Ruen takes the lead, directing our group through the Academy hallways towards the Gods' wing. The closer we get, the more sweat beads pop up along my spine.

Theos walks next to me, casting worried glances my way every few minutes. I offer him a small smile that I know doesn't reach my eyes, but I can't help it. It's difficult to offer a genuine smile if you're not sure what you're walking towards—death or ... acceptance.

The burning attention of Kalix's eyes on the back of my head keeps my gaze mostly straight. I don't bother to glance over my shoulder at him, sure that he'll merely offer me another of his sardonic and threatening smiles. I swallow roughly, my throat bobbing with the action, when I see the painted windows and murals of the Gods' corridors. I know the Gods of the Mortal Gods Academy of Riviere live and work in these places, but surely the God Council would have even better accommodations. Wouldn't they?

My silent question is answered a moment later as Ruen leads us past the offices—including the door to Dolos' office that I remember from my sentencing several weeks back—to a staircase. We ascend the stairs, one after another with Kalix, once more, bringing up the rear. When we reach the next floor, something slithers over the top of my foot and I bite down a scream, jolting to a halt as I grip my skirts and look down to spy the smallest snake I've ever seen slip over my foot and around my ankle.

The creature's little black scaled head tips back gazing up at me briefly before it closes its eyes and settles against my skin as if it means to fall asleep like that, wrapped around my leg.

"Leave him," Kalix orders at my back, finally forcing me to turn and look at him.

"He's yours?" I clarify. Though I've never minded my own familiars crawling over my arms and legs—it had felt natural to let them do so—this creature is not mine. I cannot meld their mind with my own or reach out and sense their feelings.

Kalix nods in response. "Should the Gods wish to separate us and talk to you alone, I will be able to see and listen to everything."

He likely won't be able to see everything, I think with a grimace, not with the snake's body and head covered by my skirts. Another thought occurs to me. Will he be able to see up my skirt with the snake's presence? I whip my head around to glare at him and for a moment, I part my lips to tell him to take back his perverted familiar when a hand reaches out and latches on to my wrist, stopping me.

"Kiera." Theos' choked voice has me turning back to face whatever it is he's trying to capture my attention for. When I do see it, my whole body goes cold.

Caedmon stands outside a set of crimson double doors with similar carvings to the painted scenes on the first level of the building etched into the wood. His hands are clasped behind his back, but his face is tight with concern and tension. One of the beads of sweat on my spine pops and sends the liquid sliding down my back.

"Thank you for coming," Caedmon begins. The doors crack open and the sound of voices exits as a familiar face appears, quickly slipping free of the room and closing the door behind them.

Dauphine stands next to Caedmon, her face paler than usual. My gaze pans down to her dress. Gone is the plain gray of the Academy Terra attire and in its place is a more ornate gown of pale yellow muslin. A little detail decorates the front and bottom of the skirt and her puffy short sleeves make her shoulders look a bit more mannish than ever before. The only thing that does anything to accentuate her body is the thin ribbon tied around her torso just under her breasts. The color does nothing for her countenance, but the dress itself is pretty and far more expensive than I'd expect any human Terra to be able to afford.

"Th-they are ready, Your Divinity," Dauphine says without looking in our direction.

"Thank you, Dauphine." Caedmon nods to her. "You may return to your regular duties."

Dauphine doesn't need to be told twice; as soon as Caedmon's dismissal has left his lips, she practically sprints down the corridor. She keeps her head down, not even bothering to glance up as if she doesn't want to know who's been called to the God Council as she bypasses the Darkhavens and me on her way to take the stairs down to the ground floor.

Once the resounding clap of her feet on the stairs has receded, all of our attention returns to each other. Caedmon and I gaze at one another for a long moment. When he finally releases a breath, he unfolds his arms from behind his back and holds one out for me.

"Come, Kiera," he commands. "The God Council awaits."

I take a step forward, but Theos' hand on my arm hasn't released me. I pause when the hold keeps me from moving more than that single step and look back. "Theos?" His attention isn't on me but on Caedmon.

"We're going with her," Theos says, directing the words to Caedmon.

Caedmon lets his hand drop and then shakes his head. "I'm afraid not, Theos," he replies. "You may wait out here, but you cannot go in with her."

Ruen shifts his stance from slightly in front of me to completely there, his big body stepping between me and the path to the God of Prophecy. The snake around my ankle rubs its head against my skin and I jerk my gaze back to Kalix's. His eyes aren't on mine but as he raises a palm to warm the small of my back, he directs me forward.

Theos' grip on my wrist eases and then falls away as Kalix urges me around Ruen and further down the hall. Caedmon seems just as surprised as I am because his eyebrows rise and continue to do so until they're as high as I suspect they can go before Kalix and I stop before him.

"We will be out here." Kalix's voice is quiet as he speaks.

"Should she scream, we will know. Should she be harmed, we will know. Should anything happen to her that we would not approve of, we will know."

Verbally, as far as threats go, it's not very inventive. Physically, though, Kalix's eyes glitter like emeralds dipped in blood. The specs of red grow in volume and brightness as they swim through the mossy irises. Cold air wafts over the back of my neck and my braid flutters to the side. I've never been one of those petite women. Muscular? Yes. Average in height and weight? Yes. But never small or petite.

Next to Kalix and Caedmon, I feel like I've entered someone else's body. Someone far tinier and far more breakable.

Hating the strange thought, I pull away from Kalix's hand and shake my head, reaching for Caedmon. Holding my hand out for him to take, I eye him speculatively. "I'm ready," I inform him, though I feel anything but.

Caedmon's much darker fingers slide over mine, rougher than I expected. I blink and glance down, for the first time, noticing the calluses there. Calluses I know well because it took years for me to develop them enough beyond my own healing capabilities.

My eyes lift back to his face and though I don't say anything, I know that those marks can't lie. If it took me—a Mortal God—years to develop those calluses with my healing, how long had it taken him?

I'd once assumed that Caedmon was someone obsessed with knowledge and futures. Perhaps, I was wrong though. Even Gods cannot hide the signs of sword usage. He might appreciate books and art and instruction—in this world of the Divine and Mortal, he might be my guide—but I suspect he is far more than that.

This man, whoever he pretends to be, is a warrior beneath it all.

~

The room that Caedmon leads me into is long and tall. The ceiling arching over our heads is so high up that they are shadowed. As we enter the double doors, the first thing I notice is the floor. Most of the buildings at the Academy are made of some sort of stone and the Gods' buildings are no different. The floor of this room, however, is carefully painted with depictions of the Gods.

Starting with the tanned face of a particularly beautiful male whose rugged features are cut into a square jaw and glittering gold eyes. He appears somehow familiar, but I don't have a chance to continue examining the image before Caedmon's urging me forward. My eyes continue, remaining on the floor as we pass over a woman with long golden blonde hair set in waves over her high and round breasts. The next image is more than familiar.

It's Caedmon with his dark skin tone a striking contrast against the light gray of the stone. I jerk my head up and look at him, but his gaze is focused ahead. Only then do I finally turn the rest of my attention to what lies in front of me.

The God Council chambers are set up much like throne rooms of old—back before they existed in this world. I'd read of old Kings and Queens and how they'd held audiences in long rooms with a dais set up at the very end. This room is similar to those old storybooks. The pillars lining either side are separated by recessed wall insets and arching stained glass windows similar to those in the lower corridor halls. Candle chandeliers, round and unlit, hang from golden chains anchored to the ceiling and walls.

My attention finally lands on the five Gods and Goddesses waiting upon the dais with an ornate golden and redwood table stretched before their chairs. An empty seat remains at the far left side and I realize it's meant for Caedmon. He stops me before the dais and moves away from me, striding up to join the rest of them, rounding the table, and taking his seat.

I'd walked too fast to examine the other images painted on the floors, but as I gaze upon the now six faces before me, I realize that those images were meant to represent these men and women. The God Council.

Slowly, I let my gaze move from Caedmon to the others. On his right is a woman I don't recognize, her skin is a soft brown, several shades lighter than Caedmon's but no less luxurious in its smoothness. Her hair is dark, nearly pitch black as it hangs in waves over her shoulders and down her back out of sight. Upon her head sits a simple gold crown that matches the gold bracelets adorning her wrists. Her eyes are a darker brown than her skin, but soft with sympathy as she looks at me.

Stiffening at that sympathy, I turn my head quickly to the side, skipping over the God and Goddess at the center of the table whose chair backs rise higher than the rest. At the very end is the same man I saw in the first floor painting. His golden hair is darker than the artwork with various shades of brown through the locks. But just like the woman, he wears it long in thick waves. The only difference is that several of his strands are gathered together and locked in little trinkets of jewelry that pin the locks into braids.

His jawline is sharp and angled and covered by the light stubble of beard growth that reaches halfway up his cheeks. Bold gold eyes peer back at me, not with sympathy but with idle curiosity and ... boredom?

Why does he look so familiar?

Before my mind can supply an answer, my attention falls to the woman at his side. A woman with dark skin, similar to Caedmon's, sits straight-backed with her bare shoulders covered only by a light white cape tied at her throat with a simple gold chain. Her wiry hair fans out behind her head in a large puffy afro that appears like a halo surrounding her soft features. Of the rest of the men and women sitting upon the dais, her bone structure is the most petite and fragile looking.

For someone like me, that fact makes me far more cautious of her than any other. I know from experience that those who appear delicate are often the most dangerous.

As my attention moves to her eyes, I blink, realizing that she's staring back. One dark eyebrow arches at me, amusement clear in her open expression. Her eyes are the color of honey, with lighter brown rings circling the point of her pupil.

Finally, I look at the two sitting at the center. The woman is the same as the floor painting. Her long blonde hair curls over her shoulders and down toward her chest. Her features are striking and far sharper than the image had depicted. The more I stare at her, the more I realize she's not truly blonde. Instead, her hair is like a thousand different variations of the color—some of it darker, but much of it is lighter and almost the same shade of silver as mine. Her shoulders are straight back and her lips set into an ambiguous line that doesn't give me any hint as to what lies within her mind.

The lone man at her side is none other than the man I know to be Tryphone. His features are slightly different from what I'd seen in a few of his paintings and the statues of him around the Academy. There are thin, fine lines at the corners of his lips and between the dark slashes of his brows. Age lines? A shiver slithers down my spine and I try not to focus on them, to let him know that I've noticed something that I shouldn't.

Caedmon said that they are Atlanteans, not Gods. I know that. I understand it, yet still, my mind struggles to connect his truth with what I've known all my life. These are Gods that I've always feared and resented. Gods are immortal and all powerful. They shouldn't have age lines. The fact that they do only lends more credit to Caedmon's outrageous words.

My attention centers a bit more on his eyes. No painting could have shown the vibrant storms that create the color of his irises. Silver and blue clash together like seas and storm clouds. But it's not the color that makes my heart skip a beat, but the lightning flashing within them. The riot of untapped power that exudes from his very bones pours into the room, sliding over my flesh. My throat closes up and a similar power that I'd felt from Dolos slams into me. My knees buckle and I hit the ground hard.

My legs crack against the stone and the pain ricochets through my limbs. I bite back a curse, sure I've just broken something. My kneecaps feel like they've been shattered. Fissures form under my flesh as the injury throbs anew.

"Tryphone." The name is spoken with a feminine voice, admonishing.

Gasping, I try to suck air, but it never comes. My lungs collapse in my chest and my ribcage opens into a cavern for the dead. I am but a corpse in flesh, waiting to rot.

Air. I need air.

Something moves against my ankle and I nearly jerk my dress up and reach for whatever it is when I remember the snake Kalix had placed with me. The little creature is circling my leg, spinning around and around and shivering its scales against my skin as if it's trying to tell me ... what? That Kalix is nearby? That he's on the other side of those doors along with Ruen and Theos?

The Darkhavens are powerful but these ... these are the actual fucking Gods. Even if Caedmon admitted that these beings are not Gods in their world, to me, that's exactly what they are. The power rolling off them and permeating the room practically strangles me. I squeeze my eyes shut as a choked noise leaves my mouth and black dots dance behind my eyelids.

I reach down, still, though, patting the snake through the dress skirts in the hopes that doing so will make the little creature calm down and not alert Kalix.

"*Tryphone.*" This time, the woman's voice fills with annoyance. "That's enough."

Suddenly, I can breathe again. My eyes snap open as air returns to my lungs and the graveyard of my body springs back to life. I suck in breath after breath, coughing as it chokes me. My hands clench and unclench on the stone floor as I remain, kneeling on the ground before the dais.

No doors crash open. No Darkhavens come storming in. More than the fact that I haven't passed out, the fact that the Darkhaven brothers are not currently bearing down on me tells me that all of that must have happened in only a matter of seconds.

A chair scrapes back, the sound a sharp cry in my mind. Footsteps echo closer, but still, I don't look up. Afraid, I realize. I'm afraid to. My limbs tremble and my mind crawls over itself, searching for a way out—a way to escape my body and free itself.

It doesn't matter that the hand that cups my shoulder is gentle. It doesn't matter that the voice that follows it is soothing. The second someone else is near, I flinch away, scooting back slightly on my broken knees, ignoring the shriek of agony that my body responds with.

Tsking in her throat, the woman reaches for my chin and lifts my face upward. The blonde Goddess. Her full, peach colored lips purse in displeasure as she takes in my expression. Then she turns, accusingly, on the God King. "She's hurt herself thanks to your power," she snaps.

Tryphone's voice, when he speaks, is a low rumble. "She will heal, Danai."

Danai. I blink in recognition. This woman is Danai—the Queen of the Gods, wife to Tryphone. She is the Goddess of Beauty and ... of pain, I recall dimly.

Danai huffs an irritated breath and then hooks her hand around one of my arms and urges me to stand. I do, but my legs shake and tremble with the effort. Yes, Tryphone is right, I will heal. I can already feel the heat around my fractured kneecaps working faster than ever before as it repairs the damage caused by my fall. Is the speed and heat because the brimstone is gone? I wonder absently.

I'm so focused on the quickly receding pain, my brow puckered in confusion, that it takes me another moment to realize that a woman is speaking.

Lifting my head, I blink as the woman on Caedmon's right arches a brow at me. Her lips part. "Did you not hear me, child?" she demands.

I shake my head, feeling like my head managed the impossible feat of escaping because right now it feels very much detached from my body. The woman taps her long fingers against the table's empty surface.

"I asked if this is the first time you've ever received an injury," she snaps. "You appear confused by the healing."

My head tips down again and I feel something wet slide

under the skirts of my dress. Though the folds had cushioned my landing somewhat, no doubt the sharpness with which my knees had cracked against the stone had still split the flesh.

"I've never healed this fast before," I admit and am thankful that I can be honest. "It feels ... warm."

In response, the woman turns her attention to Tryphone. "Caedmon must be right then," she states, directing the words at him. "It's very unlikely that she's made it to adulthood with no wound before and if she's only now noticing the rapid healing and heat of it, then—"

"Unlikely," Tryphone rumbles, cutting her off, "but not impossible."

Danai's hand slides away from me as I straighten. As much as I want to yank my skirts up and see if the wound is still there, I won't. Instead, I lift my head, forcing the action past the threshold of my trembling fear.

"I've been wounded before," I say. "I've never felt ... this." I gesture down to my legs.

It has to be the removal of the brimstone, I decide. Before this, I'd certainly healed faster than a normal human, but never with this odd sensation of fire licking over my flesh. It's barely been minutes since I'd injured myself and yet the pain is already completely gone. The remaining wetness on my calves is likely blood from already closed wounds.

Tryphone hums in the back of his throat and gestures for Danai to return to him. She sighs and carefully releases me, pausing to see if I'll falter again. When I don't, she moves back to the dais and strides up the side steps until she circles the table to her own seat at the God King's side.

My heart thuds a rapid beat in my chest as I wait for one of them to speak again. Thankfully, I don't have to wait long.

"How did you say you found her again, Caedmon?" the man at the opposite end inquires, those gold eyes of his roving over me.

"She's been a Terra at the Academy for several months," Caedmon replies with a cool tone. "Serving your sons, in fact, Azai."

Shock slams into me. *Azai*. This man is Azai, God of Strength and Virility and he is the Darkhavens' father. My eyes snap to his face and delve over his features with a renewed intensity. The familiarity I see becomes all the more consuming. His eyes are the same gold as Theos'. His cut jawline is similar to Ruen's and the shape of his lips and nose ... they're all Kalix.

By the Gods ... how had I not seen it before?

Azai barks out a laugh, but it sounds nothing like any of his sons. Then again, I can't currently recall if I've ever heard Ruen laugh. Is this man part of the reason for that? Azai turns those burning sunset eyes back on me, assessing. "She's been my sons' servant for months, you say?" He eyes me. "Perhaps her survival for so long is a true testament to her heritage."

The implication has me narrowing my gaze on him, but I keep my lips pressed together.

The woman next to Azai is the next to speak. "This is a unique situation, Tryphone," she comments, her tone light and airy, almost too soft for me to hear. Yet, it rings in my head with all of the bells of a perfect symphony. Pinpricks of awareness dart down my spine. Her voice is the kind that would cause ships to crash straight into cliffs just for the chance to get closer to its bearer. I find myself unintentionally swaying with the sound of it tinkling in my ears like the wind chimes I'd seen women place in their gardens. The music of nature slips over my senses like a gentle caress.

"That's putting it mildly, Makeda," Azai snorts.

Ignoring him, Makeda—the soft-spoken Goddess—turns her honey gaze on me. "Tell us of your background, child," she orders. "Who are your parents?"

"I ..." My eyes span to Caedmon briefly. He nods for me to continue and I take in a deep breath. "I'm an orphan," I admit, biting down on the words even as my father's face springs to my mind.

"How long have you been an orphan?" Makeda inquires.

"Ten years, ma'am." As I answer her question, I decide to stick as close to the truth as possible. "My father and I lived in the Hinterlands, but our cabin was attacked by bandits and he died. Our home was burned to the ground."

She taps her chin with one nail. "So you entered society then? Your father never told you of your mother?"

I shake my head, wincing as I realize how tricky it will be to stick to the truth from here on out. Carefully, I lift my eyes to meet hers. "I don't remember my mother," I admit. "It was always just my father and me until he died. After he was gone, I needed to work to pay for myself." Every word is a truth, though it paints what I went through in a far different light than my mind recalls.

"How pitiable," the woman next to Caedmon murmurs.

"There is a way for us to determine her bloodline," Tryphone announces. "She is obviously a Mortal God—I can feel her power from here."

Danai nods. "As can I. It's quite strong. Her God parent must be the upper echelon."

"If her father was human," Makeda says, her voice sending those tendrils of pleasure rippling over my ears once more, "then there is a Goddess out there that gave birth and did not report her child."

"What of her punishment?" Azai leans forward in his seat and even as his question makes my muscles clench, his expression turns dark in an instant. "It is against our laws for Mortal Gods to be hidden."

"And how was she to know?" the woman next to Caedmon speaks again, irritation flashing in her eyes as she turns them on Azai.

Azai sneers at her. "Ignorance has never been a reason before, Gygaea," he snaps. "I was forced to kill one of my own lovers for hiding my son."

"If you'll recall, the mother was punished, not your son," Caedmon says quietly, cutting in without ever moving from his seat.

Azai glares over Gygaea's head to the man. "He *was* punished."

Who? My mind searches over all that I know of the Darkhavens. Which of his sons did he have to punish? Which of their mothers died by his hands? The questions circling my mind make me realize just how much I don't know about them still. The realization sits on my chest like a heavy weight. My fingers ball into fists at my sides and I bury them in the folds of my dress.

Caedmon releases a slow and almost sad sounding breath. "That was for attacking you, Azai," Caedmon reminds him. The God of Prophecy lifts his ebony eyes to mine and holds my stare as he continues. "Ruen was protecting the parent he knew. Despite that, he knew that attacking a God is against our laws. He was not punished for keeping his own existence a secret."

Ruen. My heart slams into my ribcage with this information. It was Ruen's mother that Azai had slaughtered. Had he done so in front of him? My mind supplies a horrible image—a younger Ruen in a child's body, with a child's strength viciously climbing onto the strong looking man sitting before me now, biting, fighting, and pounding little fists into the man as he cut down the mortal woman that had birthed and raised Ruen Darkhaven.

In that small image, I don't picture Ruen with the scar that now marks the side of his face, over his brow, and down his upper cheekbone. Had that been given to him as punishment from his own father?

"With the girl's father gone," Makeda states, dragging all of the Gods' attention back to her, "he cannot be punished for her existence. As for the girl's mother—we will perform the ceremony to find her bloodline and then whoever she is, we will call her here and she will be punished." She turns her gaze to Tryphone. "Is that decision acceptable, my King?"

Tryphone looks her over before turning dark eyes on me once again. I freeze, ice coating my bones to hold me in place as his power rolls over me for the second time, heavy and ... a bit curious, I think. I blink at that. Yes, I realize a moment later. The power that reaches out to me from the man seated in the center of the Council is oppressive, but it's also inquisitive. Is that heaviness on purpose as I'd suspected it had been earlier? Or is it just a natural weight to his power like that of Dolos'?

"Yes," the God King finally says after a long strained silence.

My breath still doesn't release from my chest. He holds me suspended for several more moments. It isn't until Danai's hand comes down on his arm and he turns in her direction that the feeling of air filling my lungs returns.

"She'll be entered into our records as a Mortal God while we await the date of the ceremony," Danai states. Her hand leaves Tryphone's and her gaze moves towards the end of the dais. "Until then, Caedmon, I'd ask that you be put in charge of her care. She'll have to be brought up to speed on lessons and such."

"I'm going to attend classes?" I blurt out the question before I can think better of it.

All six pairs of the God Council's eyes fall upon me. I press my lips together. It's Gygaea who speaks first. "Yes, of course," she says. "You are a Mortal God, child. Not a human. You should be afforded the same respect."

Respect? I slide my tongue along my upper teeth to distract myself from the caustic irritation caused by that comment. Mortal Gods are not respected—at least, not by these false Gods.

"Kiera will be prepared for the ceremony," Caedmon states, assuring the others. "And everything else will be taken care of."

Tryphone nods, but it's Danai who speaks next. "We'll have the ceremony the night after the second equinox. Spring comes soon."

Caedmon's lips press together, but he doesn't disagree. He simply bows his head toward her in what I assume is both an acknowledgment of her words and an agreement.

I let my gaze rise to meet his, but just as I take a step back, unsure if I should bow first or simply leave, Tryphone straightens in his seat. "Kiera?" He says my name as his brow furrows over the slanted slits of his eyes. "That is your name?"

Frowning, I nod. "Yes, Your Majesty."

At his side, Danai's face pales. "Did your father choose your name?" she asks, the question whipping out of her mouth, more of a demand than an inquiry.

"I-I don't know," I tell her honestly. "He never said."

The twisting violet of her gaze darkens and then she turns

to her husband. "I see." Her voice lowers. "Thank you, child. You may leave."

I don't hesitate or bother to ask why my name seems to be so upsetting to them. I simply curtsy awkwardly, turn, and flee the room, feeling the sharp gazes of the God Council burning into my back the whole way.

CHAPTER 13
KIERA

To my utter surprise, the Darkhavens ask me no questions once I return to them. Instead, they merely look me over for wounds, and when Kalix stomps forward and bends low, I nearly falter and collapse in a heap onto the floor. Thankfully, I'm far stronger than that and I grasp the top of his shoulder, growling low in my throat, ready to demand to know what the fuck he's doing as he gathers up my skirts and lifts them to reveal...

Shit. My mouth closes with a snap. I completely forgot about the snake that he'd ordered to stay with me as I'd gone into the room. The creature slithers off my ankle into his waiting palm and then beneath the cuff of his shirtsleeve. The animal had remained steady, silent, and completely still around my ankle even when I'd fallen to my knees. With a wince, I send a silent apology to the familiar.

Kalix trails a single finger up the line of blood he reveals with my lifted skirts. It's already dried in some areas, but in others still wet. His finger comes away red and without a word, he licks it from the digit. My lips twist in disgust but not shock. I'm learning that there is no understanding Kalix Darkhaven.

Once that's finished, Kalix releases my skirts and then stands to take my arm. He says nothing and Ruen and Theos are like silent shadows as Kalix tugs me toward the stairwell. Together, the four of us move back through the Academy grounds until we reach the North Tower without ever saying a word.

Somehow, I feel far more exhausted now after seeing the God Council than I had after having the brimstone removed from my neck. My eyelids are weighed down by the urge to sleep—a side effect of Tryphone's power? Maybe.

As we enter the Darkhaven chambers, Kalix releases me to go to the window across the large living space where a bird taps insistently at the glass. One of Regis' birds, I recognize a split second later. As Theos reaches for me now that Kalix has strode away, I rip away from his outstretched hand and dive across the room to the window.

"Kalix—" I have one hand stretched out as Kalix pops open one of the panels of the windows with a latch I didn't notice previously. The bird flies inside and heads straight for me.

Halting in the center of the room right before the fireplace, I lift an arm and the bird drops down. The animal's wings flutter lightly against my skin as its claws bite into the fabric of my dress over my forearm. I wince slightly but pull the note I see tied to its foot.

"What is it?" Theos asks, his voice growing closer as footsteps echo at my back.

"A note," I say, struggling to flip the curled edges open with the bird still on my arm. I lift the creature, and it climbs onto my shoulder, allowing me the space to unroll the scroll. I read the small script there.

"What does it say?" Ruen's voice comes closer and I ball up the strip of parchment in my hand on pure instinct, hesitating to answer him.

He knows everything now—what I am, who I am, and about the Underworld—but despite that, it's hard to ignore years of training that tell me to keep my secrets. Midnight eyes narrow on my face. I purse my lips. One second passes then two.

Theos sighs, breaking the silence. "You might as well tell us, *Dea*." His words are quiet, but unyielding. He seems to be the only one of them that I think actually gives a fuck whether I want to or not. Yet, he will still demand answers.

I close my eyes, shutting out the room and the three men eyeing me. One breath. Two. Three. I just stand there for several moments enjoying the feeling of having control over my own source of air. My limbs are trembling, I realize, when I open my eyes and look down at the piece of paper still clutched in my fist.

"Ophelia, Carcel, and Regis are leaving Riviere," I say. "They're heading to Nysa."

"For a job?" Theos asks.

I shake my head. "I don't know." And now that sending me information has been compromised, because surely Ophelia expects that whatever they tell me will get to these three and Caedmon, I doubt they'll say if I send a message back asking.

I stride over to the fireplace, the embers of the dead fire illuminating the barest bit as air wafts over the ashes and the lone log that's inside, half burned and ashy. Without waiting for any of them to ask to see the parchment, I rip the paper into tiny little pieces and scatter it over the remains of the fire.

My head pounds fiercely, the dull ache taking up residence at the back of my skull and spanning outward as if it has little fingers clutching at any area of my mind it can reach. I sway on my feet and the bird on my shoulder flaps its wings, the barest hint of wind against my throat as it lifts up and away. Distantly, I hear the window latch reopen and the rustle of those wings growing further and further away.

Leaning over the hearth, I place one hand on the stones surrounding the inset of the wall and heave a great breath. "What now?" I manage to ask.

Silence meets my question and my lips twist in irritation. I'm debating on whether or not I have the energy to face them when I finally receive an answer.

"You stay here," Ruen states. "Caedmon will send notice of what the Gods have decided and then—"

"The Gods have decided to have me inducted as a Mortal God here," I say, cutting him off as that throbbing in my head grows worse.

"What?" Theos barks. "They accepted you without punishment?"

I turn my head in his direction without moving the rest of my body and send him a baleful look. "Do you think they would have allowed me out of that room if they intended to punish me?"

He blinks as if startled by the question and his expression twists—part flush of what I assume is chagrin and part turmoil. "No," he says after a bit. "I suppose not."

"Nothing changes, then," Kalix says, reminding me of his presence as he leaves the window and strides closer. Unwilling to keep my back to him, I release the stone and turn to face him, reclining onto the side of the fireplace. "You stay here and you attend classes with us."

I shouldn't be surprised that he knows. Other than what it means to be inducted as a Mortal God at the Academy, no doubt his little familiar had heard all and relayed it to his master. I stare back at the forest green eyes that rove over me now.

"You're pale."

I grimace and admit, "My head hurts."

Theos turns towards the door. "I'll go get Maeryn."

I reach for him, intending to stop him, but he's gone before I can get another word out—the door shutting silently behind him. *Fuck*.

"Come, you should lie down." Ruen takes my arm, startling me.

I want to argue. I want to fight against them and demand that he release me, but just as I go to do so I realize how fucking tired I really am. I nearly falter and go down on my knees again as Ruen tugs me away from the fireplace. Even though I manage to stay upright, it's not without issue. I stumble along at his side, my feet tripping over one another in a way I'm not accustomed to.

I'm a damned assassin. Trained. Cautious. Strong. Why can't I walk straight? It's the simplest of tasks.

"Kiera?" Ruen's voice sounds as if it's coming down a long dark tunnel. My eyes stay fixed on the floor, my shoes winking in and out of my vision despite knowing I haven't pulled my gaze away.

Cold dread slips through my veins and into the rest of my body. My ass hits something soft, but almost as soon as that happens, I start sliding. I'm going to slip right off whatever it is and onto the floor, I just know it. How fucking embarrassing.

Before I can, solid arms lift me as if I weigh nothing at all. My feet disappear from view entirely and no ground meets them as I'm hauled close to a wide chest. My hand slaps the rock-like muscle and my head sinks back. A pair of midnight eyes meet mine, the brows above them creased with ... could that be concern? From Ruen?

"What did they do to you in that room?" The question is so quiet that I'm not entirely sure if I just read it from his lips or if he really whispered it.

Unable to hold my head up any longer, I let myself rest against him as the world starts moving around me. It takes a beat for my addled mind to catch up to the fact that the world isn't so much moving as he's walking with me—right towards the room I woke up in. Ruen carries me into the bedroom I know is his and lays me down on the bed. The skirts around my legs get tangled up when he tries to pry the sheets out to cover me and he finally gives up with a grunt. A low voice speaks from the doorway and his head turns towards it. I can't hear what's being said, though I think it's Kalix. My ears seem to be filled with some invisible substance that feels like rushing water and everything around me is muffled.

Try as I might, the room swims around me and an imperceivable amount of time later, another familiar figure appears over me. I blink wondering belatedly when Ruen disappeared and Maeryn took his place. Her features are creased with worry as she sets one cool hand on my forehead.

She closes her eyes and then something warm emanates from the palm on my head. It fills me and lifts away the running water taking up space between my ears. Something pops and the water is completely gone. I can hear again. I flinch at the loudness of sound—from the crackle of fire in the hearth of the bedroom someone must have lit to the pounding of my own heartbeat.

Maeryn sighs and I look up as she opens her eyes once more and gives me what I assume is an attempt at a reassuring smile. It's less reassuring and more tense, but I don't say anything as she turns back to someone just behind her. My gaze flits over her shoulder as I spy Ruen with a thunderous expression.

"It's just the aftereffects of having the brimstone removed, I think," Maeryn starts.

"You *think?*" He glowers at her. "What do you mean, you think?"

Maeryn's shoulders bunch and though I can't see her expression, I can tell by the stance she takes—the slight widening of her feet as she plants them on the floor and the tension radiating down her spine a moment before her low, annoyed voice enters the air—that she's not happy with him.

"Yes, Ruen, I think. Perhaps you should try it sometime," Maeryn snaps. I repress a snort. "I've never known or met anyone that has lived with a sliver of brimstone in them for years much less the decade Kiera had it. There's no telling what kind of effects she's suffering from. This is all new. Brimstone damages us as you are well the fuck aware. She's still—" Maeryn keeps going, her words shooting out one after the other like daggers sailing through the air, but I stop on her last statement. My attention shifts up a bit more from Maeryn's shoulder to Ruen's face and the scar that cuts through the side of his handsome features. The thin, raised line dissects his brow and then, thankfully, skips his eye, before continuing to travel over his cheek as it tapers off.

The memory of the Council room returns to me. Something Azai had said—he'd had to kill one of his children's mothers and then punish the child. Ruen had been that child. Is that scar from his father? My lips twist even as the cold, dead thing inside my chest pumps blood through the rest of my body. It aches for him.

I had only had my father for a short time. The blink of an eye in a God's—or Atlantean's—lifetime, but I knew for each and every moment of that time together that he would die before he would ever scar me the way Ruen's had done to him. Shutting my eyes against that thought, I recline against the pillows and sheets, unaware of just how tense I'd been.

"I'm tired," I say, the words croaking out to halt Maeryn's tirade.

"Of course you are," Maeryn says, sounding as if she is just as tired as I am. "Get some sleep. We can speak again tomorrow. Your head should feel better now."

I open my eyes and peer up at her. "It does," I admit. "I don't know what you did, but thank you."

Her lips curve into a light smile and she nods. "You're welcome." With that, Maeryn sends the others in the room a seething glance and leaves. My lips twitch in amusement, but almost as quickly as my burst of energy came back, it leaves again and my eyelids slide down once more.

It isn't until I feel a masculine hand on my cheek that my eyes startle open once more. Ruen's expression is pinched tight as he releases my face and then turns away. That's it. Just that single touch and then he's gone. They all are and I'm left alone in the room with sparks of something vibrant and hot sliding through my body.

With a shaky hand, I reach up and touch the same place he had. The heat is long gone, or at least, it should be. Yet, something lingers there beneath the surface and no matter how many times I rub my fingertips over the section of flesh on my face, it doesn't go away. I fear it's embedded into my skin now and I have no idea what that means.

CHAPTER 14
RUEN

White lines mar the inside of my forearm. Only slightly paler than my skin, each slice was cut with a shaft of brimstone sharpened to a fine point. Each of them is so faint that most can't even perceive them. Just in case, though, I almost always manage to cover them with my clothes. The ones on my back are different. Deeper, whiter, more noticeable.

I remember each and every one of them, though the reason for them has long been lost to me. Instead, I merely recall the way that the blood had welled up from beneath my flesh as it poured down my skin and smudged across the blade and my fingertips.

I drag a washcloth covered in soap over my arms and chest absently. It takes a concentrated effort to ignore those markings. There are dozens on each forearm, more than that if you count the scars I'd repeatedly cut open and made deeper to ... well, I'm not entirely sure what I'd wanted to do when I started the process.

I grab handfuls of water and rinse away the suds before

standing and getting out of the tub. Water sluices down my body, running between crevices and indentions made by the muscles I've packed on since I was that skinny, half-starved child when Azai tracked us down. The room is colder now that I'm no longer sitting in the waist-deep water. It had cooled significantly since I'd first gotten in but it was still warmer than the air is now. I ignore that and reach for a drying sheet, wrapping it around my waist and tucking the end into itself before I swipe a hand up my face and shove the dripping strands of my hair out of my eyes.

My fingers still over the one mark that was not made by my own hand. The slightly raised line that dissects my brow and skips my eye to taper off on my upper cheek is tight with age. I close my eyes and let my hand drop away. I itch to go back to my room and find the brimstone blade I keep hidden beneath the floorboards and use it on myself. It would distract me from the very sensual and dangerous woman now sleeping in my bed. It would ... be useless, I ultimately decide with a shake of my head.

Opening up old wounds won't do more than create problems. I'd stopped for a while after Theos had found the blade —forcing me to change my hiding spot for the damn thing. I'd intended to start back up just when I needed it, but then she'd come into our lives. Like a storm bent on wrecking freshly built cities, Kiera Nezerac had torn through our mundane reality and ripped large gaping holes in our foundation. No, perhaps, it would be more apt to say she'd merely unsettled things enough for our foundation to be ripped from its roots. Caedmon had done the actual ripping with what he'd revealed.

The Gods are not Gods at all but creatures from another world.

I can safely say I had never seen that coming.

With slow steps, I pad across the bathing chamber to the mirror against the far wall and to the waiting pile of clean and dry clothes on the stool next to it. I quickly finish drying my body, ripping the sheet away to use it against my skin with rough movements, ridding myself of the water droplets still clinging to me before sliding into fresh black trousers and doing up the row of buttons. Beyond the window, a low hum of thunder echoes closer. I pause on the final button and lift my gaze to the glass and the skies beyond. Another rumble sounds in the distance, and almost as soon as I take a step toward the window, the clouds part and rain begins to pour. Just a perfect fucking shit ending to the perfect fucking shit week.

The smattering of clicks and taps of the rain slapping the side of the tower fills the room and the lights in the sconces on the walls flicker as if they can sense the wind of the storm on the outside. For several long moments, I stand there, letting the last of the water on my skin dry in the too cold air as my eyes find my face in the window's reflection. Down, down, down my eyes sink until they're, once again, fixated on the scars smattering along my arms. I close my eyes briefly, shutting out their image before turning away from the window and moving to finish dressing.

I rip a long dark tunic over my head and yank it down my arms, covering the evidence of my pathetic weakness before leaving the bathing chamber. The main floor is empty. Quiet. Dark.

The others are either asleep or closed off in their rooms. As I reach the hearth, I pause and for the longest moment, I debate making a bed for myself on one of the lounges. A rustling sound draws my eyes towards the stairs again and I spy, with no small amount of disgust and unease, one of Kalix's familiars slithering over the bottom step and moving its way up to the railing for easier grip as it makes its way up to his room.

Yeah, guess I'm not bedding down out here after all.

I head for my bedroom door and crack it open to peer inside. The room is dark. No candles are lit. I take that as a good sign and slip inside before letting the door snick shut behind me once more. It takes only a second for my eyes to adjust to the darkness. Almost as soon as I do, though, thunder rumbles in the distance and the whole space lights up with a flash as lightning cracks beyond the barrier of the Academy grounds—likely somewhere over the seaside.

A figure is sitting up in the bed, pale and smaller than I've ever noticed before. My breath catches in my throat.

"Sorry," I say immediately. "I didn't mean to wake you."

"You didn't." The lightning is gone in another instant, but my eyes adjust quicker than before and I can still see where Kiera rests with her back against the headboard and her legs drawn up to her chest. The evidence of her claim—that I hadn't woken her—seems accurate because she's no longer wearing the dress she went to see the Council in.

I scan the room once more and find it in a heap in the corner, near one of my reading tables. Staring at the dark wash of fabric crumpled there, I try to recall if she'd been naked when I looked at her last—her skin is as pale as her hair, but had she been wearing something else other than her flesh?

A desire that I know I shouldn't feel beats at me like the winds outside the tower.

Don't fucking look, I urge myself.

It's like telling a dying man to keep breathing. *Impossible.*

I look and my breath catches in my throat, freezing there as I look over the long, white limbs of her arms delicately draped over her knees. She's not naked. At least, there's that, but she's certainly got a lot of skin revealed by the tunic she's dressed in. My tunic, I realize a moment later when she shifts on the bed and straightens her legs out, dropping her arms. That fact doesn't seem to help the sharp stabbing pain in my chest.

It's big on her even with the sleeves pushed and folded up to her elbows. It covers her lap, but the skin of her thighs remains available for my eyes to peruse. They lock onto her legs and picture what they'd look like wrapped around me, hooked at the ankles as I drive my cock between that hot, wet place that's hidden from view.

I swallow roughly, a low growl threatening to spill out. I turn back to the door. "You can sleep here tonight," I snap. "I'll—"

"Why would I sleep here?" she asks before I can finish. "I have a room below." Rustling follows that statement. The muscles of my back bunch and tighten with each sound that slithers through my ears like one of Kalix's serpents.

Then her words catch up with my thoughts and I turn, slowly, to face the woman in my bed. "You're not going back to your old room."

Kiera turns and slides her legs away from the rumpled covers and sheets. Long pale legs appear over the side of the mattress and her bare feet touch the floor.

Eyes up, you fucking prick! I tear my gaze away from her flesh and settle on her face.

"Why?" Stormcloud gray eyes stare at me.

Why? I repeat her question in my head, trying to recall what we'd been talking about. I blink at her. "Because you are a Mortal God, and that is a Terra room."

Kiera stands up and as she does, another flash of lightning breaks through the room. *Holy ... fucking Gods.*

"Why does that matter?" Kiera asks as she moves closer.

If I thought it was a struggle to tear my gaze away from her before, it's impossible now. Not only had she chosen an old tunic of mine, but this one is so pale and thin that when the flash of light takes over the darkest parts of my bedroom, illuminating everything in its path, it does more than just ... shed light on her. It peers through the fabric and casts a glow around her form, outlining every curve beneath the cloth.

What might have been—in the once dark room—a somewhat overly large night dress on her becomes practically nothing in an instant. The image burns into the back of my mind through my eyes and I know that this moment, this memory will be etched into me forever.

Thunder fades over the sound of waves crashing in the near distance—disturbing the cliffside outside of the Academy walls. The light disappears, fading from existence, but not the image of Kiera standing from my bed in little more than transparent fabric. Volcanic heat pours through my veins, directing a pathway straight to my groin.

"Ruen?" Kiera's voice is curious, not angry as it usually is when directed to me. I'm standing here, beating back my internal beast with each passing second and forcing myself not to rip that damn tunic from her body and she ... knows, I realize when I raise my gaze to meet hers.

Even in the dark, my eyes sharpen on her face, my sight far better than mortals as I now know hers is as well. The corner of her lips is curved upward and her brow is lifted. The challenge in her expression sends the growl I'd been holding back up my throat. It unleashes and, in an instant, I spring forward, grabbing her with both hands on her too-skinny waist. No, perhaps, not too skinny. She's not a delicate woman, her body is built for athleticism. Her muscles are obvious under my palms.

Still, she doesn't fight as I catapult her back onto the bed and land on top of her. Her back presses into the mattress and I come down hard, my legs encasing her thighs. I'd wonder why were it not for the fact that, a moment after we collide, she's rearing up to clasp my shoulder and canting her hips into mine. The damn woman uses my momentum to push me onto my back so that she can swing a leg over my hips when we flip and she falls against me in the dominant position.

"Oh, don't look so shocked, Ruen," she says. "You were practically begging me to kick your ass with the way you were eyeing me."

My hands grasp her hips. Instead of lifting her up as I know I should, I grip her tighter and bring her down further into my lap. I know the exact moment she feels my problem because Kiera stiffens all over, her head turning down where my cock is straining against the inside of my trousers, pressing up against the center between her thighs. The taut silence in the room is disturbed only by the sounds of the storm outside and still, that's not enough to break the spell that has somehow found itself cast over both of us. I have to be the one to do it, I know, but it's quite possibly the most difficult thing I've ever done in my life just to clear my throat and speak.

"I want to see it," I tell her.

Gray eyes widen. "What?"

I sit up, and to my surprise, Kiera doesn't lean away from me as I expect her to. Instead, she remains right where she is until my chest is a hair's breadth away from hers. "I want to see where the brimstone was in your neck."

She blinks and then, slowly—as if she's not sure I'm telling the truth—rises up off my lap. I know only a moment of peace as she gets off the bed and allows me to move forward. She turns away from me and just as I'm about to stand, she's back again. The round globes of her ass settle over my lap. My heart stutters to a stop in my chest.

"Go ahead," she murmurs.

Is this a dream? It must be. Or is she ... perhaps, teasing me?

Women go after Theos, and a few of the crazier, masochistic ones go for Kalix. They do *not* come for me. They had—long ago—when the three of us had first entered the Academy, but I'd shut that down quickly. Despite the herb we're forced to take annually to mitigate Mortal Gods procreating, other than a few dalliances here and there with discreet women who knew where they stood with me, I don't seek out females.

I don't understand them, I don't trust them, and I don't wish to. The damage my mother suffered because of her relationship with my father will always remain in the back of my mind, reminding me just why it's a damned bad idea. Females cause complications and this one is no exception. In fact, she's likely worse than other females and far more dangerous to me and my brothers.

I don't order her to stand up though. I catch the heavy wave of her silver hair in one fist. The strands slide between my fingers like the finest of spider webs. The material is stunning, not sticky like a web's strand, but silky to the touch and devoid of any viscous sensation.

Slow, calm breaths, I tell myself. I force them out of my lungs even as they seize against the inside of my chest. I lift the mass of her hair and move it to drape over her shoulder. The corner of Kiera's mouth is in near shadow to me, but just once, she turns her head in my direction and I spot the way it lifts.

She *is* teasing me. Devious little wench. My cock hardens impossibly further. I close my eyes and pray for patience. Though, I can't say who I'm praying to. The skies are empty and the Gods have all descended.

The moment her hair is out of the way and I can see the thin raised line at the back of her neck that marks where the brimstone had been buried beneath her flesh, the flames of my desire dampen. My lips press together as I ignore the throb of my cock and lightly brush over the skin beneath her hairline. The silence in the room is heavy and thick. Light flashes outside of the window, illuminating everything again, but if there's thunder, I'm too focused on the woman perched on my legs to hear it. What I do hear, however, is her voice as she speaks in a raspy, obviously uncomfortable tone.

"It doesn't hurt anymore," she tells me.

No, I don't imagine it does. I touch the pad of my thumb to the top of the mark. "It's a scar now," I tell her. "Even if it doesn't hurt, you won't heal from this." Not like she had from the whip marks, I notice as the back of my tunic gapes away from her spine and I can see straight down her back through the wide-open neck. The flesh over her spine is as pristine as it had been before her punishment. Carefully, avoiding the heart shaped ass just beneath her back, I lift the tunic back up into place even as my cock throbs against the inside of my trousers, begging me to do something about its condition.

"Scars don't bother me," Kiera says. "I'm surprised you care though."

I don't. The lie freezes on my tongue, and I swallow it back.

The scar is a pretty pale pink and I know from experience that it'll whiten over time, fade, and become barely perceptible unless she repeatedly opens it up and lets it form fresh scar tissue over and over again.

"...Ruen?" My name comes from Kiera tinged with a bit of confusion and frustration as if she's already said it several times with no response.

My hand falls away from her neck and Kiera leans forward, her head turning back to peer over her shoulder at me. I clear my throat and reach for her waist. My hands grip her there for a moment and though I had intended to remove her from my lap, my fingers freeze against the warmth permeating my palms through the thin fabric of the borrowed tunic. My mouth goes dry. Even with the cloth of the shirt separating our skin, I can still feel the heat of her and it makes me realize—perhaps, for the first time—just how fucking cold I am. She is fire and life and I've never wanted to burn as much as I do in this moment.

Let her go, I urge myself. *Release her waist. Stop touching her.* The words are commands stabbing through my skull. I want to make myself listen to them, but my hands don't seem to care. They act on their own volition, tightening against her and pulling her closer.

"Ruen, what are—"

Kiera's words dry up as my head sinks down. I can't let her go, I realize, but I don't need to perform the vile actions I've got spinning through my mind. I can distract myself with something else. Words. Talk. Yes, I'll do that.

As images of Kiera on her back against the darkened sheets of my bed and my hands drawing the tunic up and off her to reveal her naked flesh dance through my mind, I squeeze my eyes shut and press my forehead to her shoulder blade.

"Tell me what the Council said," I practically beg her, needing something to distract me from the insanity of my own thoughts and desires.

She's stiff in my arms. I don't blame her. I've caused her

nothing but damage and pain. She doesn't trust me and she shouldn't. Even I don't know what I'd be willing to do to save my brothers. Even knowing how deep we all are with her lies and secrets—with Caedmon playing puppet master alongside that fucking ... mortal woman who has kept Kiera indebted to her for the last ten years—I cannot be trusted. We both know that, she and I.

At the end of the day, my brothers are all I have. I will protect them even if that means risking her, even if it's not what I want.

A beat passes and I'm sure Kiera will deny me, but once again, she surprises me. Her body relaxes against mine and my cock takes notice, prodding against her lower back with decided interest. I bite down on my tongue and curse internally.

Vile. Disgusting. Pervert.

Kiera ignores it. "There were six Council members," she says, her voice lowering to a whisper. Her head turns towards the window and I open my eyes to look up at her through my lashes. She doesn't look at me as she continues. "They debated on how to determine my lineage—who my God parent is."

Will they be able to? I wonder. According to what Caedmon had said, her father was also of Divine blood even if her mother was the Goddess that birthed her. I contemplate asking, but considering how new she is to much of the Academy's inner machinations, it will likely simply distress her further. I keep my mouth shut.

"They decided on performing the ceremony around the Spring Equinox celebration."

My muscles tighten at this news. Kiera glances over her shoulder at me as she feels that change. "I see," I murmur against her body.

She arches one brow. "Is that a problem?" she inquires.

I shake my head. "Not a problem, exactly," I say. "I'm simply surprised they would wait that long."

Kiera frowns. "Could they do it sooner?"

I nod. "Yes. The ceremony can be performed whenever—they often do it, though usually with younger Mortal Gods who've simply been left by their mothers on the steps of the Academies."

"Why would mothers leave their children on the Academy steps?"

With a sigh, I sit up and pull myself away from her heat. Kiera lifts herself from my lap and though I want to stab myself for the reaction, my body mourns the loss of her. I keep my gaze trained on her face as she stands and turns to face me. Her silver hair pours over one side of her chest, hanging in long waves.

The rumble of thunder echoes in the distance—sounding as if it's growing further away despite the rain still slapping against the glass.

"Many mortal women leave children they believe are of the Gods on the steps of the Academy if they don't wish to be acknowledged as their parents. Gods do not marry mortal women. Any relationship a God might have with a mortal is purely physical, rarely anything more. Many of the women become bitter or angry and don't wish to keep their children." Or so I've always been told. The lies of the Gods make me wonder if anything they've ever said is true, but then I think of Theos and I know, sometimes the truth is worse than the lie.

Kiera is quiet for a moment and then she shifts to the side and the mattress sags with her slight weight as she takes a seat next to me. "Your mother didn't do that."

It's not a question, but I still answer. "No," I agree. "She didn't."

"Did Kalix's?" The lightning flashes have moved away, but even in the dim interior of the bedroom, I can still see her face and her eyes as they lift to meet mine.

"No." Olivia had been obsessed with the idea of being Azai's wife. Though she never cared for me, even now, I still feel a twinge of pity and sorrow for her and her end.

"What about Theos' mom?"

I press my lips together and return my focus to Kiera's face. "Why do you wish to know?" I ask.

She shrugs. "Well, this is the first time I've ever really been able to talk about being a Mortal God and ask about parentage with anyone that might actually have some answers—or be willing to give them to me," she says.

"Your father never..." I let the question trail off when she answers before I'm finished speaking.

"No, of course not." She snorts as if the very idea is amusing to her. She turns her eyes away from mine and looks down, picking at the hem of her borrowed tunic. I force myself not to stare after the initial look. "I think he still loved her—my mom, whoever she was—but he didn't like talking about her with me. So, I don't know what she did. If she stayed during a time before I can remember or if she left immediately. It's also a little different, too, the fact that your God parent was male and mine was female."

"I know there are places where young Mortal Gods are kept before their powers have manifested," she continues. "I heard as much after I joined the Underworld, though I'd never seen them. Do the children who are left at the Academies go there?"

"Yes." Cold, dank, dark places those facilities are. Disgusting and foul. My upper lip curls back from my teeth on instinct as I remember the hovel of a room Darius, Kalix, and I had found Theos in. "It isn't a place fit for children—mortal or mortal god."

Kiera's head lifts. "You weren't in one of those, were you? I thought Azai found you and your mother?"

Shock cuts through me deeper than any blade and my hands clamp into fists on the mattress's edge in an effort not to rip her up from her seat and demand she tell me where she gained that information. Slowly, I turn my head to peer at her. "And how would you know that?" My words are colder than ice as they slice from my throat.

Kiera stares back at me, eyes clear of any fear as she answers. "The Gods talked about it," she admits. "Your father is on the Council and it was mentioned that he was forced to track you and your mother down and..." She pauses, her brows pinching down as she bites her lower lip.

My eyes shoot to the little depression there—her white teeth flashing as they sink into the petal pink color of her mouth. I want to see those lips wrapped around my—*fuck! No.* My attention returns to her eyes and creased brow.

"And. *What?*" I demand, growling the words as I feel something sinister curl through my gut. It's the same darkness that lives within my brothers, a likely curse from our father's blood—a cruelty that I refuse to acknowledge.

When I expect her to look away, she doesn't. Her eyes lock with mine. Open and intense as if she's testing herself to see if she can hold my gaze. I have to admit, she does a damn good job. "Your punishment," she says, the words a near whisper.

A muscle jumps beneath the skin of my neck, right next to the pounding beat of my heart. As if she hears it, Kiera's eyes move down to the side of my throat before returning to mine once more. Whereas someone else would be smug about that knowledge—might mistake knowing who I received the scar on my face from as a weakness—she doesn't even seem particularly interested in that.

I let more silence pass between us, each second ticking by as the storm outside drifts further and further away and the shadows in the room shift as the clouds part and moonlight peers inside. Finally, I break that silence.

"No," I tell her. "I was not one of the children left outside of the Academies. Neither was Kalix." I release the edge of the mattress and stand, striding across the room to the armoire.

"What about Theos?" she asks as I open the door and reach inside for one of the many extra blankets kept there. I withdraw two.

"What about Theos?" I repeat, shooting the question back at her.

She growls in frustration and the sound makes my lips twitch in rare amusement. No wonder my brothers both seem so obsessed with her. She brings life back to the cold dead thing that resides in my chest and has since my mother let herself die for my sake.

"Was he or was he not abandoned on the steps of the Academy?"

At her words, I shut the armoire one-handed and a bit harder than necessary before carrying the blankets across the room towards the window settee. "That's something you'll have to ask him," I reply coolly. "His story is his own and not mine to tell."

"*You*—what are you doing?" Her tone changes as I get to the settee and drop the blankets onto the thin cushions that stretch the length of the window.

I unravel one and lay it out along the cushions. "Getting ready for bed," I answer her absently. "It's been a long damn day and I'm exhausted."

"Yes, but..." She drifts off as I take the second and shake it out. I bunch the blanket up at the makeshift foot of the settee and turn to face her.

She's peering at me with her brow creased as she looks beyond me to the window settee and then to the bed. "Why aren't you sleeping here?" she asks, gesturing to the mattress beneath where she's half turned in my direction.

"You're sleeping there," I say with an arched brow. Did she think I would sleep next to her? With the way my cock seems to seek her out against my own wishes? I shake my head. No, that won't happen. If I let myself sleep near her then there's no doubt in my mind that I'll wake up to find my body moved against her, pinning her to the sheets with a knee between her pale thighs, and my lips devouring the skin of her throat as my hands move over her breasts.

As if encouraged by my mind's supply of that image, my cock throbs against the inside placket of my trousers. If I could punch the thing into submission, I would. Unfortunately, I truly am exhausted and I have no wish to remain awake on what promises to be a too small settee sore from my cock and back.

I turn away from Kiera and climb onto the settee, reclining against it with both arms folding behind my head. One side is pushed against the cold glass of the window and the other just barely manages to keep from hanging off.

"Go to sleep, Kiera. We will talk in the morning." I say the words, knowing that they're a partial lie. Yes, we'll talk again, but I have the feeling that without the storm and the darkness, the light of day will bring back my sense of propriety and—hopefully—dampen my desire to strip her bare and sink my cock into her hot depths.

I grit my teeth and shut my eyes against those thoughts, though doing so doesn't cure me of them. A beat passes and though I listen to the soft shuffling sounds Kiera makes as she climbs back into the bed and under the sheets, I don't sleep. Seconds tick into undetermined minutes, hours, and an eternity passes before I sense the soft breaths of slumber coming from her. Only then do I, too, allow myself to fall into oblivion and dreams of the woman who lies not but a short distance away.

CHAPTER 15
KIERA

The back of my head burns with awareness. There are more than a dozen eyes on me. Mortal Gods, Gods, and Terra alike all stare as I pass them through the corridors. Gone is the dark mark of my unique Terra uniform, and in its place are the long dusky skirts of a royal blue gown, one of Maeryn's.

Why Maeryn's? Because I don't really have anything of my own and the Darkhavens decided that the pathetic excuse of a clothes collection I *do* own is unacceptable. For some reason, wearing this dress makes me feel more like their servant now than when I actually was.

"I'm surprised I don't have to tell you to keep your eyes forward," Ruen comments from my left.

I bite down on my lip and don't respond immediately. When I woke up that morning, he was gone from the settee. I must have been truly exhausted if he managed to sneak out without waking me—or perhaps, my energy is still drained from the recent brimstone removal. There's no telling, but I ignore the small voice in my mind that suggests maybe I don't see Ruen as the betrayer he once was. That maybe ... somewhere, *deep down*, I might trust him.

After a beat, I finally give him a response. "Why would you have to tell me that?" I ask without looking at him.

The answer to my question comes from my right. "Because everyone is staring at you and he expected you to glower back at them," Theos says with a hint of amusement.

My response is a low hum in the back of my throat, but I do pause as we come to the mouth of a corridor and the open doorway of a familiar classroom. Divine History—one of the handful of classes I'd been informed I'd be required to attend on top of extra tutoring to help catch me up to the same level of education as the other Mortal Gods. The tutoring, however, has yet to start and I can only hope that Caedmon will be placed in charge of that as well.

"Where's Kalix?" I ask curiously as the three of us enter the classroom to more open stares. It almost reminds me of one of the many auctions in the Underworld that Ophelia had brought Regis and me to in an effort to warn us what would happen if we disobeyed her—beyond torture, maiming, and death.

A blood servant who doesn't listen to their master ends up at those horrible places. A shudder works through me at the memory, and it doesn't take much effort to shove it back into its little dark box in the back of my mind and refocus on the present.

I sense rather than see the look Ruen and Theos exchange. I don't know how—maybe being around them so much for the last few months has given me some sort of extra Darkhaven sense. They are a language and culture to themselves and understanding the way they work leaves me feeling like I'm learning a whole new species of Mortal God.

"He has another class," Theos says as one of his hands

finds the small of my back and he directs me up the steps to seats toward the back of the classroom.

"No, he doesn't," I reply evenly, repressing a snort.

The flash of golden white hair whips past my periphery as Theos turns his head sharply in my direction. "Yes, he—" Ruen begins, ready to back up his brother.

I glare at Ruen before cutting him off. "I've spent the last several months as your servant—trailing you to every class," I remind him. "I think you forget that Terra aren't actually invisible. Just because you didn't acknowledge me but to order me around doesn't mean I wasn't there. I've got your schedules memorized by now and I know damn well, the three of you share this class."

Ruen frowns. "I wasn't ignoring you," he says quietly.

"Yes, you were." Or rather, I suspect, he was trying to even if it was a poor showing.

Ruen opens his mouth but whatever he's about to say is silenced as Theos steps between us. "Kiera, don't start this here. Let's just take our seats and get you through your first day."

I want to argue. The desire pounds at me, a strange need to unleash all of the sensations of the sudden upheaval of my life out on the man behind Theos. I don't know why *him* of all people. Perhaps it's because I'm still reminded of what he did —of the humiliation of being dragged before the entire school and whipped, something they all seem to have forgotten, thankfully. Or perhaps it's because our conversation from the night before, and the odd sensations he brings to life within me, are still lingering, keeping me on edge and off kilter.

Instead of unleashing that frustration, though, I inhale a long breath and turn, striding up the steps to the very back of the classroom. At the very least, I'm hoping it'll keep the stares to a minimum since I'm sure no God will appreciate attention anywhere else but on them. Gods are vain creatures after all and so fragile in their egos—just like the Darkhaven brothers.

I reach the final row of chairs and take a seat, soon followed by Ruen and Theos, who take up residence on either side of me. I grit my teeth and shuffle forward as Theos scoots behind me to take his seat as more students and their Terra enter the room.

The sight of the mortal servants of the Academy reminds me of something. "Now that I'm no longer a Terra, will the three of you get a new servant?" I ask curiously, turning my gaze to first Theos and then Ruen.

"No," Ruen says, keeping his eyes pinned to the front of the room. The door at the front of the classroom opens and Narelle enters in a wash of robes and skirts, slamming the door as she strides across the open space before the students until she reaches the board. My body goes rigid as she casts a look up, freezing for a mere second when she spots me sitting.

I half expect her not to realize that my station at the Academy has changed and to say something, but she doesn't. In fact, other than that single slip, she doesn't even acknowledge my existence in the seats—forbidden, of course, to Terra —as she launches into her lesson.

A little over an hour later, my back is tight with tension and my head is throbbing. It isn't until we're leaving the classroom, however, that I notice something off with both Ruen and Theos. For the fourth or fifth time, one of them lifts their head and peers over the crowd of students as they leave the room and gather in the corridors.

"What are you looking for?" I ask, frowning as the throbbing in my temples increases.

Almost absently, Theos moves to my side and takes my

arm, urging me to the side as several female Second Tiers pass by, their heads swiveling to stare at me as they do.

I grit back the urge to bare my teeth at them before I realize I don't have to anymore. At least ... I don't think I do. I flip my gaze to Ruen as he steps in front of me and continues to scan the sea of students on their way to their next classes. "What Tier am I?" I ask suddenly.

Ruen jolts as if shocked and turns, blinking at me with a stunned expression. "What?"

"What Tier am I?" I repeat. When that still doesn't elicit an answer, I sigh. "You and the other Darkhavens are First Tiers, right? Do I need to take a test to determine what Tier I am—"

"First." I'm so focused on Ruen's face as I speak that when that answer comes, I'm confused because it's spoken without his lips having moved to shape that one word.

I turn to Theos, but he shakes his head as if he already senses my question—or perhaps it's written all over my face. When Theos jerks his chin to the right and I follow the silent urging, I realize Kalix is standing there between us and the crowd.

Ah, I realize. *It wasn't a* what *they were looking for, but a* who. *Him. Kalix.*

"I'm a First Tier?" I clarify, frowning as Kalix begins to move towards us, cutting through the crowd like a hot knife through butter. The other students part, several nearly falling all over themselves to get out of his way as he moves. I don't blame them. Kalix is so far from a normal person—Mortal God or otherwise—that there's no telling his reactions to things that other people would consider normal. Who's to say he wouldn't straight up rip the head off someone who steps in his path, accidentally or not?

When Kalix smiles as he approaches, I nearly stumble in

my own surprise as the others nudge me forward to meet him. The picture of Kalix's expression far more confusing than anything he could've said. When he smiles, he almost looks ... normal.

It's a mask, that's for damn sure. My body still remembers how he'd nearly drowned me when he fucked me in the Terra baths. A shiver skids down my spine as if recalling that memory has my senses reacting on instinct.

Kalix's lips widen as if he scents the sudden wetness that I'm almost half ashamed of soaking the place between my thighs. His teeth appear sharper for all of a second before he stops before the three of us and answers my question that he obviously heard over the crowd's low hum. "Your Tier will be determined during the ceremony at the Spring Equinox," he states. "But if any of us would guess, we'd say you'll likely be a First Tier. Few Mortal Gods can wield as much power over familiars as we've seen you do."

"But you—"

"First. Tier." Kalix repeats the words with that grin of his.

Right. He's a First Tier and I have to admit, he's right. In the months I've been at the Academy, I haven't seen many other Mortal Gods openly use familiars, and the ones I had seen were considered First Tiers as well.

"Don't forget that you were also able to wield at least some of your powers even with a sliver of brimstone in your neck." Ruen's voice lowers as he dips his head closer to the side of my face. His nearness as well as the warm breath he sends over the shell of my ear reawakens that odd emotion that flutters in my lower belly.

I'm pulling away from him before I even realize I'm doing it. I recognize the action for what it is—self-preservation. "Why is that so shocking?" I ask, trying not to sound as breathless as I feel.

Three sets of eyes spear me. "Not here," Ruen finally answers. He nods somewhere over Kalix's shoulder. "We'll talk about it later, but for now, we should head to our next class."

I must make a face because when Theos looks at me, he snorts out a laugh before casually moving closer and slinging an arm around both of my shoulders. "Oh, don't be like that, *Dea*," he says jovially. "You'll like the next one—it's battle practice."

Battle practice? Oh shit. Shock slams into me along with a new realization. *The Battles.*

Now that I'm a Mortal God out in the open, I, too, will be expected to fight in them if I'm called. Theos' hand tightens on my shoulder.

"Don't worry," he says. "With your ... *previous training*" —he lowers his voice at that before returning to a normal tone—"and all that we'll teach you, we'll make sure that you're in fighting shape before they announce the next rounds."

I shrug his hand off before shooting him a scathing glare. "If anything, Theos," I reply, "you should be worried about yourself and your fellow Mortal Gods."

Though I never expected it, now that I no longer have to hide my skills or who I am, I'm more than ready to show these men what my 'previous training' taught me.

Theos grins. "I look forward to kicking your ass," he says.

I smile sweetly back at him, showing him my teeth. "That's if you can touch it," I reply.

Golden eyes glitter brightly. "Is that a challenge I hear, *Dea?*"

I move closer to him, lifting my hand to his chest. Sparks dance beneath my fingertips and something sharp and painful jumps beneath the touch. Yellow glowing tendrils of lightning waft off the edges of Theos' hair. Dangerous. Oh, so fucking dangerous. And addictive.

"That's exactly what it is," I tell him honestly. "I want to see what you can do, pretty boy."

His head dips towards my own and his tongue comes out to swipe across his full lower lip. My eyes lock onto that little action, my throat going dry. "What do I get if I win?" His question is whispered so low that I almost don't hear it despite how close we're standing.

It takes me a moment to respond. "What do you want?"

Cool air slides over my shoulder from behind, lifting one strand of my hair and fluttering it towards my face. Theos reaches up and captures it between two fingers. Instead of tucking it back over my shoulder or ear as I expect, though, he lifts it to his lips, pressing the silvery lock against his mouth. Memories of that mouth on other parts of my body attack my mind. My muscles ache deliciously at the reminder.

"A boon," he finally says.

I blink. "A boon?" I repeat.

He grins and releases my hair. "Yes," he affirms. "You win and I will offer you a boon and if I win, you offer me one."

"And I assume this boon will be like a favor or..." I drift off as he begins to shake his head. "Then what do you—"

"It can be a favor," Theos states. "Or it can be a benefit. Perhaps that boon will be to have you in my bed instead of Ruen's."

I roll my eyes and take a step away from him, turning to go. "Sure, then," I toss my answer over my shoulder. "I don't expect that to happen, but if that's what you wish—it makes no difference to me."

I stride towards the end of the now nearly empty corridor —all of the students having moved on to their next courses— and pause to look back. "I'm going to get changed and I'll meet you at battle practice soon, boys," I announce before offering them a grin. "I look forward to wiping the sand with your asses."

When I turn to leave this time, the responding burst of laughter at my back carries a twisted sort of promise with it. Whether this challenge is our way of forgetting the other issues plaguing us or inciting a closer connection, I have a feeling that now that I'm officially a Mortal God, my relationship with the Darkhaven brothers has taken a new course through uncharted waters.

No matter what happens in the future, we are bound together on this ship. If it goes down, we all do.

CHAPTER 16
KIERA

"This is going to be fun."

"I think our definitions of fun are two very different things."

Those comments from first Kalix and then Theos have me biting my lip as I—along with the Darkhavens—line up in the sand of the battle arena for practice. Fun does seem to have an obnoxiously large number of varying definitions when it comes to these men. Unfortunately for Theos, I have to agree with Kalix. Now that I'm no longer hiding my powers, being able to unleash some of this pent-up energy in a violent way will certainly be ... *fun*.

"Are you sure you're ready for this?"

Tilting my head down and to the side, I meet Ruen's eyes and smirk. "Why? Are you scared I'll beat the shit out of your brothers?"

Midnight eyes widen and one corner of his mouth lifts ever so slightly. He doesn't answer my question but turns his attention back to the front where Axlan strides with two Terra struggling to keep up with his pace.

I scowl at the big brawny God as he stalks toward the

front of the current class of Mortal Gods we're surrounded by. Despite the struggling mortal Terra stumbling behind him, their arms filled with spears and swords and all other manner of materials, Axlan's hands are completely free and hang loosely at his sides.

Turning my head, I scan the exterior wall, going down the line of other Terra until I come across a familiar brown haired male. Niall spots me looking his way but when I offer him a smile, he ducks his head and stares at the ground beneath his feet. My smile falls away abruptly and I stare at him a moment more, wondering if I've done something to upset him.

It isn't until Ruen nudges my side that I realize the class has started. I jerk and whip back around as Axlan begins to speak.

"Today, we will continue with sparring practice," the God of Victory announces. "Find a partner and get into your circles. We will mimic the same rules of a tournament. Winners of each round will go on to fight another and another until..." He pauses and grins. "The final winner left will have to battle me."

I stare at the God of Victory with no small amount of disgust. No doubt this little exercise of his doubles as a way for him to find a high of his own abilities. Vain, greedy, fucking Gods. I shake my head and blow out a breath.

Axlan claps his hands together before gesturing to the Terra who finally stop at his side, panting and sweating though they are. "You may choose any weapon we have available or you may choose to fight without," he states. "It matters not to me, but I shall be coming around to watch the rounds. Don't disappoint me."

The moment Axlan releases us to our own devices, Kalix's hand reaches out and snags my wrist. Before he can open his mouth, Ruen growls out a denial. "Don't even fucking think about it, Kalix," he snaps.

Kalix groans. "I won't kill her," he promises.

Both of my brows shoot up and I glance from him to Ruen. "Let him fight me if he wants to," I suggest. "I'm not going to lose."

The grip on my wrist tightens and Kalix's grin turns feral. His eyes flash something red and wicked before morphing back to the forest green I've come to know so well. "See that," he says, directing the words to Ruen. "She's up for it."

"*No*." Ruen reaches forward and deftly removes Kalix's hand from my wrist. "I'll not have you killing her with your tendencies—no matter what you say."

Kalix sags in defeat, and for a moment, I'm struck with a bolt of confusion. Eyeing the two of them, I don't say anything as Kalix turns and curses under his breath as he approaches an amused looking Theos. Theos, for all the world, appears as if this kind of exchange isn't abnormal to the two and perhaps it's not. I'd seen over the past few months just who made the decisions in their little group.

Ruen is their leader and Theos and Kalix fall in line ... until they don't. Even when they don't listen to him, though, Ruen never abandons them. He simply deals with the fallout just as he dealt with me. Cold precision is his ability and I find that I want to see that mask of his break. I want to see what hides beneath the ice of his exterior and then I want to set it on fire and watch it burn.

"Does that mean you're my partner, Ruen?" I ask, arching a brow as Theos grips Kalix's shoulder and leads him away.

Ruen watches them go, being careful not to look my way as he answers. "Yes."

My grin turns into a full-blown smile. I guess there are

some things to be said for coming out in the open as a Mortal God. Now I have the opportunity to kick some Darkhaven ass.

"Sword or spear then?" I ask. "Which will you choose?"

Finally, he looks at me and meets my gaze. Flickers of something I can't name spark in the depths of his eyes. I don't dare look away from it.

"Neither." Ruen's voice is low, gruff. "I want to see what you can do without a weapon in your hand."

I purse my lips and shrug as I step away from him before turning and striding across the arena until we're far away from the others into one of the empty rings that has been drawn out in the sand. Only then do I stop and turn back, placing my hands on my hips as I wait for him to approach. Ruen narrows his eyes on me briefly before he moves forward, his stalking footsteps jerky and uneven as if he's being led to the gallows rather than a sparring ring.

I snort and shake my head before reaching up and over my shoulder. I grip the white tunic I'd changed into for this class and quickly tug it off over my head. Despite the winter chill in the air, the arena down here never seems to get cold. Perhaps it's because the sun is directly overhead, heating the stone walls surrounding us, or perhaps because the sand bakes for hours before we arrive and the warmth from it seeps up through the soles of our shoes.

Whatever the case, I know that after a few minutes in the ring, I'll be coated in sweat and a loose tunic will do nothing but get in my way.

Lowering my arm to my side now that I'm free of the billowing fabric, I catch sight of Ruen's face. Jaw slack and eyes wide, he's focused on the front of my body and the leather I've revealed. It's neither a corset, nor is it a true vest, but almost a combination of both. Specially designed for fighting in the Underworld, I notice several of the female

Mortal Gods in the class eyeing me speculatively, their own gazes taking in the garment.

Their attention, however, is vastly different from the Darkhaven who stalks forward into the ring and doesn't stop moving until he's standing in front of me, nearly blocking out the sun. "What do you think you're doing?" he demands, eyes burning with that untapped fury, and he might deny it, but attraction.

I don't know why figuring that out makes me feel powerful, but it does. This dark cold man is attracted to me, and even if he doesn't want to be, he can't deny it. Seeing me like this, covered in leather and ready to do battle, does something to him.

When I toss the tunic to the edge of the ring and spot a Terra jolt away from the far wall, running to pick it up, I frown. "You don't have to—" The Terra freezes halfway to my shirt and looks up at me, eyes wide in horror.

"Let him," Ruen orders, gesturing a hand towards the Terra to continue his task.

"I can take care of my own clothes," I snap back, glaring at Ruen as the Terra quickly lifts the tunic, dusts it off, and then returns to the wall.

"Worry about your fighting skills, Kiera, not your clothes."

At that, I jerk forward and swipe my foot out, kicking both of his ankles together. His eyes widen in shock and a grunt leaves his lips as he stumbles, and I watch with sickening satisfaction as Ruen Darkhaven goes down in a heap on the sand.

"Why don't you worry about your fighting skills, Ruen, instead of concerning yourself with mine," I suggest sweetly as I take several steps back and don't offer to help him to his feet.

A burst of laughter erupts to my left and I turn my head to see Maeryn in her own fighting clothes—brown breeches and a tunic. She covers her laugh with one hand but offers me a thumbs up that sends a warmth sliding through my chest. Sand sprays the tops of my boots and my attention swaps back to the man who gets up from the ground and towers before me once more.

I arch my brow, waiting for his response.

"Point to you, Kiera Nezerac," Ruen states, eyeing me with more than irritation. There's amusement in his stoic gaze. Whether he realizes it or not, I think he likes it when I surprise him. "But don't think just because you caught me off guard that it means you're the better fighter."

"No, of course not," I agree. "I'm the better fighter for other reasons." Bait meet fish. I wait to see his response, but instead of outrage, Ruen merely arches one dark brow at me and takes several steps back, falling into a fighting stance as Axlan prowls closer—nearby, but just far enough to not involve himself.

It hits me that there's another reason for these sessions. Axlan is a God like the rest—no doubt he's under strict orders from the God Council to watch me and determine how powerful I actually am. Should I keep my abilities hidden? Or should I show them off?

Ruen jerks his chin in my direction and I meet his eyes. My breath catches as he tucks his head to the side and swipes it back and forth. The movement is so small that I know Axlan can't see it from his position, but it gives me an answer to my internal debate. Don't show off everything, but don't appear weak.

I fall into my own fighting stance, rocking back on my heels and lifting my hands into fists. Eyes sharpen. My senses blossom. I don't know how I didn't notice it before now, but the world is louder, brighter, more colorful. When I reach out with my senses, I can pick up thousands of tiny minds toiling away—some in the sand, some in the crevices of the stone walls. Spiders.

They flutter against my mental walls at the lightest brush of my attention. There's something else, though, a darker creature that has lain dormant. A shadow of something powerful. I don't reach for it, instead choosing to push it away as I refocus on the man in front of me. Whatever it is—my gaze flicks to Axlan and then back to Ruen—it's not for the Gods' eyes.

When Ruen moves, he's speed incarnate. Despite the mass of his body and the bulk of his shoulders, he's fast. Dodging first one way and then the opposite, he circles me and just as he's about to take me to the ground, I burst into action myself and avoid his barreling form, spinning in a circle. We switch places and he comes to a stop immediately when he doesn't reach me, slowly turning back to face me once more.

"You need to do more than simply avoid me," he warns.

I shrug. "I'll do more when you prove you can touch me."

"Oh, I can touch you, Kiera. Of that, have no doubt." I know he doesn't mean it *that* way—not Ruen—but the words he speaks do something horribly wicked to my insides, heating them up and lighting them on fire.

Prove it, I want to tell him. *Touch me.* Before the words can escape my tongue, however, Ruen attacks.

One moment he's feet away and the next, he's not. Ruen moves with the fluidity of someone who has trained for years. I dodge, duck, and weave—narrowly missing some of the blows he tries to land. He gives me practically no time at all to form an attack of my own. Instead, putting me completely on the defensive. Sweat beads pop up along my spine and over my shoulder blades. I knew I'd start to get hot despite the cool air sooner or later and I was right, but I don't appear to be the only one. As we circle each other once more, there's a thin sheen of sweat on Ruen's face and neck as well. Several other male Mortal Gods have stripped away their shirts and tunics, but not Ruen. Then again, his tunic is thinner than theirs and it molds to his body, not causing any resistance as he moves.

Panting, I curse the lack of action I've had in the last few months. Though I'm holding back so as not to give away too much of my own training, Ruen is no easy prey. The minutes churn into an hour and then another. He shows no signs of wavering and already my muscles are weary. They shouldn't be. I've spent far longer than this training, but perhaps it has something to do with the brimstone that's been removed from my neck. Since that incident, I've found myself tiring quickly, almost as if something is sucking up my energy to replenish a part of me that has been starved for too long.

Faces hover closer to the ring Ruen and I face each other in. I slide one foot to the side, through the sand, my brow puckering in annoyance as the movement is slowed. I hate sand. It always makes things difficult. Ignoring that, as well as the students who have lost their own mock battles, I refocus my attention on the man in front of me. Ruen's face is as dispassionate as ever. Not even by a twitch of his lips does he reveal his innermost thoughts. That is both the most frustrating and the most intriguing part of him. His ability to hide what he's feeling so completely that it makes me want to tear him open.

On our next pass around the ring, he dives for me and I'm too slow to react. My back slams into the hot sand and a split second later, I'm rolling. The two of us tumble as I buck my hips up, slamming my hand into his throat and swapping our positions until Ruen is with his back to the sand and I'm straddling his hips.

"If I had a blade in my hand, it would be at your throat," I chastise him.

"If you had a blade in your hand, I would have taken it by now," he replies as he grips my hips, and then with nothing more than pure unfettered strength, he lifts me off him and tosses me backward right. Out. Of. The. Ring.

"Winner: Ruen Darkhaven!"

I lie like that for several seconds, trying to understand what just happened. I had him on his back. I had my hand on his neck. I ... lost?

A hand appears in front of my face and I glance up to see the man who just threw me out of the ring like I weighed little more than a sack of laundry holding it out to me. Sweat coats his brow.

"You fight well without powers," he pants as I grit my teeth and ignore his hand, getting up off the ground under my own strength.

Exhaustion trembles along the muscles in my calves. I straighten my spine and send him a withering glare. "You didn't even use yours," I snap.

He blinks and nods. "Yes, because you never did."

I pause at that. He's right. Other than the naturally increased speed and strength we both have, neither of us had attempted to use our abilities during the fight.

"I've never had a sparring match last this long," Ruen comments, nodding up to the sky.

I tilt my head back and realize that the sun has already begun to set. I'd thought we were sparring for a good amount of time but not more than half a day.

"Here." That soft voice pulls me out of my reverie and I peer over my shoulder as Niall approaches, my tunic in his hand—obviously given to him by the Terra who'd picked it up earlier. He holds it out, offering it to me.

"Thanks, Niall," I say, taking it from him.

Niall dips his head in deference. "Of course, my lady."

My hand freezes, the tunic still gripped between my fingers. "My lady?" I frown at him. "It's just Kiera, Niall. You don't have to call me that."

"I would never presume to say your name, my lady." Niall's bow deepens and my frown turns into a scowl. "I apologize if I've ever said anything disrespectful. I know now that you are—"

"Niall, stop," I bite out. "Stop bowing to me, for fuck's sake. Just—"

"*Kiera*." Ruen's sharp tone stops me from saying more and when I lift my gaze to his, he flicks his eyes to the side—to Axlan.

Right. The hierarchy. I'm no longer a Terra and therefore Niall isn't allowed to speak to me so casually. A bottomless pit opens up in my stomach, a vile, angry thing. I bite down on the words I want to say and jerk my head in a nod of understanding.

"Thank you for the sparring match," I say instead, directing the comment to him.

Ruen inclines his head slightly. "It was informative," he replies.

"Informative, huh?" I huff out a breath as I pull on the tunic. The fabric immediately clings to the quickly drying sweat on my flesh.

"Yes," Ruen agrees. "It's good to know where you're at so that I can train you later."

I blink. "Train me later?"

He nods. "There's no telling when the Gods will announce another official Battle tournament," he states. "If you're called, you need to be prepared. Though your fighting style is good, you're uncontrolled in a lot of your movements."

"I'm not uncontrolled," I snap back. "I evade and counter. If I'm controlled then I'm predictable."

"Predictable and control aren't synonymous," he argues.

Heat burns up the sides of my neck as I feel eyes on me. I know without looking that Kalix and Theos are done with their sparring session. In fact, a subtle glance around tells me that everyone is. Now, they're all watching Ruen and me with assessing gazes.

I stomp forward and though Ruen frowns in confusion, he doesn't move. I don't stop until our chests are nearly brushing and then I lean up on my toes, letting my lips skim the bottom of his ear as I speak in a low voice.

"You might have won this round," I tell him, "but don't think you'll win if I actually give it my all." Then before I can think better of it, I add another note to the already tense air between us. "I am everything you can't control, Ruen," I say, leaning closer so that the heat of my breath slides over his earlobe. "And I know that *kills* you."

With that, I turn and walk away, putting a little bit more stomp in my step as the sun slowly slips over the horizon, and the burn of Ruen Darkhaven's eyes settles on my back and stays there until I'm well and truly out of sight.

CHAPTER 17
KIERA

Later, after I've washed away the sweat and sand from my skin, I sit alone in the Darkhavens' rooms contemplating the strange buzzing under my skin. The sun has long since set and still they have not returned. The fire in the hearth is dying as well, and I have no desire to get up to tend to it. Instead, I just sit there. In the near darkness, covered in the sensation of little insects crawling under my flesh.

It's not like when my spiders come to me. That feels ... different, though I'm sure many others would not agree. To most, spiders are just as much insects as a fly or a bee, but they're not. They're far more intelligent creatures than even many Mortal Gods.

As if sensing my inner thoughts, Ara comes creeping out of the shadows and marches towards me. My lips twitch in amusement as she latches on to my trouser leg and crawls up until she reaches my knee. The moment she stops, reclining on her perch on my leg, she peers up at me with her numerous black eyes.

Curious. That is the emotion that comes from her, slipping more easily than ever into my mind. That, too, is different. Whereas before, it had been somewhat difficult to find the creatures that claim their place as my familiars, now it's as natural as breathing. I used to have to work at finding them, at calling out to them. Now, they are there. Always. Perhaps I would be frightened and disturbed by that were it not for the fact that, in many ways, their presence feels like comfortable company. They don't demand anything from me. They don't pressure me for anything. They are simply there, silent and waiting.

I lift a finger and pat the top of Ara's little head, the short fuzz making my twitching lips turn into a full-blown grin. "I'm alright," I assure her. "I'm just feeling off."

Maybe because I lost a fucking battle to Ruen or maybe because I felt like neither of us had even really been trying. Or maybe because since I woke up that first time back after having the brimstone removed, I've felt a growing sensation building within me. A pressure that swells with each passing day.

A knock on the door pulls me from my thoughts and I cup a hand beneath Ara as I stand. For a moment, I contemplate taking her with me, but I don't know who it could be on the other side of that door, and other than the few people who frequent the Darkhaven quarters, not many know of her existence.

Ultimately, I decide to leave her behind, setting her gently on the lounge I'd been previously sitting on before petting her head and heading for the door as the person on the other side knocks again. I'll call for her if I need her.

I know before I turn the lock that it's not one of the Darkhavens. None of them would knock on their own damned chamber door. Still, I find myself repressing both surprise and confusion when I spy a Terra on the other side.

Not one I know well as I don't recognize her face, but the clothes she wears tell me that she's a servant just like I used to be.

"Yes?" I frown down at her as she stares up at me with wide doe brown eyes that remind me of the deer my father and I used to hunt for food when I was a child.

Her head dips back down as a flush creeps up her neck. "M-my a-apologies, my lady," she says. "I-I was sent to retrieve you."

My lips curl down instinctively at the 'lady' comment, but I ask instead, "Who sent you?"

"L-Lord Caedmon," she stutters.

Caedmon. Of course, it must be about my tutoring. I suppose the Gods decided to give him that task. Despite my earlier wishes, I'm not yet certain if I'm grateful for that or not.

Carefully, I step out of the chambers and seal the door shut behind me. The fire has died down more than enough, I don't have to worry about going back to put it out. If it does suddenly spark up and catch on something nearby, well … I don't exactly care if the entire Academy burns down or not.

"Lead the way," I tell the mousy girl, gesturing back towards the stairs.

Her head comes up slightly and this time, instead of peering at me openly with gaping curiosity, she's a bit more discreet. Her gaze moves over me through the veil of her lashes and the dishwater blonde of her hair before she bobs her head and turns to go first.

The change in my status—and more specifically, in the way I'm being treated—leaves my insides rioting in annoyance. There is nothing about me that has changed. I look the same. I sound the same. I even act the same, though a little less polite than I'd been previously, especially with the Darkhavens. Yet, somehow, I *am* different from those around me now that my heritage is no longer hidden.

As I consider that, though, I'm reminded of Niall. I should talk to him soon, I decide. Tell him that nothing has changed between him and me. No matter that he knows my secrets, I am always and still just Kiera, the ex-servant who never quite fit and the girl he befriended when she had no one else.

My heart aches at that. Yes, Niall is my friend ... just as Regis is ... *was*.

The female Terra in front of me leads me down the stairs of the North Tower, out and through several outdoor corridors before surprising me and leading me down a different set of stairs I don't recall ever having traveled before. I know it from the blueprints Regis had given me what now feels like a millennia ago. Even in those details, though, there had been nothing more than short notes and lines to draw out the walls and exit routes.

In person, this section of the Academy is much brighter than I expected. Wall sconces light up the curving staircase, illuminating the path without any windows, but when we get to the bottom, the walls disappear entirely and reveal glass all around. Unlike the darkness that had been outside the windows on the way here, the windows here are full of light. Someone with Divinity must be in charge of taking care of this place, but it's the only excuse for the bright, almost sunny, interior. Unnatural warmth permeates the air, sliding over my face and shoulders, seeping past the clothes I'm wearing as a sweet scent lingers. I sniff and frown. There's a hint of floral but also something deeper and richer.

"Miss?"

I hear the Terra, but my focus is on the man standing several paces in front of me. Shrouded in a light golden long coat that folds lopsided over one half of his chest, Caedmon stands like a King of old surrounded by leafy trees and sprouts of colorful blooms. The foliage shivers as if there's an invisible wind only they can sense. Somehow, it pulls them toward him before fluttering back as Caedmon lifts his head and meets my gaze.

"That will be all, Desireé. Thank you for bringing her to me."

The girl—Desireé—bobs her head, bowing slightly before she scuttles away, back towards the stairwell, and out of sight. Caedmon and I are left alone in silence. I wait for him to begin, to explain why I'm here even if it's for the tutoring I was informed I would be subject to, but he doesn't speak. Not even when I chance several more paces into the ... well, room would seem an odd thing to call it now that I realize what it truly is. A greenhouse. Or rather a green corridor.

On the map, this section of the academy appeared like a long-forgotten hallway with no end. Seeing it in person makes me realize that it had always been built for this—to house great palms and miniature trees and buds of a floral nature. I pass around where Caedmon stands in front of a stone table with two seats set out. If he expects me to sit before him without ever saying a word to me, he'll have to think again.

I keep my side facing him even as I bend over a particularly fat bush and lift one of the leafy stalks that protrude from its top. Little dots of red line the stalk and when I touch one gently it unfurls, going from what once looked like a berry to a full-blown bloom in a matter of seconds. That rich, heady scent gets stronger.

"I would be careful around that one," Caedmon murmurs quietly. "She can become a bit testy when touched without permission."

I straighten and face him fully. The God of Prophecy is

dressed like he's attending some party later. The gold stitching on his coat edges all the way to his knees and the billowy white pants that cover the rest of his legs only serve to make his skin even darker. When I look into his face, it's like looking into the night sky.

"Why did you call me here?" I ask, not bothering to hide my displeasure with him.

Not because he called me here. Not even because he was Ophelia's client which means he—along with practically everyone I've trusted for the last few months—has been lying to me. I don't trust him and I'm certainly not happy to be in his presence when I don't know what to do with him. Yet, he still holds a lot of power over me.

Caedmon closes his eyes with a sigh and when he reopens and fixes them on me, it's with a creased brow. "You don't need to act so defensive around me, Kiera," he says. "I don't wish you any harm."

"You've lied to me once already; what's to say that's not a lie as well," I shoot back.

Ebony eyes glitter dangerously, and I get the distinct impression that the face Caedmon has shown me up until this point is not all there is to him. I believe that feeling; it's an instinctual reaction that has saved my life more times than I care to count. Right now those instincts are roaring at me with a good dose of apprehension. I might be an assassin—or I suppose *was* an assassin—but I'm still mortal. God blood or not, I've always been and always will be mortal. To stay alive as I have, relying on my senses and my intuition, isn't just an option. It's a necessity.

With soft, but deliberate movements, Caedmon moves around the stone table at his side and takes a seat. When he lifts his hands to the box perched in the center there, gold rings glint across three of his fingers, two on one hand and one on the other.

"Come." The word is an order. "Take a seat."

Biting down on my lip, I leave behind the leafy bush and take the five or so steps to the table. I sit down gingerly in the seat across from him. Caedmon lifts the lid of the wooden box and then begins to withdraw small objects.

"Do you know what this is?" he asks as he lays out a flat checkered mat and then sets the smaller objects atop it.

"Chess." I haven't seen a board in a long time, not since the early days of Ophelia's training. Even then, it was a rarity. Ophelia didn't love chess the way those of the gaming persuasion did, but she did find its value in teaching strategy. Regis and I had played many times that first and second year in the Underworld.

Is he still in Riviere? The question pops into my mind before I can stop it and I close my eyes, hating the wave of pain that assails me. I'm angry with Regis, and though I know that anger is rooted in hurt, that doesn't make it any less volatile.

"That's correct." Caedmon's voice pulls me back and I lift my gaze to collide with his as he finishes setting up the board.

"I thought I was here for the tutoring I was told I needed," I say as he flips the lid of the wooden box shut again and sets it to the side.

"You are."

The rings on his hands glitter again as he lifts one hand, hovering it over a pawn on his side of the board. I frown at his words. "Then what is *this*?" I gesture to the game set in front of me.

Caedmon doesn't answer right away because of course he doesn't. Why would anyone want to give me an answer to a question when I ask it? Instead, he takes his time, glancing over the pieces from the pawns to the rooks and bishops. Finally, he settles on one pawn and moves it barely an inch from its original position.

"Tryphone wishes to set you up with another God from the Council for tutoring," he says as he lifts his fingers away from the piece.

My spine straightens and my eyes flash from the board to his face, but he's not looking at me. He's still looking at the damn pawn. "Who?" I demand when he doesn't elaborate further.

"I am not sure yet," he admits. "Though, if I were to choose, myself, I think it might do you some good to speak with a female God. Perhaps Makeda or … Danai would also be a good choice."

I want to spend one on one time with the Queen of the Gods about as much as I want to toss myself out a window. I sit forward in my seat and place my elbows on the edge of the stone table.

"Is this what you consider tutoring or are you just here to torture me with information you'll never fully give me?" My tone is sharp. It's definitely not how anyone of a lower status —Mortal God or not—should speak to a God.

Unsurprisingly, though, Caedmon doesn't admonish me. He simply gestures to the board and says, "Your move."

With gritted teeth, I turn my attention to the checkered mat. I consider my choice for a moment. In chess, there are few ways to start but many to end. Though it's a game of strategy, it's a board with pieces and a finite number of endings. There are only two players and therefore only two choices.

I move a pawn and return my attention to Caedmon. "Do you truly think I can pull off what you want me to, especially without the full details?" I'm careful not to speak the truth aloud. Though it seems as if we're alone, I know I'm not the only one who has familiars, and with Tryphone on the Academy grounds—as well as the God Council—I'm not taking any chances with my own life that I don't have to.

Caedmon doesn't answer immediately, instead moving his rook up right behind his pawn. I roll my eyes and move another pawn. Finally, after what feels like an untold number of seconds that have passed in tense silence, Caedmon's next turn ends and he raises his gaze.

"I know that you can do what needs to be done," he says, his words just as discreet. "I do not doubt your skills, Kiera. Both what you have learned and what power you have naturally will aid you in this quest."

"There is no quest," I snap and his eyes flicker up to meet mine. "This is not a storybook. This is my life—the life of dozens, hundreds of others."

"Try hundreds of thousands." Caedmon's full dark lips pinch downward as his face takes on a contemplative look.

My jaw tightens in irritation. "Tell me what the taboo is," I order. "What have the Gods—"

"No."

The exposed skin over my face and neck grows tight. "Then I can't help you."

"You can and you will," he says, his attention returning to the board between us. "I did not invite you here to discuss what your future will be."

"Then what did you—"

He doesn't let me finish the question, sitting forward and steepling his hands together in front of him. "Have you felt any different since the brimstone was removed?" he asks, his voice lowering until it's a strain to hear it.

My eyes dart from side to side, but there's no one else here other than the plants. Almost as if my body is responding to

Caedmon's words, that earlier buzzing under my skin comes to life again. The wave of pinpricks roll over my shoulder blades, up my arms, and down my thighs.

"Different ... how?" It's my turn to move and my eyes focus on the pieces in front of me. No one has been taken yet, all the porcelain black and white miniature statues are still there. My mind, however, is eons away.

"The more powerful of the God children have control over various elements," Caedmon says instead of giving me a true answer. "Familiars are a sign of an exceedingly powerful Mortal God."

Mortal *God*. One corner of my mouth turns up in sardonic amusement. When he's not a God at all. None of them are according to him.

"Mastery over elements comes with certain physical reactions," he continues when I don't speak. "Brimstone is the one thing that can stifle those abilities."

"I still had them," I say, looking up. "Even with the brimstone."

"Yes, you did."

The buzzing grows louder, filling my ears. A dull pain begins to throb behind my eyes. I plant my hands on the edge of the table and lean forward. Lifting one, I take my rook and shift it closer to one of his pawns. One more move and it'll be mine.

"Whose garden is this?" I ask, changing topics.

Caedmon blinks, and for the first time, I think I've actually surprised him. I try not to let the satisfaction show on my face, but it's hard. Brown eyes flash down to the board and then back to me again. A beat passes and then he moves the pawn closer to my rook.

I narrow my eyes on the placement of his piece before I take it, lifting the now captured pawn in my hand.

"The owner of this garden is a friend," is all he says as I turn the porcelain shape over in my palm, watching the false light smooth over its surface.

"Do Gods have friends?" I ask. "Or allies?"

"Why can't it be both?"

I want to deny him either but I can't. "What would you consider Ophelia then? A friend or an ally?"

Caedmon hesitates a moment and when I glance at his face, it's to see the skin between his thick perfect brows pinched. "Ophelia is…"

He doesn't need to answer, I think I get it now. I hold the pawn up between us. "She's a pawn," I say, answering for him. I look down at the chessboard with more interest now. Pawns. Rooks. Bishops. Knights.

I set the pawn down and gesture to him. "Your move."

Just like that, the game restarts. Caedmon moves his pieces and I move mine. Despite what he said about Tryphone wanting a different tutor for me, to Caedmon, this game *is* his version of tutoring, I realize. I'm not entirely sure what lesson he means to teach me. The Gods and their manipulations. I wonder if there's some spell that's been cast over them that forces them to do everything in their strange roundabout ways. It would definitely save everyone time and energy if they could simply do away with all of the social cloaking.

Even the Academy is a game. The grounds are the board. The students are pieces, separated into hierarchies. The only difference between the game in front of me and the one we're playing in real life is the fact that these pieces have no emotions and no autonomy of their own.

If I lose a pawn, I lose a pawn. Not the game.

In life, though, losing a pawn means losing a person. Each

loss chips away at you until all that's left is the husk of the player.

Caedmon and I play in near silence for a long time. The only sound is that of our breathing and the soft whoosh of an invisible wind that flutters at the plants surrounding us. That rich, enticing scent of the blooms seems to sink into my skin, into my very bones.

Finally, when it's down to just a few pieces on either side of the board—Kings, Queens, a knight, two rooks, and a pawn—Caedmon looks up at me again.

"You play the game well."

I've been playing a game since the night my father died. A game of survival.

"I'm trying to learn your lesson," I tell him before lifting my eyes to meet his. "How am I doing?"

He sighs at that. "I'm not entirely sure yet," he admits before sweeping his hand over the pieces on the board. "You're an offensive player and that's not necessarily a bad thing, but I think you play by your emotions. You're angry right now and anger makes you quick to decisions that you might otherwise take more time to consider."

Angry? He thinks I'm angry? Am I? I briefly consider his words. Yes, I suppose I am angry, but I've been this way for so long that I've forgotten what it feels like to be anything but *enraged*.

I pick up his King and turn it over in my palm. "Whatever it is that Tryphone has done, he couldn't have done it alone, could he?"

Eyes the color of burnt umber bore into me. For several long seconds, he doesn't answer. I start to think he won't, but then he does. "No," he admits. "There are Gods that know, Gods that—though they disagree with the cruelty of the taboo—have been complicit because of the benefits."

Benefits? So, it has something to do with giving the Gods what they want. I consider his words, trying to puzzle together everything he's giving me. There are holes, but the image is becoming clearer. Immortality. Power. Oppression. I need more information. I tighten my hold on the porcelain King in my hand.

"One man cannot control a population just like one can't turn the tide of a battle. It must be more. You say you wish to stop what's been happening, but how long did it take you to decide to take action?" Did it start with me? Or before? Has he already failed once? Am I just to be another dead pawn in his effort to right the wrongs that he and his brethren have committed?

Caedmon is silent at my question, but I'm far from done. I set the King back into its place, harder than necessary, and the sound it makes is a giant *clack* in the near quiet of the greenhouse.

"How many pawns have you killed to get here, Caedmon?"

The abrupt inhalation tells me I was right to ask. I close my eyes, unwilling to look at his face as he answers. I don't want to see what I know will be guilt or shame. It doesn't matter if that's how he feels now. When you take a life, you make that decision yourself. You accept whatever the consequences may be. Guilt or shame cannot bring back the dead or erase the past. I know this better than most. The world is a merciless place, and sometimes to survive, you must be just as ruthless as the monsters you fight.

"I don't pretend to know how you feel, Kiera," Caedmon begins and it doesn't escape my notice that he refuses to answer my last question. "But I did not bring you here—to the Academy—because I do not see a future. You *are* the future for your generation."

Fuck. Him. I want to scream in his face, punch him, rail against the unfairness that surrounds not just me but every unfortunate soul born into this world less powerful than a God. "No, I'm not," I tell him. "I'm nothing but a pawn in your game." The words cut through me and then through the air, but once they're out, I refuse to take them back. They're true after all.

I thought I'd learned well enough already that there is no one I can truly rely on but myself. Regis went to Ophelia and Ophelia already knew things—for ten. Fucking. Years. She knew. Still, she never told me the truth. Is there anyone in this Gods forsaken world who is on my side? Who prioritizes *me* above all others? The desire for something so ridiculous as loyalty is pathetic, and yet, I want it still.

"If you are anything at all, Kiera, you are a *key*, not a pawn. But if you were, I'd like for you to remember this ... at the end of the game, both the pawn and the queen end up in the same box." As if to punctuate that fact, he lifts one of the pieces on the board and ironically, it's the only remaining pawn. The porcelain shell of it glints under the pseudo-light shining through the murky glass.

I have nothing to say to that. There's nothing I can say. He's right, but we're also speaking in hypotheticals and hyperboles. Not reality. The reality is this:

The Gods are liars, and if I don't find some way to resign myself to whatever prophecy Caedmon is trying to force to fruition then it's not just my life in danger.

At the end of the day, it never has been. First, it was mine and my father's. Then it was mine and the entire Underworld. Now, it's mine and the Darkhavens. If I were less than my morals, it would be so easy to turn away, to refuse to play these games.

I can't.

I have no interest in saving the lives of the Mortal Gods of this Academy or the others for that matter. I have no interest in saving the lives of mortals or Gods alike. They're all cogs in this clock tower of horrid hierarchy. Just because they've sat back and let this society grow and fester the way it has, why do I have to be the one to fix it? Why must I be the one they turn to?

It's not fucking fair.

I didn't ask for any of this.

I don't want it.

I just don't want the people I have actually come to care about to be killed because I know too much, because I'm a threat.

"What you need is a hero," I tell him. "Someone from the storybooks." I pick up my queen and reach for the game box. Slowly, methodically, I take each piece off the board and put it back in the box before I fold up the mat and place it inside as well.

Then, and only then, do I lift my gaze to meet his. "I am no one's hero," I say. "And I'm certainly no one's salvation."

CHAPTER 18
KALIX

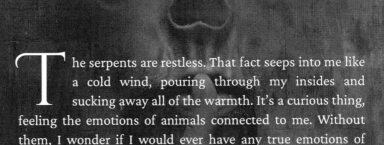

The serpents are restless. That fact seeps into me like a cold wind, pouring through my insides and sucking away all of the warmth. It's a curious thing, feeling the emotions of animals connected to me. Without them, I wonder if I would ever have any true emotions of my own.

That thought drifts away like mist though as the chamber door opens and Kiera steps inside. Her head is down, her hair covering half of her face as she turns to quietly shut the door behind her. Ruen and Theos are both asleep already. They would have stayed up for her, I suspect, had a Terra not stopped by to inform us that she'd been called away by Caedmon.

I, however, could not rest until her return. Now that she has, though, I'm curious as to why she appears so agitated. From my position against the low burning fire in the hearth, my shoulder propped against the stone, I watch as the woman moves further into the chambers. She shoves her long silver hair back over her shoulders and marches towards the door leading to Ruen's bedroom.

About halfway there, she stops, though. Her muscles tense, and in incremental movements, she pivots to face me. The shadows upon her face nearly hide her expression. What I can see of her features are the soft but strong line of her jaw, the petite ridge of her nose, and the side of her forehead. The rest is encased in darkness.

"Kalix."

That's it. One word. I never knew my name could make my cock stand at attention so quickly. Yet, here it is and my serpents are squirming inside the walls, behind closed doors, sensing my impending burst of arousal. Does she know yet that we can affect our familiars as much as they can affect us?

I don't speak. Instead, choosing to wait for her. Kiera turns more fully towards me until the shadows pull back from her features, revealing more. Her plush bottom lip disappears as she bites down, drawing it into her mouth before releasing it abruptly.

"Where were you during class today?" she asks.

I tilt my head to the side. "Do you want to know?"

She blinks and frowns, stepping towards me. The sudden movement captures my attention as I look down at her clothes. She's changed out of the sand caked trousers from earlier and is now dressed in a similarly dark pair and a black tunic that molds to her chest and sides. The brown leather belt around her waist gives me insidious ideas and before I can stop myself, I feel a smile blossom over my face.

"I really don't feel like playing any more fucking games tonight, Kalix," she snaps, her tone tight with irritation. My cock hardens further at the sound. The serpents hiss in my mind, hungry.

Pushing away from the stone wall next to the hearth, I stride towards her with slow, measured paces, not stopping until her chest is barely a hair's breadth from mine. Her face is aimed right at my throat, but she tilts it back until she's looking up her nose at me.

"You seem upset," I comment.

She blows out a breath. "Can you blame me?" she replies. "This whole ... everything is..." She waves her hand and rolls her eyes, unable to finish the statement.

Unable to help myself or the craving I find to touch her, I lift a hand to her face and brush a lock of silver hair back behind her ear. It's thin, softer than anything I think I've ever beheld, ever so much like a spider's silk. The urge to wrap it around my fist and yank is so violent within me that it's a shock I manage to hold myself back.

"Kalix?" Stormy eyes, the color of monstrous seas and clouds, stare up at me, through me. I suspect she knows exactly what I'm planning for her. My lips widen further. Still, she doesn't run away.

My little liar is brave.

"*Sssssssss...*"

My smile drops and my gaze flashes up to the serpent peeking its head out from the railing above us. A bolt of fear shoots through the creature and it disappears from sight in an instant.

The absence of warmth against my front alerts me to Kiera's movements and I drop my hand to my side as she backs up a step and shakes her head. "I'm tired, Kalix," she says. "Whatever you're doing, I don't—"

Reaching out, I latch on to her wrist and drag her back into me. Her chest slams into mine as I round the back of her neck with my other hand. My head descends and my lips slant over hers in an instant. Her frozen body is rock hard against mine, unyielding, but I've learned what it takes to get what I want. Even if I don't understand it, I know what she needs.

I part my lips and tease the seam of her mouth with my tongue. "Open," I command.

She doesn't. Not right away. Kiera remains still in my arms, against me, as I pry her lips apart and delve inside. My shaft strains against my trousers. She tastes of darkness and shadows and wickedness.

When, after several beats, she doesn't soften up or return my affections, I pull away and arch a brow down at her placid expression. "Now is really not the time for this," she says, glaring up at me.

I offer her my most pleasant smirk. Usually, it makes others scramble away from me, but not this one. Not my little liar. She merely hardens her stare.

"I can think of no better time."

Her hands plant themselves on my chest and push back. I don't move, but she does. "Go to bed, Kalix," she snaps. "And I'll—"

Enough is enough, I decide. I don't let her finish her statement as she turns away from me, I whip her back around and lift her, hauling her smaller frame over my shoulder. Pivoting to the end of the stairs, I leave behind the main room and start walking.

"What the fuck!"

"The others are sleeping," I remind her, though it doesn't matter all that much to me if she wakes them. They'll get their turn with her when I'm finished and not before.

When she next speaks, though, her voice is lower, though no less angry. "Put. Me. Down."

"Of course," I agree, pleasantly as I take the stairs two at a time, hurrying now that she's in my arms and more than ready to unleash my plans.

"I mean now," she snaps, punching my lower back. I pause and reach out with a hand to grip the railing. Pain flares against my kidneys as she punches it again. My teeth sink into my lower lip as I close my eyes and relish in the heat that spears through my groin.

Faster. I need to get her to the room.

I open my eyes and race the rest of the way up the stairs, not stopping even when she protests and curses me until we're in my room and the door is shut behind us.

"*Sssssssssss...*"

Kiera's body goes rigid over my shoulder as the sound reaches her ears. "Kalix..." The word is a warning, one I don't listen to. She hasn't tried to fight me off, yet, not truly. Not like she had in the baths. I release my hold on her, letting her body slide slowly down mine until her booted feet hit the floor.

Her muscles bunch and jump beneath her flesh, pulled tight over bones so small, I wonder how she hasn't shattered before now. Will she break if I use her too hard? I want to find out.

One of my braver snakes unfurls from the nest they've built upon my bed and slithers over the side of the mattress. Dropping to the floor, the creature chances moving closer, slinking across the stone floor until it's upon us, curling around her leg and making her entire frame jolt at the sensation.

Wide eyes turn up to meet my gaze. Shadows haunt her. Anger. Wrath. It practically vibrates off her in waves and she has nowhere to unleash it.

Lifting another strand of her hair, I rub it between two of my fingers, wondering what it'd feel like wrapped around my cock. "We're not doing this." Despite her words, her voice is breathless. I almost chuckle aloud at them, but somehow manage to keep the bark of laughter back.

"We already are," I remind her, releasing her hair to reach

for her tunic. I don't bother pulling it off her head, instead, I grip the neckline and rend it down the middle. The sound of tearing fills the room and at the sharp noise, the serpents waiting begin to move faster, curling over each other, hissing and rattling as they sense the incoming storm that bubbles in all of our blood.

The under corset that had been hidden beneath her shirt makes me scowl, but she doesn't stop me when I reach behind myself and remove a blade from the hilt at my lower back. I cut through the laces with brisk, sharp movements until that too becomes useless. The shredded remains fall to the floor.

She doesn't bother to cover herself, making me smile, but just because she doesn't pretend modesty like many others would, doesn't mean she isn't annoyed. The little v that forms between her brows smooths out after a moment and when it does, I narrow my eyes. She takes a step back and bends. The snake circling her ankle hisses and though she pauses at the sound, it's only for a brief second before she lifts her pants leg and withdraws a blade of her own from a hidden sheath.

If it were possible for my cock to harden any more, it would. It fucking *does*. An image of her dragging that blade of hers over my flesh, up and down my chest, my arms, holding it to my throat, makes me want to sink inside her.

"You're a fucking asshole, Kalix Darkhaven," she bites out as she uses her own knife to cut my tunic away. The end of the blade grazes my abdomen. I can feel a bead of precum slip from the head of my shaft.

I lift both hands and part my fingers. The dagger I'd been holding clatters to the ground, leaving her the only one with a weapon.

"Take your anger out on me then, little Thief," I challenge her.

Gray eyes narrow further upon my face as if she's trying to decide if I mean my words or not. I've never meant anything more than I do right now.

Slowly, I lower my hands to my side as the remains of my tunic fall to the floor, colliding with the scraps of her clothes. She fights it—I can see the battle waging upon her expression—but inevitably, she can't help herself. She looks down and then so do I.

I suck in a breath at the sight of blood that greets me. A thin line tracks up the center of my stomach, droplets of red dribbling down to the crotch of my tented trousers. The small wound is already healing, much to my disappointment.

Kiera doesn't apologize. Instead, she reaches out and presses the pad of one finger into the line. My blood smears across her paler flesh. My hunger for more burns inside me. I want her. Crave her. Need her to hurt me the way I know she wants to.

Only then will it be okay for me to hurt her, I suspect.

If I've learned anything from my brothers and our stint here at the Academy, it is that few will ever understand my needs. Fewer still would like them. That never mattered before. Causing pleasure was a side effect of getting what I wanted. She is different.

I've never wanted something so much as to wish for another's enjoyment.

Kiera withdraws her hand and shakes her head. Before she can wipe off the minuscule amount of blood from her thumb, I capture her wrist and bring it up to my face. "Kalix?" My name is a question on her lips.

In response, I bring her hand closer, turning her thumb until it's right beneath my nose. The smell of my own blood sends arousal pounding through my limbs. Slowly, keeping my gaze locked with hers, I enjoy watching her eyes widen as

I part my lips and suck the pad of her thumb into my mouth. Hollowing out my cheeks, I suck and swipe my tongue over the blood still there.

Her breaths come faster, each one attempting to catch up with the other, but inevitably failing to do so. Once wasn't enough and I doubt many more will make it so. I don't care if I must share her with my brothers, having her is still making her mine.

My wicked little thief.

CHAPTER 19
KIERA

Kalix's hot mouth on the tip of my thumb sends spirals of horror through me, but that horror is not alone. I should *not* be turned on by his actions, but I am. Licking his own blood off my skin is ... disgusting. I *should* be disgusted.

I'm not.

My insides squirm like a million little spiders are swarming my organs, crawling all over every inch of them. I can't pull my gaze away. I'm locked upon Kalix's face like a drowning man upon land. When he finally drops my hand and releases me from his physical grip, I snatch it back and hold it against my chest.

What the fuck is wrong with me?

"Come now, little Thief," Kalix says, using that stupid nickname yet again, reminding me of our first encounter. "Show me your teeth."

Keeping my eyes on his, I release my own knife to reach for the front placket of his trousers and undo the laces. Without pulling my gaze away from his face, I let my hand slide against his washboard abs straight down into the front until my fingers collide with the hot, hard length of him. The root of his cock is solid as I free him from the fabric of his pants.

A muscle in his jaw jumps and pulses as I slowly squeeze him against my palm and then stroke him once from base to tip and back again. When I reach the head of him a second time, I pause to let my thumb—the same one that had been coated in his blood—move over the slit there. The pad comes away wet and a low growl erupts from his throat.

There is so much wrong with what I'm doing. So much to be worried about. The Gods. The Council. Caedmon. The Underworld. Should I really be getting distracted by having sex with the Darkhavens? No. Am I going to fuck Kalix anyway?

Yes, I decide a moment later as Kalix tilts his head and crashes his mouth down on mine.

We kiss like we fight. Violence tinging every movement. His teeth sink into my lower lip, drawing blood. A moment later, my mouth is flooded with the taste. It's raw and enticing. I open my mouth wider, tilting my head as I fist him in my hand.

Harder. More. I want this dangerous man to fuck me until I can't think.

And as if he can read my mind, Kalix's hands come up and he lifts me from the floor. My hand falls away from his cock as he steps out of his pants and carries me across the room to the bed. It's the gentlest he's ever been and it confuses me a split second before he lays me down and I realize, I'm not on the mattress.

No, I'm on a bed of snakes.

My eyes slam open as he withdraws from my mouth and something slithery creeps over my body. A shudder works through me. I'm alright with spiders, but that's because I've been able to control them for years. I feel myself in the little creatures, learn their thoughts through their emotions, and share my own. I can't do the same with these animals. They aren't mine. They're *his*.

Hands grip my own pants and shred them down my thighs until they're completely gone and I'm left naked and vulnerable beneath Kalix's gaze. I try to reach for him, but a heavy weight moves directly over one arm and then the next. My head snaps to the side as I realize that the serpents decorating Kalix's bed have pinned me down.

Some of them are larger than the rest, resting across my belly the same thick length of an arm. I hold incredibly still as my legs are pulled apart and then also strapped down with the weight of the snakes holding me in place for Kalix's perusal. I swallow roughly before lifting my gaze to the man who stands over me.

Kalix looks flushed. His eyes are wild and his thick cock stands at attention between his legs. He fists himself as he continues to look at me.

"I thought you wanted me to show you my teeth?" I ask, trying for a casual tone as I contemplate if I'm in any real danger here. I never know when it comes to him. That note of insanity lingers in his green eyes, glittering with some emotion I can't quite place. Whatever it is, though, it seems to be designed specifically for him and it sets my senses on edge.

My heart races within my breast, growing louder in my ears with each passing second as he doesn't respond to me. Kalix tilts his head to the side and with his other hand, he strokes careful fingers over me. Starting at my throat, his touch drifts from my throat down between my breasts and over my belly—which goes concave as I suck in a breath at the same sizzling sensation—before he stops right above my mound.

As dangerous as he is, as much as I don't know what his intentions are, I know I'm wet. Soaked. I want him to go further, to touch me between my legs. I close my eyes and inhale deeply. My skin is abuzz with sensory overload. Fuck, he's going to make me beg.

My eyes burst open and I glare at him. *I do not beg.* "Either you fuck me, Kalix, or I'm leaving," I grit out.

Those moss green eyes of his glow unnaturally, red pouring into the irises and taking over the otherwise ordinary color. His hand makes the rest of the trek in silence, and I gasp as two thick fingers penetrate me. They slide into my core, eased by the juices leaking from my cunt. My breath rasps out of my throat.

"You will not leave until I have had my fill of you, little Thief." Kalix's words are so quiet in the room that I almost don't hear them over the pounding of my heart in my ears.

I find his gaze once more and bite back a moan as his thumb turns and presses over the bundle of nerves above my opening. The muscles in my thighs tremble and jump as sensation assails me.

"Then stop playing with me, Kalix," I growl, unable to help myself.

His shadow falls over me in an instant, his cock pressing into my belly as he climbs atop the bed of snakes. It's strange to feel the cold scales sliding over my flesh—quickly growing warm as they steal my heat. I want to touch him, to reach for him and force him to give me what I want, but they continue to hold me down. I know that I could rip them to shreds, that I could free myself at any moment if I truly wanted to. But I don't want to ruin this. I want Kalix to drive me into the dark and make me forget everything about the last few weeks. To forget Regis' betrayal, Ophelia and Caedmon's secrets, and the God Council's threats.

For this moment, I want to forget everything but pain and pleasure.

Does it make me crazy to desire that solace from a psychopath like Kalix? Yes. Do I care? No.

I've lived in the shadows for long enough, denied myself any hint of freedom. I'm done.

Kalix's palms graze along my ribs, moving up and over to my breasts as he squeezes them between his hands. The snakes around me shudder as if sensing our emotions. He pinches my nipples harshly, twisting them, and sharp spikes of pain go through me, traveling directly to my core. I arch into him, away from the snakes, and straight into his chest. My nipples are hard little pebbles and I have to bite down on my lower lip to keep from crying out at the sudden pain. The red in his eyes has yet to recede and they glow down on me as he does the action again, gripping my nipples between his thumb and forefingers. The harsh stings make me bow up again and a groan finally escapes from my clenched teeth.

Kalix's chest rumbles in satisfaction. That had been what he was after all along—the sound of me. I pant as he releases the sore buds and continues his exploration. Fingers dipping over my stomach until they return to my core.

He moves down the bed, the snakes not seeming to get in his way at all. In fact, they aid him. Their little bodies moving and positioning me, pushing against my legs until my feet are planted on the mattress and my thighs are spread apart before they circle my ankles once more, holding me in place—open and waiting for him.

Lips steal over my core and a gasp locks tight in my throat. Hot breath wafts across my wet, sensitive flesh. Hunger like I've never known pools low in my belly. I bite down so hard on my lip that fresh blood wells up and fills my mouth. I can't seem to care as Kalix latches on to the bundle of nerves at the apex of my thighs. His lips and tongue move over it, sucking and laving until stars burst before my eyes. My hips roll of their own accord. More, I desire more and if he doesn't give it to me soon, I'm going to kill him.

My blade is close enough. I can still see it out of the corner of my eye, lying there on the floor. I eye it speculatively even as his tongue burns a path over my clit, and his teeth nip until my insides are molten. I lift my head to look down on him and freeze when I realize that his eyes are up and squarely on me as he devours my vulnerable flesh. Glowing red above cold green as his teeth flash and he nips me again. My whole body jerks at the sensation and the evil man grins before slipping his fingers up my parted thighs and into my pussy. He penetrates me with two fingers again, moving in and out in a sensual dance that mocks me. My hips cant upwards, demanding more as he turns his head and bites down on one thigh.

I cry out as his teeth sink past my flesh, drawing blood. When he withdraws to lave the wound, I realize that he's changed. He didn't bite me with just teeth, but with fangs that protrude. Sharp and dripping with something...

My head goes hazy as I realize what it is.

Venom. The crazy bastard injected me with his venom.

The world shudders and moves out of focus, spinning around and around until all I can feel is heat and scales. The serpents move over me, around me, heightening my pleasure as Kalix devours my cunt. He doesn't just stop at one bite, but delivers another to my other thigh, making me jolt in pain. Almost as soon as the sharp sting hits, more arousal pours from me. I feel too hot, like my skin has been stretched over a fire that burns inside me. Being naked isn't enough. I want to peel my flesh from my bones to release myself from the confines of this mortal realm. Moans pour from me more freely as Kalix forces my body to the edge again and again. But he never lets me fall from the cliff.

I become delirious as his venom takes effect. His fingers fuck into me, first the two and then three and then four. I swear he's trying to spear his whole fist into my core. My legs shake and my body gyrates atop this bed of serpents, unable to fall off the precipice he's driven me to.

"Kalix…" My voice comes out as a croak, sounding more animal than anything human or God.

I feel fingers retract from my core and nearly whimper at the loss. The emptiness leaves me feeling hollow and aching. A moment later, though, Kalix's face is before me and the prod of a hard, hot cock at my entrance has me holding my breath in anticipation.

Almost there…

His eyes are glowing that unnatural red still, but his pupils have cut themselves to half the size, turning to slits as he gazes down at me. Knuckles bump against my clit as he fits himself right to my pussy. The head pushes in just the barest of inches.

I scratch and claw at the snakes beneath me, a growl rumbling up my throat. They squirm and slither, trying to continue holding me still, but it's no longer working as well. I shake them off, reaching for Kalix as I latch one hand to his shoulder and push my hips up, forcing his cock to take me another inch. My nails dig into his flesh, piercing his skin. Droplets of blood fall from him to my breasts. The blood only incenses me. "More," I demand, thrusting my hips up further. He backs away, smiling as his fangs peek out from his lips.

"Fight me for it," he replies.

Oh, that, I can do.

I arch up and use my own teeth—blunt though they are—to bite down on his throat. His chest rumbles a groan and one wide, masculine hand comes up and cups the back of my skull to hold me close as I sink my teeth into the corded muscle of his neck. Harder and harder, until his blood floods over my tongue. A fresh wave of groans emit from him, and finally—blessedly—he thrusts into me. His cock spears my insides with a single sharp movement that causes my lips to part and a gasp to escape me. More blood rains down on me. It covers my lips, my chin, and drips down my throat towards my breasts.

The snakes surrounding us are forgotten as the ride begins. The sex is raw and angry and full of a frenzy I didn't know I possessed within me. Kalix fucks into me harder and harder. His hips withdraw only to pummel back into me like a battering ram. I grip him tight, pulling my legs from the snakes to wrap around his waist as he takes me. Long scratches form on his chest and I can feel more skin peeling away on his back as I claw at him. Animalistic. Violent. Wicked.

Euphoria erupts within me as I make him bleed. He hisses and scrapes his fangs up the column of my throat. I don't even care anymore about the venom that leaves me feeling as if I've consumed enough ambrosia to kill a horse. My core squeezes against him, demanding more—more blood, more passion, more pain, and more pleasure.

Until this moment, as fire burns hot behind my closed eyelids, I never knew how much I'd been craving the liberty of his insanity. What this is isn't sex. It's not lovemaking. It's a murder. A death of whatever purity I still had, and together, we slaughter that innocent creature until we're bathed in her blood and licking it off each other's bare flesh.

When his climax hits, it's a lightning bolt through my chest and into my veins. Scalding hot cum spurts into me as Kalix slams me hard against the bed and his snakes. His hand wraps around my neck, holding me captive as he rears up—his fangs dripping with more of that venom. When he pierces my throat one last time as his cock stills in my depths, my whole world comes apart. The venom sinks into my blood, heating it beyond possibility. It becomes one with me until I feel as though I'll never be cold again.

There is nothing but the fire and release and I let it consume me into oblivion.

CHAPTER 20
KIERA

I wake up alone, and for that, I'm grateful. My limbs are shaky and my head feels full of lead. Slowly, I climb out of Kalix's bed and pause only once my feet have touched the cold floor to look back. The snakes are all gone and I half wonder if I imagined them there—but they had been there before Kalix had bit me and injected his venom into my veins. They must have been there. A shudder works through me. Spiders are one thing. Serpents are another. A large part of me shies away from the memories of what happened between Kalix and me. The act of not thinking of them isn't difficult considering that those images feel warped as if I'm trying to look at them through the bottom of a jar.

I quickly gather the scraps of my clothes, but when I try to pull them on, I realize that they're torn beyond repair. With an annoyed huff, I leave them on the floor and go through his wardrobe. Pulling on a pair of smaller trousers that were left in the bottom that are still somewhat too big on me, I grab a dark tunic and haul that on as well.

When I exit his room and peek over the railing, the Darkhavens' main room is blessedly empty. I hurry down the stairs and to the door. At this point, I don't care about their reasons for keeping me in their tower. I head down a floor to my old Terra room and steal inside.

Thankfully, my old things haven't yet been removed. I dig through the small number of items I own and frown when all that's left is the one dress Regis had forced me to bring when I'd first entered the Academy all those months ago. Holding it up, I glare at it and debate if I'd rather walk around with my trousers falling every few steps or just give in and wear the damn thing.

Being reminded of Regis doesn't exactly endear me to the fabric, but I release a long slow breath and give in. Stripping out of my stolen clothes, I don the dress. It's far less elaborate than the ones I'd had to borrow from Maeryn, but I still dislike the feeling of so much fabric around my thighs and legs. Despite the flow of the skirts, it feels more restrictive than breeches.

I sink onto the creaky cot I'd once called my own and drag my hands over my face. My cheeks feel dry and stiff. I reach for my neck, intending to scratch the side only to pull away when dried flecks of blood come off at the scrape of my nails. Standing, I go in hunt of the small mirror I'd kept in my sack and lift it to look at the damage Kalix had done.

Any evidence of Kalix's bites is gone now though. They had obviously healed over sometime during the night. The only remainder is the darkened flecks of crusted blood. I scratch them off and let them fall where they may.

A *taptaptap* at the window pauses my actions. Shock rolls through me as I turn my head and spot none other than Regis' crow outside the window with its clawed feet hooked around the bars and its little beak tapping repeatedly on the glass. Forgoing my task, I move to the window, quickly pulling it open, and retrieving the little scroll tied to the animal's foot. For several moments, I just hold the piece of paper without opening it. If it's from Regis, then I have half a mind to burn it without reading the contents. He should know, though, that it's far more dangerous now than ever before to attempt to send me notes.

I'm no longer a Terra in the eyes of the Gods but a newfound Mortal God. They're watching me and I'm not so naive as to think they don't have eyes everywhere. I peer around the room and then close my eyes, calling out with my mind.

Almost immediately, a hundred little minds respond—their emotions nearly overpowering in their strength. I flinch and focus on the loudest and brightest one. *Ara*. I convey my need with a thought and she quickly responds. The other spiders' minds fade as I pull away and I know that they'll be watching and keeping an eye out while I deal with this.

Protection in place, I slip my nail beneath the end of the scroll and unravel it. The words scrawled on the parchment are short. One line.

Can we meet? — R

Fresh anger burns hot within me. I close my eyes as I crumple the paper in my fist. What would be the point? I know who his loyalty lies with now, and though it should not have surprised me—I admit that it did. It had hurt far worse than all the torture Ophelia had heaped upon me at a young age.

Not stopping to think of my actions, I move to the candle sitting on the nightstand and light it. Holding the parchment over the flame, I watch as it eats away at the paper until there is nothing left but ash falling from my smudged fingertips.

Then I blow out the flame and wave the crow away, shutting the window without writing anything back.

Even if it weren't far more dangerous now than before, I don't think I'd be willing to meet with Regis. He was part of my life in the Underworld and that life is over now. The brimstone is gone and I've been released from my contract. There is nothing left for me in the past. So, there is no use dwelling on it.

Still, I watch as Regis' crow flaps its wings outside of the tower window a few times before it turns away and flutters off. I'm sure I confused the animal with my actions, but that's no longer my problem. My problem is finding a way to survive this new chapter of my life—in the Mortal Gods Academy.

I turn back to my things and start to pack them into my satchel, intending to bring them to the Darkhavens' quarters. I'm mostly done when I spot the old volume that Caedmon had gifted me back when I thought he knew nothing of my heritage. Ice fills me, erasing whatever heat had been poured into my veins the night before as I realize the title has changed again. The stitching has been reworked into new words. Lifting it in my hand, I drift a palm over the front.

To Those Who Have Been Stolen

I FROWN down at the words, but because I can't seem to help myself, I flip the book open once more and watch in fascination as words begin to form.

~~*Demetria Gyllmare*~~

~~Atticus Varlane~~
~~Philomena Deveras~~
~~Cecil Marr~~
~~Seline Xarxis~~
~~Abeyance Wellbriar~~
Malachi Ortison

I SCAN the names that appear on the first page, stopping only on the last one as I recognize it. It's the only one without a line crossed through it. I know none of the other names, but from them, I don't think they sound like any mortal name I would know. Instead, they sound like ... the names of someone with status. Names of Mortal Gods. With the final name, too, still sitting there on the front page like a beacon, my mind rolls over the list with confusion.

Frowning, I flip the book closed once more, staring at the title. "To Those Who Have Been Stolen..." *What does that mean?*

The only person I could ask who might have some idea is Caedmon. I grit my teeth and shake my head, turning and shoving the book into my sack before hefting it over my shoulder and stomping to the door. I'll ask him when I'm forced to be in his presence again, but until then, I will simply remain silent.

Whatever the book is trying to tell me, it all leads back to him anyway. I don't know what to ask the book to get the answers I need, the truth that Caedmon won't give me.

I leave behind my old Terra room and return to the Darkhaven chambers. After all, where else am I supposed to go?

My stomach rumbles with hunger as I approach the door and when I open it and step inside, I'm greeted by two familiar faces. Ruen and Theos are standing in the middle of the room, dressed for the day. They both stop talking the second I enter. Ruen's midnight eyes fall to the strap of the satchel over my shoulder.

"You went back to your room," he states.

I don't acknowledge him and instead, stride across the room to his reading table. Once there, I unload my burden and drop it into his seat before cracking my neck to one side and then the other.

"We're about to leave for breakfast before we head to our classes," Theos speaks up, drawing my attention. "Would you like to come with us?"

I face the two of them, ignoring Ruen's disapproving glare as I reply. "I didn't know you deigned to eat with the rest of the Mortal Gods." For the most part, when I was their Terra they'd either skipped meals or ordered me or one of the numerous kitchen Terra to deliver their food to the North Tower.

Theos flashes me a smirk. "We go with the masses on occasion," he says with a shake of his head. "Are you coming or not?"

"She is," Ruen snaps before I get a chance to answer.

My eyes jerk to his. "*She*," I hiss out, "can speak for herself." Though I know I wasn't using my full strength during our sparring match, the fact that he won still burns through me with violent annoyance. I hadn't been trying—not really. It wasn't like I could reveal my training right there for all to see.

Ruen arches a brow at my tone but doesn't say anything. It's Theos who darts a look between us before leaving his brother and moving across the room in my direction. As he gets closer, though, and notices my attire, he pauses and glances me up and down.

"You're not wearing that, are you?" he demands.

I shrug. "I don't have anything else."

The scoff he releases is followed by a shake of his head as he turns and disappears through the doorway that leads into his bedroom. A moment passes and I say nothing. Not even when Ruen drags a hand up his face and through the dark strands of his hair, mussing them. I'm not going to ask what his problem is.

Theos returns quickly with fabric tucked over one arm. He approaches me and hands over what looks like a new tunic and a pair of trousers. I take them but eye the pants. "Will these fit me?" I ask, arching a brow.

He snorts. "Yes," he says.

"Where, may I ask, are you getting clothes for me?" I peer at him curiously. "And why don't I know where you all are keeping these?" I lift the clothes now in my hands.

"There are clothes for you in each of our rooms—well, save for Kalix, I suppose." Theos frowns at that and glances up. "Have you seen him this morning?"

I stiffen. "No," I say quickly—too quickly if Ruen's sharp look is anything to go by. I ignore it as I turn and head towards his room. "I'll get changed and be right back," I toss over my shoulder as I enter Ruen's bedroom and slam the door shut behind me.

Heart pounding, I repress the heat spearing through my face as I quickly strip out of the dress and pull on the trousers—sans underwear since none was provided. Thankfully, the dress had an under corset that could be separated and I leave it on as I don the tunic as well, tucking it into the waistband that molds perfectly to my hips.

Taking a moment to stride to Ruen's wash basin, I splash some water onto my face before patting the skin dry. I peer into his mirror and am relieved to find that all hints of crusted blood are now gone.

When I return to the main room, I think I've calmed my face enough to deceive Theos and Ruen. While Theos merely offers me a smile at my new attire and gestures me towards the door, Ruen hangs back, eyeing me with an analytical interest. Theos is easier to fool than Ruen and I hate that about the eldest Darkhaven.

Ruen Darkhaven sees past my flesh into all the things I want to keep in the dark.

The smile he gives me when I glance back at him over my shoulder is full of teeth.

Maybe he's not Kalix, but he unsettles me in a different way, and he knows it.

CHAPTER 21
RUEN

I stare at the woman seated across from me at the breakfast table. She refuses to meet my gaze and that only serves to make me more suspicious. Terra surround us, laying silver-topped trays down in front of us, and quickly pull away the covers, leaving a feast of meats, breads, and cheeses. They gather the tops and leave, hurrying away as more Mortal Gods enter the dining hall. Kiera immediately sets to work filling her plate and diving in to eat. I continue to watch her with caution and interest even as Theos nudges me to begin eating.

Once again, when we woke this morning, Kalix was gone. The difference today is that Kiera was as well. Though Theos hadn't bothered to go searching for Kalix, I had, and his room had smelled of blood and sex. Knowing how obsessive Kalix has become with the girl—with Kiera—in the last few months, I'm sure it was she he spent the night with. I'm curious to know why the ripe, raw scent of blood had filled his chambers though.

My eyes scan her throat and collarbone revealed at the parting of her tunic. Of course, there's nothing to be seen though. She's a Mortal God and therefore has extraordinary healing ability. Her brimstone shackle is gone now as well, which only means she heals even faster.

Kalix's disappearance is still a conundrum though. Her blood hadn't been the only one spilled in his room. The sharp, acrid scent of his had also permeated the space. The lack of broken furniture, though, speaks of consent. Even before her secrets had been revealed, Kiera Nezerac was not one to sit back and allow herself to be used and harmed against her will.

That knowledge is what finally allows me to direct my focus on the food in front of me. I select a few choice cuts of meat and cheeses and eat methodically as the morning wanes. By the time I finish my meal, the first warning bell of the day chimes across the Academy, ringing into the dining hall and hurrying along students who fear tardiness.

Together, the three of us—Theos, Kiera, and I—push our seats back and start to make our way towards the exit. As we leave the dining hall behind, though, a rather harried looking Terra male stumbles right into our path. His brown eyes are blown wide, the pupils dilated as the scent of terror wafts off him. Kiera frowns as he comes to a bumbling halt before us, but Theos goes rigid as if he recognizes the scent underlying the fear.

"M-Master Ruen," the Terra bows deep. "Y-your presence has been requested by—"

"I know who sent you," I snap, cutting him off. I don't want to hear my father's name.

Kiera glances at me, finally looking at me for the first time since we left the North Tower.

The Terra peeks up through his shaggy hair. "H-he's requested y-you, sir."

I wave him off. "Fine." Ice fills my veins, fueled by my

rage. The arrogance of Azai to call me out. I knew he would do this—which is why I'd gone to Caedmon all those months ago to demand to know if the God Council would be called here.

That bastard can never resist calling his most hated son before him. My whole face tenses and the skin around my scar pulls tight. I close my eyes and try to ease the tightness in my chest by sheer force of will as I sense Theos move closer.

"I can go in your place."

My eyes shoot open at that offer. "*No.*" The word is a brand against the inside of my throat. I would rather relive Kiera's whipping in real time, every inch of my flesh shredding from my own back, than allow my brothers to stand before the monster that sired us.

I jerk my chin to the girl. "Take her to class, and if you find Kalix, keep him close. Let him know where I've gone. I will return."

Theos' mouth firms and his expression hardens, but I'm already striding away before he can argue. The sound of the Terra scrambling after me, his footsteps uneven but agile despite his obvious ungainliness catching up within seconds as he takes the lead, a necessary allowance since I don't know where Azai resides within the Academy ... or what he plans for me.

The Terra leads me away from the classroom buildings of the Academy and closer to the section reserved only for the Gods. Each step closer to my tormentor brings back old memories. Every little scar that lines my arms and on my back tightens and tenses as my muscles jump beneath my flesh.

It's been so long. Too long, some might say. I've almost forgotten what punishment feels like. Air saws in and out of my chest as the Terra leads me up a familiar set of stairs, but instead of stopping before the room where Kiera met the God

Council, the Terra leads me right past the double ornate doors. Sweat beads on the back of my neck and slides down over the ridges of my spine beneath my tunic.

The human's steps finally slow as we near the end of the final corridor. A much smaller set of double doors awaits with a similarly ornate style. A knocker shaped like that of a monster of old—spikes along the side of its head and within its mouth a circular ring of metal that the Terra takes and uses to rap upon the wood once, twice, three times. Each sound drives my mind further and further back as a familiar numbness descends.

The door creaks open and, trembling, the Terra steps out of the way. I don't bother to wait to be allowed entrance via a sound, but instead stride into the room, letting the heavy door close behind me, sealing me inside.

My eyes remain on the floor—a cool black marble with trails of gold and white moving through the glimmering mirror-like surface—for several moments. Then, slowly, I lift my head in incremental movements until I'm standing straight and staring across the vast space of what looks like a bedroom fit for a King of old.

My expression remains blank, devoid of any emotions as Azai ignores me and continues to sit with his back to me in a high-backed winged armchair. The top of his head is visible over the top of the chair; with his height that's not surprising.

His bulky frame is an outline facing the window and it takes several moments for me to realize the noises coming from him. No, not from him ... my upper lip curls back in disgust and as if I need to prove it to myself, I take several steps forward and around to the side.

I stop at the sight of the woman on her knees, the neckline of her gown open and pulled down beneath her bared breasts. Her mouth is locked around Azai's cock and she chokes and gags as the man she's currently sucking off, keeps hold of her head with a palm nearly double the size of her skull. A rumble of a groan unleashes from him as he forces her head down and holds her.

My hands tighten into fists as her eyes widen and then dart to me. Humiliation turns her face bright red as Azai unleashes his seed into her mouth and throat. Tears gather at the corners of her eyes and drip down her face. Once Azai's done, though, that's it. He releases the woman and flicks his hand at her as if dismissing an animal. Quickly gathering herself, the woman yanks her neckline up over her breasts and covers her mouth with the back of her hand as she stands on shaky legs and hurries past me. Her footsteps are the only sound in the room until the click of the door shutting leaves the space in silence.

I close my eyes, trying to rid myself of the scene I just witnessed. I shouldn't be surprised, and I'm not. What I am is sickened and weary.

The creak of the chair as my father shifts and stands has my eyes shooting open. I keep my eyes fixed on his face, but in my periphery, I know he's tucking his saliva covered cock back into his trousers and lacing them shut.

"You're here," he states with a nod. "Good. We have much to discuss."

I don't speak. I simply wait and turn, watching him as he passes around the chair and moves toward the wet bar on the other side of the room. He pulls a glass down from a shelf of them, uncaps a decanter, and pours himself a hefty amount. Azai looks down at the glass and then pulls down a second, filling that as well.

It's barely late morning and yet, already he's drinking. I narrow my attention on his face, noting the fresh lines bracketing his eyes and lips. He looks older since I last saw him.

That's odd. He's never seemed anything but young. Now, though, he looks old enough to actually have fathered children of my age. I take note and secret the information away in the back of my mind—it's surely something I'll have to ask Caedmon about. He said that the Gods aged, but it seems odd that it would happen in the span of a few years when they live centuries.

"Come." Azai flicks his fingers at me. "Drink with me, Son."

With gritted teeth, I take slow measured steps towards him. When he hands me the second glass full of amber liquid, I don't wait for him to taste it first. I put it to my lips and down it all in one gulp.

Azai pauses, his own glass halfway to his lips.

I slam the glass down. "Thank you," I bite out the words. "It was most pleasing."

A smirk passes his lips and he snorts as he takes a sip from his glass. "I doubt you'd know," he comments. "You drank it so fast, I doubt the rum even touched your tongue."

He would be correct. I'd assumed the alcohol was brandy, not rum. I hadn't even tasted the stuff, but I would have known that if I had. I offer him a smile full of teeth, wishing that I had Kalix's ability to produce fangs.

"It's not the type that gives the liquor good taste," I say, "but the company we keep." And no matter if it were a vintage or not, I'd say that whatever this man gives me will end up as little more than shit on my tongue.

"I see you've learned to hold your tongue appropriately," Azai says, his words half amused and sardonic as he sips lightly at his glass. "But I didn't bring you here to discuss liquor. Tell me, I hear that your Terra was found to be a Mortal God. What do you know of her?"

A dangerous emotion blooms inside of my chest,

spreading a darkness I didn't even know I possessed outward until it creeps through each of my limbs. My body reacts as though it's been atrophied. *This meeting is about Kiera?*

Now, I really wish I still held my glass in my hand. It would at least give me something else to focus on instead of the awareness of how close Azai is to me and how easy it would be to plant my fist in his face.

Do not let your anger control you, my son, for anger will make you weak to poor choices.

I close my eyes as the soft, almost lyrical sound of a memory penetrates the rage pouring through me. The voice is tired, but loving. Feminine.

Your anger changes no one but yourself. You may use it as fuel, but do not let it consume you or you will cease to be everything that you are—the child of my heart.

My skin becomes impossibly tight, stretched over muscle and bone that wishes nothing more than to shatter into a million pieces. When I reopen my eyes, I feel as if years have passed. My whole body is sore with the effort it took to hold myself back and it has aged me—inside, if not externally.

"You wish to know more about the new Mortal God?" I say, lifting my tone at the end to form the question. "Why?"

Azai continues to sip at his drink. Sometimes, I wonder if he's able to see into my head and know just how many times I have held myself back from attacking him. The last time I'd been a mere child of ten. It was inevitable that I would lose and pay a price for insulting a God, no matter that he was my sire. Things have changed since then. I am older now, wiser.

My anger has not abated though. No, it has festered and grown in the years since he killed my mother and gave me the scar over my eye. As my mother always warned me not to use my anger too quickly, I've taken her lessons to heart. She might have meant for me to let it go entirely, but that's not who I am.

I am a man who feeds on his anger like a dying wolf. I am a man who will show this one—this God—that he made a mistake in letting me live all those years ago. Perhaps not today, and not even tomorrow, but somehow, someway, I will be his death and I will relish in it.

"The girl is staying in the North Tower, is she not?" Azai replies, arching a brow. "Surely you see her around. She was your Terra. What was she like then?"

See her around? I almost want to laugh. Of course Azai wouldn't even know the details of his sons' lives. He doesn't even know that we're the only First Tiers to inhabit the North Tower—other than Kiera now. He must think she stays within the Tower in different quarters. I have no interest in changing his thinking. The less he knows of us the better—even if this information is something he could easily find out for himself considering how many Terra and other Mortal Gods are aware of our living situation. It says more about him than it does me that he still is blind to the facts.

Pathetic.

He might be the God of Strength, but intelligence will always conquer pure brawn. I'm thankful to my mother for giving me that much even if this bastard's genetics have given me more of my features.

I choose my words carefully as I reply. "She does live in the North Tower," I tell him, "and yes, she was our Terra."

Azai nods. "And?" He gestures for me to continue. "What else?"

I tilt my head to the side and eye him warily. "What else do you wish to know?"

He scowls. His golden eyes—eyes nearly the same shade as Theos'—flash with irritation. He slams his glass down on the wet bar and the delicate material shatters upon impact. I don't even flinch as the glass fragments ricochet in several different directions—the wood beneath where Azai had landed splintering with a loud *crack!*

This right here is why my mother warned me against using my anger without thought.

I meet my father's gaze with barely a glance at the now broken bar and the glass that litters the floor at our feet.

"Do not toy with me, boy." His voice deepens with a low, thunderous rumble. "I want information on this new addition. What of her powers? Have they materialized yet?"

In this, I must be cautious. What I know of Kiera's abilities are small, but I don't yet know what information he's already been given—or if there is any.

"Caedmon discovered her heritage," I say slowly. "Has he not given you any information regarding the girl?" I refuse to say her name before a piece of trash like him.

Azai is a tall God, towering over most others with a bulky frame that seems traditional for the God of Strength. When he turns from me and stomps away, the room appears to tremble at his harsh footsteps. The floor wavers and dust that once clung to the open beams above rains over my face. Azai stalks across the room and in yet another fit of anger, he grips the chair he'd been previously sitting in and hurls it into the wall. Upon impact, the chair breaks. Another loud crack rebounds through the room, echoing into the arched ceiling as wood splits through the otherwise pristine fabric, shredding through in sharp broken pieces. Little bits of stuffing fall to the floor as the chair collapses.

Chest heaving, he breathes harshly and stares at the mess he's made before he scrubs a hand over the top of his dirty blond hair, most of which is separated into long braids with various trinkets attached. The baubles woven into his hair glimmer with the movement.

"As my son," he starts, "it should be your honor to answer my summons and to give me the information I demand."

Honor? How laughable. There is nothing honorable about being his son.

"Caedmon is hiding something." His hand moves to the equally long beard at his chin, stroking through the glittering trinkets there as well. My eyes flash to him and narrow at his words, but he isn't looking at me. Instead, he's looking to the window.

"There are things you do not know, *boy*." I narrow my eyes on the man standing in the remains of his anger as he moves closer to the window to gaze at the cliffside and ocean beyond.

Gods may be hard to kill, but they are not hard to hurt. Brimstone makes them vulnerable, and as I stare at the back of Azai's head, braided in a plethora of valuables, I imagine myself smashing his face through the glass and throwing him to the jagged rocks below. If those rocks were brimstone, all the better.

"She has abilities like the rest of us," I say instead of making that dream come true. Now is not the time, but the future is still unknown. I may get my opportunity if I play my cards right. "Coercion. Added healing and strength."

Azai looks over his shoulder at me. "Nothing else? No hint as to who her God parent could be?" he demands.

I shake my head, a silent lie. To my knowledge, he doesn't yet know of her familiars and control over shadows and spiders. That, more than anything, tells me that when Kiera does come into her true powers, it will be a magnificent sight to behold. She might even be more powerful than my brothers or me.

"Even if her powers were revealed that doesn't necessarily mean it'll reflect who her God parent is," I remind Azai. "Some powers are more reflective of a Mortal God's personality than their lineage."

Azai frowns at my words but he bobs his head up and down in an almost absent movement. "Yes, yes of course." He turns back to the window.

"Is there anything else?" I ask, hoping against hope that he'll release me from the confines of this room and his presence.

Silence greets my question. Azai continues to stare through the glass, fixated on something in the distance. I wait, trepidation swirling within me. The anger and outbursts from him are normal. They are expected. This silence ... is not.

Several more minutes pass and I remain where I am. I know better than to try and leave without permission. Each tick of the clock on the mantel above his hearth, however, stretches my flesh further, tightening everything within me. When he finally does speak, I fear my skin will shred itself with the relief.

"I know you do not understand the choices I have made, Ruen," Azai speaks, his voice that continuous low rumble. He doesn't turn to look back at me. "None of your brothers do, but what I decide must be done for the survival of God kind, and as my sons, you are part of that. Whatever happens, that is most important."

God kind? I have to force my face to remain calm and expressionless when the muscles in my jaw begin to throb and my upper lip tries to curl back. I don't speak. I hardly even breathe, locking the air inside of my chest as if doing so will save me from having to inhale anything this man exhales.

Azai is quiet again for a long moment and I have the

strangest thought that there is more he wants to say. Instead, though, he merely shakes his head and flicks out a hand, dismissing me with the gesture.

I don't wait to clarify. I'm out of his door and stalking down the corridor of the Gods Council's quarters before he ever turns around. I head directly for the classrooms, peering at the sky as I exit the building and trying to ascertain the time of day with where the others will be.

If Azai wants information on Kiera, then I need to talk to the others. They need to know and we need to close ranks. Whatever he wants it for, I can only be sure it's nothing good.

CHAPTER 22
KIERA

If there were a prize for the most aggravating and bothersome males in the entire world, the Darkhavens would win first place, hands down. This is a fact I didn't quite realize until I was forced to spend weeks locked in close quarters with the three of them. We eat together, we attend classes together, we train together. They hover and I've never been hovered over before.

I dislike it. *Immensely.*

They're even now aware that Regis is attempting to set up a meeting with me. I would have thought that my obvious snub—and the lack of reply would give him at least a hint to leave me the fuck alone. It seems, however, that my ex-friend is a stubborn asshole.

His crow has figured out that I no longer go to my old room and has been tapping outside the Darkhavens' window every few days with a fresh note. I've stopped reading them altogether, but merely take them from the crow and toss them into the hearth before sending the creature off with a wave. Ruen, despite his sudden quietness since meeting with his father, has attempted to argue that I should at least give a response.

I find both him and the others overbearing.

The only times I gain some bit of freedom from their presence is when I sneak off or must attend tutoring with Caedmon, the former of which consists of a lot of roundabout God talk.

The days pass into weeks and Kalix continues to disappear periodically without telling anyone where he goes or what he does. When he returns, he sometimes smells of blood and decay. Even Theos and Ruen seem to be unaware of his activities, but they both act as though it is normal for him.

Perhaps, it is.

Every day in the Academy reminds me of the invisible noose that continues to tighten around my throat, cutting off my air. Blood is in my lungs and it is what I now breathe.

I've managed to keep the book Caedmon had gifted away from the Darkhavens' prying eyes. Most shockingly of all, from Ruen—who, since the meeting with his father, has taken to himself more so than ever before.

Why does it feel like the four of us are simply waiting for the start of a storm and there's nothing more we can do to prepare? There must be something. There is *always* something.

"Kiera?"

I blink and glance up as Caedmon calls my name, sounding as if it's not the first time. We are, once again, in the strange garden that is lit with divine power with a spread of a chessboard before us. The scent of floral blossoms surrounds us and invades my nostrils with each breath I take. I shake my head and refocus on the board.

"Sorry," I mutter. "My turn?" I reach for a pawn, stopping

only when a dark-skinned hand comes down on mine, halting the movement.

"Your mind is elsewhere," Caedmon says.

I sit back, pulling my hand out from under his as I look up towards the lights glimmering from every surface of the ceiling. If I didn't know any better, I'd say that this place is coated in real sunlight and that the windows are true visions of what lies beyond the walls. But I do know better and I know that it is all an illusion—much like these 'tutoring' sessions with Caedmon.

Perhaps now is the perfect time to bring up the changes to his book. I contemplate that even as I sense Caedmon's eyes boring holes into the side of my face.

"What is bothering you?" he asks after several moments of silence.

A heavier question, I'm not sure I've ever heard. He still hopes that I will accept his request to attempt to kill the most powerful being to exist within this realm. Kalix is keeping secrets and Ruen has pulled into himself. I'm confused and frustrated. The weight of all of their expectations as well as the building pressure within my own body now that the brimstone has been removed is slowly driving me to the brink of insanity, and I fear that when I fall over the edge there will be no coming back.

I don't say any of that but instead, go back to something far simpler. "The book you gave me has changed again," I admit.

I sense rather than see Caedmon shift forward. The light creak of the chair beneath him and the scrape of fabric on the stone table echo back to me. Thankfully, I manage to maintain a straight face and not wince at how loud it seems.

Maeryn informed me that it's only natural for my senses to get stronger with time as my body is now acclimating to having full access to my abilities. That doesn't make dealing with it any easier though.

"What has it shown you this time?" he inquires.

"Names," I say, glancing in his direction. "Some are crossed out but others aren't."

Caedmon's face doesn't change as he absorbs that information. "Are they in any sort of order?" he asks.

"The ones that are crossed out are at the top," I say. "And the ones that aren't appear at the bottom."

"Do you recognize any of them?"

I hesitate to answer him, but my hesitation, I realize a moment later, is answer enough. "I recognize a few, but they haven't been crossed out yet." Another beneath Malachi had appeared in recent days. Enid Duskhorn. Though I'm not entirely sure since I don't know the girl's surname, Enid is the name of the Mortal God Theos had recommended for advancement before the battles. She'd won and still lives, but her name appearing in the book has me on edge for some reason.

"What is the book's new title?" Caedmon asks, disrupting my thoughts.

I swallow before answering. *"To Those Who Have Been Stolen."* The only response from him comes in the form of a small twitch over his left eye. I narrow my gaze as he sits back. "What does that mean?" I mean the question to come out soft and curious. Instead, it comes out harsh and annoyed. I suppose trying to hide my frustration at this situation is not within my current skill set.

I find when there's no reason to hide my personality any longer, I simply can't. Caedmon knows all anyway. My past. My present. And a future he still refuses to divulge.

"I cannot say," Caedmon says as he reaches for a tea cup set a few inches to the side of the chessboard.

"You cannot say or you *will not*?"

His elegant fingers still as they latch on to the cup's fragile looking handle. Ebony eyes lift to meet mine. "You are angry." Yet another statement.

I can't help but bare my teeth at him. "*You don't say.*"

His sigh only serves to irritate me further. He releases the tea cup and steeples his fingers together, setting his elbows upon the edge of the stone table between us.

"I told you once that that book is special and that it is quite ancient and spelled," he begins, his voice quiet enough that even my heightened senses strain to hear him. "But it is more than that. The book you currently have in your possession is a book of prophecies of a sort."

"A book of prophecies?" I repeat. "But it told me of the past as well. I thought prophecies only dealt with the future."

"All prophecies that come to pass eventually end up in the past," Caedmon replies gently. "That book is more than special." He pauses and his brow creases, lips turning down at the corners.

My heart hammers in my chest as a peculiar sensation takes root inside me. It's a warning and I know why the moment Caedmon seems to resign himself to something before speaking again. "That book is a part of me," he finally admits. "It is bound in my flesh and therefore, holds some of the same powers as myself."

My lips part and my jaw loosens in pure shock. *The book is bound in his flesh?* The leather I'd held in my hands was not of any animal but a God? Horror sickens my insides and Caedmon must see it upon my face because, in the next instance, he's out of his seat and around the table, kneeling before me as he takes my hands in his.

"It was purposeful, Kiera," he says. "Do not worry—I was completely consenting in its creation. I bound it myself. Were

I to perish, I wanted there to be something left behind. Something that could aid you."

My breaths come in fast pants, filling my ears even as he squeezes my fingers in his grip. He's still talking, his voice soothing and gentle, but I cannot understand. Why would anyone purposefully flay their own flesh to bind a book? What does he mean he wanted to leave something behind to aid me?

My gaze lifts to find his. The skin around his eyes crinkles at the corners reminding me of the same happening to Tryphone the only time I'd met him within the God Council's chambers. Those lines, though beautiful and speaking of many amusements, are marked by age. Something that should not be possible for a God, another piece of evidence to back up Caedmon's claims that they are not Gods at all.

After a lifetime, however, of thinking of them one way, it's difficult to completely shift my understanding of the world around me. Knowing does not always mean truly believing. That is something entirely different. Faith in Caedmon's words doesn't come from my mind, but a separate place entirely. I'm starting to feel its spark now.

Before, I thought I'd understood all that is now on the line. It isn't until I stare down at Caedmon's otherwise smooth face and the hands that hold mine—hands that cut his own flesh from his body and bound it into an object of permanence—that I realize I was wrong.

The act of stripping flesh from a person's muscles is a torture I've received. The pain that I'd felt and the elongated time of healing after is an enduring reminder. I shudder as the memory comes back to me. I repress it once more and try to catch my breath upon this new information.

"Are you alright?" Caedmon's voice which had fallen into the muffled timbre of sounds returns in words.

I'm not sure I have a real answer, but I nod anyway. He retracts his hands and stands to his full height. I tip my head back, staring up at him. I focus on his face so that I don't try looking for scars from his ordeal as I know they won't be there. Even I healed from mine so there's no doubt in me that he did as well.

"I know it's frustrating that I'm not able to give you more information about prophecies, Kiera," Caedmon says. "Believe me, I wish that I could be straightforward. I do not enjoy the hints I must leave you rather than simply telling you what you need to know. The downside to having these abilities is that we are often controlled by them and there are consequences of stepping outside the boundaries they have set for us."

"So you can't tell me anything that isn't shrouded in some metaphor or mental puzzle that I must first unravel?" I ask plainly.

Caedmon's lips twitch and he offers me a beseeching smile as he returns to his seat. "I am sorry," he admits. "The disadvantage of my power is my inability to know the prophecies if I reveal the secrets of the future."

I just stare at him. Heat fills me. Frustration. I've already told him that I am no one's hero, least of all his. Yet, still, as he stares back, I see the truth in his eyes. He still has hope. Hope that I can somehow manage to overcome all of these obstacles.

He's one of them.

Whatever future he knows but cannot reveal to me, sits in the shadows like a monster waiting to strike. Like the creature parents tell their children about in secret whispers to make them behave lest the being come to steal them away in the night.

I will not be frightened by an imaginary monster. I have more than enough real ones to face.

I lay a fist on the stone table between Caedmon and me and fix him with a harsh look. "So you can't tell me what those names mean?" I ask.

Caedmon's gaze shifts to something unexpected. I've seen broken men before. Witnessed their demises in darkened alleyways and shunned their existence simply for the fact that to acknowledge their cracked souls would harm my own ability to live on. That is exactly what Caedmon becomes though at the mention of those names again. He doesn't speak, but his lips part as if he wants to. They close again and he answers with a shake of his head.

Again, because he *can't* tell me.

I lower my eyes to the chessboard. The porcelain pieces—the same as every other time I've been here—seem to dance in front of my vision. I know this feeling well. I close my eyes against it, but that doesn't erase the truth.

Trapped. I am well and truly trapped.

I can try to gain more information from Caedmon, but I have the feeling that no matter how many questions I ask, no matter how many times we come back to this place, I will never get what I seek. Maybe because what I seek is not in him. It's not here in this false garden with its false light and its confined flowers.

The irony is not lost on me. The Academy is just like this greenhouse. We, the Mortal Gods, are the precious blooms that smell of sweetness and power. We grow under the light of the Gods, but it's not true sunlight that shines upon us. The primary difference between me and the rest, though, is that I was not raised as a greenhouse flower. I was raised outside. I was carved from blood, sweat, and bone.

My eyes shoot open. Of course ... I blink at Caedmon who

is peering at me, his expression a mixture of curiosity and concern.

Those names have made me realize something. I'm still not sure what they mean, but they remind me that I'm not alone. I can't kill Tryphone and I refuse to do so without knowing the truth—a truth that Caedmon knows but can't tell me.

I must go hunting for it myself.

I stand abruptly. "I think this session is over," I say, blinking as my blood rushes through me, speeding along my movements.

I need to find out the truth, and then, once I've decided what to do, I need to find out how to use the others. There are far more Mortal Gods than there are Gods. Using them isn't a choice but a necessity. The greenhouse needs to be opened and the flowers need to be released from captivity. Only then can they truly grow into what they were meant to be.

Only then can the Gods' oppression end.

CHAPTER 23
THEOS

"Is Kalix not here?"

I unfold my arms and turn to greet the speaker of that question. Ruen looks a little worse for wear with his hair in disarray and his eyes sunken in a bit with shadows that have been growing for weeks creating a permanent place for themselves beneath the sockets.

"No," I answer. "What's wrong with you?"

Ruen waves off my concern as he has each time I've asked. I frown but don't push. If he doesn't get better soon, though, I'm going to have to push. Whatever is eating at him can't be good.

Together, we turn back to the sandy area of the arena where several Mortal Gods are locked into mock battles in their own circles. Axlan isn't here today. It happens on occasion, the Gods forget that they have duties and classes to attend to here, and they simply don't show up. Had this been any other class, everyone would have simply gone on their way and enjoyed the free afternoon. This isn't just any other class. This is battle training and everyone knows that keeping up with this is more of a means of survival than actual education.

Enid is doing well and I'm glad I recommended her for advancement all those months ago. Even if it'd put her in danger, she's more challenged here and her skills are improving quickly. I watch her duck and weave out of the reach of her attacker, using her much smaller body to circle him and then leap onto his back. Her forearm encircles his throat as she chokes him out. His face begins to turn a splotchy red.

"What about Kiera?"

I pull my attention away from Enid to face Ruen. With a frown, I scan the rest of the arena. "She should be here," I say. "She wasn't with you?"

Ruen shakes his head. "No, Caedmon pulled her out of the last class for more of her private sessions with him."

I frown. "He normally waits until all of her classes are finished for the day," I comment.

"I know." Ruen nods. "Which is why I find it odd."

The sound of flesh hitting flesh echoes into the air around us followed by grunts and curses. Ruen glances back to the other Mortal Gods, eyes scanning them. My attention goes to my brother, from the shallow bruises beneath his eyes and the haunted look in his gaze down to his hands. My sharp inhalation has his head turning quickly back in my direction.

When he notes the direction of my stare, he snaps his hand back as if he can hide what I've already seen. Anger flares bright within me and I grab ahold of his arm, dragging him further from the others and turning my back on them as I lower my voice.

"Tell me you didn't," I hiss out the words, each one coated in the rage that's currently spearing through my insides.

Ruen doesn't answer but that's answer enough.

"You said you'd gotten better," I growl. "That you stopped."

"I did." He won't meet my eyes.

Fire sparks at my fingertips, white gold light flaring brightly against my palm. I release Ruen and close my hands into fists, stifling the lightning that threatens to spill forth.

"How long?"

He doesn't need clarification. He knows what I'm asking. Without looking at me still, Ruen answers, his voice quiet. "Since seeing Azai." The words are tinged with shame and I want to scream at him that he *should* be ashamed.

All these years ... all this time...

Rash words full of hurt and anger hang precariously on the tip of my tongue. They cling to my teeth as I grind them together. Instead of giving them a voice, I scrub a hand down my face, pulling at the skin.

"I want the fucking blade," I say.

Ruen doesn't even argue. He has no right to. He merely nods. It's rare, after all, when our roles reverse like this. I am not the level headed one. He is. Usually.

"If it's not in my room by the end of the day, I will personally rip apart yours until I find every single one of them," I grit out.

Dark eyes that appear even darker in the sunken features of his face meet mine. "There's only one," he says.

But he can always get more. It's dangerous but possible. After all, the mere fact that Ruen has yet another brimstone blade in his possession when I took and disposed of his last one should be evidence enough that if he wants to retrieve another, he will.

I jerk my chin to the end of the field. "Go," I snap. "You're likely in no fucking position to be training today. Contact Maeryn and see if—"

"No." Ruen stops me.

I arch a brow and wait.

"I don't want anyone to know," he says. "I'll take care of it myself."

My upper lip curls back and I turn, grabbing ahold of him once more. The two of us spin until I slam his spine into the nearest wall surrounding the arena. I sense several eyes upon us, but I ignore them as I get up in his face.

"Your *'taking care of it'* has left you like this," I snarl at him. I grab ahold of one of his arms and lift it, reaching with my other hand to yank back the sleeve of his nearly skin tight tunic. Freshly scabbed over cuts greet me on top of old ones.

Bile threatens to come up my throat. "Kalix and I rely on you," I snap as he yanks his arm away and jerks the tunic sleeve back into place. "We listen to you. You owe me the same Gods damned courtesy when you're being a fucking idiot."

Ruen's expression goes blank. He stares back at me and my stomach rolls.

I have to force the next words out without puking. "*Go. To. Maeryn.*" The order is an angry, pain-filled plea. "You don't even have to tell her to heal you herself. She'll have herbs that will expedite the process." I release him and step back. He still doesn't move. His eyes are empty, devoid of life, of anything but shame and resignation.

"You can't break on us, Ruen," I tell him. "Not now."

Not ever.

CHAPTER 24
KIERA

Nothing. There is absolutely nothing in the records of the library that is even marginally useful. With frustration, I slam closed the book in front of me, sending a waft of dust out from between the pages. I cough and swipe a hand in front of my face to clear away the last vestiges of the particles that have become airborne. The cover itself hadn't been covered in dust, which is more of a testament to the work of the Terra and caretakers of the books than its time off its shelf. Even now, a subtle glance around the stacks of shelves and the darkened corners of the quiet space reveals that I'm one of the few Mortal Gods here.

When I was forced to work here, it had felt more like a retreat away from the Mortal Gods than the actual punishment it was meant to be. Few students venture into this space. If they need the volumes within, they usually send Terra with notes on which ones to pull and deliver to them.

A familiar figure appears around the corner of one of the shelves, her pallid face half hidden by the wash of brown and gray hair over her shoulder. Sylvis moves quickly and quietly through the arching shelves like a ghost and I wonder at how much longer she has. The last time I'd seen her, she'd been, in essence, one of my prison guards when I was forced to work here. She had never been unkind though.

Absently, I find myself scratching the inside of my wrist as I watch her go. The memory of her secretive discussion with Caedmon prickles at the back of my mind. She looks more tired than she had before and I know it's not all because of age. Mortals don't age that quickly in the span of a few short months. Whatever Caedmon had given her is obviously not helping her as much as either of them had hoped.

My eyes fall to my wrist again. For a moment, I contemplate slicing open a vein and finding a vial to fill it with my blood. It would help her, I know. It would be a kindness for her lack of cruelty when to the rest of the Academy I'd been nobody, just another mortal Terra whose life was subject to the whims of the Mortal Gods and their sires.

Almost as soon as the thought takes over, I shake it away. Even if I could afford to risk giving my blood to her, there's no telling if she would accidentally reveal the gift to another Terra, someone who might go tattling to the Gods. A Mortal God who'd lived her life as an unknowing human wouldn't have the idea of sharing their blood to heal a lowly servant.

I push the volume in front of me away, standing up from the table and wincing as my back throbs in protest. Stretching up on my toes, I start to gather the books I'd taken down from the shelves of past graduates of the Academy, pausing when I spot a book beneath the others that I've already reviewed.

Sitting back down, I flip it open and scan the index. This is last year's list of Riviere attendees and graduates—whereas the others were older. This is the one I'd been looking for to begin with. I scan back to where it had been—*why hadn't I placed it on top? Why hadn't it been the first one I'd looked at?*

Frowning, I return my focus to the tome and then start to

go through it. Minutes later, my pulse begins to race. Excitement pours through me and my hands hover over the names with a fine, barely there tremble. I hurriedly flip the page and start scanning the next. Then the next and the next, until I find them all.

DEMETRIA GYLLMARE—TRANSFERRED.
Atticus Varlane—transferred.
Philomena Deveras—transferred.
Cecil Marr—transferred.
Seline Xarxis—transferred.
Abeyance Wellbriar—transferred.

THEY'RE ALL THERE. Every. Last. Name. Each one is marked with a transfer, but to where? These are the list of the ones my book had given me. All save for Malachi.

I continue reading and after a few more minutes, I'm rewarded for my efforts with the answer. The Mortal Gods Academy of Ortus.

A shudder works through my body. The image of sharp, glistening ebony spikes that appear more like jagged knives spearing up through the land and ocean flickers in my memory. Upon further review, each of the names of the Mortal Gods listed come up as either First or Second Tiers.

I'm not entirely sure why so many strong Mortal Gods with powerful backgrounds would be transferred to the Academy of Ortus, but without stopping to think about these findings, I write them all down on the last page of the book, an empty extra. With a hurried glance around, I quickly rip the page from the volume and fold it before stuffing it into my pocket and standing once more.

My mind is awhirl with the knowledge, though I'm not sure yet what to make of it, I do know one person who might be able to help. Of all the Darkhavens, Ruen is the most studious. His wicked intelligence is one of the few things I admire about him. Even if I'm still smarting from our spar weeks prior, I know that he'll be the best to help me figure out the meaning behind it all.

⁓

I LEAVE the books behind where they lay, shooed away by the Terra of the library when I even attempt to put them away myself. I don't argue. I'm in a hurry to get back to the North Tower anyway. The paper in my pocket is burning a hole right through the fabric of my trousers.

My legs eat up the distance and when I see the stairs inside the door of the Tower, I take them two at a time. My body buzzes with excitement and the fresh wave of adrenaline that's flowing through my veins. It's been a while since I felt quite this enthusiastic and the minor physical exercise is a good way to release the extra energy.

In a burst of energy, I fly up the rest of the stairs, straight past my old room until I'm standing in front of the door of the Darkhaven quarters. I don't bother to knock. I don't anymore. Turning the handle and letting myself inside, I scan the room, finding no one else. Ruen's reading table is empty too.

Damn it. It's the middle of classes. I'd completely forgotten. They're all likely away and wondering where I am. I pause and release an annoyed breath, but as the door swings shut behind me a sound reaches my ears.

Hope blossoms in my chest when I turn my head and notice that Ruen's bedroom door is slightly ajar and a shadow moves around inside. I don't even stop to wonder why he's back early when it's obvious the others aren't. I'm across the room before my mind can catch up with my body, pushing the door further open and stepping inside.

"Ruen, I found something that I want to ask—"

The sight that greets me freezes all movements and the words that had been on my lips fall away, forgotten. The silence that follows my sudden intrusion stretches into what feels like centuries, but I know, logically, it can only be a few seconds. Ruen is shirtless. His body chiseled to the perfection only capable of being immortalized in statues and art. Each muscle of his chest and shoulders is cut like granite and the most stony of all is his face. Drawn into a complete mask of nothingness—no anger, no happiness. Every minuscule inch of his expression is devoid of the emotion that breathes essence into living beings.

For all I can tell, Ruen Darkhaven has simply ceased to exist as anything more than a memorial of the Mortal God I've both come to hate and unwillingly trust.

My eyes fall to where his hands are locked in place with a wet cloth coated in what looks like green and brown mush. They hover over his forearms, both of which are lined with sharp wounds.

I take a step further into the room and then quietly shut the door. My back touches the wood a moment later as I lean against it, needing the help to hold myself up. The physicality of touching an object grounds me as old memories swarm the back of my mind. Each cut is a perfect line. No wavering signs of hesitation. Precise. Cold. Callous.

The light outside the window appears to dim as I take a breath and push away from the door. Ruen doesn't move a muscle as I approach and I don't stop until I'm standing over where he's perched on the side of his bed with the nightstand acting as a placemat for the bowl of water and what looks like a bag of herbs. The scent of soil and the tang of turmeric along with the softer aroma of lavender hover between us.

"What are you doing here?" Ruen's voice is husky.

I peer from his arms to his face. "What did you do?" I demand instead.

To his credit, he doesn't flinch. My question does, however, seem to give him the energy to move. He lowers the cloth until it covers one of his forearms, and then he rubs it back and forth over the scabs that have now formed.

I eye those markings. They're dark, suggesting that they aren't new wounds. There are only two things that can harm a God or Mortal God and keep it from healing so completely. I don't detect a hint of poison in the air, which can only mean that he used brimstone.

Several minutes pass as Ruen strokes the medicine covered cloth up and down his forearms and still, he doesn't respond. I narrow my gaze on him. "*Why?*" I ask instead of repeating my earlier question.

Ruen pauses his actions with his head bowed. His breath shudders out of him, lifting his shoulders and lowering them once more. This close to him, I can see the fine details of scars marking his shoulders as well, the lines disappearing over his back.

"Ruen. Answer me."

"It's none of your concern." I'm not surprised by his gruff response. What I am, is angry.

"Those cuts aren't jagged." I lick my dry cracked lips, feeling devoid of anything but wrath and pain. "You didn't get them from someone else."

He doesn't reply, just continues scrubbing at the scabs. My gaze lands on his chest, the dips and hollows of a well-trained and muscled body. I bite down, grinding my teeth together.

I want to circle him to see where the lines along his shoulders and back end. Deep down, I know they don't. The scars might come to a point somewhere along his spine, but they go far deeper than the flesh. I know because no matter how many times I've healed from my own scars, sometimes, I still wake up from old nightmares covered in their ghosts.

Ruen curses and my eyes jerk down to find that he's scrubbed himself so hard that one of the scabs has peeled away completely and blood flows freely from the freshly opened wound. I don't think. I just react. Capturing his hand and stopping him from slapping the cut across the opening, I reach for the extra cloth lying on the nightstand. I ignore the herb concoction and dip the fresh cloth into the waiting water, wetting it before bringing it to his skin.

"Irritating the scabs won't help them heal," I state. "But you know that, don't you?" My tone is even, my words clinical as I press the wet fabric to his wound and watch the blood seep through in a way that it wouldn't were these wounds made by anything other than brimstone.

My motions are moderate. I don't press down too hard, but meticulously clean the wound before I set the cloth to the side and steal his from him. He doesn't fight me, much to my astonishment, but I don't comment as I press the herbs into the opening of his skin. A hiss escapes from him a moment later and the forearm under my grip tenses as I assume pain flares through him.

"I don't know why you're acting like this," I finally say. "Didn't you want to feel the pain?"

He doesn't answer and my gaze flickers up to meet his. Midnight eyes with pupils blown wide nearly encompassing the color of his irises are locked on me.

"Or is there another reason why you flayed yourself open

like this?" I continue. My voice leaves behind the cold, clinical tone and delves back into anger.

Of all the Darkhavens, I didn't expect this of him. Then again, Ruen is the Darkhaven I know the least about. Perhaps, had I been paying closer attention, I would've noticed that he rarely undressed in front of others. That I'd never seen him without a shirt—not even in sparring practice when so many other men had stripped to just their trousers.

"It's not always about pain," he murmurs.

"No?" I continue my ministrations with his forearm, finishing smearing the herbs over the wound before moving onto the next scab. "Then what is it about?"

Ruen doesn't answer. His expression doesn't change, but I suspect he doesn't have an answer—at least not one that he wants to admit to. The grinding of my jaw persists and I finish with one forearm, reaching for the next. Ruen lets me take it, lifting it as I spread more of the herbs that seem to sink into his flesh until merely a thin sheen of the gooey liquid is seen over his skin.

There are older lines here, so pale that they're difficult to see. My fingers pause over an older line, at the end of his wrist, right over the twin veins that meet. This line is different from the rest. It's deeper, cut vertically along where the blood thrums a consistent pulse. It's older, but it tells a story. This cut had meant to kill, not harm.

I release Ruen's forearm and drop the cloth into the bowl on his nightstand. Finding the wrappings discarded behind it all, I lift his arms once more and start the process of circling his forearms and dressing the wounds to keep them from getting infected. Ruen doesn't speak when I finish the first and move to the second. In fact, he remains completely still and quiet as I perform the task.

My gaze lifts to meet his, and I see nothing of the man and

everything of a barely restrained beast reflected back at me. Ruen Darkhaven may not have the same abilities as his brother Kalix, but that doesn't make him any less deadly.

I cinch the last of the dressing, completing the task, before taking a step back and fixing him with a look. "We need to talk."

CHAPTER 25
KIERA

"What are you afraid of?"

A low growl leaves him at my question, rumbling in obvious warning. Ruen's eyes glow a little brighter, the dark blue tint still left as a small ring around his pupils illuminating as it tinges the slightest bit in red. I disregard the implied threat of that change and stare back at him unflinching. Waiting.

"*I am not afraid of anything.*"

Silence echoes between us at Ruen's hissed statement. I wait a bit to see if he'll say more, but when he doesn't, I'm not surprised.

A sigh slips free from my lips and Ruen narrows his eyes on me. Before he can open his mouth and say anything else that'll leave me further annoyed, I speak. "That's not the first lie you've told me, I'm sure," I say slowly, meaningfully, as I lift my gaze to meet his. "But if we're going to do this—you and me and your brothers—if the four of us are going to work together, then I intend to make sure it's the last."

The look Ruen gives me is full of unending cold rage. Something skitters beneath my skin, a match to that frost coated fury of his. I meet his eyes with resolute determination. If anyone can understand him, it's the child that still dwells within me—the child of my past.

Phantoms enter the room. Each one a monstrous creature, unseen to most but not us. We know these ghosts quite well, Ruen and I. They're part of the darkness that resides within our souls. Ruen's body unfolds from itself, and it isn't until he rises from the bed to his full height that I realize just how much smaller he seemed with his shoulders hunched and his head tilted down to his arms. Now I have to raise my chin to keep my gaze connected with his.

"Who are you to demand that of me?" Each word is accompanied by the throb of distant thunder, but I'm not so naive as to think it has anything to do with the perfect weather outside.

It might be cooler than the summer months, but there is no storm hovering in the near distance. The only storm is right here in this room. Between him and me.

There is something enticingly stimulating about two powerful beings facing off against one another and a strange sort of energy crackles through the room. The air is hot, wafting over my throat as it remains bared while my attention stays trapped within his eyes. Eyes that are flickering between midnight and crimson. The line of civility that he has walked since our first meeting is being erased.

"Who do you want me to be?" I finally ask in response. A question for a question.

Full masculine lips part, and I can't tell if it's shock or consideration. Ruen takes a step toward me, but the distance between us doesn't shorten. It takes me a moment to realize it's because my body moved on its own accord and forced me back in the same instant. As if my instincts are warning me to avoid this monstrous creature that's appeared before us.

Ruen is a man in the thinnest sense right now. The body he resides in may appear like that of a Mortal God, but there is a creature of great power and strength that lies beyond his flesh, and every primordial sense I possess is cautioning me to be careful. Irritation flares to life within me. I don't like to be ordered about—not even by my own senses. I am the one in control now in a way that I haven't been in a very long time.

There is no brimstone in my neck. No blood contract sealing me to do someone else's bidding. In this room, it is just Ruen and me. No one else should come between us when we are so close to uncovering something I sense must be unveiled.

Some wounds fester if you leave them wrapped for too long. I suspect Ruen Darkhaven has many that need to be excised from him and there's no one else around to help him but me.

This time, when he takes a step towards me, I force my traitorous body to remain stone still. Being so close to him, nearly touching the wide warrior frame of him reminds me of all the ways I can't compare. In the Underworld, I'd learned to use my smaller stature to my advantage. Focusing on speed and honing what advantages my God blood had brought me had saved my life more than once. In the end, though, I'd always been destined to work in the shadows, hiding my talents even when my Divine ancestry was discovered.

The same cannot be said for the Darkhavens. Watching them train, seeing them fight in the battles—it had given me a true understanding of what it means to be in the light. To not fear showing off one's true abilities. Knowing that Ruen Darkhaven has a particularly dangerous set of powers that implicates the mind doesn't detract from the intimidation of his physical form. He is as much a warrior of the flesh as he is an assassin of the mind.

Ruen's hand lifts towards me, fingers trail up a lock of my hair and capture the pale, web-like strands. "I don't know who you are," he whispers. "I don't know who I want you to be either."

The truth of those words ring between us like the Academy's bell. I lower my gaze to the gauze coverings on his forearms. Reaching up, I trail a single finger down the side of one arm.

"Can you tell me why you cut yourself?" I ask, keeping my voice quiet—almost a whisper.

Ruen releases my hair. The loss is a blade slicing through my chest, but I don't let the invisible pain stop me from pushing harder though.

"*Don't,*" I warn, grabbing ahold of his arm when he would step back. "If you will tell no one else, then tell me."

"Why should I?" The question is a sharp taunt. "You are no one."

Tilting my head, I answer. "Because you know that's a lie. I'm not no one, Ruen. I never have been. Not even when you thought I was a mere Terra. I was always someone that intrigued you, and if anyone can understand wanting to hurt yourself—it's the woman who survived the Hinterlands and then the Underworld."

He scoffs but doesn't pull away from my touch and that fact is more telling than any insult he could fling my way. He's a wounded animal, pride the only thing keeping his tongue, and I know wounded animals. I've been one for years.

"What would *you* know of anything?" Ruen snaps back. "You had the freedom we so desire. You were raised outside of these walls and away from the prying eyes of the Gods. What truth could you so yield to me that would change anything?"

I arch a brow. "You want truth?" I release his arm and step away. Then, as if I need to be away from him lest I punch him in his stupid perfectly chiseled face, I stride towards the window on the other side of the room. My breaths come sharp and uneven as I consider what to say.

Moments pass before I feel calm enough to face him again without unleashing the riot of rage that dwells within me—it's always there, ever present, just waiting to be liberated. To free it from its confines, however, would result in chaos so catastrophic that I almost wish Ophelia's brimstone were still embedded within me. Maybe then it wouldn't be so dangerous. Maybe then *I* wouldn't be so dangerous.

"Fine, I'll tell you the truth," I say. I turn and face him. His eyes clash with mine, full of fury and a hint of fear. Of course, he fears—even if he's powerful, even if he's half God, he's still *mortal*. He, too, can *die*.

Those wounds on his arms do more than hurt him, they reveal far more of what lies beyond the surface than any words ever could.

I take a step forward and another and another until the two of us are so close the heat of his breath touches my face. That's when I graze my fingertips over his abdomen. The ridges of his abs are as hard as rock. At my touch, his muscles contract and his lips part. I repress a smirk. It feels good to know that I affect him in the same way that he so often affects me.

"You could avoid all of these scars," I tell him, careful not to touch his forearms again. "You don't. Instead, you acquire them purposefully. You want your scars to remain because they're evidence." My fingers trail further down, over the solid lines of each individual mass of muscle. His skin tightens. He grits his teeth as his eyes lower to watch the movement of my hand. "You hurt yourself..." My throat grows thick and heavy and the rest of what I want to say remains buried in my head for several moments.

I work through the deep ache this new knowledge assails me with. Ruen Darkhaven hurts himself. Not all of his scars were made by others and even though he hasn't said as much, I know it for what it is. The truth. He asked for it and I found it.

Fuck me, but I don't want to care. I hate what the Darkhavens represent. Power. Prestige. Dominance. Even if I didn't already know it before ... even if I hadn't already seen the proof of it, this realization—more than anything—tells me that they are just as trapped as I am.

I close my eyes, not wanting to look at him as the last of the truth leaves my lips. "You scar your own body because you feel like you need to be punished for living." But he's not living and survival isn't a sin. "Whatever devious deeds you may commit, whatever pain you endure—all of it is purely out of your own selfish desire to compensate."

Through bared teeth, he speaks. "What *the fuck* do *I* need to compensate for?"

That's easy enough, though I'm sure he doesn't really want to know the answer. Perhaps giving it to him will show him to be careful of what he asks for, to stop and consider his words before he spits them out.

"The death of your mother," I say. "The loss of control you have. The powerlessness you and your brothers suffer under." They might be Mortal Gods, but they are just as much at the mercy of the God Council as humans are. They're just slightly more useful—like beloved pets rather than the rats that slink about in the walls of homes that reject them.

His hand springs up and grabs ahold of my wrist, stopping any further movement right as my fingertips graze the skin above the laces of his low-slung pants. There are lines that carve out a delicious v with the end disappearing beneath the fabric. My lips twitch. My eyes lift and meet his.

"I am Ruen Darkhaven. Son of Azai, God of Strength and Virility." The words are spat into my face. Knowing what I know about his feelings towards his God parent, I never expected him to use his father's name in describing himself. That, too, I suspect, is another punishment.

"Yes," I agree without trying to remove my wrist from his grasp, "and because of all of that ... *I pity you.*"

His lips part and his brows draw down into a deep v. His features contort into abject shock. "You *pity* me?" He repeats the word as if he can't believe that I've said it.

With my free hand, I reach up and touch the curl of dark hair hanging over his ear. I tuck it back and surprisingly enough, he doesn't move away from the brush of my fingers over his skin. "You are alone in so many ways," I say. It's not as if I can't relate. For as long as I've known what I am and had no one to protect me, I, too, have been alone. "You might be strong, but you, your brothers, and every other Mortal God in this place are all under the control of those who sired you."

Us, I remind myself.

Ruen remains silent for a moment more. When he next speaks, it's with a harsh breath. "I am *not* powerless." Oh, how he wants to deny the truth in my words. I can't blame him. If I weren't forced to see the truth, I wouldn't want to admit it either.

I smile and lean forward. He releases my wrist as I turn my cheek, pressing my chest against his, letting him feel the swell of my breasts against his pecs. I arch up onto my toes and lift my chin. My lips touch his jawline and then smooth upward, stopping at his ear.

Finally, I do what I've been wanting to for the last several days. I gift to him the challenge I want to see him complete.

"Then prove it," I whisper against his ear. "Show me how powerful Ruen Darkhaven is. Not because you're the son of Azai, God of Strength and Virility, but because you are *Ruen*, a Mortal God with just as much ability, just as much strength as any pure-blooded Divine Being."

"You are a temptress," Ruen hisses back at me.

I laugh. I like that title. Temptress. Maybe I am. No, I *know* I am. And I'm okay with it. If being a temptress will get him to realize that he's bound by more than the walls around the Academy, then I'll be whatever he needs me to be. I'll sow the seeds of doubt and make him and the others realize that they—like I—were not born to be pawns on someone else's chessboard.

CHAPTER 26
RUEN

She is ... inevitable.

That is my one consolation as I wrap my hand up in the silvery strands of her hair and drag her to me. *She always has been.*

Kiera comes to me willingly, her lips parting even before my mouth is on hers. Her body against mine is everything I imagined it would be. Fire and ice dances between our tongues and I lose myself to the mindless eroticism of the kiss.

I flip her around and urge her towards my bed. No more. I can't hold my desire in stasis any longer. The need for her is a grotesque beast that consumes me and I think she knows it—sees it, understands the volatile animal far more than I ever could. As angry as this woman makes me, the knowledge that she connects to the darkness that often dominates my mind only makes me crave her more.

The backs of her knees hit the mattress and her hands slap against my bared chest, stopping me from dropping her onto the surface. I pull away, only enough to give her a sliver of space. Few have ever been allowed to touch me like this.

Fewer still have ever touched me beneath my clothing. Those rights belong to her now, and I will not take them back.

I am starved of touch and my hunger for hers beats at me like a never-ending ocean wave against the cliffside's edge.

"Do not stop this." I don't care if it sounds like I'm begging. I will beg if it means I can have her.

She shakes her head, the strands of her hair whispering against my chest as she reaches down and grips the hem of her tunic before drawing it up and over her head. Her skin is a supple honey color, pale in many lights and golden in others. I grip the under corset and rip straight through the strands with nothing but my strength. What might normally take a blade to unleash comes apart under my harsh desire for her to be bare to my eyes. The discarded clothing falls to the ground and I cup her jaw in my palm again. Just before I lean down and press my lips to hers, I hear her sardonic chuckle. "You Darkhavens are so costly to a woman's wardrobe..."

"I'll buy you as many clothes as I can rip apart." I answer her comment with a harsh kiss. Kiera responds to the meeting of our mouths with the kind of fervor I expected from her. Violent and needy, she doesn't just let me devour her. Instead, she meets me stroke for stroke.

As small as she is, I can picture a number of positions that would bring the both of us to the height of fast pleasure. I don't want fast. I want to linger, to coax, to tease, to torment her the same way she's done to me with little more than her fucking scent. Unfortunately, my body and cock throb with demand. Each brush of our skin sends my senses into erratic amplification. Every touch is heightened and it doubles as it separates and bounces off the need pulsating inside me.

She feels it too. That much I'm sure of as her breasts brush against my muscles, her nipples peaked and hardened into the finest points. They scratch through the thin layer of hair between my pectoral muscles. I cup one deliciously full mound, flicking a thumb over one nipple and dragging a sharp inhalation from her mouth.

In this moment, the most uncontrollable flame of a woman becomes a spark that dances for me and me alone.

I can't stop. Even if the logical part of my mind somehow managed to crawl from the depths of wherever it went and tried to rip back control, I know that I'd squash it in an instant. It's been too long and she and I have been circling each other for what feels like ages. I don't want to stop this and if anything comes between me and this woman right now, I know that even Kalix wouldn't be able to stomach the atrocities I'd commit just to keep her by my side.

"Let me have you." The words are a caress, a demand.

Her hands skim up my sides, over the dips and hollows of my body, and up my chest. Silver lightning eyes open, practically glowing out of her face as she gazes up at me. There is a fire inside her, so brilliant that it's a wonder I haven't seen it before now. No. Perhaps it isn't that I didn't see it, but that I purposefully ignored it because to admit to it would mean that I'd have to also admit that this woman intrigues me and she has since the first moment I laid eyes on her.

Guilt eats at my insides. That vicious part of my mind that takes over and won't be assuaged until I see the glint of dark ebony brimstone against my skin and freshly spilled blood bites at me.

This vibrant, beautiful creature—part of the darkness and part of the light—was hurt because of me and I deserve to be flayed alive for it.

"*Stop.*"

Sharp nails dig into my cheeks and my eyes shoot open. I hadn't even realized I'd closed them until they land on Kiera's face and I recognize the fury there. How she senses my inner turmoil, I don't know. I only know that I am grateful for her interference because I could feel myself slipping back into that dark place, the very same place that my life as a Mortal God was born. A place I detest with every fiber of my being.

"If you're going to be with me, Ruen, then *be with me*." Her pupils are wide, but her eyes are narrowed on me. "Do not fall into that place. Do not ignore me and return there when I am right in front of you. I know you are not that weak."

No. I'm not. I've survived loss and pain and torture. I've survived death, but I've also survived something so much worse. I've survived life and all of the torments therein.

My arms close around her once more, squeezing her tightly and pulling her so hard against my chest that I wonder if some subconscious part of my brain wishes to meld her to my very existence. If it were possible to tie two souls together, I would do so to her. I would do whatever it took to ensure that she could never regret this choice and leave me.

The feel of her in my arms drives me into the darkness I knew I possessed. Except, this time, I am not alone.

There is no turning back now.

Kiera has awakened a monster within this Divine blood of mine that even I didn't know existed and it's her responsibility to feed him.

CHAPTER 27
KIERA

Ruen's body is a mass of jumping muscles and barely restrained violence. He clutches me like I'm a life line and I let him. I have the strangest sensation that if the two of us were set adrift in a stormy sea—if we were drowning—his hold alone would be enough to keep me tied to this plane of existence. As if I can't die unless he gives me permission.

When next his mouth lands on mine, it's even harder than before. It's raw and powerful and crushing. I part my lips, letting him take what he needs and feeding that beast I sense within him.

He's different from Theos and Kalix. As well as they move together as a unit, each of them is an individual creature with different needs. Kalix is a hungry beast, devouring everything in its path to sate some unknown desire and he won't stop until he's drawn the blood of his prey. Theos is a healer, a seeker of love and compassion and affection.

Ruen is neither and he is both. He is the perfect mix of animal and man.

His hips bump against my stomach and I feel the hard

press of his erection straining beneath his trousers. My insides turn to liquid in the most molten sense and I reach for the man currently devouring my mouth and every small sound that escapes it.

My nails rake down his back and his hips jerk in pleasure at the sharp sensation, pressing harder against me. The side of the mattress bumps against my calves, but I don't lie on it. Not yet. Pulling my lips from Ruen's, I use the mattress as an aid as I climb up his body, hooking my legs around his waist as I grip his head between my hands.

"Show me what you want, Ruen," I demand. "Show me what you're so terrified of showing everyone else."

Blue-red eyes glitter back at me dangerously, the soft fall of his long dark lashes casting shadows over the sharp angles of his cheekbones. He is a barely restrained man, teetering on the knife's edge of civilized. He doesn't need civilized. He needs wild and untamed and so do I.

As if he senses that, too, Ruen's eyes shift from half midnight and half red to fully crimson in an instant. My back slams down against the mattress. He drives me up the cushioned bed reaching for my hands and stealing them away from his flesh. I blink and he pins them above me. Solid metal locks onto my skin and my eyes jerk up, seeking the manacles that now encircle my wrists. Something wicked uncurls within my lower belly. I test the chains that now lock through the heavy wrought iron of the headboard before flicking my attention to the man that prowls over me with more intensity than any animal I ever saw in the Hinterlands.

"These weren't here before," I say. Not a question, but then again, I don't mean it as one. I know what brought them forth, I just never expected Ruen to lose control so completely that he'd use his powers on me during sex.

Ruby colored irises track over my face with dilated pupils

blowing out nearly all of the color, leaving behind very little but a small ring of fire. "My illusions are as real as you or I," Ruen whispers, lowering his lips to my throat. "For as long as I control them, they exist."

The beast licks over my pulse and then moves down, his fabric covered legs sliding against mine until his mouth touches my collarbone. My nipples pebble harder and I bite down on my lower lip, forcing my need back as it threatens to make my hips buck against him.

It's when his words enter my ears that I realize Ruen hasn't lost control at all. No. He's nothing like Kalix or Theos. He is discipline and dominance, a creature with far more patience than I ever gave him credit for. To lead two other Mortal Gods with such volatile powers and abilities, he's had to maintain this precision of his and I fell for the false display of instability like a fool.

Sweat beads pop up along my skin as he licks the taste of it from my flesh with a hungry moan. "You taste like salt and sin," he says.

My stomach muscles contract and I suck in a breath, hollowing out the area as I tug at my restraints. I don't know how it's possible, but he's right about his illusions. It feels more real than the bed itself, more tangible than the illusion I'd felt the day I'd been whipped before the entire Academy.

"Ruen—"

"Shhh," he hushes me as his mouth descends over one nipple and sucks it between his lips. His teeth sink down against the pale pink flesh and I grit my teeth as my back arches at the pleasure-pain that pours through me.

Little pinpricks of light flash behind my closed eyelids as he tortures my nipple before switching to the other breast and performing the same action. Breathing heavily, I don't reopen my eyes until he finally, blessedly, lifts his lips, tongue, and teeth away from me—freeing my wet nipple to the now cool air.

"Look at me." I can't help but answer that command with a sharp look. There's no denying it. Ruen's crimson gaze locks onto my face, searing into my eyes like he's trying to burn me with just a look.

There's too much clothing still between us. "*Ruen.*" His name is a groan in my throat. "If you don't get rid of both of our pants in the next ten seconds, I'm going to—"

Whatever threat I'd been about to make is swallowed by the sudden rending of fabric. I gape down as Ruen shreds the sides of my trousers before he peels them far too slowly down my long legs. Then his body leaves me as he moves down the mattress until he's at the end of the bed and he's able to untie his laces and drop his pants to the floor.

My eyes lock onto the hard shaft that juts out from the ring of dark hair at his crotch. It's long and thick, with a pulsating vein that arches up the underside. That's not the only thing that makes me stare open-mouthed though. It's the series of metal bars that run the length of that veiny underside of male flesh.

"H-how..." The question doesn't make it past that one word in my throat as Ruen takes himself in hand and strokes the length of his cock once—up and down from root to tip.

"Pain means nothing," he says by way of an answer, even though I never finished the curiosity. "I had to prove that to myself."

Rage blossoms in my breast. Another form of self-harm then. I want to chastise him, but the words aren't there as he slowly climbs back onto the mattress and moves forward like a stalking Hinterland *panthera*. I can just imagine the hulking cat-like beast inside him. Hungry feline ready for its prey to fall under fang and claw.

Ruen releases his cock and touches my legs. "Open for me, Kiera. Spread your legs and let me into the most Divine of realms."

If anyone had told me that Ruen Darkhaven would rival both of his brothers in terms of sexual deviancy months ago, I might have laughed at the idea of the cool and indifferent Mortal God being a creature of pure fire and sensuality. Now, I have no other recourse but to follow that command of his, spreading my thighs at the soft touch of his sword-roughened fingers.

My teeth ache to sink into him as my hands curl, my nails digging into my palms as the need to draw blood becomes a burning desire inside me. I pull at my restraints. "Release me," I growl.

"No." That's the only answer I get right before Ruen's head dips and the harsh rasp of his tongue steals over the bundle of nerves above my core. My legs jerk in shock and then clamp down on either side of his head. Ruen doesn't miss a beat, gripping my thighs in his palms and slamming them back open, even going so far as to push them slightly up and out so that he has a wider seat for his face to make a meal of my most vulnerable place.

Heat flashes through me, turning my chest a light shade of pink. My head thrashes back and forth and I struggle beneath the illusioned bonds he's put me under. The moment these damn things are gone, I'm going to wrap my hands around his throat, force his cock inside me, and ride him until I'm cresting the wave of release.

Ruen releases my clit and then drags his teeth down the soft inner flesh of my thigh and then up the other. "Stop fighting me."

"I'm not submissive," I tell him through clenched teeth.

"If you didn't want me to fight then you would be beneath me, not the other way around."

His dark head lifts and his gaze looks up my body, over the valley of my hips and stomach, and between my tightly budded breasts. "You may not be submissive for others," he concedes, pausing a beat before he continues, "but you will be for me."

The dry laugh that scrapes out of my throat is anything but amused. It's a challenge. "No, I won't."

When Ruen tilts his head to the side it's with that same feline grace as the *panthera* I'd thought him before. One finger slides between my folds and flicks my clit, forcing my body to bow in response. "Yes," he repeats, "you will."

Little fractures of power spark through me. My core seizes at the challenge in his tone and my breasts swell with anticipation. For several long, breathless moments, the two of us are tied together like that. Neither of us speaking, both of us wanting, needing, craving more than what the other is willing to give.

Perhaps this wasn't such a good idea. Pushing the iciest of the Darkhavens past his limit was a risk. Now, there is no turning back.

"I should have known that you would bring me to the edge," Ruen murmurs almost absently, breaking the silence as he moves up my body and then takes a hardened nipple between his teeth.

I gasp with pleasure and then pain as he bites down. My hands close into fists as I crave to clutch at the back of his head. My teeth clamp together while he switches to the other breast and performs the same action all over again, wetting the nipples he'd ignored as he'd teased my core.

In adolescence, when I'd been around many other members of the Underworld—more specifically, the few female members—I'd listened in on their stories of lovers and bed partners. The talk of love had always confused me as it seemed to be equated to the feeling of butterflies in one's stomach and a strange sort of giddiness that overtook a girl's mind.

My mind is filled with neither, but instead with cruel talons that scrape around my organs, demanding satisfaction. My pussy clenches with carnal insistence.

Ruen freezes and backs his head away as his eyes slide shut and he groans. "I can fucking *smell you*." That admission is pulled from his throat as if the words are being dragged over sharp rocks. His voice is lower than it's ever been, gravelly in the way that only a man lost to the haze of lust can be.

He opens his eyes and fixes them on me.

"Kiss me," I growl, giving him an order of my own.

As if he's possessed by the sudden need, he moves up further until our mouths hover a scant inch from one another. His lips, when they land on mine, taste of me. Just to punish him, I sink my teeth into his bottom lip hard enough to draw both blood and a masculine groan. We are a tangle of teeth and tongue. A clashing storm of two overpowering wills, neither bending for anything save for the other. Feminine delight swims through me as Ruen worships my skin with that fine attention to detail that is something purely *him*.

Muscles flex as he holds himself above me. With a vicious little grin, I lift my legs and lock my ankles around his hips, feeling the prod of his hard cock against my pussy. "Give me more," I demand, nuzzling little nipping bites along his throat. "You know you want to."

A hard grip seizes my hair and rips my head back. Ruen arches a brow down at me. "Do you think you're in charge here, Kiera?" He shakes his head without waiting for a response. "No, I will take you when and if I decide—not before."

If? What the fuck does he mean 'if' he decides? A snarl threatens to rip free of me. It's only stopped by the feel of his palm landing against my throat. My whole body goes still, my heart thudding an inconsistent beat against the inside of my ribcage as I realize how trapped I truly am.

His hand holds my hair in his grip, keeping my head immobile as his other hand grips my throat, squeezing tighter and tighter until I can hear the rush of my own blood blasting through my ears. Oddly enough, I can still breathe. Sparkles flicker before my eyes, little visual hallucinations dancing around me like stars. The low, thrumming sound of Ruen's amusement rumbles from his chest into mine.

"Look at you now, Kiera." His voice shifts deeper than I've ever heard it before. "The great, strong assassin brought so low by her target."

I try to shake my head. We both know that Ruen was never my target, but ... he could have been. They all could have been.

Ruen leans down, setting his teeth on my bottom lip as he tightens his grip and those stars begin spinning. Around and around they go, driving my hazy mind into a distant land.

"Do you know why I don't fuck around like my brothers?" Ruen asks as he releases me to the taste of my own blood on my tongue.

I'm set adrift on the wind. My insides clenching and unclenching in an unfamiliar need. His hands remain on me as I feel his hips move to lower themselves between my spread open thighs. I arch myself against him, feeling the graze of his cock against my wetness. A groan sears my throat.

"No, not yet." The hot length of him moves away again and I almost whimper—*almost*. I'm not that far gone yet.

"I prefer to dominate women who are as powerful as me, if not more so," Ruen says, answering his own earlier question. "I've fucked Goddesses, but few Mortal Gods." Sharp pain attacks one nipple and I realize he's stopped talking to bite down on my breast again.

My hips buck. *Fuck him.* I part my lips to voice that thought, but the hard hand squeezing my throat releases and a heady rush of blood fills my ears once more and all that escapes is a gasp of both pleasure and relief.

Ruen keeps the hand against my head still tangled in my hair as he lowers the other one to the outside of one hip. Then I feel the underside of his shaft drag slowly along my soaked cunt.

This time, I can't stop the whimper of pure unadulterated need. His responding growl resonates against my nipples and I feel the vibrations all the way down to my throbbing clit.

"I should have known," Ruen grits out as his hand slides along my outer thigh to my inner thigh and then down. "You would be the one to drive this need out of me."

I glance up at him through my lashes, begging with my eyes though I won't with my words. *Never.* To part my lips and beg him with words would mean to cross a line inside me that I refuse to even go near. The hand in my hair loosens marginally.

"Don't worry," he says, face moving to poise over mine. "I won't take your darkness from you, Kiera. I simply want you to accept mine too."

Darkness is all I've ever known. If he wants to share his with me then that's something I can do.

The hard ridges of his knuckles bump against my clit and I suck in a sharp breath. He shushes me with a strained but amused smile. "Almost there, sweetheart," he says as I feel him take himself in hand and line the head of his cock to my entrance. "Almost..."

Feral eyes and an even more feral grin split his face and in the next instant, a scream is ripped from me as he slams into me without any further preamble. My interior muscles make way for the hard length of him, slicked by my own juices, but still shuddering under the sharp too-fast intrusion, and my back bows off the bed.

"Fuck, you're so tight." Little shock waves ricochet through my cunt, rippling the muscles up and down the heavy length of him, squeezing down on both his flesh and the metal that pierces him. "So fucking perfect..."

Gasping, heaving, begging for air where there is none, the sparkling stars are back. Lips press into my own.

"Breathe," Ruen orders. "Breathe for me, sweetheart."

I do, and with each inhalation, all I can smell is *him*.

Something dark moves through Ruen's face. Not an expression or emotion, but something wholly different. "*Release*." The word is a whisper, but it's all that's needed to liberate me from the chains holding my hands captive.

The second my wrists are free, my nails are in his flesh, sinking into the skin of his shoulders as I ride the wave of ecstasy that crashes into me. I can feel his cock twitch inside me, pressing those ridges of metal against my inner walls and making the fissures of power spread further inside me. Now that he's fully seated inside, Ruen's hand falls to my ass as I cling to his powerful frame and he cups the fleshy underside, gripping tight even as his hips pull back. The motion drags his cock from my depths and then he thrusts back inside with the same crude violence as before.

Fire and glory. That is what we are. Two beings of domination fighting for the right to control the other.

"*Kiera*." I blink at the razor blade of his tone. He glares down at me. "Focus on me."

I release one shoulder and stroke one hand up into his hair, curling my fingers into the dark, almost inky black of the strands until they disappear completely. "Who else would I focus on but you?"

A fresh scream shoots up my throat as he chooses that exact moment to cant his hips, withdrawing nearly completely from my body and then thrusting his wide, thick cock back into my pussy. Soft, feminine flesh parts as he forces my insides to concede to him. I lock my hand in his hair and hold on.

"...handle more?" I'm so delirious with pain and pleasure that I don't hear the first part of his question, but I don't need to in order to know what he's asking.

I nod my head rapidly. "Yes," I say, squeezing my legs tighter around him as if that could stop him from pulling out of me again. "Yes. Give me everything." I kiss his lips. Sink my tongue inside to twine it with his. He kisses me back, tasting of blood and rawness that I never thought would be so addictive. "Fuck me into the dark, Ruen," I growl as his hips stutter in their movements. "Drive me to the brink of insanity and then drop me over the edge."

Ruen's head lifts, and for a moment, the crimson recedes the smallest bit, allowing the midnight color to resurface once more. Sweat drips down his straining throat, droplets falling from him to land on me.

We are not soft lovers, but two swords clashing. Violence and sparks flying off each other as we war for dominance. He drives me higher and higher into the darkness until the lights start to go out. Each star drowns under shadows as they crawl up over the stones of the room around us.

What little illumination is left on the window winks out

of existence and I don't know anymore if this is his illusion or my own darkness. All I know is that I cannot pull my eyes away from his and he keeps his eyes trained on me with each thrust.

Then, as his jaw clenches and I feel him pulse inside me, seeding me with his cum, Ruen reaches between us and pinches a thumb and forefinger over my clit, sending me into a shattering orgasm that steals the breath from my lungs.

His responding roar as he empties the last of himself inside me echoes in my ears as my heartbeat slows and the darkness completely descends for the last time.

CHAPTER 28
RUEN

10 years old...

I know the moment I wake up that today won't be like the others. It's time to leave. That much is clear because when I finally finish rubbing the grit of sleep from my eyes and sit up in the cot style bed pushed against the back corner of our one room shack, I can see my mom's face as she moves around the slight kitchen area.

It's not so much a real kitchen—like those houses she cleans in the villages and larger towns we pass through—but more a collection of chairs and tables put together next to the fireplace that acts as both our oven and stove. Only the people who live in real houses have those.

Mom's old tea kettle whistles from its position over the fire and she quickly grabs a cloth to remove it from the handle that hangs over the flames before moving to pour the steaming hot liquid into two bowls. Soup for breakfast... again.

A dull groan rumbles up my throat as I swing my legs over the side of my cot. "Don't we have any bacon?" I plead as I settle a hand over a stomach that bites at me in hunger.

Mom passes me a guilty look. "Not today, sweetie," *she murmurs before setting the now cooled kettle onto one of the tables that make up a counter.* "Vegetable soup is good for you. Come sit. We need to pack after breakfast."

I'm halfway to the table, but at her words, I slow to a stop and lift my eyes back to hers. "Do we have to?" *I want to snatch back the words the moment they're out of my mouth. I know better than to beg, but I thought this place was different.*

Yette is a small village near the Hinterlands. Surely whatever searches for us wouldn't dare to come so close to a place even the most dangerous of criminals avoid. I thought it was safe here. That we were safe from whatever shadow stalks my mom's dreams. I should have known better though. She had another dream last night—and unlike the others, this one seems to have her more on edge.

Mom sighs and comes around the table, wiping her hands absently on her already stained apron as she bundles me into her arms. "I'm sorry, baby," *she says quietly, patting her hands on my back as she holds me to her.*

I cuddle closer. Even if I am ten, almost a man by my standards, I still love the smell of her in my nose. All powdery and lemon scented. Lemon is my favorite and I wonder if it's because it reminds me of her.

"I liked it here," *I say, the childish hope to convince her to forget whatever nightmare held her in its thrall last night and stay still bubbling inside me.*

When she pulls back, though, I know it's a false hope. "I know." *Mom pushes a lock of my hair back and tucks it behind my ear.* "But it's time for us to move. You knew that we wouldn't stay long."

"We stayed longer here than anywhere else," *I argue.*

Her brows pinch and her expression turns stern. "Eat your breakfast," *she orders, straightening as she gestures for the table.*

I stare past her at the gross vegetable soup that sits, waiting, on the rickety wooden table that had been here when we first moved in. That, too, I know will be left behind. Everything but what we can carry will be.

"Can I at least say goodbye to Ralf?" I half-plead.

Huffing out a breath, she places her hands on her hips to glare down at me. I don't care, I place my hands together and gaze up at her, trying to make my eyes as big as they can be until I feel like they're about to pop out of my head. With a huff, Mom rolls her eyes and drops her hands, and with that one action, I know I've won.

"Fine," she says. "But hurry along. You have to eat before we leave and I'm not reheating your soup, so if you go now, you'll have to eat your soup cold."

I've had cold soup before, and honestly, hot or cold, it never makes it any better, but I at least want to have some time with my first ever friend before I say goodbye to him forever.

"I love you!" *I cry as I slam myself into her lower half, squeezing her legs as I press my face into her stomach.* "I'll be quick, promise."

Her laughter as I release her to jump about the room, pulling off my night clothes and jerking on my breeches and tunic and boots, follows me as I race out of the shack and into the street.

Unlike other places, even the slums of Yette are clean. The people living here prefer to take care of whatever they have even if it's not much. After three months, I know the way to Ralf's by heart. Hanging a left, I jog lightly down the road closer to the city. Ralf's shack is similar to ours except that it has two rooms instead of one, each one stacked atop the other with a ladder that acts as their staircase. When I stop outside Ralf's door and knock lightly, I hear his elder sister, Mira, call out.

Creeping inside, I offer the older pretty girl with eyes like a doe and freckles smattered over her cheeks a smile. "Is Ralf up?" *I ask, peering around the room where no one else moves about.*

Mira huffs out a snort. "This early?" *she shakes her head and points the ladle she's using to stir something over the fire towards the ladder.* "Feel free to wake him and Samson up. They need to head out to gather some meds from the forest edge soon."

I'm already nodding and heading for the ladder, setting my hands into place and making short work of the effort it takes to head up to the lone room that sits above their living space. My head peeks through the opening to see that it's far darker up here without windows. The ceiling is lower than the first floor with barely enough room to crouch as I scoot down the row of blankets and straw mattresses spread out on the floor for Ralf's family of five including his sister, brother, and parents to sleep.

"Ralf!" *I whisper-hiss into the darkness.* "Ralf, wake up, I need to talk to you."

From the back of the room, a low grumble sounds. "Five more minutes, Mom," *Ralf replies, his voice heavy and still mostly asleep.*

I roll my eyes and head straight for him, grabbing the foot I see sticking out of the bottom of his straw mattress and yanking hard. "Wake up," *I order, getting a little bit louder when I remember that Mira had said I could wake both him and Samson.*

At my voice, Samson's little head pops up next to his brother's and he blinks eyes the same color as Mira's at me for several long seconds. Then he smiles. "Hi, Ruen," *he says, reaching up to rub his eyes with his fists.*

I smile back at the five-year-old, thankful that both of their parents appear to be out for the day and already working to provide for them. "Hi, Sammie. Mira has something cooking for you downstairs. You should go eat breakfast."

"'Kay," *the little boy responds around a yawn, but unlike his brother, Sammie is awake and already crawling across the mattresses heading for the opening that leads below.*

Ralf kicks at my hand, making me realize I've still got a grip on him. I tug again. "Come on, Ralf, I'm serious."

He half sits up and glares at me. "What is so important that you have to wake me up at the ass crack of dawn?" he gripes.

"If Mira heard you talking like that, she'd tan your hide," I warn him.

Ralf shakes his head. "Nu-uh, Dad talks like that and she can't tan his hide."

I don't argue the fact that Ralf's Dad is also Mira's and that though the man seems like a gentle giant, I doubt Mira would feel comfortable telling her dad not to curse around the young ones. Not when the man himself doesn't even seem to realize it. Instead, I just tug at Ralf again.

"Come on," I wheedle. "Mom says we're moving today and I didn't want to leave without saying goodbye to you."

That has Ralf fully awake in a split second and he tosses back the covers. "You're moving?" I release him so that he can crawl to the end of his mattress and sit up more fully.

I nod. "Yeah. I told you that my mom and I travel a lot. Well, she said it's time for us to go to the next place."

"Why?" Ralf looks at me in what I guess is the same way I'd looked at Mom this morning. "Can't you stay a little longer? We were supposed to go to the Day of Descendance Festival together."

I drop down to sit cross-legged on the floor as Ralf starts searching through the side of his bed for the clothes he'd been wearing the day before. Scratching out a line on the grain of the wooden floor, I wait for him to finish dressing.

"She seems pretty set on leaving today," I say. "I asked her if we could stay, but she..." I shake my head and lift it again to see that Ralf has his trousers on over his hips and is tying the too loose waist

tight with the laces practically folded in half under his belly button. "I'm sorry, Ralf."

Ralf quickly tugs on his tunic and then grabs my hand. "Come on, let's go to the clubhouse."

I don't argue as I let Ralf lead me back to the ladder. He releases me, and together we climb down to the first floor to see Samson sitting at the table, his dangling feet swaying back and forth. Mira waves at the two of us as Ralf offers her a quick goodbye and pulls me towards the door.

"Don't forget the herbs you need to gather with Sammie!" Mira calls out.

"I'll be back soon," Ralf promises, and then the two of us are off.

We run back up the street, towards my house, and past it. Though no one dares go too far into the Hinterlands, the edge woods that linger closer to the outskirts of Yette are safe enough. About two weeks into our new friendship, Ralf and I had discovered a hollowed-out tree facing the city, big and dry enough for the two of us to sit in during a light summer storm. Since then, it'd become our secret clubhouse and hideout when neither of us wanted to return home for one reason or another.

I wave to a few familiar faces of the other inhabitants of the slums of Yette—men and women who'd welcomed my mom and me with open arms and even helped her to gain work closer to the village's center. It was thanks to them that I'd come to love this place so much and I'm going to hate trying to set up somewhere new. Few villages are as kind as Yette.

Ralf and I pause at the edge of the woods and then track along its exterior until we spot the three marks we'd made on one tree to mark our path. Once we see it, we climb over the roots and underbrush off the normal path that other villagers take when they come to collect herbs and other roots to sell in town.

Our clubhouse is a massive tree that's wider than any of the smaller trees that hover around it like sentinels guarding their King. We circle it and Ralf pulls off the web of moss that we'd woven together to hide the interior during the times we had to leave it unattended.

"Come on." Ralf waves his hand for me to go first and I do, hooking one foot over the side of the massive trunk's opening and then dropping to the floor of crushed leaves and foliage. In the next instant, Ralf is next to me. The inside of our clubhouse isn't big to begin with, barely a five-foot perimeter. With both of us inside, it becomes smaller, but it's private, and more importantly, it's ours.

"Okay, so talk," Ralf demands. "Why does your mom say you have to leave?"

I shrug. "I don't know. She just does. We've never stayed in one place for very long."

"Hmmmm." Ralf hums in the back of his throat and crosses his arms over his chest. I kick at a twig sticking against the toe of my boot. "That's suspicious, don't you think?" he asks.

"I don't know. I never really thought of it." It's a lie. Of course, I'd wondered why my mom and I had to move so often. I'd asked and her answer had always been vague, but I think I know the truth. It's because of me, because of what I can do. More than that, though, I have the sneaking understanding that we're running from something or someone. Whoever it is scares her, though, and despite my earlier begging to stay, I know that I don't want my mom to be afraid. If that means moving, then so be it.

"Listen, Ralf, I'm sorry," I say, blowing out a breath. "But I promise when I get older and I can make decisions for myself, I'll come back to see you."

Ralf eyes me and then drops his arms. His eyes grow glassy just like I expected. He sniffles. "I don't want you to go," he confesses.

I don't want to go either. I hug my friend, squeezing him tight. Suddenly, I have the thought that the two of us could grow up together. We could keep coming back to our secret clubhouse and when we have muscles like Ralf's dad, we could build it bigger— maybe even make it a real house.

That hope blossoms inside my chest and swells bigger and bigger until it consumes my whole mind. Around us, the wind whips through the trunk of the massive tree. Ralf and I pull away as the ceiling of the tree hole widens and expands, growing upward. My eyes widen. The wind swirls faster and faster, fog rolling in and spreading over the floor to sweep away the dust and debris. When the wind settles, the clubhouse is transformed. It's become a real place, no bigger than my mom's shack, but wide enough with carvings into the interior wood and even a window.

"Whoa, what in the world..."

My heart beats faster when I realize what I've done. Almost as soon as that thought occurs to me, the illusion vanishes and Ralf blinks at me with big, almost owlish eyes. "What was that?" he demands.

I repress a flinch and instead offer him a laugh that sounds too sharp to even my own ears. "What was what?"

Ralf narrows his eyes. "Our hideout, it just got—"

I stare at him. "I didn't see anything," I lie, cutting him off. "Are you okay?" Guilt eats at me, but I say the words anyway.

Ralf pauses and then shakes his head. "I don't know, uh, never mind, I guess."

Relief spreads through me and I hold out my hand for him to climb back through with me. "I can't stay for much longer," I say. "Mom wants to eat breakfast and pack."

Ralf lets me help him out first and we spend some time talking —reminiscing over the last few months of friendship—as we walk back to the slums of Yette. It isn't until I get to the end of our street that I realize something is very wrong.

All of the people I'd waved to on our way out are gone. Doors are shut. Window shutters are closed. There's no sound. Ralf doesn't seem to notice the sudden silence, but it slides over the back of my neck in warning, drawing me to a standstill.

"Ruen?" Ralf's voice is distant as I gaze down the street towards the middle shack amongst others. Mine and my mom's.

There's a carriage outside it. A big one.

I start running, ignoring my friend's shout of surprise behind me. My legs fly over the grit and dirt road, faster and faster until I can hear the sound of crying. My mom's crying. White hot anger like I've never felt before gives me the energy and power I need to burst through the front door of our temporary home to find her on her knees before the fireplace with a tall muscular man standing in front of her, sword drawn.

"Get away from my mom!" I scream, diving for the man before it hits me.

The second my little body slams into his legs, not that it does much good—he's built rock solid, like a mountain unwilling to crumble, the power he's exuding crushes into my lungs. I fall, my back hitting the dirty floor as all of my breath escapes me. Blackness creeps into my vision at the edges, but I still see the man turn to look at me. Those golden eyes assess my face and then turn back to my mother with a nod.

"Good, we have him then," the man says. Two figures I hadn't noticed standing further back in the room come forward.

"No!" Mom screams and reaches for me. "Not him. You cannot take him! He's mine! He's my child!"

"And mine, Gabriela," the man states. "You knew that and that's why you hid him. Hiding a Mortal God is a crime punishable by death."

Someone grabs ahold of my arms and drags me to standing. The man lifts his sword and my mom's eyes swing my way. She opens her mouth and I know what she's about to say—look away, baby—*but I can't. I'm locked onto her face, watching with horror and helplessness as the man—the monster—brings his sword down and severs her head directly from her body.*

Blood squirts and then gushes from her body as both fall lifelessly to the floor. The spray of it rained so far that I can feel wetness on my cheeks. The arms holding me feel light as a feather. My body ascends from the natural plain and I feel nothing but the prickling sense of emptiness.

Hollow. I am hollow.

It isn't until the man starts talking again as he wipes his sword against a cloth that one of the other men in the room hands him that some emotion returns to me. "Burn the body. She doesn't deserve a burial for keeping my son from me," *the man says before turning to me.*

Confusion fills me. His face is stark and angular with a heavy thick beard. The man bends slightly to look at me, eyes roving with clear intention. "You are well built," *he comments.* "Although, a bit underfed."

I stare at him, unblinking. Then my eyes turn to the small hilt of a weapon on his side. The handle is silver and black leather. A dagger. If I can just get my hands on that, I can cut his throat. I can make him pay for what he just did. I can avenge my mother.

"Do you know who I am?" *the man continues to ask, though I haven't spoken yet.* "My name is Azai, I am the God of Strength, and you, boy, are my son."

No. I shake my head at that. There's no way I could be this man's son. I am not. I will never be his son. I'm her son—my mother's. I am Gabriela's son.

Blood stains the wood grain beneath my hands and feet. The man—Azai—lifts his head and jerks his chin at the man gripping my shoulders. "Release him and go ready the carriage." *The command is followed without a sound, but all I hear is the booted footsteps of someone leaving the two of us.*

My eyes move from the hilt of his dagger to my mom's apron. I don't know why I focus on it. Perhaps it's because I can't bring myself to look at the horror of her headless neck—the splintered bone jutting out or the unseeing eyes of the head that has rolled against the wooden frame of our hearth.

Whatever the case, my eyes latch on to the dirty no-longer-white color of her apron. Stained with green and brown splotches. Vegetable soup. She made vegetable soup for breakfast. I should get up and eat it. Even if I don't like it, she always looks happier when I'm eating.

No. Wait. I have to do something first.

"*Are you listening to me?*" *the man snaps, sounding angry.*

My head turns as if it's being pulled on a string until my eyes meet his. His lips part and I don't hear what he's going to say next because I'm already moving, jerking forward, hand wrapping around the hilt of his dagger as I draw it free and then twist, slamming it into his gut right past the leather of his tunic.

The man freezes, and for a moment, the two of us are suspended in a single instant in time. Our eyes, together, move down to where the silver blade is embedded into his abdomen. He doesn't cry out in pain. No, instead, the man backhands me so hard that my hands leave the grip of the dagger. I fly across the room—harder and faster than I ever expected. My side slams into our kitchen table, the piece of weak furniture crumpling under the weight of my body as it kicks out two of its legs.

Bowls crash to the floor around me, the smell of my mom's vegetable soup spilling over the wooden slats under me. It seeps into the space, filling my nostrils until I swear I'm going to choke on it. Blood coats the inside of my mouth and I turn my head, spitting a harsh wad of it out ... along with a tooth.

"*You are going to regret that, Son,*" *Azai says coolly.*

I look up to see him pulling the dagger from his stomach as if he doesn't even feel it. How is that possible? The blade slides out, and he cleans it on his thigh before placing it back in its scabbard.

Something wet trickles down the side of my face. My head throbs.

Azai straightens and then reaches for a second dagger, one that had been hidden at his back. This one isn't silver, but as black as stone, and it glints in the sunlight streaming through the doorway.

In the distance, I hear Ralf crying out my name. Azai jerks his head to the lone other man in the room. "I want everyone cleared out of this village," *he orders.* "When we're through here, raze it to the ground."

"N-no." *My protest is breathy and my chest feels tight as if it's caving in. Ralf can't lose his family too.*

Azai doesn't even bother to acknowledge that I've spoken as he approaches me. I try to scramble back, but when I move, my knee screams out. I suck in a harsh breath as Azai bends over and captures my head with his hand tight in my hair. Pain sears through the back of my skull and when I look up at him, fear and anger swelling in my gut, I think I know now who my mom was always running from.

It was from this man. This monster.

"Look at me, boy," *Azai commands, brandishing that black blade.* "This is your first lesson as the son of a God." *He brings the knife closer and closer to my face. Sweat beads on my brow, but I don't close my eyes. I keep staring back at him.*

When he sets the edge of the dagger to the skin above my brow, I almost lose control of my bowels. Fire stretches over my flesh, parting it as blood gushes out, flowing into my eyes—eyes that I keep open and locked on the man in front of me.

Blind or broken, I will know the one who stole my life from me and if it takes a thousand years, I will kill him for it.

CHAPTER 29
KIERA

Present Day...

Malachi doesn't show up for class the day after my liaison with Ruen. Though I don't owe the bastard the Darkhavens had manipulated into humiliating me on my first day as their Terra a damn thing, his absence as well as his name in Caedmon's book, is a distraction that follows me through the day. When classes finish and we're released to the arena for battle training, I fall behind Theos, Kalix, and Ruen.

Even knowing he doesn't share the same training time as the four of us, I still search for him in the corridors on the way. I see several familiar faces but not his. When I checked the book this morning, its contents had changed. More names had been added and Malachi's is now crossed off. That has me on edge.

"You're falling behind," Theos says, pausing and turning to the side as he glances back at me. He tilts his head at my face, a lock of white-blond hair falling over the top of his forehead as he does so. "What's wrong?"

"Do you know where Malachi is?" I ask.

His expression changes to reflect his surprise, brows raising, and lips parting. "Why do you want to know?"

I shake my head. "Not here."

Ruen and Kalix stop too, several paces ahead of us. "He was transferred to the Academy at Ortus," Ruen says.

When he looks at me, the place in my lower belly pulls taut like a string. I ignore the sensation and nod my acceptance of his answer. "Is that normal?" I ask. "For a transfer between academies? Also mid-semester?"

Ruen's eyes narrow. "It happens," he says slowly, but I hear what he doesn't say. He finds it odd as well.

With little else to do about it now, the four of us continue until we reach the sandy arena and take our places before Axlan as he stands with his arms behind his back and his legs spread shoulder-width apart.

"Good afternoon," he calls out, sounding far more formal than usual.

It doesn't take long to spot why. Above our heads, in the balcony reserved for the Gods during actual battles, there are two figures perched and looking down on us. I recognize their faces from the one time I'd faced the God Council.

The dark-skinned Goddess known as Makeda sits straight backed with her hands resting on the stone armrests on either side of her. Her wide cloud-like hair is pulled back into a single puff that encircles her head with a golden crown set amidst her curls. Curious but reserved eyes fall to me and I straighten almost instinctively under her scrutiny.

At her side, Danai sits in a similar posture as Makeda. Her presence is the one most of the students of Axlan's class recognize. The Queen is here.

Whispers echo to me from where I stand towards the front of the crowd.

...What is she doing here?

...Do you think they're planning to host another battle to entertain the God Council?

I'm going to impress her with my abilities, just you wait and see...

They flow into my ears and then back out. The other students' excitement doesn't touch me. Ruen leans close to my side, dropping his voice as he whispers to me. "Keep the animosity down, Kiera," he grits out. "Show them respect."

Why should I? They don't deserve my respect, I want to snap back. I don't. Instead, I listen to him for a change and lower my gaze back to Axlan. I don't know why two of the God Council members have deigned to watch us practice for their bloody entertainment, but I refuse to let it distract me.

"As you're aware, we have an audience today," Axlan continues talking. "Therefore today will be slightly different from your usual training. Today we will have mock battles, one on one, each at a time. You may use the length of the arena as if you were in a true battle."

Someone behind me raises a hand. "Will these mock battles be to the death?" a deep voice inquires.

Axlan shakes his head. "No. Today we will simply be watching to see who has come the farthest. Some of you are in a position for advancement." Axlan's eyes fall over the three Darkhaven brothers, and for a moment, I think he's going to ask them to recommend someone. Instead, he points to a girl in the second row and then a male in the furthest one.

"Davina and Raze. You two will start us off. You may use any ability you have. The battle will go until either one of you is unconscious or I say so."

A firm hand grips my arm and begins dragging me backward. "Come on." I glance up with surprise to see it's Theos.

"What? Where are we going?" I ask.

"The stands," he answers.

Ruen and Kalix follow us as we head out of the arena, leaving behind the two chosen to start the mock battles and I find myself being led towards the same place the Darkhavens had chosen to sit for the actual battles all those weeks ago. This time, instead of being forced to stand at their side, Theos drags me down onto the cushion at his side.

"Why are they doing this now?" I ask, curious to know if the Darkhavens have a better idea of what the Gods are planning than I do.

"They're likely planning to see if another battle will be entertaining," Ruen says.

"Or perhaps they're looking for new playmates," Kalix replies with a deep chuckle.

He leans forward around his brothers and winks my way. "Should we show them what you and I can do, little liar?"

I flip him off, earning another amused sound from him before he's forced back by Ruen's hand on his chest. "Keep it in your pants," he huffs.

"Now, now," Kalix says, "I know for a fact that our little no-longer-a-Terra likes me out of my pants."

I roll my eyes at his jab and focus on the arena as the two students who'd been called upon step into the middle of the ring, facing each other. Davina is a tall willowy female with plaited blond hair and almond shaped eyes. In contrast, her opponent—Raze—is a muscular male with golden skin that can't be replicated under any amount of sunlight.

The two of them stand face to face as Axlan repeats the rules of the battles. Then, as the God turns and leaves the arena, they continue to wait until he appears above them on the balcony alongside Danai and Makeda.

"You may begin!"

Fire explodes into the sand, sending up a plume of dust so thick that I have to lean forward and squint to see anything. The shapes of two people dive out of the cloud a split second later as Davina and Raze race across the arena sands, eyes moving from where they're going to their opponent with clear intent.

"Davina's not playing around," Ruen murmurs.

"Of course not," Theos replies. "The Gods are watching."

I glance around, noting that the stands are mostly empty. The only people watching are those who have training at this time and the three Gods presiding over this mock battle. Once again, I find myself turning my attention to the balcony.

Danai's eyes are heavy-lidded as she watches the two Mortal Gods fight each other. She looks disinterested and it makes me wonder why she bothered to come in the first place. Makeda, however, is different. She's sitting forward, eyes focused and sharp on the two battling it out in the arena as if she's trying to pick apart their strategies.

Then again, from what I now know, she's the Goddess of Knowledge—no doubt it's something she's always interested in. Knowledge of others.

The fight between Davina and Raze ends in a draw, called to an end by Axlan who announces the next opponents. A male named Parvan Rockwell and ... Ruen slaps a hand out against Kalix's chest when he moves to leap up when his name is called.

"Don't kill him," Ruen growls.

Kalix frowns down at him and then huffs out a breath. "Fine." He points to me as Ruen drops his arm away from his brother. "But then you owe me a night."

"What?" I gape at him. "Why me? I didn't ask you not to kill him."

Kalix hooks a leg over the edge of the several foot drop

instead of walking around like any sane person would. "Doesn't matter. I agreed. You'll be paying up when I win this, little liar."

A growl fills my throat as he turns and then disappears over the side, appearing only a moment later as he strides confidently through the sand until he reaches the center ring where a dark-skinned man with wide shoulders and a tapered waist waits for him.

I lean into Theos' side. "What's Parvan's ability?" I ask.

Theos glances at me. "Worried about Kalix?"

I snort. "Hardly. Just curious." If anyone deserves my concern, it's Kalix's opponent. I do not doubt that the only reason Parvan won't be leaving this arena without a heartbeat is because of Ruen's order.

Theos returns his attention to the arena once more. "He's a nullifier."

"A nullifier?" I frown. "What's that?"

Ruen is the one to answer this time. "He nullifies the powers of others," he says. "It's probably the reason why he was selected to go against Kalix. If he touches him, Kalix won't be able to use any of his Divinity."

I sit up straighter in my seat and sharpen my eyes on the new match as it begins. A nullifier is something I've never heard of before. Is it possible that this man's powers affect Gods as well? I wonder.

Unfortunately for Parvan, Kalix quickly demonstrates that his power is not tied to his physical abilities. Even as Parvan's hands grab hold of Kalix and attempt to get him to the ground, Kalix laughs openly and lifts the other man, deftly picking him up and tossing him into an arena wall that's at least fifteen feet away.

Parvan collides with the hard wall with a grunt, and a fresh cloud of sand goes up when he lands. It's too late for him though. Once Kalix smells weakness, he's on top of the other man with fists flying. His wide smile flashes white as he grins and pounds into the other man over and over again. Blood sprays into his face and that fact only seems to incite him further. My pity for the other Mortal God blooms in my gut.

The battle doesn't last long, but Axlan doesn't call an end to it until Parvan is unconscious and several Terra are led onto the arena grounds to remove him from the space. Barbaric doesn't even describe it. My eyes turn to the rest of the students, scanning with curiosity to know who will be called next when I hear Axlan's voice ring out over the arena.

"Kiera Nezerac and Theos Darkhaven. Take your places in the arena."

CHAPTER 30
KIERA

Oh, they're good. I slowly rise from my seat, feeling the heat of three gazes fixed on me as I turn and make my way out of the stands. *Very, very good.*

The Darkhavens warned me in the privacy of their chambers that the Gods were curious about me. Azai calling Ruen to him to specifically ask about me and my abilities wasn't even the first hint that they want to know more about me and what I can do. Caedmon had all but alluded to it. Now here I am—about to show them exactly what I can do and I have no other recourse.

Fast footsteps fall into line behind me. Theos' voice, low and throaty, reaches my ears. "Don't worry," he murmurs. "We have contingency plans. We'll get through this. You're good with a blade. We'll grab swords on our way out to the arena and—"

"It's fine," I say, cutting him off as I cast a glance over my shoulder. "I'm not worried."

What I am is pissed.

The two of us leave behind the stands and enter the darkened interior of the inner corridors that lead back down to the center of the arena. Theos catches up and walks alongside me.

"They're getting suspicious because they haven't seen my abilities yet," I say. "They want to know what I can do. Even if, technically, not all God Children have the same abilities as their Divine sires, sometimes they do. I have no doubt that they want to see if that's the case for me."

I sense Theos' shock. "You're going to actually use your abilities?"

I don't see how I have any other choice. "Not right away," I tell him, sliding a glance his way out of the corner of my eye. "But if there's one thing I've learned, it's that you cannot appear weak in front of a strong enemy."

Sunlight pours into the end of the corridor as we grow closer to the opening. A slender familiar Terra stands to the side with his arms laden down with swords and other weapons.

"Niall..." I stop in front of him. My chest squeezes tight. "How are—"

"Not the time, Kiera." Theos grabs two swords and passes one to me. "Move."

Niall dips his head and backs away. I snarl a curse at Theos but stomp forward regardless into the bright cold sun of the battle arena.

Axlan, Danai, and Makeda are all standing now, side by side, with those glittering Divine eyes of theirs pinned to the two of us as we make our way to the center of the arena. None of the students are shouting. There is nothing but the sound of my heartbeat pounding in my ears, in my blood, and the wind as it whispers over too-hot flesh even though it's still somewhat cold outside. Winter is clinging to the air, though it's long since needed to be over. I'm grateful for the slight brush of wind over my skin as Theos and I take our stances about twenty feet apart in an invisible ring that's far larger than it would have been had we simply been sparring.

I close my eyes and feel a bubble of darkness slither up my chest and into my head. I can win this if I so choose. Theos is a strong Mortal God. His power an electrifying mark of the sky. I've seen it—the flecks of white-hot gold that spring from his fingertips at his command.

Darkness swallows the light, though, and I will swallow his whole.

No. That thought rings inside my head as the edge of competition threatens to cause me to make a mistake in this arena. The Gods don't yet know who my God parent is. There's no telling if my powers come from me or from the unknown Goddess who birthed me and then disappeared from my life. My hand tightens on the sword handle. I must handle this situation with care. *Fight with enough to show them not to see me as weak, but just enough to not be a threat.*

I reopen my eyes. *What a precarious string we walk along.*

"You may begin!" Axlan's shout sends Theos sprinting.

I guess he's not going to pretend that fighting doesn't get his blood pumping. Amusement rises inside me as I let him go. Around and around, Theos runs, discarding the sheath of his sword along the way as I slowly draw mine.

All of the training that Ophelia beat into me pours through me. Not just the torture I endured, but the days and nights of lifting a sword over my head, the daggers I nicked myself on time and time again as I learned to wield them, throw them, handle them like an extension of my own body. The blood flow in my veins freezes for an instant as Theos' feet leave the ground and he flies towards me, sword raised.

I react purely on instinct. Metal on metal clashes and sparks fly in front of my face. Heart slamming against my ribcage, I feel my face split into a smile and Theos blinks.

"Fuck, *Dea*," he mutters, just low enough for me to hear. "Do you have any idea how crazy you look with that light in your eye? You look like Kalix."

Good. Kalix is a psycho and psychos always win. Ruen might have beaten me before because I underestimated him, but I'm not going to let Theos go as easily. My smile widens as I step to the side and slide Theos' blade down my own. The shrieking sound it makes echoes against my ears. It's sharp and it would be debilitating if I weren't already used to the noise. Without waiting for Theos to guess my move, I jerk my elbow back and slam it into his face.

"Fuck!" This time his curse is loud enough to be heard by all as his head snaps to the side.

We part and I move, faster than the wind circling me, I dive on top of him, lifting my sword. Despite his surprise, he manages to hit the ground and roll out from beneath me, and my blade slams into the safety of the earth. I turn my head, following him with my eyes as he lifts his sword again.

"Fine," he mutters, turning and spitting out a wad of blood—likely from a cut on the inside of his mouth after the blow to his face. "You want to play it that way, baby? Then let's play."

And just like that, we do.

Theos is a fine sparring partner, his body languid in his movements but no less strong. He may not be as bulky as his brothers, but what he lacks in muscle he certainly makes up for in speed and agility. After a while, the two of us are coated in a fine sheen of sweat, and what I once thought was cool air has become unbearably hot.

Panting, I roll and stab my sword into the ground. Red liquid slips over my forearm where he'd cut me after his last strike. My eyes glance to the balcony. The Gods are still watching us with eyes full of judgment. They're not even bothering to look at both of us. No. Their gazes are trained purely on me, evaluating me. They're not going to have us stop until I reveal something and we've already been at this far longer than either of the others.

The distraction costs me. Solid hands close over my arms and lift me up and I let them. Dropping my weight throws Theos off when I know he expects me to react violently. Suddenly handed the full breadth of my body, he stumbles as he meets not just feeble resistance, but no resistance at all.

Off balance, Theos attempts to right himself. Before he can fully adjust, I rear back and slam the soles of my feet into his legs, kicking off and catapulting myself out of his arms. Whirling back to face him, the world fades away. My vision narrows. One breath. Two. Three. Too many. Faster and faster. That's not right. They should slow down. I should be calm. I've done this many times before.

Darkness stretches over my vision. Theos' face twists in the center of the long tunnel that my sight has become. "Kiera?" I can barely hear him over the roaring in my ears. Heat burns a vicious path up my spine.

"By the Gods, stop her!" I hear someone else say—sounding like Ruen. Is it Ruen?

I turn my head, trying to see him, but the end of the tunnel is becoming smaller and smaller. The light is far away and all I see is the dark. Shadows swarm me. Fear closes long skeletal fingers around my throat. Mentally, I reach out for some sign that it's not real. That I'm still in the arena. Almost immediately, there are dozens if not hundreds of tiny little minds that respond to my own. They ground me, pull me back from the brink. Their emotions are a whirl of fear and anxiety, but they reply to my silent plea without a second's hesitation.

That's the thing about spiders. So many think they're no

more necessary than any other insect, but the world wouldn't have them if they weren't meant to be natural to this plane of existence. Spiders are pure in a way that no Mortal or Divine being could ever be. They are innocent and when I ask them for help, they don't stop to consider how it will hurt them or not. They simply reach out their tiny little minds and feed me what I need to ground myself.

When the light returns, I see that I'm standing in the middle of the arena with Theos on top of me, shaking my shoulders.

"Kiera!" he's screaming my name.

I part too-dry lips. "We're ... still fighting," I croak out.

His eyes widen a split second before I send a blast of power at him. Theos' body goes high into the sky as he's flung into the wind. For all his supposed power, though, he never used his lightning on me. I watch it now as it arches around him in rippling waves as he uses that agility of his to twist mid-air.

In an instant, Theos is back on the ground, one knee planted into the sand along with a fist and his gold-blond hair hanging in sweaty clumps around his face.

"Enough!" Both of our heads jerk up at Axlan's announcement. Panting, heart thundering in my breast, I look up into the balcony as Axlan raises his hand to command everyone's attention.

"The mock battles have ended. This battle is a draw," he calls out over the arena. "You are dismissed."

My chest rises and falls with my heavy breaths as I get up off the ground and watch as the trio of Gods each turn and leave the balcony. Axlan is the first to go and then Makeda, but to my surprise, Danai is the final one to disappear from view as she pauses at the edge of the balcony and glances back. Her golden hair appears to glow around her as eyes dipped in the purest of honey delve into me. There's an emotion I can't quite recognize on her face, but as my brow creases, trying to understand it, she turns and then the God Queen is gone.

Across the arena, Theos collapses onto the sand with a grunt. "Fucking Gods," he mutters.

Distant voices echo from the stands as the students rise, talking amongst themselves—both about the battles and the Gods' presence. Two nearby *thumps* following each other back-to-back has me turning towards the end of the arena to find that both Kalix and Ruen have jumped over the partition into the middle of the arena and are quickly heading our way.

"What was that?" Ruen's voice is a dark angry growl as he approaches.

"What was what?" I ask, frowning as the pair reach us, Kalix moving to help Theos to his feet.

"Your eyes went completely black," Theos tells me as he and Kalix come up on my right side. He dusts off sand from his trousers before reaching for my arm. "Did I cut you too deep?"

I shake him off, pulling my arm from his grip. "Of course not," I say with a roll of my eyes. "I'm not as delicate as you think I am."

"Oh, I know you're not delicate, little liar," Kalix says, somehow appearing closer than he was a moment ago.

With a grimace, I arch a brow his way. "Is that your idea of flirting?" I ask.

He shrugs. "No, my idea of flirting is having you on your back, legs spread for my—"

"That's not flirting," Theos bites out, cutting his brother off.

I turn away from the lot of them and start to dust myself off as well. "They wanted to see what I could do," I say absently, trying to figure out what the hell Danai's expression had been. What emotion was she showing? There had been something different about her today. Something I hadn't seen the first time I'd met her.

Not being able to figure it out is driving me mad.

"Come on," Ruen huffs, stomping forward and snatching my arm up before I can slap him away. "We need to talk."

The only reason I don't yank myself out of his hold and punch him in his too-perfect and stupid face is because he's right. We do need to talk. I haven't forgotten the original reason I went in search of him last night.

As we exit the arena, I search for Niall, but he's nowhere in sight. I'll have to find him too. Make sure we're okay because no matter how my status has changed, he'll always be the first friend I ever made outside of the Underworld and I don't want him to think that he's become nothing more than another Terra. Not to me. Never to me. But before I can do that, I need to get Ruen's insight.

Something is happening to the Mortal Gods and I don't believe they're being transferred.

My instincts are screaming that this has something to do with the taboo the Gods have broken, but I don't know what.

CHAPTER 31
KIERA

Days pass after the mock battles in front of the God Queen and Makeda. I inform the Darkhavens about what I'd found in the records of the Academy library and then, for the first time, I show them my book.

"This isn't leather," Ruen states as he palms the exterior of the beautifully crafted tome. I swallow roughly, but I don't tell him what it's made of. Every time I touch the thing, I try not to think about it.

Theos peers over his shoulder at the pages he's flipped the book open to. "There are so many names." His tone is strained, as if he's forcing himself to show less emotion. "You're right, that's Malachi's surname—and Enid's."

"Her name isn't crossed out yet," I say, "but Malachi's name was. Then I found out that he was transferred."

Across the open space of the Darkhaven's living quarters, Kalix lounges in a chair by the fireplace, flipping a silver dagger up into the air before deftly catching it between his thumb and forefinger. He repeats the actions over and over as his eyes haze over with barely contained boredom.

"The rest of these pages are blank," Ruen murmurs as he flips through the book. His midnight gaze lifts to mine. "Is there a reason for that?"

I shrug. "I don't know," I admit openly. "Caedmon gave me the book when I was just a Terra—it was originally just information about the Hinterlands. Then it changed. He said it's a book of prophecies."

"So these names are a prophecy?" Theos frowns and then jumps when a dagger flies past all of our heads and embeds itself between two stones in the wall.

"Kalix," Ruen's cold tone is a chastisement.

The response is a low deep groan of annoyance. "This is stupid," Kalix snaps. "The book isn't telling us anything."

I turn when the chair beneath Kalix creaks as he gets to his feet, boots slamming onto the floor. "I say we go to Caedmon and make him tell us what the damned prophecy is."

"You can't threaten a God to get information," I remind him, though honestly I wish we could. Though I'm frustrated with Caedmon's secrets and I'm not entirely sure if he's with us or against us yet, something deep within me says he's not trying to harm us.

Kalix's lips split into a wide smile. "Oh, *little liar.*" He tuts at me. "You should know better. There are other ways to get someone to spill their secrets."

I suck in a breath and narrow my eyes on the most unhinged of the Darkhaven brothers. "You can't torture one either," I grit out.

Another groan and he collapses back into his chair. "What is the point of being so powerful if I'm not allowed to have any Gods damned fun?" he demands.

When no one answers him, he withdraws another blade that, until this moment, had been completely hidden somewhere on his body. The distinct *thwip thwip* of his return to the flipping of the blade into the air and catching it is all that lingers in the air until Theos speaks.

"Why can't Caedmon just tell us what the prophecies are instead of giving you a book that only gives hints?" he asks.

"He said it's something about his ability—a barrier," I answer him. "I guess if he were to tell us straight out what the prophecies are or what the future is, it would change and he wouldn't be able to help us at all."

Despite my words and the fact that I *do* now understand where Caedmon is coming from, Theos' frustration matches my own.

"Divinity is complicated, but it does have its own laws," Ruen says with a nod. "So that makes sense."

I look at him. "It does?"

"Yes." Ruen's eyes lower to the pages of the book, one thumb hooked between two of them, but holding the current side in place as he stares at the names listed there. "Even the Gods have to answer for their powers. It's why Axlan needs victory. Why Dolos needs oppression. Why Maladesia is in charge of raising young Mortal Gods—they need praise as much as she needs to give it. The Gods are controlled by their abilities and they have to continue to feed them."

"But ... why doesn't the same apply to the Mortal Gods?" The sounds of Kalix's dagger toss and catch cease. All eyes turn to me. I look around the room. "What?" I demand, frowning at the three of them.

"What did you just say?" Ruen's question isn't so much a question as it is a command worded as one.

"Mortal Gods don't have to feed their powers the same way the Gods do, unless ... they do?"

Gold, green, and midnight gazes clash. "I've never

thought of it like that," Theos murmurs as Kalix gets up and his dagger disappears back beneath his clothes.

"She's right though," Ruen says. "We don't need to feed our abilities like the Gods."

Kalix strides across the room, cutting through the throng of us until he's at the wall and jerking his earlier blade from its place in the wall. "What does that mean?" he asks, turning to face us.

"I don't know," Ruen admits, "but it could be another reason why they've made it a crime to hide Mortal Gods, why they've ensured that all God blood children are sent to their academies."

"Does it matter if we need to feed our powers or not?" I ask as I fold my arms across my chest. "The fact still remains, Gods are naturally more powerful than we are."

"*Are they?*" The silence that follows Ruen's quiet question is loud enough to be a sound on its own.

The four of us remain still and silent long after the echo of Ruen's voice has dispersed from the air. If the Gods need to feed their power and we don't ... does that mean that their rules do not apply to us?

"Caedmon said that they lied about mortals being able to kill them," I whisper, half afraid of disturbing the odd sort of dark peace that hovers between us. "He said they aren't Gods at all."

"And if they'll lie about that, then what else have they lied about?" Ruen offers.

Our eyes meet and clash.

"Can we even trust the knowledge of them needing to feed their powers?" Theos asks.

Kalix nods. "Yes, I believe so. I don't think that's a lie."

"Why?" I jerk my attention to him. "What do you know?"

Kalix is frowning as he settles his hands on his hips and

stares down, though I know from the look on his face—more concentrated than it's ever been—that he's not seeing just the floor. "Hatzi," he states.

I try to remember which God he's speaking of. "The God of Travel?"

He nods. "Hatzi went with me when I was taken to Talmatia's region, Mineval." My spine stiffens as cool green eyes lift and his lips twitch.

I should've stabbed him harder and twisted. As if he senses my thoughts, his smile widens.

"Why is that of any import?" Ruen asks, disrupting the invisible battle of wills between us.

Kalix's attention goes to his brother. "He seemed quite agitated on our way there, but the moment we were traveling he settled. When the Terra set to go with and serve him asked, he said it had to do with his power. He doesn't just like to travel, he *needs* to. He can remain in one place for a short period of time, but if he goes too long without traveling then he grows more than agitated, he becomes like an alcoholic in need of a drink."

Ruen nods and his expression turns contemplative as he closes the book in his hand. I reach for it, taking it from him and holding it closer to my chest.

"Okay," I say. "So the Gods need to feed their powers and we don't. That doesn't help us figure out what's going on with the Mortal Gods. Enid's name is next on the list. If we don't do something then she's going to be transferred."

"What if that's all it is though?" Theos asks. "What if she really is just being transferred to another academy? There's nothing wrong there."

I shake my head. "No, the book wouldn't mention it if it weren't important," I argue before flipping the book around with the front facing outward. "Look at it." I point. "Look at the title."

"To Those Who Have Been Stolen," Theos reads the title aloud and then sighs. His shoulders slump in defeat. "You're right. That doesn't exactly sound like the title for a list of names of people who are okay."

"They've been stolen," I insist. "But what does that *mean?*" Frustration colors my tone, and to my surprise, it's Ruen who steps closer and puts a hand on my shoulder.

"We'll figure it out," he says.

The sharp bolt of heat that spreads from his palm through the fabric of my tunic makes me look up at him, my eyes fixating on his lips in remembrance of how they felt against mine. He'd been so heavy on top of me, controlling, commanding. My thighs press together. *Would he be the same if we did it again?*

Thankfully, my thoughts don't lead me to do something stupid like lean forward and place my mouth back on his to find out. Because, in the next instant, a loud cracking against the window has all of our heads turning in that direction. A groan rumbles up my chest and I quickly thrust the book back into Ruen's grasp as I turn and stalk across the room. Flipping the lock and opening the glass, Regis' crow flutters into the room.

"Caw! Caw!" The bird flaps its wings and circles overhead before landing on my shoulder in a fury of feathers. Its beak pecks lightly at my head.

I glare sideways at the damn creature before ripping the scroll off its leg. I'm already halfway to the fire of the hearth, intending to toss this note where all the others have gone when I stop. There's a splotch of something dark, a stain, on the side of the scroll. When I lift it to my face, the scent of blood hits me.

I slip open the note with fast, trembling fingers. There are only two short sentences, but they turn my insides to pure ice.

Underworld has been breached. *Stay safe.* — R

Breached? *The Underworld has been breached? When? How?*

"What is it?" Ruen is across the room and at my side in a split second. He takes the note from my hand and curses. "Kiera?" He looks at me. "What does this mean?"

I lift my gaze to his. "It means the Underworld is collapsing," I say.

"How?" he demands.

Regis' crow nuzzles its beak against my cheek as if seeking comfort. I reach up, absently rubbing my fingertips over the bird's feathers along its neck. No wonder the animal was acting odd.

"I don't know," I answer Ruen without emotion. "It's never happened before. The Underworld has been around for decades—hundreds of years—Ophelia is only the most recent head."

"Do you think the Gods…" Theos' question drifts off as my eyes move sharply to him.

"*No, they can't know.*" I don't know if I say the words because I believe them to be true or because I want them to be.

Regis is alive though. If he weren't then he wouldn't have been able to send me this note. I straighten and glance at the bird perched on my shoulder. Regis' crow looks back at me with deep black eyes.

"We need to go," I say.

"Go?" Ruen crumples the piece of parchment in his fist. "Go where?"

"To the city," I snap, storming forward. "To the shop."

I hurry past Ruen and then Theos, both theirs and Kalix's eyes watching me as I rush for Ruen's room. I grab my cloak and thrust it on. Regis' crow caws at me again but he leaves my shoulder to allow the movement and then circles me as I head back into the living area.

"Kalix, I need—" A little tap on my booted foot nearly sends me jumping out of my skin and I cut myself off to look down and spy a snake with a glimmering shimmer of jade green scales peering up at me. There's a dagger handle sticking out of its mouth along with a leather strap.

Bending, I take it from the creature and look at Kalix, who's looking at me rather smug, and nod my thanks. The snake slithers away now that its task is complete and I hook the strap of the dagger sheath around my thigh, buckling it into place.

"You're not going alone," Ruen barks. "So don't even think of it."

"Then hurry up," I snap back. "I'm going with or without you and I'm going *now*."

"If the Underworld is breached then they're likely not at the shop anymore." Ruen's reasoning is solid, but so is mine.

"It's the last place they were known to be," I reply. "I can try to pick up a trail to know where Regis has gone, plus—" I lift my arm and Regis' crow lands on it. "This one can lead me to him if we get close enough." Crows are intelligent creatures with long memories and each crow trained by the Underworld knows their primary agents. This one will know where to find Regis.

Ruen's hands ball into fists and he turns towards his brothers. "Talk to her!" he yells. "Make her see reason!"

Theos groans. "I don't think we can stop her."

Kalix moves for the stairs. "I'll grab a few more weapons."

Good. Yes. Weapons we might need. "Another dagger for me," I call after him.

Ruen thrusts a hand into his hair, grabs a chunk of the dark inky strands and yanks. "This is ridiculous. We can't risk leaving the Academy right now. The God Council is here!"

"Risk or not, I'm leaving," I state. "Are you coming with me?"

Blue-purple eyes glow red. "Fuck you," he growls. "Yes, of course, I'm coming, damn it."

The tightness I hadn't realized was coiling in my chest eases the slightest bit. Relief slides through me. "But not all of us," he says when I'm about to thank him.

I scowl. "I'm not—"

"You'll go," he assures me, dropping his hand from his hair before I can tell him that there's no way I'm staying behind. "Kalix and I will go." He turns to Theos. "You will stay."

Theos blinks and then scowls. "What? Why me?" he practically yells. "Why do I have to stay behind?"

Through gritted teeth, Ruen responds. "Because we need someone here to act as a look out in case any of the Gods comes looking for us."

Theos grinds his jaw but doesn't say anything which, to me, means that he sees the logic in Ruen's words.

"And," Ruen continues after a beat, "I'll need you to call for Maeryn. Have her Terra bring her here."

"What for?" I ask, frowning as the door above opens and Kalix appears at the stairs, quickly moving downward.

"You're going to the shop to find your fellow assassin, Kiera," Ruen replies. "If the spot of blood on his note is any indication, he's hurt. We're going to find him and bring him back here. That's the mission. Can you handle it?"

The last words, a question, make my back go ramrod straight. Insulted at him even bothering to ask deepens my voice to my own growl. "*Yes.*"

Ruen nods and Kalix finishes his descent, handing me another dagger upon passing. I take it and Regis' crow lifts away from my arm to allow me to strap it to my other thigh. Kalix tosses Ruen a cloak and then dons his own.

"Good," Ruen states, "then, let's go."

CHAPTER 32
KIERA

I don't recall a time when my feet moved with such swiftness. Now, I'm running with a near impossible speed as I race away from the Academy wall and down towards the city of Riviere. Even with my anger at Regis for what he'd done—how he had betrayed me—I don't want him hurt or dead.

Regis' crow flies overhead, the creature's black wings nearly eclipsed by the darkness of the night as I'm followed by two silent figures. Kalix and Ruen. They run with me, quiet and fast. The tingle of Ruen's power threads an illusion over all of us, hiding us from the view of those who guard the walls of the Academy.

That power calls to my own, reminding me of what had happened in the arena merely days before. The long dark tunnel that had obscured my ability to see. I still have no clue what it was other than my own power needing an outlet. At least, I hope that's all it was.

We make quick work of the distance between the Academy and Riviere, reaching the city's edge in far less time than it's ever taken me. When I slow towards the first street, I find myself breathing evenly as if I'm not even winded. Ruen's hand comes up to cup my shoulder.

"With the brimstone out, you likely have more stamina than before," he says as if he can read my mind. "Your body is already working to catch up with your new abilities."

I open my mouth to reply, but Regis' crow chooses that moment to *caw* down at us. Jerking my gaze to the sky, I watch as the animal flaps its wings and circles us before heading off down the street. Sliding out from under Ruen's hold, I trail the creature. The Darkhavens fall into step behind me, never wavering, and never dropping back.

Regis' crow leads us through the streets of Riviere in the dark, but not towards the place I'm used to going. We pass the coffeehouse that Ruen had taken me to the day he'd found out my secret. I barely offer it a passing glance as the crow turns a corner, its beady eyes looking back over its wing as if to make sure we're still on its tail. It's heading away from the shop, not towards it.

I follow regardless even as we enter a section of the city I don't recognize. The townhomes are closer together than even those near Madam Brione's shop. I thought that it had been the slums of Riviere, but I soon realize that it was merely a run-down section, not the slums themselves. Because the part of Riviere that Regis' crow is flying towards is in far worse condition.

Cracked windows full of darkness. Dust and dirt and grime on every doorstep. Some houses have doorways completely open to the elements with nothing but dirty sheets to block intruders. I slow my steps, and behind me, so do Ruen and Kalix. They don't say anything as the crow slows above an intersection.

"I thought we were going to the shop," Kalix says, his voice a careful whisper.

I shake my head. "We're following the bird," I reply. "It's leading us to Regis." *I hope.*

Wind beats against my face as the crow lowers itself and then lands on my shoulder. I stare at the creature, but it's not looking at me. Instead, its eyes are scanning our surroundings. Its beak twists this way and then the opposite way.

"Do you think it's lost the trail?" Ruen asks.

"Just give it a moment," I tell him.

As we wait for the animal to come to some sort of decision, I take the opportunity to glance around the street. The roads here are even smaller than that near Madam Brione's shops, hardly wide enough for the three of us to stand shoulder to shoulder and certainly not big enough for any carriage. There are broken objects littering the stones beneath our feet, cracked pieces of furniture left to bleach in the daytime sun, and rancid food in garbage cans where several glowing eyes of vermin peer out toward us. A shudder works through me. Regis hated the dirt in Madam Brione's shop. I can't imagine him here where filth is caked into each corner and crevice.

The crow on my shoulder spreads its wings, feathers drifting over my cheek as it takes flight. "Come on," I say, though I don't need to. Kalix and Ruen are already moving with me.

Regis' crow flies further up the street, the dilapidated townhouses turning into wooden shacks stacked on top of one another, each in worse disrepair than the last. Then the animal takes a sharp left turn down an alley.

Ruen curses and reaches out to grab my arm, pulling me to a halt when I would follow after the creature. "Wait. We can't all fit down there."

"I have to—"

"Let me go first," Ruen insists, stopping my argument before it can begin.

"But—"

Ruen doesn't wait for me to finish what I'm about to say. He lifts his head and nods to where Kalix stands behind me. Hard hands grip my shoulders, keeping me in place. A snarl rips past my lips as Ruen turns and disappears into the darkness.

"*Release me.*" I hiss out the command, but Kalix merely chuckles and tugs me against him, my back to his front. Something hard presses against my ass. I snap my head around and gape up at him. "Are you fucking serious right now?"

Kalix merely shrugs. "Blame yourself, little liar," he replies. "You're irresistible when you're feeling violent."

I flip him off and then turn to face the opening of the alleyway again. Seconds pass and then minutes. The longer we go without any hint or sign of either Regis or Ruen, the more my body tenses as if preparing for something horrible to come walking out of the darkness at any moment.

My eyes flick back and forth, up and down the street. There are no lamps here—not even burned-out ones, just ... none at all. As if this place is a part of the city that's long been forgotten by all. Metal crashing onto stone makes me jump, but Kalix remains perfectly still at my back.

"It's just the rats," he tells me.

I glance over my shoulder to be sure, but he's right. One of the trash cans overflowing against one of the shacks has been tipped over and several of the rodents that had been making meals of the insides pour out and disappear into the shadows. Disgust rolls through me. Regis would not be fine here. If he is in this place then he must be either dead or dying. The smell of urine and decay invades my nostrils like a foreshadowing of impending doom. I wrinkle my nose against it.

Kalix's fingers squeeze tight around my upper arms, dragging my attention back to the alley as he speaks. "Ruen's returning."

My breath catches when I see him—a figure darker than the shadows as it steps out of the gloom beyond. In the next second, my eyes fall to the man he's holding in his arms. Regis' face is pale and bloodless. There are dark purple bruises beneath his eyes and a black stain over the side of his throat. No, not black, I realize as they draw nearer. Dark red. It's dried blood.

"He's badly wounded," Ruen states, stopping in front of us. "If we want Maeryn to see to him, we need to get him back to the Academy fast."

As Ruen grows closer, I reach up, shaking off Kalix's hold. Brushing one of Regis' dirty blond dreads to the side, I bite down on my lower lip at how cold he is.

"Are you sure he's still..." I don't want to say it, but from how he looks...

"He's still alive," Ruen assures me, "but he won't be for much longer if we don't get him help."

I nod and step back to allow Ruen to take the lead this time as we retrace our steps back to the Academy.

CANDLELIGHT FLICKERS over the hollows of Regis' face a few hours later as Maeryn bends over him, running her hands up and down his chest. My face blanches at how he smells just like the place where we found him. *Like death.*

"Can you help him?" I ask her.

Maeryn doesn't answer for a long moment, her power

spreading in a thin layer of whitish gold over his body as she works. When it sinks into Regis and she blows out a long breath, I know she's found her answer.

"I can," she says over her shoulder, "but he'll need time and rest to fully recover."

"What if..." I take a step forward. "What if I were to give him some of my blood?"

Maeryn's hands pull back and she turns to gape at me. "Kiera, that's not something you should offer."

"It will help him heal faster," I press.

"Yes, but it's illegal."

I stare at her. "Half of the things we've done over the past few months are illegal," I remind her. "This hardly seems like the time to pick which crimes I'm willing to take part in. It's not even the worst one."

Her lips press together as if she doesn't want to admit that I'm right.

A hand locks on my shoulder. "Why don't you let her do what she can first," Ruen suggests. "If she decides he needs it, then we can give him some Divine blood to speed up the healing process."

My gaze moves back to Regis, still and so damn pale that I wonder how the hell she can do anything when he looks like he's already knocking on death's door. I grit my teeth and jerk my chin in a nod of understanding.

"Fine," I concede, "but if he's not at least somewhat improved within the next day or so, then I'm doing it anyway."

Maeryn shakes her head but doesn't argue as she turns back to her patient. Regis' crow sits perched on the back of the couch, watching his master and the red-headed Mortal God that pushes more of her healing into him. My shoulders droop. Maybe if I'd been born with an ability like hers, I wouldn't have become what I am. Useless unless it's to kill someone.

Ruen removes his hand from my shoulder and steps back. His presence doesn't leave though. Not right away. As the night draws on, the minutes stretching into hours, only when the early light of dawn begins to stretch its long fingers across the sky outside the window does he retreat to his bedroom. Kalix does as well, leaving Maeryn, Regis, Theos, and me alone in the main area as we wait for some sign from Regis that he'll pull through.

When birds begin to chirp outside, Theos moves to my side. Without saying a word, his arms come around me and he unbuckles the strap at my throat. My cloak loosens around my shoulders and he catches it before taking it away and returning a few seconds later.

"Come on, *Dea*," he says, wrapping a strong arm around my waist as he pulls me into his warm side.

I'm so cold. Frosted over with the knowledge that Regis could be dying and I've spent the last weeks hating him. I've burned every note he's tried to send and only by some twist of fate did I manage to stop myself from burning the last one. He knows I'm angry at him. He knows I hate him for what he did.

Yet, still, in what could be his last moments, he sent me a note trying to warn me of danger.

Does that make what he did okay? No.

But does that make him my friend still?

I don't know, and yet, I'm the only one who can answer that question.

When Theos tugs at me again, turning me away from where Maeryn still bends over Regis' still body, sweat coating her brow as she works at him with her healing, I go. My footsteps stumble as we move away from the couch and Theos doesn't stop to right me. He simply reaches down and plucks me off the ground, hauling me into his arms and against his chest.

Theos carries me into his room, kicking the door closed behind us. He doesn't stop until he's at the bed, lowering me onto the mattress with careful kindness. I close my eyes when they begin to burn, but remain awake enough to know he's unbuckling the daggers strapped to my thighs and removing the weapons. Then he's tugging my boots off. Firm fingers touch the laces of my pants next, undoing them before they, too, are being dragged off me.

My body is lifted back into his arms and with somehow practiced movements, Theos holds me to him as he pulls back the blankets on the bed and places me against the pillows. I listen to the sound of him moving away from the bed, his footsteps tip-toeing around the room.

After a while, the covers are pulled back on the other side of the mattress, and a hot male body slides beneath them. Theos' scent moves over me, into me. The smell of rum and spice is hot and soothing despite the burning in my eyes that has yet to let up. My lower lip trembles and I bite down on it to stop the tick. Arms move around me, drawing me against a naked chest. Lips touch my hair, pressing a kiss I don't deserve to my head, and it's too much. It's all too much.

Before I give in to the oblivion of sleep, the last thing I feel is the tears building against the back of my eyelids give way, streaking down my cheeks in the darkness of Theos' room.

If Regis dies, it won't be anyone else's fault but my own.

CHAPTER 33
KIERA

It's been a long time since my dreams were just dreams and not nightmares dragging me back down the streets of memory. In Theos' arms, though, that is all they become. I'm drifting down a long dark river full of black skies and diamond stars. It's warm and safe here. Far away from blood and death and decay. I snuggle deeper into the space that smells of rum and spice. It invades my nostrils threatening to slip through to my very soul. A contented breath escapes me and a breath blows across the crown of my head. Baby hairs flutter at my temple and I wrinkle my nose at the sensation, trying to go deeper into the dream. Then wide, firm hands move over my front, down the plain of my stomach towards the place between my legs.

The sigh turns to a gasp as the first electrifying sensation of lightning sparks against the sensitive bundle of nerves above my sex. I jolt from the half-asleep state into one of full wakefulness to find that the hand is real and it's Theos'. His name is both a groan and a scolding as it's ripped from my lips. He pulls his hand back, but his mouth presses a kiss to my nape as he holds me in the same way we fell asleep. His naked front to my tunic covered back. That doesn't last long. Theos' hands push up the fabric so that he can touch me, skin to skin. I glance down to find a golden glow surrounding his fingers. The sparks of his Divinity light up the shadowy room as he flattens a palm against my lower belly. A shock rippling of energy moves through me. That strange buzzing that I've felt tingling beneath my flesh rises to greet this new sensation. The muscles beneath my flesh bunch and jump to meet the heat coming off the hand belonging to the man at my back. Theos' body is like an inferno against mine, chasing away the last vestiges of the ice that filled my insides until there's no hint left.

"*Theos.*" My nails dig into the muscled forearm around my side as my spine arches. More lightning glows at the tips of his fingers trailing from him to me, making the nerves beneath my skin shudder in a mixture of pleasure and pain.

He nuzzles against the side of my neck. "I love it when you say my name like that."

I shake my head, trying to clear it from the erotic fog he's somehow woven over me. "Now … is really … not…" *the time*, I mentally add when yet again more of his lightning appears, this time jumping and dancing over the exterior of my flesh like tiny little sentient creatures.

Theos ignores my words and parts his lips. Sharp, sweet agony spills through me as his teeth sink into the column of my throat, and the evidence of a hot hard cock prods my ass.

"*Regis!*" I half gasp, half moan, trying to remind both myself and the man torturing me of the reason we shouldn't be doing this.

Unfortunately, all it does is result in a low male growl. The world flips and my front is suddenly turned, my back pressed into the mattress beneath me as a very angry very erect Theos Darkhaven appears above me. My legs are spread and in the next second, I'm filled to the brim. My spine arches and my lips part in a silent scream as Theos is suddenly inside me, his cock sliding through soft not-quite-ready-yet flesh.

"I might not mind letting my brothers have you, *Dea*." His voice is a quiet dangerous rumble—sounding nothing like the usual Theos. "But if you ever call another man's name while you're in my bed ... I will gut him upon this mattress and then fuck you in his entrails."

As if intended to punctuate that threat, Theos withdraws from my cunt and then slams back inside with fervent desire. My hands are on his shoulders, my nails digging into his flesh until they draw blood.

"Don't. Fucking. Threaten. Me." Each word is marked by a low animalistic growl, and it takes several moments after the words are out to realize that the noise is coming from my own throat.

Liquid treasure eyes bore into me as Theos pulls back, his hips twisting before he sinks back into me. Lightning the same color as those eyes of his appears along the length of his arms. The scent of something smoldering, hot and wicked reaches my nostrils a split second before the sheets around us catch fire. Flames lick at my side, eliciting a gasp as I mentally prepare for the heat stealing over my skin and searing into me. Arms close around my body and Theos spins us, ripping the sheets from their position as we tumble to the opposite side of the bed. When I reopen my eyes after realizing I'd closed them in preparation for pain, I find myself sitting astride the big golden eyed Darkhaven beneath me. Other than a scorch mark on the otherwise pristine sheets, there's no other evidence of his near lack of control.

"Off." Theos yanks at the edge of my tunic.

Shaking off the sudden change, I stare down at him—confused and aroused. Perhaps it's because I just woke up, but I don't have any of the usual barriers I normally would. My mind isn't focusing as hard as it should on all of the reasons why I shouldn't let this man do what he wants.

When I don't immediately do as he demands, Theos reaches up and grips two sides of my tunic. The sound of rending fabric reaches my ears a bit too late as he peels away the remains of my shirt and then does away with the under corset, leaving me completely naked astride him. He slaps my hip lightly—just enough to sting, though not to cause actual pain. "If you don't want me to fuck you into unconsciousness, I suggest you ride me, *Dea*."

My hands curl into fists against his chest. "Theos—*fuck!*"

Whether he senses my impending protest or he is simply tired of being patient, the hard roll of his hips sends my body jolting up and down, my insides sliding against the hard shaft between my legs. Theos' hands come up to grip my waist, lifting me and pulling back down until his cock is sliding between my folds in hard penetrating thrusts.

I shut my eyes again as the squeeze of my insides press hard against the cock inside me. My lower muscles contract around the intruder and the responding low masculine groan that echoes up from beneath me makes the sweat slicked hairs on the back of my neck stand on end.

"You're squeezing me so tightly," Theos pants. "It's as if you're trying to strangle my cock."

"Maybe I am," I shoot back, my lids parting so I can peer down through my lashes at his face.

His neck is craned back, the sharp lines of his jaw no longer shadowed as the veins bulge beneath his skin. I look to where his hands are holding me down against him and curiosity has me lifting slightly on my own, rubbing up and down and back and forth. A hiss escapes him and then me as I inadvertently rub my clit against something. It feels good, so I do it again.

Up and down. Back and forth. Grinding. Hungry for a bit more of this pleasure when I should be focusing on anything —everything—else. Just once though. I want to steal a bit of time for myself, for privacy to reward myself for all that I've given up and all that I've yet to give up but know that I eventually will.

I can't keep them—these deranged devious Darkhavens. They are not mine, and I'm not theirs. But I can take this with me when it's all over—the memories of something good, of something pleasurable.

If I don't die here in this place, in this academy at the hands of the Gods, then this will be all that I will allow myself for the future. A memory of once when I wasn't so in control, when I allowed myself a short reprieve from everything else. Hopefully, it'll be enough.

"Fuck!" Theos' sharp cry as I feel his cock swell against my inner walls leaves me panting for more as he uses his hold again, slamming me up and down upon his shaft.

Wetness trickles from between my thighs, soaking his lap and the dark hairs at the base of his shaft. Sweat coats my flesh—my thighs, my shoulders, and everything in between.

"Kiss me." Theos' plea is a soft purr, hypnotic. So much so that I find myself leaning down to offer my mouth to him.

The second his lips touch mine, though, I realize my mistake. His hand comes up and clasps around the back of my head, holding me in place as he takes what remains of my sanity and completely obliterates it. The world spins a second time and he's over me, his body moving like a lithe predatory animal as he powers into me. Our hips are locked in an age-old dance, my legs spread open for him. He grasps me by the throat now that my head is pressed back into the mattress and ravages my mouth.

Tongue, lips, and teeth collide in an explosive fury that I knew we both possessed. As hungry as he's turning out to be, I'm more so. I bite back, sucking his tongue into my mouth and tormenting him with little needy sounds in the back of my throat. A hand squeezes against my breast. Fingers tweak my nipple, pinching down hard until the kiss is interrupted by a sharp cry from me.

"*Gods...*" I hiss out as Theos' head dips and he takes my other nipple between his teeth.

He pauses and lifts his head. "Don't bring those bastards into this moment, *Dea*," he orders, eyes dripping with icy gold. "The Gods have no place between your legs. Only me. When you cry out, I want to hear you scream my name."

I have no words for his command, but as he dips his head again and begins to move inside me once more, I lose all other rationality that allowed me to think in the first place. With his cock buried in my cunt, Theos drives me to the brink again and again, but he must still retain some of his own sanity because he has no problem stopping just before we ever reach the point of no return. I pant. I curse him. I scratch at his back like a wild creature.

When he tries to kiss me again on the mouth, I bite, drawing blood and eliciting an amused chuckle from him. "So violent." He doesn't sound angry. "So perfect."

My eyes burn at that statement and all I can do is cling to him as fresh tears well up, soaking through my lashes. *No,* I want to tell him. *Don't ruin this with lies no one would believe.*

I'm a killer. I'm a monster. I am one of the dangerous creatures in the dark. That's why Caedmon came to me. That's why he believes I'll be the one capable of killing the God King. No one *good* can be asked to do something so heinous.

"With me, Kiera." I blink as Theos rocks into me, sliding back and forth between sore folds. Hands come up to cup my face. "Look at me." I do and frown. "You're with me, right now," he tells me. "No one else."

How had he known?

Wet slick sounds squelch through the room as he continues to thrust into me. A thumb slips over the bundle of nerves that is my clit and Theos is not the only one who can produce lightning. It ricochets through me, stealing away my breath and leaving me a mindless, sobbing mess of pleasure as I come all over him. It only takes an instant for him to follow me into the drowning darkness of release and then the two of us collapse against one another, panting, trembling, and shaking with the aftereffects.

I don't know how long we lie like that, our skin pressed so close together that it begins to stick. I'm not the one who interrupts the peace that settles into my bones in a way that nothing else ever has.

"We need to talk."

I roll my eyes at Theos' now calm tone as his hand strokes up and down the goosebump speckled flesh of my back.

"Yes, because you're *so* good at talking," I mutter.

His hand leaves my spine and comes down in a sharp strike against my right ass cheek. I lift up slightly on his chest and arch a brow at him.

Theos scowls at me. "I'm serious," he says.

Propping myself up on his chest with one hand, I wave my other in a gesture for him to continue. "By all means, Master Theos, talk."

Another half-hearted slap and another roll of my eyes.

Finally, he speaks. "I need you to know that we will protect you."

I stiffen at the implication his words bring to mind.

Rolling away from him onto the other side of the bed, scorch-marked sheets dig at my backside. "I neither need nor do I want your protection," I tell him.

"Tough shit."

I ignore him and sit up in bed, pulling the straggling strands of my hair away from my face and twisting the spiderweb-colored locks into a knot on the back of my head. "Forget it, Theos," I say, sliding off the mattress to pad across the floor. I scrub a hand down my dry face. Old remnants of the tears I shed last night still linger on my skin—I can feel the dried, salt-scented tracks on my cheeks. "We're allies, I'll give you that, but after this mission is over, you'll go your way and I'll go mine."

"Are you fucking serious?" His sharp tone penetrates my mind but doesn't dissuade me from moving about the room, gathering my trousers from the night before along with my underwear. I don them first before I grab my under corset up—thankful, at least, that he hadn't torn apart this bit of clothing.

Tying the laces at the front of my pants to keep them closed, I slip into the under corset and redo the laces Theos had loosened. With the clothes covering my skin again, I feel stronger—like I'm putting on armor instead of thin fabric.

"*Kiera.*" I don't turn to look at him even when I hear the angry note in his voice. "You're insane if you think after *everything* we've done that you're going to walk away at the end of this."

If there even is an end. My fingers still at that thought. It's a sensible consideration. We could die. All of us. If the Gods find out the truth of everything, they could just as easily execute us and no matter how many secrets we uncover, if the rest of the world remains ignorant to the secrets hiding in the corridors of these academies then we have no real protection.

I hear the soft whisper of sheets moving and then footsteps on the floor. "We couldn't have a relationship before because I thought you were a Terra—a human—but now—"

I pivot to face the lightning-eyed Darkhaven, stopping him with a hand raised against his chest before he can reach for me. "Nothing has changed about that other than the fact that you know the truth about my bloodline," I state coolly. "There is no relationship here. Not with you."

Gold turns to wounded bronze. "And my brothers?" Theos asks.

"Not with them either."

He stares back at me with silent rage. The emotions swarming in the depths of his gaze batter at my soul like a wicked storm wanting to be let into the safe haven of a castle that has withstood hundreds of its kind. I lock the doors and windows and let him see the icy control that has returned reflected in my own expression.

"I see." Theos steps back, taking the warmth of his body with him. I curl my fingers into my palms, nails stabbing at the soft flesh there to keep from doing something ridiculous such as reaching out to bring him back.

I watch him carefully as he strides away from me and bends to pick up a pair of discarded pants. The hard planes of his muscled frame ripple as he steps into them sans underwear and does up the laces before turning back to face me. There is blood in my mouth. I blink and realize I'm biting down on the inside of my cheek so hard I've broken skin.

"Go." Theos gestures for the door. "Go check on your friend."

With a frown, I take a step toward a chair and lift a tunic that's too big for me before pulling it on over my head. "Theos, I—"

He stops me with a snarl. "I don't want to hear it," he

snaps. "You want to be a fucking coward, then do so with someone else, Kiera. I am not the man for you to use and discard as you please."

"That's not what—"

Lightning crackles along his arms, glowing golden in the dim light of dawn pouring in through the window. "*Go.*"

I swallow roughly, an apology poised on my lips, but I know with a single look it won't be accepted. So, instead of offering any more justification for my decision, I just do as he asks.

I turn away from the kindest of the Darkhaven brothers and I leave, each step creating a staggering fissure of pain through the shattered part of my soul that I thought died long ago—before I ever met any of them.

CHAPTER 34
KALIX

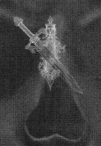

Light rain collects and slides in long rivulets over the external side of the glass that makes up the window overlooking the ocean in the near distance out of the North Tower. I stand by it, watching one drop slip away from the others to disappear between the crevices of the stone alongside it.

Vexing.

The low continuous hum of voices echo behind me as people hover over the man still sprawled, unconscious, on one of the lounges in our main room. I turn ever so slightly and peer back, a scowl overtaking my face.

Why did I allow this again?

Almost as soon as the question slips through my mind—along with images of slaughtering both the unconscious, nearly dead man and the red-haired annoyance still working him over with the low thrum of her pathetic excuse for a Divine power—the answer walks out of the bedroom belonging to my brother, Theos.

A room once devoid of anything worthy of being in it becomes a museum of all the things *she* enjoys and desires.

The darker emotions of anger, frustration, and boredom amongst others that have been a battering ram against the closed doors of the inside of my head die down.

It isn't until she completely ignores my presence in favor of going to the lounge where that *man* lies that it returns in full force.

"How is he?" Kiera asks.

My eyes narrow on the sallow face of the human that Ruen had pulled from the gloom the night before and brought back on behalf of her. I quickly calculate the chances of killing him so that she may turn her attention back to me. Ultimately, though, it's the way she places the back of her hand on his forehead, as if looking for a change in the human's temperature that reminds me that she cares for him. To kill him would upset her.

It's odd. I've never cared before about upsetting anyone other than Theos and Ruen, but my brothers are of my blood. They are part of me. In essence, they are me. To upset them would be to upset myself.

She is different.

She is separate.

She is *mine*.

"He's breathing more evenly," Maeryn murmurs, her tone full of exhaustion. Though she'd slept sometime in the night, she'd been back at checking over her charge by the time I'd woken at dawn. "But he's still yet to wake."

"Do you know how long that will take?" Kiera asks, her hand leaving the man's face as she turns towards Maeryn. Her brows are creased with what I recognize as worry. There are the slightest tracks, too, that rain down from her eyes. She's scrubbed them away, of course, but I see them—the evidence in the streaks of silver lining her face barely perceptible to most.

A door creaks open and Ruen appears in the doorframe of his bedroom, hair tousled uncharacteristically as he enters the main room.

Sssssssss. I bat away the serpent's thought that threatens to intrude in a silent request.

"How is he?" Ruen's question has me turning away from the room once more to stare out the window.

Everything is once again ... *vexing*.

Ssssssss. That request returns. A growl threatens to spill from my throat as my lips curl back in agitation.

What? I snap, demanding an answer from the creature that should know by now when I wish to be interrupted and when I do not.

There is silence and then...

Ssssssss. I straighten away from the side of the wall and frown.

You're sure? The creature sends through an image of them nodding their little scaled head. I'm not sure how Kiera's spiders work, but serpents are intelligent creatures with a language all their own. I've never questioned how I can translate their hissing noises into actual understanding, but right now, I'm pleased by the power.

Turning from the window to face the room, I relay the information that the serpents have passed along. "The God Council called another meeting," I say.

Three heads turn and three pairs of eyes land on me. Kiera's face twists in confusion. Maeryn's is impassable, as if merely looking my way is akin to smelling rancid meat. I bare my teeth at her, letting my fangs lengthen to fine points. Her eyes move down in instinctive submission. Irksome female.

Ignoring her once more, I lift my eyes to meet those of my brother's. "They've decided to conduct a ceremony for Kiera's ancestry."

The door behind Kiera opens and Theos steps out, his face looking far more serious than I've ever noticed before. I tilt my head to the side, curious. His upper lip curls back and he flashes me his teeth before he stomps past Kiera towards the front door.

"Theos," Ruen calls after him. "You need to hear this."

Theos halts where he stands. Though he doesn't turn back to face the rest of us, neither does he make a move to leave. His shoulders shift up and down in the slightest indication that he's still breathing, but otherwise, he's as still as a statue. My gaze flicks to Kiera who seems to be intent on not looking his way.

Interesting.

"Kalix." Ruen's commanding voice spears through me, interrupting my wayward thoughts. "What else?"

I sigh and reach back out to the serpent's mind, seeking the information once more.

Sssssssss.

"They've sent someone to get Kiera to prepare for the ceremony."

"It's not the Spring Equinox yet," Kiera protests. "They said—"

"I'm only saying what my familiars have told me," I interrupt her with a shrug. "Spring Equinox or not, they appear to be impatient."

How very God-like of them. The thought is snide in my head but no less true. Then again, perhaps Azai is where I get my lack of patience. If that were the case, though, then why aren't my brothers more like me?

"Is it for today?" Ruen asks.

I nod my answer. "Yes, a Terra will likely be here soon."

Maeryn stands abruptly, her eyes wide with fear. "They're coming here?" she asks. "Now?" Without waiting for a response, she whirls away. "I can't be here," she directs her words to Ruen. "They can't find out I've been helping you if—"

He waves off her words. "I understand," he says, cutting her off as he gestures for the door. "Go ahead. We thank you for your assistance."

"Wait!" Kiera reaches out for the red-haired Second Tier. "What about Regis?"

Maeryn pauses and glances back at the man still sprawled on the lounge. "He's unconscious but not due to any more injury," she says, her words shooting out quickly as the sound of her anxiety trembles in her voice. *So dramatic,* I think with an eye roll. As if she can't handle a little bit of torture or death that may be punishment for aiding a mortal from outside the walls.

"Can we move him?" Kiera asks.

"Yes, yes of course. He'll wake up when his mind is ready."

"I'll see Maeryn back to her quarters," Theos says in a tight voice as the other girl nods once more to Kiera and then lifts her skirts as if preparing to run. Theos and the annoying girl are gone in the next instant and Kiera is hovering over the human male.

"How long until whoever the Gods have sent get here, Kalix?" Ruen demands as he strides across the room to stand alongside Kiera.

I scowl before reaching for my familiar yet again. A moment later, I know. "It'll be within the next hour," I say. "It appears that they're searching for Caedmon first and he is not in his chambers."

"Good." Ruen jerks his chin in an indication for Kiera to move. She does and Ruen bends, lifting the fragile male into his arms. "Then we hide him."

"Where?" Kiera asks, eyes scanning the room as if she can

divine up some secret place for the human. A snort draws her attention to me and I offer her a smile in response to her dark look.

"You may set him in my chambers," I say. "The snakes would certainly keep him company."

She blanches but Ruen seems to consider the idea. "That might not be a poor plan," he says. "You can keep an eye on him in case he rouses."

My smile drops back into a scowl. "It was a joke," I snap, not at all pleased by the idea of some human vermin being allowed access to my chambers.

"Too bad." Ruen strides past me towards the stairs. "We have little time."

"We have an hour," I state. "That is more than enough time."

He ignores my comment though to take the stairs two at a time. My scowl deepens, but I don't stop him as Kiera rushes past me to assist Ruen in getting the human male into my chambers. An assertive mental push, and I send several of my familiars to the room to keep watch over the annoying pest Kiera seems intent on nursing like a wounded bird.

Life would be far less complicated if I were permitted to simply kill all these little irritants that distract my brothers and Kiera from the important things. Me. Sex. Pleasure. Pain.

With a grumble, I stalk towards the door as a knock sounds against the wood. I open it and blink down at the sharp faced woman with shit brown eyes and a rather breakable looking fist half raised to perform another knock. I blink at the intrusion. It appears my serpents were wrong—we do not have an hour.

CHAPTER 35
KIERA

Dauphine is the one who arrives to take me to see the God Council. Her face is slimmer than I remember seeing it last with dark shadows bruising the skin beneath her eyes. She practically trembles under the dark glare Kalix is leveling her way, but when he moves to follow after us as she asks me to follow her—far more politely than she ever had when I was a Terra—Dauphine stops him.

"I'm sorry," she says, voice strong despite the fine tremor that makes her fingers shake as she holds up a hand, palm outward. "The Gods have only requested Kiera's presence. No one else may attend their Council."

The low snarl that erupts from Kalix is quickly cut off by Ruen as he grips his brother and drags him back into the North Tower quarters. I keep my gaze firmly planted on the two Darkhavens in front of me even as my mind wants me to check to make sure the door to Kalix's room remains shut, hiding away the fugitive that is Regis.

"It's fine," I tell them. "I'll be okay." I hope the words aren't a lie.

Dauphine glances my way, and for the first time, I catch a hint of regret and sympathy in her attention. I close my eyes and breathe deeply through my nose and mouth. When I reopen my eyes, I fix them on Ruen. If anyone can read the request in my eyes, it's him. Dark sea storm eyes meet mine and he nods as I step back towards the stairs that will lead me down the tower and outside. No matter what happens, at least, I know that Regis will be safe.

Dauphine wastes no more time, now that someone is holding Kalix back, hurrying me towards the exit. It's almost as if she hopes the sooner we're out of sight, the sooner Kalix Darkhaven will forget both of our existences. Though I know there's no chance of that, I let her believe so and follow her silently and amiably as she leads me out of the North Tower, across various courtyards, and through darkened corridors until we're back in the same building I'd met the God Council before.

This time, though, she doesn't take me immediately to the main chambers. I spot the man—the God—waiting at the end of the hall and immediately feel tension spread throughout my shoulders. My heart thuds a rapid beat inside my chest as sweat coats my palms. Anger. Red hot and wicked spears through me. No matter that I shouldn't care. No matter that the Darkhavens are no more trustworthy now than the Underworld—especially if Regis' last note is any indication—I still hate the sight of Azai, God of Strength.

Head tilted down, he stares at me with both arms crossed over his massive warrior-like chest. I hate him even more because of the small notes of his features that remind me of his sons. The liquid gold of his eyes makes me think of Theos. The sharp jaw that reminds me of Kalix. The stoic expression that is all Ruen.

I despise them all.

"My Lord." Dauphine stops before him and bows deep.

Though I know I should probably offer the same respect—as anyone else would—I don't. I meet Azai's gaze with a glare and wait for his response. He arches one dark brow but otherwise doesn't say anything as he turns to the side and gestures for me to enter the smaller door that is far less gilded than their original chambers. The slab of wood is plain and without any ornamentation. For some reason, that makes me dread entering the room beyond all the more.

Pushed along by Azai's attention on my back, though, I don't hesitate as I reach out and twist the knob, letting the door swing inward to reveal a smaller but no less opulent room full of familiar bodies. My throat goes dry when I spy Danai and Makeda standing side by side as they had during the mock battles in the arena. Unable to help myself, I reach out for a mind I know almost as well as my own. Ara responds without pause, and sensing my anxiety, floods my head with her own emotions. Though not as complex as mortal or Divine emotions, the sensation of her hope and care eases the strain in my shoulders and mind as I step into the room and approach the Gods.

"Hello, Kiera."

I dip my head as Caedmon appears around the corner of a large pillar. The room itself, unlike the door leading inside, is a beautifully decorated parlor of sorts. The only thing that makes it unparlor-like is the large open stone chalice that takes up a large portion of the center of the room around which are six pillars.

"Lord Caedmon," I acknowledge the God of Prophecy with a dry throat and Ara still sending me her emotions to calm my own.

Discreetly, I wipe my palms against my trousers. So fast had Dauphine come—a fact that Kalix had seemed surprised by considering he'd given us a good hour to prepare for her arrival—I hadn't even gotten the chance to change into a gown or something else that they would have likely preferred or expected. No one says anything, though, about my inappropriate attire as I approach the center of the small room.

"Do you know why you're here, child?" Danai asks, the first, other than Caedmon, to speak.

Behind me, I sense rather than see Azai enter the room. His presence is an undesired weight on my shoulders, but I ignore it and look to the God Queen as I respond.

"It's not the Spring Equinox yet, Your Majesty," I say, dipping my head in deference to her in a way I didn't for Azai.

The door at my back shuts with a harsh thump and I repress the urge to smile, knowing that respecting one God over another has certainly annoyed him. Good. If I do decide to kill the God King, then I also plan to slaughter Azai along with him. After what he's done to his sons, to Ruen, he cannot be allowed to live. My hands are stained with the blood of my kills. One more death on my conscience won't affect my already damned soul.

"You are correct," Danai says. "However, we have been watching you as of late and have determined that knowing your bloodline sooner is of immediate importance." Her gaze glints with an emotion I cannot name, but it makes me uneasy.

Despite my dread, I lift my head slightly as Azai moves around and stops just inside my periphery. He—along with the other Gods—takes up against one of the six pillars that circle the room. Overhead, a glass skylight illuminates the room in foggy morning light.

"Do you know what this is?" Makeda is the next to speak, gesturing to the stone chalice at the center with her long, shapely arm.

I shake my head. "I don't."

"This chalice is formed from the stone of Ortus Island," Tryphone's low baritone slides over my flesh like a thunderous rage. Every nerve ending in my body goes taut with expected pain. Yet, when nothing happens—neither pain nor pleasure—my muscles do not ease. "Ortus is the symbol of our benevolence in this world," he continues.

Benevolence? I bite down on my lip to keep from responding even as bile and disgust fill my mouth, coating my tongue with the too-thick sense of deceit.

Liar. I want to scream the fact in his face, but I don't. I simply nod and watch him, waiting for him to continue.

Tryphone doesn't disappoint. "The Island of Ortus is made up of the darkest stone in existence," he states, those wickedly intelligent eyes of his searing into me like a brand to my very existence. A shiver moves through me. Ara twitters, the sound of her little fangs clacking together in fear and unease slipping into my mind before I can cut it off and remove the connection. I can't fault my spider Queen for her caution. I, too, wish I were anywhere but before the God King.

My body is tense, poised as if ready to either take flight or fight for my survival. His eyes glint with knowing, but still, he keeps talking as if the fact that I'm set on edge by his voice is of no consequence to him. It's as if it matters not that I could turn and try to flee from him at any second ... as if the thought of my escape is not one he's even considered.

Fear is a tasteless rot coating the inside of my mouth.

"Brimstone is where Divinity was formed in this world," Tryphone says. "And it is from the brimstone that we may conjure the truth of your blood."

I swallow roughly before speaking. "Without the Spring Equinox?" I clarify.

"Yes." Tryphone offers no more explanation as his wide hand moves towards the chalice. "Step forward. *Now*."

My body moves before I've made a conscious decision, my legs jolting into action at the order from the God King. That, more than anything, makes the fear bubbling inside me turn into something molten and festering. His words are cloaked in a Divine power that is a pressure on my spine, pinning me to the action he demands from me and refusing to lessen its grip.

Legs trembling, I step onto the small dais holding the chalice. The closer I draw, the more I see the shards of dark chipped brimstone embedded into the rock of the chalice. The inky black of the stone glints beneath the low light. My breaths draw in short unsteady pants. I stop about a foot away from the open stone chalice and look down into what appears to be a dark watery liquid sitting in the bottom of the basin. There are dips around the sides of the bowl-like opening, and images flash through my mind of men and women being bent over those indentions with their necks facing downward. Gods—female and male alike—each step up to the chalice and silver glints as throats are slit and blood spills forth to fill the basin, frothing as it collides into a mixture of death. Vomit threatens to come up my throat. I swallow it back before lifting my gaze to the man standing directly across from me.

Caedmon's eyes are fathomlessly dark. Empty. Devoid of life. A beat passes and then he blinks and a light enters those ebony eyes of his again. His chin dips and the fear fades ever so slightly.

It's okay, I tell myself. *I'm alright. I'm still here. I'm not dead. I am not bleeding. It was simply a hallucination. Not real.*

Yet, as I turn my attention back to the inside of the chalice, I can't help but wonder where that strange scene came from. Why it had felt so real in the first place?

This is not how I expected this to happen, I have to admit to myself. When the God Council had first discussed uncovering my God blood heritage I had assumed it would be before many others, in a public ceremony. The privacy of this room and the press of the six God Council members' individual presences surrounding me have me wondering if it wasn't all a lie to begin with.

I am not sure if I'm ready to know the truth, but as Tryphone leaves his pillar and steps forward, producing a long wicked looking brimstone blade from nowhere—the dagger invisible one moment and then in his hand the next—my heart pounds with the realization that I have no control here.

Whatever the Gods find in my blood, it will decide my fate … be it life or death.

CHAPTER 36
KIERA

"Hold your hand over the chalice." Tryphone's words are a living nightmare. Not because he brandishes that brimstone dagger with such comfort that there can be no question of how adept he is at using it, but because I do as he says.

Just as my legs had moved without my consent, so, too, does my arm. How can I ever possibly hope to kill this man—this powerful deity—if the mere sound of his voice hypnotizes my body into answering his commands without hesitation?

My arm lifts over the opening of the basin and Tryphone reaches forward, taking my wrist into his grip and turning it over so that my forearm is stretched across the opening. My stomach presses into the edge of the stone and once more images of blood-soaked bodies and dead eyes assail me. I bite down on my tongue until I taste rust and raw meat. My mind is a safe place. It always has been. My haven when I was tied to chairs in the headquarters of the Underworld and beaten for no other reason than the mere fact I needed to understand pain in order to deal in it.

There's something different about pain when you acknowledge that there's no real logic behind it. The mind fights to understand, to delve into a way to avoid it in the future and when it becomes clear that there is no reason—no meaning behind the darkest of agonies—it fractures.

Blood floods over my tongue as Tryphone turns the brimstone dagger downward and slices across my wrist. The sharp discomfort of the injury has me gasping aloud, but my arm doesn't jerk back as it should. It's held suspended by the Divine ability of the God King standing before me. My breathing comes in ragged pants as sweat beads pop up along my brow and then slide toward my temples. An unfamiliar illness takes root in my stomach as I watch my own blood drip ruby red as it slides over pale flesh, into the stone bowl between the God King and me.

Pain burns against the inside of my throat with each rasping breath I take. I can't get enough air—as if it's all suddenly escaped the small room, sucked out by some unseen force. Yet, I'm the only one left with the inability and everyone else continues on—watching this ceremony with cold gazes that speak nothing of the curiosity I know they're feeling.

Who am I? What am I? Who is my God parent?

I can't deny that I want to know, that the craving to understand the reason for my birth is a hot iron in my core. Muscles jump up and down the arm I have stretched out over the brimstone embedded chalice that sits front and center. The eyes of the Gods are on me and though Caedmon's presence is a minor safety net, I feel utterly alone in this room.

Caedmon may be kind, but he, too, is a God. A liar. A deceiver.

This blood of mine—whether it be the blood of a God or a monster—will not define me, I decide. I am still Kiera.

Assassin of the Underworld. Daughter of a Mortal God who died protecting his only child. I am nothing if not resilient even in the face of the darkest of beings.

Fighting against the instinctive need to protect myself and keep my gaze away from the God King's, I lift my head. Inch by painstaking inch, the veins in my neck straining as I battle against my primordial inclination to bow before a stronger power, I raise my gaze to meet Tryphone's.

His shock is a violent reward. My lips twitch as I set my eyes on his and stare, daring him to castigate me for the action. He doesn't. Instead, he tilts his head to the side as if examining a creature he's never seen before. Then he brings the blade down a second time, searing across my flesh in a fast motion that leaves me gasping, yet again, for air that's not there.

More blood spills into the chalice.

No one speaks.

Taboo. Taboo. Taboo. My head screams the word over and over again. Is this it? Is this what Caedmon tried to warn me about? I try to look at him, but my body is not my own. Was it ever truly?

A third strike, so fast that I don't see it coming, leaves me gasping for breath. Then, there are finally three straight lines cut across my forearm and wrist where blood bubbles up and spills to collect at the bottom of the chalice. Tryphone squeezes either side of my wrist as if urging the blood to flow faster before my natural healing takes effect and closes the otherwise clean cuts. They won't heal as fast though. The brimstone made sure of it. I can only imagine that the harsh grip is little more than a minor punishment for daring to look him in the eye.

"Danai." It takes me a moment to realize that Tryphone is speaking again. Our gazes are so locked that I have to pour nearly all of my energy into holding his stare without breaking.

The God Queen steps forward at her name and ascends to the stand next to the God King at the chalice. "Begin the ceremony," he orders.

Danai glances from him to me before she dips her head in acknowledgment of his order. My arm is throbbing as more blood pours out—more, I think, than should be possible from three single cuts.

Soft, with a voice that holds a thousand years of experience and more lives than I can bear to count, Danai begins to speak. The words that spill forth from between her lips are of a language I don't recognize, one that is too old for my young mind to comprehend. As she speaks, I feel my skin begin to heat.

Her eyes are on mine, the flames of her emotions still swirling within them. *Hold on, my child* ... I blink, unsure if that was her voice I heard. It can't be. Her lips are parted, her mouth moving as she chants whatever Divine spell is creating this hailstorm of fire in my veins.

Reaching forward with my free hand, I grip the edge of the chalice as fire blazes a path over the wounds Tryphone inflicted. Gritting my teeth against the agonizing pain, I step back into my head—into that place I devised years ago under Ophelia's tutelage.

It doesn't hurt, I tell myself. *It doesn't hurt. It doesn't hurt.*

Tell a child a lie enough times, they'll start to believe it until the lie is more fact than any truth.

Another body moves up to the chalice. I cut my eyes away from Tryphone to see Makeda. Her smooth earthy skin is like a beacon for my stinging eyes as I fight against the urge to scream. At her side, Gygaea appears. Her long dark hair is pulled away from the perfect features of a face that is both ultimately feminine and jaggedly androgyne.

Shadows are all around me. Invading my nostrils, my eyes, my very being.

Caedmon appears. Azai. They surround me. All of the Gods at the lip of the brimstone basin. Their voices collide with Danai's as they speak that strange tongue that sounds all at once like a million screams of agony and a million cries of bliss. My head spins. Around and around, the room spins until I see nothing and no one anymore. The forms of the Gods become nothing but a blur. My arm is released and the smell of more blood—fresh blood that isn't my own—hits my senses.

I blink and the room appears once more, all six Gods holding their own arms over the basin with thin lines of blood welling from their own wrists and slipping over to mix with my own.

Caedmon. Gygaea. Azai. Tryphone. Danai. Makeda.

The blood of the Gods falls into the collection of my own, swirling into the dark liquid with the force of six powerful Divine Beings. Rot. Decay. Death. It coalesces into one forbidden combination that should never be.

I'm going to throw up. The thought is a sudden knowing in my mind and yet, when I gag, nothing comes forth.

My arms are shaking as I hold myself up with nothing short of sheer will. My legs tremble so harshly that I know if I release my grip on the chalice, I'll fall. Six pairs of eyes gaze down into the frothing mixture at the bottom of the basin. The blood congeals and bubbles as if it's being heated up from within. No, not from the chalice itself, but from the ancient chant they partook in.

I wait and I pray—for quite possibly the first time in my life, I pray to a deity I'm not sure even exists. I pray to the

Goddess that gave birth to me and I hope she can hear me. Because something tells me that if this works—that if this ceremony succeeds—it will mean nothing good for anyone.

Seconds pass. Then minutes. Time stretches and shortens in such a way that I know I must be under some sort of spell. There's no possible way that hours can become mere breaths. Yet, it does.

"Well?" Azai is the first to speak, his tone full of frustration. "Where is the answer?"

Tryphone doesn't respond. I'm still trying not to vomit my guts up onto the stone floor beneath my feet. My insides have liquefied. My eyes lock onto the concoction of blood in the chalice. A bubble pops and steam rises, smelling of something so old that it can only be described as decay.

The crimson color of the blend of bloods has turned it black. There is nothing but corrosion beyond, a darkness so dense that it threatens the existence of light itself. I am mesmerized by it, drawn into that darkness because of its familiarity. As if it holds a secret that only I know. Unperturbed by the presence of the inky black of the blood blend, I reach for it. No one says a word as I dip the fingers of my wounded arm into the mixture. The blood sticks to my skin and despite the bubbling of its liquid, it isn't hot to the touch.

Yes, there is something in this blood that is mine. *Is it because my blood was added or is it because there's something else calling to me?*

All too suddenly, a hand grabs my arm and yanks me back, dragging me away from the chalice. Without looking to see who it is, I start to struggle. It's not the action of an assassin, but of a deeply rooted animal desire to touch that which belongs to me.

Mine! The blood screams to me. *You are mine and I am yours.*

"Tryphone." I recognize the voice that rumbles against my back as the man holding me yanks me yet another step away from the basin. "Did the ceremony work?"

No! My lips part, but nothing comes free. The tears I worked so hard to hold back before rush back to the surface.

"No." The remark is from Danai, not Tryphone.

There is nothing but silence save for the harsh beastly noises that rise up from my throat. I have to touch it again. I was almost there. The secret was on the fringes of my mind, the truth I've spent twenty years not knowing right *there*.

"You said it would work," Tryphone says, his voice the only thing that makes me stop fighting to get to the chalice.

"With all six of us here, it should have," Danai replies.

"Perhaps your research was flawed," Azai comments.

A sound of feminine fury and then ... nothing. I sag against the chest of the man at my back. Caedmon's scent, soft and clean, invades my nostrils, calming me further. A few more moments pass and each breath I draw away from the chalice brings me closer and closer to my natural being. I shake my head, trying to chase away the last lingering effects of the spell that had woven a dark, ancient power over my mind and body.

"What does this mean then?" Caedmon is the one to ask the question that I'm sure we're all thinking.

If this ceremony didn't work ... then what are they to do next?

"Perhaps she is not of Divine blood," Gygaea's suggests, but almost as soon as the words are out of her mouth, Makeda is dissuading the rest of the Gods of that notion.

"We've kept our eyes on the girl since her presence was brought to our attention. Danai and I have both witnessed the evidence of her Divinity. There is no question that she is of Divine blood."

"Then why didn't the ceremony work?" Azai demands.

Caedmon's hands are on my upper arms, keeping me stable as I stand amid six powerful beings. Shaking him off as I slide to the side and away from the haven of his arms—a safety I can't allow myself to rely on—I eye the other beings in the room with narrow-eyed scrutiny. I knew there was a reason Danai and Makeda had borne witness to the mock battles during training, but I hadn't known it was because they wanted to be sure that I was a Mortal God. I glance at Caedmon out of the corner of my eyes. Perhaps his status amongst the God Council isn't as powerful as I'd once been led to believe. Not if the others weren't quite convinced of his support of my heritage.

Wrapping my arms around myself, I remain silent as the Gods argue over whether or not the ceremony's failure is a fault of my blood or the fact that it was never meant to work in the first place.

"*Enough!*" My whole body jolts at the dark rumble of Tryphone's command.

All other sound ceases—even the light tap of wind against the glass above our heads goes quiet as if the world itself cannot help but bow to his orders.

"We will keep to the original plan," Tryphone's words hold no room for argument. "The Spring Equinox is but a mere two weeks away." Cold eyes that hold the power of storm and lightning fall upon where I stand. Just like before, I react by fighting my own instincts to look away, to cow to the man who is far stronger than I will ever be. I meet the God King's gaze.

His lips twitch as if amused, this time, rather than surprised by my show of silent defiance. I can sense the God Queen's attention on my face, but I don't turn to face her. To pay attention to another predator when one that is far more dangerous has me in its thrall would be the height of both arrogance and stupidity, and I am neither arrogant nor stupid.

"Then the Spring Equinox ceremony will continue forward," Caedmon speaks, interrupting the disquieting force of wills between the God King and me with his words. "Perhaps this is for the best."

Tryphone jerks his chin in agreement. Massive as he is, the God King looks once at his Queen before turning and striding from the room, and the moment he is gone, I feel as if the entire space has opened up. The air is easier to breathe and my insides don't feel quite as riotous. I don't move a muscle nor do I speak as Gygaea is the next to leave with Makeda quietly following after, offering me a passing glance as she exits the room. Azai scowls down at me and thunders past in a fury of stomps. I resist the urge to roll my eyes. The God of Strength is nothing if not a petulant child.

Nails score the sides of my arms as the last remaining male God moves past me, towards Danai. "I know you wished to uncover the secrets of her blood, my Queen," Caedmon says. "I am sorry that the ceremony was a failure."

Directing my attention past Caedmon's shoulder, I meet the golden ringed gaze of the God Queen, her focus centered on me in such a way that it feels penetrating to my very soul. Her eyes hold untold stories, and though they seem benevolent, I have to remind myself of Caedmon's words. The Gods are all liars and she is no different. Even if she is merely complicit in the oppression of the people of Anatol, the fact remains—Danai, the God Queen, has built her throne on the blood and bones of mortals. I squeeze my arms tighter to my chest.

"Yes," she murmurs almost absently, as if it takes a moment longer than it should for Caedmon's words to truly take root in her mind. "You may be right, Caedmon." Her eyes never leave my face. "I shall discuss the Spring Equinox ceremony with Tryphone. I have the sense that this child holds a secret we all must know. He is right. Even if we must wait, two weeks is but a blink of time to us."

Caedmon is good. Though I find him difficult to trust completely, I must acknowledge the fact that he is nothing if not unbending. Not by the flicker of an eyelash does he reveal what he knows. As the God of Prophecy, and what little he's revealed to me, he already knows the secrets of my blood.

"Yes, my Queen." Clasping a gentle hand on the God Queen's arm, Caedmon bows his head in respect and silent agreement to her words. Then, without further hesitation, he releases her and turns to me. "Come," he orders, striding past me towards the door. "I shall return you to your quarters."

CHAPTER 37
KIERA

"Caedmon!" I call after the God of Prophecy even as I force my protesting legs to move faster.

In the time that has elapsed inside the God Council's chambers, the light sprinkle of morning rain has ceased. The dark figure that strides before me grows more and more distant as I struggle to catch up with him, my legs somehow not moving with the natural grace and expediency that I'm used to.

"Hey!" The second I get close to the tall ebony skinned man who has both frustrated and helped me over the last few months, I reach out and snag the edge of his fine-silk coat. He draws to a stop and glances back at me with those all-seeing eyes of his

"What the fuck was that?" I demand, shockingly breathless. My head swims and my fingers tremble as I reach up and shove back a massive lock of silver hair that falls into my face.

Caedmon doesn't speak. He merely reaches back and grabs my arm and starts walking again, this time dragging me with him. I stumble and nearly go down on my knees.

"What's wrong with me?" I ask this time, unable to pull

myself from his grasp. I haven't felt this weak since my first sparring session in the Underworld at ten years old. It's as if a decade of muscles and careful training has evaporated from my body, leaving behind a fragile collection of bones beneath my skin.

"It is the blood loss," Caedmon says, his tone curt as he directs me down an outside pathway that passes through the very courtyard in which I met him for the first time.

I glance over the fountain where I found my Spider Queen briefly before I return my attention to the God at my side. "It's not just that," I insist. "What was that ceremony? That wasn't the"—I lower my tone—"the taboo?"

Caedmon's head rears back. "*No.*" The fabric of his clothing twists slightly with the abrupt action. I glance down to see that his free hand is clenched so tightly that the normally dark skin over his knuckles has turned an ashen gray. "The ceremony was simply an attempt to discover your bloodline."

"Why didn't it work then?" I ask. "Did you do something to disrupt it?"

Caedmon unclenches his hands and sighs. "No, I didn't do anything to disrupt it. Doing so wouldn't help. The God Council is determined to find your God parent and they will."

"You said you know who she is," I reply. "Is it dangerous if they find out?"

His expression turns contemplative. Ask the right questions, he'd said. Is that one? The hope in my chest is stomped out when, a moment later, Caedmon shakes his head. "That is a question I cannot answer, Kiera."

"Cannot or will not?" I bite back, anger rising.

Again, I'm left with no answer. I stop walking and when Caedmon nearly pulls me straight off my feet without any effort, I yank back, digging my heels into the dirt beneath my boots. Left with little other choice than to either carry my ass or stop, Caedmon finally halts. His hand falls away and I cross my arms over my chest to glare at him when he turns to face me.

"Enough," I state. "You need to start giving me answers."

Gold trinkets dangling from one pierced earlobe glitter in the soft sunlight that now peeks out from behind gray clouds as he shakes his head. "I've already told you why that's not possible, Kiera," Caedmon replies. "The book—"

"—is only offering me more problems," I snap, cutting him off, "not solutions!"

His skin is smooth, no crease between his brows and no lines bracketing his lips as they might a mortal. Of all the Gods, Caedmon is the one that appears most like a statue. Flesh the color of uncut brimstone. Eyes of deepest chestnut and unlit night sky. Sometimes, I'm not sure if his darkness is only external or if somewhere beneath the facade of Divinity, he's just as evil as the rest of them.

I don't want to believe it. Caedmon, after all, is the only God, so far, that has offered me even a modicum of truth. Unfortunately, it's not enough.

"If you want..." I drift off, my eyes turning to scan the area —up the face of the stone walls of the buildings that surround us and towards any exit to see if there are any unwanted ears. When next I begin to speak, I lower my voice so much so that not even a potential familiar unseen in the grass or crevices of stone could hear. "You need to offer me some sort of explanation, Caedmon." I let him see the conviction in my gaze. I step closer until I can scent the lemon and bookish smell of his office. "I received a warning," I tell him, "that the Underworld was breached." I leave out the mention of Regis and how I managed to find him, waiting, instead, for

Caedmon's response. "If you want me to kill the God King then—"

"I do not *want* you to kill anyone," Caedmon finally says after a brief respite where his eyes bore into mine with no amount of emotion that I can decipher, "but this mission is what you were born for, Kiera. Of that, have no doubt. Regardless of what you desire or think you're capable of—what you are fated to do cannot be changed."

My own brows crease as I frown. "What—"

Caedmon turns away from me. "I assume you can get back to the North Tower from here on your own," he states as he begins to walk away.

My lips part in shock. "Wait!" I yell for Caedmon to stop, but as I drop my arms and try to race after him, black dots dance in front of my vision and I barely make it ten feet before I have to stop and hunch over, bracing myself on my knees for breath.

When I next lift my head, he's gone. A bell chimes somewhere in the Academy, the sound ringing across the grounds with an air of finality that sounds more like a death knell than the start of a day of classes.

For all we know, each ring of that damned bell is exactly that. The signal that we're all drawing closer and closer to our ends ... and all of it at the hands of the Gods we're meant to serve.

THE FAILURE OF THE GODS' ceremony accompanied by the fact that Caedmon still remains an enigmatic figure that I'm not entirely sure if I can trust swirls in my head as I slowly make my way back to the North Tower. The second I enter the main room, Ruen and Kalix are there, blocking me from going any further.

"What happened?" Ruen demands.

"Why do you look like that?" Kalix frowns and reaches for me, sweeping me off my feet and into strong hands that I've seen do deadly things like ripping another Mortal God's head from her shoulders. I should not feel as safe as I do right now and I remind myself that up until a few weeks ago, the Darkhavens were potential targets for my mission.

A mission that no longer exists in the original sense. After all, the brimstone chip keeping me bound in blood to Ophelia's Underworld Guild is gone. The client I was meant to serve is none other than the God of Prophecy himself.

Kalix carries me over to the same lounge that Regis had occupied and as he sets me down, I straighten. "How is Regis?" I ask, casting a look to first Ruen and then Theos, as he enters the room through the doorway leading to his private chambers.

Theos doesn't say a word to me as he moves to take a seat near the fireplace, hooking one ankle over a knee and crossing his arms over his chest. I grit my teeth. Now doesn't really seem like the time for him to be throwing such a childish tantrum about what happened between us this morning, but I return my attention to Ruen as I wait for an answer to my query.

"He's still in Kalix's room," Ruen says. "His condition is unchanged. Now, tell us what happened."

Before I can answer his demands, Kalix reaches down and plucks my arm up from my lap. "*What. Issss. Thissss.*" All else in the room goes still at those three cold dangerous words.

Kalix's upper lip pulls back and his tone takes on a distinctly serpentine edge as the s's elongate through fangs that press down from his gums. The three lines marking the cuts Tryphone had made are revealed as the sleeve of my tunic is pressed up towards my elbow.

Theos stands abruptly, golden lightning sparking at his fingertips.

"I'm fine." I jerk my arm, but Kalix's fingers contract, holding me in place.

"Kiera?" Ruen's voice draws nearer and I turn my head, blinking when I realize I've suddenly been surrounded by three increasingly angry Mortal Gods.

Ruen's normally purple and blue eyes are a stark crimson as he gazes down at the thin lines cut into my forearm and the dried blood crusted around the now closed wounds that should be sealed by now thanks to my Divine blood. That is ... they would have been had Tryphone not used a brimstone blade.

Exhaustion thrums a steady beat behind my eye sockets. "Please don't." My plea is a hushed whisper, one that is ignored when Ruen manages to pull his eyes from my skin to meet my gaze.

"Explain." Just like that, I know, the Darkhavens will accept nothing less than an exact retelling of every single thing that occurred between when I left their quarters to when I returned.

I sink deeper into the lounge and close my eyes. Giving up on pulling my arm from Kalix's grasp, I'm only half startled when I feel him release me. A second later, I'm being shifted forward as a hard male body climbs in behind me and pulls me against a wide warm chest.

Don't get used to this, I order myself. *This will not last. It's not real.*

Despite that internal warning and my dry throat, I spend the rest of the morning explaining in detail everything that happened between the God Council and me. I tell the Darkhavens of the strange room, the brimstone chalice, and the failed ceremony.

Halfway through, both Theos and Ruen take seats on the low-rise table before the lounge, their legs bumping against mine. When I get to the part of Tryphone cutting my wrist as part of the ceremony to combine my blood with that of the God Council, Kalix's muscles twitch and he moves to get up.

I press a palm flat against his chest and glare. "If you move, I will not tell you the rest," I tell him.

He freezes, eyes narrowing on my face as if assessing whether or not I will follow through with my threat. I don't know if he believes me or not, but he doesn't move again and that's enough for me to continue. Several minutes later as I finish explaining the confrontation with Caedmon in the courtyard, Ruen shifts forward and takes my arm in his grip. I let him and watch as he turns my wrist over, his thumb coming up to stroke along the three markings that the God King had made. My head tilts to the side. Ruen's touch is the barest whisper of flesh on flesh and when he lifts his head once more, his eyes have returned to midnight.

"Caedmon is no longer to be trusted." No one argues against the words he speaks. Not me. Not Kalix. Not Theos.

Kalix steals my arm away from Ruen, but unlike his older brother, he isn't gentle with the injury. He presses the edge of one nail into the corner of one scab, peeling it back as fresh blood wells. A hiss escapes me as he lifts the lesion to his mouth. Forest green eyes with slitted pupils hover on my face as he presses his lips to the wound. My stomach churns and then tightens for a reason I'm not wholly aware of as his tongue laps at the blood, taking it into himself.

"They will not take you again." Kalix breathes the words against my bloodied skin.

Nothing, I mentally insist. *It means nothing.*

Even I know, though, that I, too, am lying. To them and to myself.

Because the one thing I didn't tell them about was the way Danai had looked at me. The piercing quality of her gaze that I feel knows far more than she's said. The God Queen has suspicions about who I am and I am more than a little fearful of what that must mean.

CHAPTER 38
KIERA

It is by the mercy of some unnamed power—certainly not the fucking Gods—that all returns to normal over the next two days. Everywhere I go, I can sense eyes upon my back, ever present, ever watchful. It's as if the Gods do not fully believe that their ceremony failed, as if my heritage will reveal itself in the minute details of how I eat my damned breakfast or read books within the Academy's library.

The Darkhavens—even Theos, despite his coldness towards me—refuse to allow me a reprieve from their presence. At least one of them follows me wherever I go as if the Gods will appear out of thin air at any moment and drag me back to their chambers for yet another ceremony that will see me bled for information.

It's to no one's shock that out of all of them, Kalix is the most suffocating.

"How much longer?"

I roll my eyes at that question—the tenth repetition in the last hour—and flip a dusty page to scroll a finger down the list of names of earlier transferred students.

"Until I'm done," I say, giving Kalix the same answer that I'd given him the last nine times.

A low, reverberating groan echoes into the rafters of the Academy's library stacks. I flip another page, ignoring Kalix's pleading expression. Another hour passes and still, I'm nowhere closer to an answer than I was when I started. My vision begins to blur and I blink dry eyes, looking up as booted footsteps sound around the corner. Ruen appears a moment later, eliciting a whisper of relief from Kalix who slips out of the chair to round the table I've been sitting at for the last several hours. He doesn't wait for me to admit defeat. Kalix simply snatches the volume I'd been using and snaps it shut, shoving it to the end of the table before bodily lifting me from my chair.

"I wasn't done with that." I deadpan, annoyance a bite in my tone.

Kalix grins my way and encircles me with one arm. "Too bad." He bends and sets teeth to my earlobe, making my whole body tense in surprise.

"You're in public, Kalix," Ruen growls. "Behave."

"Semi-public," Kalix replies lightly before biting me again, this time on the side of my neck.

I reach up and shove a hand against his face. "You heard him," I say, trying not to let it show just how unsteady his attentions have made me. "Listen to Ruen."

His arm retracts. I move towards Ruen and arch a brow. "Is there a reason why you came to get us?" I ask.

Ruen glances back, and instead of nodding or answering me, his hands grip my hips over the blue-gray fabric of the dress that had been left out for me that morning—a silent punishment, I assume, from Theos. He pushes me back, directing me into the darker parts of the library, away from the caretakers and librarians.

"Kalix, keep watch," Ruen orders, and just like that the two of us have our own personal bodyguard. Kalix moves to the end of one stack and leans against the curved frame of the shelves in a deceptively casual stance. I don't mistake the movement, though, for one of true indifference despite the expression of ease and boredom he dons.

Ruen has information and now is the time to find out if all of this sleuthing and research has paid off. Once Ruen has directed me into the shadows of the library, far closer to the statues that line the walls at the furthest end from the entrance, I stop him with a hand against his chest.

"Tell me," I say, looking up into eyes the darkest of indigo colors swirling with hints of bruised skies.

"All of the students on your list were first taken to Dolos before they were transferred," Ruen announces. "But not the latest ones—not Malachi."

I tip my head back further. "Who was Malachi taken to?"

Ruen's expression darkens. "Tryphone."

Lifting a hand, I bite down on my thumbnail and consider the implications of what that could mean. At first, students were taken to the Dean of the Riviere Academy—the most powerful God in the vicinity. Then, when the God Council arrived, Malachi was taken to the God King.

"Were any of them seen after they were transferred?" I ask.

Ruen shakes his head. "After they visited the Gods, they were transferred immediately," Ruen says, his hands squeezing tighter against my side, making me realize he still hasn't released me. "They weren't even permitted to pack up their belongings."

I shift on my feet, the skirts of the damned dress Theos left in place of my trousers swishing uncomfortably around my legs. After so many years in tighter breeches, the feeling of nothing but air on my legs leaves me feeling exposed, and Ruen isn't helping.

Focus, I order myself.

"How did you figure this out?"

One of Ruen's thumbs begins to stroke my side as he speaks and it takes considerable effort to pay attention as every nerve ending in my body seems to want to move towards that one spot.

"Your little Terra friend," Ruen answers.

I blink. "My Terra friend?" Who could he—"Niall?"

Ruen's lips twitch and if I didn't know better, I would swear he's amused. "Yes." He nods. "It appears your mortal friend is far more apt at spy work than I would have originally expected. He's very unassuming."

Realization slams into me with such ferocity I almost slap myself in the face for forgetting one of the most important lessons of the Underworld.

There are thousands of invisible people in this world, Kiera. Ophelia's words echo in the back of my mind. *Maids. Butlers. Cooks. Barkeeps. Humans, all of them. You'll never catch a God doing menial labor, but what they often forget is that those servants they love to order around are always there for every moment of their long lives. They see even if they don't speak and those who see things know more than the Gods would ever believe.*

I could absolutely curse myself for being so shortsighted, but even as I think that, worry edges into my mind. I lift suspicious eyes to Ruen's face.

"You didn't threaten him to get him to do anything, did you?"

Ruen's face grows closer as he bends, dipping his head

towards me. "I know you care for the Terra," he says, breath warm against my cheeks. "I did not threaten the boy."

"He's—" I start to disagree with Ruen calling Niall a 'boy' when I know for a fact that he's at least my age if not slightly older.

"You've shared your body with me, but you still don't trust me not to hurt a mortal?" Ruen asks.

I shut my mouth. All amusement dies in my throat. "So, we're talking about that," I say, feeling as if the words are being ripped over shards of glass as they move up my throat.

He tilts his head to the side, keeping his gaze pinned to mine. "We haven't had a moment to discuss it." When I don't say anything, Ruen releases my hips and straightens. "Do you have nothing to say?"

"You didn't ask a question," I remind him, taking a step back.

"I hope you're not going to tell me the same thing you told Theos—that it meant nothing."

I flinch. "He told you?"

Ruen arches one fine cut brow. "My brothers and I rarely keep secrets from each other and certainly not when we've all bedded the same woman."

Instinct has me crossing my arms over my chest as if that will, somehow, protect me from this conversation. "I didn't mean to hurt him," I admit.

"Clearly." Ruen's tone suggests more than a little sarcasm.

I scowl. "We're not children, Ruen." My voice comes out strong despite my discomfort. "Sex is sex. I should think you would agree with me that we have more important matters to focus on right now than a damned *relationship*."

"Just tell me something," Ruen says, lifting a hand to a nearby statue and stroking the pad of a finger down the side of the icon's arm. It comes away coated in dust. "Have you considered the consequences of sleeping with the three of us?"

Considered it? I've damned myself by falling into bed with them and I know it. Now, I'm just postponing the inevitable for as long as I can.

Dropping my arms, I turn away. "This is ridic—"

"*Coward.*"

My feet freeze at that one word. I pivot back to face him ... slowly. "Excuse me?"

"You heard me." Ruen rubs the pad of his thumb and dust-covered finger against one another. "I called you a coward and that's what you are."

"You have no fucking idea who I am." Ice touches my voice, frosting over each word.

"Does anyone?" he replies.

"What do you *really* want to ask, Ruen?" My hands curl into fists, nails stabbing at my palms. "Come out and say it."

Ruen's gaze sparks with a dangerous light that reminds me of Kalix. "*You* came to *me,* Kiera," he states. "You demanded I crack open my soul and reveal all of my dirty little secrets, or have you forgotten?"

Heated flesh on flesh. Open mouths. Tongues. Lips. Teeth. Moans swirling in a darkened bedroom lit by the window and smelling of parchment and ink.

No, I haven't forgotten a damn thing.

"Say. It." I bite the words out, angry at feeling so damned vulnerable.

Ruen steps closer. I refuse to move, and when he takes a second and then third step, not stopping until our chests are nearly brushing, my lungs contract to inhale the scent of him as if it needs the added reminder of what being this close to him is like. I don't need to remember—it's already burned into my memory.

"You know as well as I do that all power demands a sacrifice." My eyes lock onto the column of his throat as he speaks. "The four of us have made a deal with a God—one that could betray us as easily as he could save us." *Caedmon.*

My lashes flick upward. "And?" I prompt him.

"Are you so blind that you don't see that Theos is reaching out because he thinks he's found a woman who doesn't give a fuck what or who he is?"

"I'm not."

"Then are you so heartless that you'll turn him away—turn all of us away because you don't want to deal with the idea of a *relationship*." As Ruen speaks, he uses the same tone that I had before when he says the final word.

I lower my arms to my sides, wetting my lips with the tip of my tongue, and inhale a breath before slowly releasing it once more.

"How many Mortal Gods have you watched die in the Academy?" I ask.

Ruen's head goes back. "What does—"

"Answer the question."

His lips part and after a moment, he responds. "Dozens, at least."

"And how many of them did you care for in some fashion?"

The silence that follows is answer enough. I nod. "*That* is why I avoid it," I tell him honestly. "You're right—we are trapped in this deal, for lack of a better word—with Caedmon. He could decide that we're not what he needs to make the future he wants come true. He could betray us to the God Council. He could *kill* us *all*."

"Kiera—"

I hold a hand up, stopping him. "*Vincere aut mori.*"

His eyes darken with confusion. "What—"

"In the old language, it means 'conquer or die,'" I answer his unfinished question. "We have not conquered anything, and death hovers over each of us. It doesn't make me a coward to want to protect myself, Ruen."

"Yes, it does." His argument is swift. "The uncertainty of life means that you should take everything it gives you with both hands, not run from it in fear of getting hurt."

My chest is caving in. I look down and it seems the same. Whole. It's not. "I can't." *I can't.*

Blood-soaked snow. Black cloaked bandits. A house on fire. The old memories cling to the raw inside of my skull, molding into my bones with one understanding.

Everyone can die. Everyone can leave. Trust no one.

Even Regis had taught me that in the Underworld. Regis, who had eventually betrayed me. Regis, who now may die—another loss on my conscience.

When Ruen lifts a hand to me I step out of reach. "I *am* sorry that I hurt Theos," I say. "But I will never be sorry for protecting what's left of my heart."

"I see." Fury lights the fire in Ruen's eyes, turning the storm into a sea of red. "So, you don't wish to be vulnerable then." He nods, and for some reason, I feel my skin heat. "Yes, I see," he repeats, seemingly more to himself than to me. "You're not a coward then, you're just weak."

"I am the furthest thing from weak." The words cut through me like the edge of a sword.

Ruen sets his gaze on me once more. "You're glass," he half whispers as if imparting a secret.

"Don't you dare—"

"What?" He cuts me off. "Treat you like glass? Why not when that's what you are—beautiful, broken glass."

I sneer at him, but his next words stop me from responding. "Glass is fragile until it's shattered, and after that, it becomes sharp. Deadly." My heart beats a steady rhythm in my chest, in my ears. "That is what you are. Shattered. Sharp. Deadly. And ... a pretty little liar."

I turn away from him, unable to see the look in his eyes anymore.

"Thank you for the information," I say, ignoring his words and not deigning to give them a reply. "But I think you should leave Niall out of it now." Even if Ophelia was right and servants make the best spies, I'm tired of watching those around me die.

Ruen doesn't respond, but I've said all I need to, so I turn and leave him behind, sliding back through the stacks until I reach Kalix. When Kalix spots me, he leans away from the bookshelves and follows me to the exit. A figure appears in the doorway as we pass through and I glance up, absently expecting another student. My heart slams against my ribcage as a familiar pair of golden eyes land on first me and then Kalix.

Azai.

Kalix pretends as if he doesn't even notice his father's presence and merely nudges me to keep going. I place one foot in front of the other, not even aware of my direction and it isn't until we're halfway back to the North Tower that I wonder if Ruen ran into their father in the library.

Perhaps it makes me a hypocrite for caring when I just informed him that I wouldn't consider them to protect myself. Then again, hypocrisy is how we met. A Mortal God who hated her own kind, forced to serve them, and now I know the truth—we're all the same in the eyes of the Gods. Bugs to be squashed. Pawns to be used.

CHAPTER 39
KIERA

I return to the North Tower and leave Kalix in the main room as I ascend to his bedroom which has now become Regis' sickroom. Pushing the door inward, I peer at the bed where Regis lies, his face a pale sallow color. I nudge the door further open and enter, striding across the space—past the weapons hung on the walls and the hiss of Kalix's snakes under various pieces of furniture—until I reach the curtains against the massive window on the other side of the room.

Gripping large handfuls of the thick fabric, I snap them outward, revealing the fading afternoon light and letting it spill into the otherwise dreary room. A scaled creature slithers out from beneath a nearby chair, coming cautiously closer until the snake sidles up next to my booted foot beneath my skirts. I arch a brow at the animal before shaking my head and going to the bedside. The quiet wheeze of Regis' breath is accompanied by the short rise and fall of his chest. *At least, he's breathing,* I think. *That's something.*

I tap my hand against the wall, high up where a small crevice creates a space between the headboard of the bed and a crossbow hung sideways from a hook in the stone. A moment later, a familiar set of fuzzy black legs appear and Ara sticks them out to crawl from her little nesting place down to my upraised palm.

"Any changes?" I ask.

The emotions she pushes into me are both good and bad news. No change means he's still alive, but it also means he's still not awake.

I lower my Spider Queen to the nightstand as I lift a pitcher of water and pour it into a small basin. Dipping a cloth into the water, I use the wet fabric to stroke the side of Regis' face, cleaning his skin of fresh sweat.

"You're starting to look like a true Nezeracian," I tell the unconscious man absently. "Only a man of the Hinterlands would have a beard so thick."

Lightly tracing that very beard with the wet cloth, I feel my chest grow tight. I dip the cloth, getting it wet again, before wringing it free of the added water.

"I'm still mad at you," I say. "You fucking betrayed me to Ophelia. I know you'd tell me that we're all hungry in the Underworld—hungry for power, for freedom, for what we're all searching for and hungry dogs are never loyal, but I..." My hand stills over the side of his cheek. "I expected better from you. I expected better from my best friend."

Hot coals burn behind my eyes, threatening to send the emotions I've kept bottled for so long into an explosive eruption. Blinking back the tears, I turn away from Regis and drop the wet rag into the bowl before taking a seat. The conversation with Ruen and being unable to leave the North Tower without someone spying on me has made it nearly impossible to catch any true rest and I'm beginning to fade from the constant vigilance.

I sink further into the cushioned chair at my back, staring

at the familiar face in the bed and hoping against hope that one day soon, he'll wake up. When the dream starts, I don't even realize it because it's not a dream at all, but a memory.

11 years old...

HOT BREATH SEARS *the inside of my lungs as I run. My feet slap the stucco stone pavement as I race after the sandy-haired asshole that is at least several paces in front of me. I grit my teeth and force my legs to go faster, knowing that to call after him and demand that he slow down would only earn me another trip to the dark room.*

Pain, *I can hear Ophelia say,* is only temporary. You cannot expect others to help you, so you must help yourself.

If I were a betting kind of girl, I would bet all of my worldly possessions—which equals the clothes on my back—that she stuck me with the kid from my induction simply because he's a sadistic monster who likes it when I get in trouble.

I lift my head as we near the next alley and realize with mounting horror that we're almost at the end of our training obstacle course. I can't come in last again. I can't.

The back of my neck burns with the effect of the brimstone sitting beneath my flesh. It's an ever-present ache that often leaves me crying into my cot in the middle of the night when the pain becomes too much to bear. One day, I'll be able to ignore it. One day, I won't even notice the constant buzz of the ache that ricochets up the back of my skull to invade my thoughts at all hours of the day or night. One day, I'll be strong.

But even if that day is not today. I will not *come in last again.*

Putting on a burst of energy that forces me to feel the tug of power pulled through the sharp stab at the base of my skull thanks to the brimstone, my feet fly over the stone beneath me and as I round the next corner, I spy the object of my victory. Without stopping to think about my actions, I hang to the side and race right up the half broken wooden slat that is propped against the wall and use it as leverage to leap onto the rooftop of the building to our right.

The loud snapping noise of the wooden slat is my only warning as the too-weak plank gives way, but I'm already airborne. My hands slap the wall, two fingers hooking onto the rooftop shingles. I flinch as I feel a hard tug on one of my nails, but I don't hesitate to swing my body upwards, grappling onto the shingles and using what pathetic little arm strength I have to yank myself the rest of the way up.

When I get there, rolling onto the steaming hot roof and feeling my skin burn when it meets the stone that's been cooking under the sun for the last several hours, I pop back to my feet, shaking off the pain in my hands. Regis is already way ahead of me, but our end goal is in sight and he'll still have to stop to climb towards it.

I take off running again, flying over the shingles and barely noticing when a few break free under my boots, sliding towards the street and alleyways with loud crashing noises. I'm panting, sweating, praying to the Gods—almost there. I'm almost fucking ... there.

A cry of victory leaves my throat when I see Regis finally stop at the end of the next row of abandoned homes that act as part of our training ground today. I'm moving faster than ever before, the wind shoving the sweaty strands of my hair off my face. Relief is an initial sensation that's quickly overcome by a strange sort of rush that I haven't felt in a long time. I recognize what I'm feeling in the next instant—it's triumph. I haven't won one of these training exercises. Not even once since I was thrust into the program after my deal with Ophelia.

The pain of the runs and sparring exercises is nothing

compared to the senseless beatings of the dark room, but at least here, I have a chance. The pain here is my body strengthening itself. The pain in the dark room is my body losing its control while my mind takes over the task of being strong.

Today, though, will be different. Today I will be the victor.

Glee floods my veins. Below, Regis bites out a curse and then takes several paces back from the stone wall that is now his obstacle. He takes a running start, leaping several feet more than any normal kid would be able to and hooks a hand over a jagged, uneven rock that juts out from the wall. As soon as he grasps it, however, it crumbles and he's falling back to the bottom.

My heart beats a faster rhythm as I sprint towards the white flag that sits at the top of that wall. I leap from one house to the next as Regis tries again, taking another running jump and finding another hand hold. The second one holds stronger than the first and I force my body to hurry in response.

Sweat streaks down the sides of my face and my body, coating every inch of visible skin, but I don't care. Regis scales the wall below, moving slow but still with decisive steps.

Don't think about him, *I urge myself, refocusing on the flag that hangs against the pole just ahead. There's no breeze save for the air that slides past me as I run. It makes these exercises all the more difficult and all the hotter.*

One step. Two. Regis' hands closes over the edge of the roof.

No! I mentally scream as I turn the last ten-foot difference between me and the flagpole into nothing as I stop and jump. I soar forward, catching the flag with the tips of my fingers. Just as Regis rolls to his feet upon the shingles, I tear it away and hold it up.

"I won!" I cry, chest heaving. Holy shit. I actually won.

Adrenaline still shooting through my body makes my steps shaky as I take one stumbling step towards Regis and hold up the flag as proof of my victory. "I won," *I state again, brandishing the white piece of cloth.*

His lips twist into a scowl. "You probably used your Divinity," *he sneers.* "Can't take a human without that power of yours, huh?"

I blink at him and slowly lower my arm and my prize with it. "I didn't use my Divinity," *I snap.* "I beat you fair and square."

He rolls his eyes and turns away. "Fucking Mortal God."

Regis doesn't get two feet towards the edge of the roof where I'm sure he's planning to leap back down so that we can be on our way to meet up with our trainer. He doesn't get there.

I throw the flag against his back and it hits him right between his shoulders before thumping to the shingles below our feet. Regis looks back, noting the fallen flag, and then pivots to face me slowly.

"Why are you such a dick?" *I demand, planting my hands on my hips as my chest rises and falls in sharp, stuttering breaths.* "I haven't done anything to you!"

"You're of Divine blood," *he snaps back, nose wrinkling as he toes away the white cloth at his feet as if it's been contaminated now that I've touched it.* "That's reason enough to dislike you."

I jab a finger at him. "You're ... you're..." *I don't know what to say but my fury hasn't abated and all I really want to do is punch him. So, that's what I do. I drop my finger and take a running jump at the jerk who's made my training miserable for the last year.*

I see the widening of surprise in his eyes right before I slam into Regis. The two of us fall to the rooftop in a tangle of limbs and tiny fists. I punch him in the gut, relishing in the soft whoosh of air that escapes him before he flips me over and slams me into the curved shingles.

Kicking and punching, I feel the prickle of angry tears at the corners of my eyes and shove them back. Even if he's a dick, I still remember the words he told me when we met in the induction area of the Underworld—no one will care if I cry anymore, least of all him.

Regis knocks me off himself when I attempt to crawl back on top of him to get a better position for punching. "For fuck's sake!" *he snaps, getting back to his feet.* "Just leave me alone, you little runt."

"We're both in the Underworld," *I huff as I, too, clamber back up on shaking legs, holding my fists up as I wait for him to try and hit me back.* "We have to work together."

He doesn't. Instead, his upper lip curls back in disgust and he shakes his head. "I don't know why Ophelia took you in and I don't care. I don't care about you and I certainly won't help you with any of our future missions." *He points to me and glares.* "I'll give you this one warning, runt. You are nothing to me and it's because of your people that my brother was taken from me. I don't care what Ophelia says. Don't ever expect me to help you."

With that, Regis turns and stalks away. I frown, lowering my fists, and glance down as his booted foot stomps right over the white flag—the first one I ever won. This time, when the tears come, I don't hold them back. I let them roll over my cheeks for several minutes before wiping them away and reaching down to pick up the now stained flag.

Holding it close to my chest, I sniff. "I didn't do anything," *I whisper.* "I'm just trying to survive."

My only audience, the flag, doesn't reply.

∽

17 YEARS OLD...

The whisper of my dagger slides through flesh like a hot knife through butter. Blood spills, drenching my fingers. I wait a beat and then release my victim's mouth as he falls to the ground, lifeless.

Wiping the stained edge of my dagger against the black fabric of my trousers that won't show the blood stain, I step over the corpse and keep moving into the dark tunnel leading from the edge of the mountain towards the God city, Nysa. The sound of footsteps and low voices in the vicinity echo off the stone surrounding me. I plaster my body against the wall, the bite of ice stabbing through the thick cloak I wear to penetrate my senses.

"Hurry, bring him this way." The words are courtesy of a fat bulbous man with a ring of thin hair circling his head. He lumbers ahead of two men dragging a third between them. Despite the first man's obvious access to food, the two following him and his orders are rail thin, their eyes sunken with cheekbones jutting from their faces from lack of nutrition.

I lick my dry lips and keep to the shadows as the group passes right by my hiding place. The fat one holds up a single torch to light their way, his eyes bouncing right and left. None of them see the body of the guard I've killed.

Pathetic. *I shake my head.* Truly pathetic.

"Where is Krychek?" the fat man gripes. "Damned guards are worthless."

My eyes glance down to the corpse at my feet. The 'Krychek' the man is talking about, I guess. I almost feel bad about the man getting a bad reputation, but then again, he's dead so the fat man is right. He is worthless now.

"Mr. Guillot, he's too heavy, we can't carry him much further," one of the skinny men says hefting the much larger figure between himself and the other servant, his voice sounding strained. The man they're dragging along the floor moans lightly, his booted feet nothing but dead weight between them.

I'm going to enjoy rubbing this rescue in his face. He once told me he'd never help me if I needed it and now the one person he hates more than any other in the Underworld is here, ready to save his *ass from a mission gone sideways. He won't hear the end of it for years to come.*

"Keep fucking moving!" the fat man, Mr. Guillot, barks. "I swear to the Gods if you disobey my orders, I'll whip both of your hides until you're bloody."

My smug smile falls away completely and becomes a scowl. My fingers clench the dagger still in my hand. Rescuing Regis isn't the only reason Ophelia had sent me. I can't kill the fucker holding him just yet—I need the information we were contracted for first. So, against my own wishes, I remain a shadow as Gideon Guillot —merchant of stolen goods and secret peddler—orders his servants to carry Regis' unconscious body deeper into the mountain tunnels. Following them for several minutes on silent feet, I stop when they finally come to a halt at the end of one offshoot of the main cavern.

Guillot glances back and licks his wide lips before finding a rock on the side of the flat, dead-end wall. Lifting the rock and putting it against a small indention, I release a low breath at the ingenuity of the secret passageway. The rock, innocuous and loose against the wall, becomes the key needed for the dead-end wall to move inward, the clanking of mechanics soundlessly opening the door that leads beyond.

"Hurry it up!" *Guillot snaps as he steps to the side and gestures for the servants to carry Regis' body ahead.*

Just before Guillot steps into the opening, he turns back and tosses the rock key back out and the door slides shut. I wait a beat and then a few more, until I'm sure they're far enough ahead for me to use the door myself.

Finding the rock key, I use it and watch the masterpiece of a hidden door open before dropping the key and hurrying after my quarry. Guillot doesn't get far into the new section of the mountain before it opens up into a massive cavern. I bite down on my lower lip in shock and amazement as lights become clear—glittering in long strings held at the end of the tunnel to reveal the city beyond.

And what a city it is.

The scent of cooking meat and the smoke and ash of fires filter through the open series of caves that have been dug out to make room for the stone houses. Guillot takes a rock staircase with an iron railing to the left that leads down into the streets below, trailing after his servants.

There aren't just people here, I realize, but families—children. Peering out from behind the tunnel entrance, I watch as a ball skitters across one of the pathways between stone huts, a boy of no more than five chasing after it.

"Ophelia is going to be pleased about this," I mutter to myself. I'd assumed that I'd get some hint as to where the Hollow City was. I never thought I'd find it myself.

The hidden city beneath the mountains surrounding the God city Nysa has been on Ophelia's list for as long as I can remember. I step up to the railing, confident now as Guillot and his servants make it to the end of the staircase and move toward a shadowy alcove. Now that he's in the Hollow City, Guillot stops glancing back, his shoulders straightening, and his steps more assured.

I shake my head in disgust. How the fuck had Regis gotten caught by such a stupid bastard?

I mentally catalog the location that I've entered through, sure there are other entrances hidden throughout the other caves. Those will have to wait though. I've got the information that Ophelia wants. Now, it's Regis' turn.

Turning towards the stairs, I take them down two at a time, keeping my eyes scanning, ever assessing. The air beneath the mountain is hot, stifling, but I can't help but understand the reasoning of the people living here. As far as anyone knows, no God or Divine being has ever been here. If people like Gideon Guillot, with their secrets and betraying ways, continue to inhabit it much longer, this place will soon become like all the rest. My chest aches at that thought.

This place, this city, is a safe haven—the one, sole mortal-run city on the entire continent. For hundreds of years this place has been kept hidden, and as I follow my prey, I know that there will be more blood on my hands before the night is through.

No one can ever find this place. I refuse to let someone like Gideon fucking Guillot—who'd sell the information this place holds for a handful of denza—ruin what has held strong for so long. Even if it means it'll displease Ophelia. I have to hope that finding the city, itself, will be enough to save me from punishment because before the end of this night, Guillot's blood will run over my dagger and his life will become another in a long line of those I've taken.

Shaking away the thoughts of my impending target's death, I hurry along the streets, keeping my cloak up and my hood covering my face. I pass a few others, though not nearly as many as one would expect in a normal city. Like me, they, too, often wear face coverings. Identities are as secret here as the city itself, it seems.

I catch up with Guillot as he stops in front of a stone hut and bangs on the door. A moment later, the door slides open and he waddles inside, followed by the panting, sweating duo carting Regis' body.

There are two windows, bare slits into the stone, on either side of the door, and I wait until the coverings over those are closed before I creep closer. I cross the path and sidle up against the outside of the hut, tilting my head as I listen for what they're doing inside. Reaching mental fingers out, more than a few little minds react to my phantom touch. I close my eyes and let their minds meld with my own. Suddenly, I'm in the hut. Though the point of view I'm watching from is obviously from the floor, half hidden behind some large wooden crate, it's enough to show me everything.

One. Two. The servants following Guillot drop Regis' body to the floor and hunch over. One gags and is promptly slapped by Guillot as he strides across the dirt floor and brings his meaty fist down on the other man's head.

"Don't you dare," the fat man sneers before he turns to the unknown.

The woman who steps out of the shadows is trailed by another man. Unlike the servants that brought Regis, this man is more than just a lackey. He's obviously also the woman's bodyguard with his big shoulders and square cut jaw dotted with scars. He'll be my main focus, I decide. The first one I'll need to take out to get to Regis.

My attention turns back to the woman, taking in more details. Her dress is long with ruffled skirts the color of deep indigo. The color, although expensive and beautiful, does nothing for her pasty skin tone. She appears so pale that at first, I think she's ill. Then she flicks her finger at Guillot and I realize her hand is a shade or two darker than her face. Makeup, I conclude.

Guillot takes the woman's fingers and bends, pressing his fat lips to her knuckles. "Madam Rose, you're as beautiful as ever."

She shakes him off with a huff. "What have you brought me?"

Guillot doesn't take her actions as offense and straightens away from her. "This man was sniffing around my businesses looking for information on the Hollow City. He's of good stock—tall, muscled—I thought perhaps if he wanted to know about the Hollow City so much then you might make use of him."

The woman, Madam Rose, takes a step towards Regis and with the toe of her boot, she nudges him. A moment passes and Regis doesn't move. She snaps her fingers and her servant jolts forward. "Turn him." Her words are crisp but denote a strange accent I've never heard before.

Her bodyguard follows her command and hefts Regis' body up, flipping him so that he lands on his back. "Oh my." Madam Rose bends over him and the image of Regis' bruised face disappears from my view. Gritting my teeth, I soften my irritation lest it make the spider, whose eyes I'm borrowing, uneasy.

"He's quite beautiful," Madam Rose comments. "He'd make a good addition to my harem."

Guillot rubs his hands together almost gleefully. "My thoughts exactly, Madam."

"Did you have to mar his pretty face?" She straightens away from Regis and sniffs in disdain.

"He fought my men; it was necessary," Guillot replies. "But of course, he'll heal. We didn't damage him further."

"Why is he unconscious?" *she asks. A question I certainly would like answered as well. Regis, for all that he's a big stupid asshole brute, would never normally allow himself to be so vulnerable for so long.*

"Drugs," *Guillot says, confirming my suspicions.* "They should wear off before too long. I wanted to make sure he wouldn't escape or attempt to harm you when I brought him."

Damn it. If I have to carry his ass out of the Hollow City, I'm going to throw him off the mountain itself.

"I'll likely need more if he's that dangerous," *Madam Rose says. Obviously, the fact that Regis is there against his will matters not to this woman. At my sides, I clench my hands into fists.*

Nudging the spider to take a look around to see if there is anyone else in the vicinity, I keep an ear out for their conversation.

"I can provide you with enough drugs to keep him docile, Madam Rose," *Guillot continues.* "For a price of course."

"Of course," *Madam Rose replies as if she expected as much.* "But will they disrupt his ability to ... perform the tasks I'll expect of him."

At that slight intonation, I feel the blood in my veins go ice cold. Guillot's reply when it comes, is barely heard over the rushing in my head.

"He shall perform for you quite well, Madam," the secret peddler says, no small amount of amusement in his tone. *"I've even procured some herbs that will ensure he remains ... ready for your attentions."*

Vomit threatens to spew from my lips. I barely even register the sound of Regis' low groan before I'm already on the move. I slam my booted foot into the door, and it splinters at the seams. A second kick sends the damn thing inward. My dagger flies across the room, embedding itself into the man at the Madam's back a split second before I duck and jerk out a leg to knock one of the two servants Guillot brought to the ground. The man collapses with a pained cry and the second one doesn't even bother to fight me. Instead, he goes to the ground next to his friend and cowers with both hands over his head.

Guillot splutters, stumbling back into the wall and reaching for the dagger I'd spotted strapped to his waist as he'd walked through the tunnels. I'm on top of him before the fucker can even get it fully freed from its sheath. Ripping it from his hand, I use the blade to stab his hand down into the dirt at my feet before whirling on Madam Rose.

The scream of Guillot as he struggles to free his bloodied hand from the ground is dull to my ears as I freeze. Madam Rose isn't running as I expected. No. The woman blinks back at me, eyes with pupils blown so wide and dark that they nearly swallow the thin ring of copper that I guess is her natural eye color. This close, the powder on her face becomes more evident.

Her lips part as she gapes at me. "By the Gods..." *Her hand rises to her chest.* "It's not—"

I don't let her finish whatever she's about to say. Rearing back, I channel all of my disgust into my fist and punch her. Her nose breaks under the contact, blood spurting free as she goes down to the ground.

"You disgust me," *I growl, reaching for my second blade. This one isn't meant to kill mortals, but I don't give a fuck. Ophelia can beat me all she likes when I return. I won't leave this place without ensuring that this woman—this rapist—dies at my hands.*

Madam Rose holds up a shaking hand, not even seeming to notice the ruby red blood that dribbles down over her lips and chin to stain the indigo of her gown. "Y-you..." Her breath comes in harsh pants and her eyes glisten with unshed tears.

"Don't fucking try begging," I warn her. "Those who take what is not freely given will see no mercy from me."

The brimstone dagger falls in the next second. The blade pierces the woman's chest, straight down to the plain black handle. Red bubbles up around it as I pull it free and she chokes, eyes going glassy with the first hint of death as it descends.

I take a step back, my chest pumping up and down in a combination of effort and rage. A cough and a moan capture my attention and then a hand locks around my ankle. Jerking back, I kick out and Guillot goes flying into a bleary-eyed Regis as he tries to sit up.

I'm on the merchant in the next second, ripping the blade he'd pulled free from his hand and using it to slit his throat. Blood sprays over the side of Regis' face and he gapes at me, blinking as he attempts to work through the fog he's no doubt experiencing from the drugs.

"What the—"

"We have to go," I say, cutting Regis off as I roll the fat merchant to the side to get off him.

A glance over my shoulder reveals that Guillot's two servants are missing—no doubt having run at the first opportunity. Madam Rose's bodyguard lies dead with a dagger in his eye a few feet away.

"Get up," I snap out the command as I stand and move over to the dead man. I pull my dagger free, wipe it, and sheathe it along with the others.

Regis curses as he places a hand on the side of the stone hut and staggers to his feet. Shoving my shoulders beneath one of his arms, I hoist him against my side. He hisses in pain, his already bruised face a molten shade of purple and black. No doubt there are more beneath his clothes.

"Suck it up," I order. "We need to get out of here before anyone else comes to check out the noise."

"Why the fuck are you the one rescuing me?" Regis grumbles.

"Because Ophelia ordered it," I snap. When he leans against me as we shuffle towards the open doorway, I know he's not quite recovered. There's no other way he'd allow himself to rely on someone like me.

I bite down on my lip and glance back at the gray faced, glassy-eyed woman on the dirt floor. Frowning, I notice the black veins that have stroked up the sides of her neck and face, visible even through the makeup. I glance away and move forward.

"Is this the Hollow City?" Regis asks, his voice full of grit, confusion, and also a little bit of shocked awe as he glances up at the light-filled cavern we're in.

"Yes." I nudge him forward. It isn't until Regis and I make it to the staircase leading up to the tunnels—the path having taken twice as long as the first time as we pause to hide from passersby—that I decide to tell him some of what I uncovered.

He takes one step onto the bottom of the stairs, reaching for the iron railing and hefting himself to the next. I follow a step or two behind, ensuring he doesn't fall even as I continue to survey our surroundings.

"Regis..." My voice is quiet, nearly a whisper, but he hears it.

Glancing over his shoulder, Regis arches a brow at me. "What?"

I take a breath. "When we get back to the Underworld, you should ... see one of the medics."

He rolls his eyes and takes another two steps before he replies. "I'm bruised, not broken."

I grit my teeth, not wanting to say the next words that come out of my mouth. "The merchant that took you was planning to sell you to that woman," I tell him.

Regis pauses on the next landing of the stairs. "He ... was going to sell me?"

When he looks back, I nod. Regis turns ahead and after a moment, he starts walking again. This time, his movements are far more stiff and uneven as if they're suddenly extra painful.

"He didn't..." Regis states. It's not a question, but I answer it as if it were.

"No."

We climb the final steps and stop at the entrance to the tunnel.

"Nothing happened to me while I was unconscious." Another non-question. "Drugged," he mutters. "I had to have been drugged." I can practically hear the thoughts circling in his head as the hands at his sides clench and unclench into fists. He sways where he stands.

"Regis..." His shoulders hunch inward away from me at the call of his name. Unable to help myself, I reach out and touch his back. He flinches and my hand drops away.

"Yes, you were drugged and I don't think anything happened while you were unconscious," I say. "But ... if it'd been me, I'd want to know for sure."

Ocean blue eyes look back at me, darker than I've ever seen them and full of phantoms I've seen too many times in the last seven years. I never expected to see them in his.

"You came for me because Ophelia sent you."

I nod.

"Did she tell you to kill for me?"

I blink. "What?"

He turns to face me. "Did Ophelia tell you to kill for me?" he repeats the question.

"Regis, I—"

"I'll keep this secret," *he says, cutting me off.* "Just this once." *He holds up a finger.* "We're not ... friends."

I breathe a sigh of relief. This is what I'm used to from Regis—anger, annoyance, distrust. I roll my shoulders back. "I don't have to be your friend to know what's right and wrong, Regis," *I tell him.* "I would've killed anyone who attempted to commit rape. It had nothing to do with you."

Regis snorts a strained laugh and shakes his head, dropping his hand and finger. "Right." *He nods and then, absently, he repeats himself,* "...right..."

"Come on." *I gesture toward the tunnel opening.* "Let's get out of here and back to the guild."

It isn't until the two of us are through the secret passageway and take that final step from out of the hot interior of the mountain tunnels that he speaks again. A wash of cool night air slides over my skin, the drying sweat on the side of my neck making me feel sticky with grime.

I move towards the forest, stopping only when I feel a hand close over my shoulder. Frowning, I look back to Regis who stands, half in the tunnel and half out. His body is illuminated by the moonlight shining down, but his face remains in the shadows.

"Regis?" *I turn back.* "Are you okay? Do you need to rest?"

He shifts and lowers his arm. "No." *The word is a croak.* "No, I just wanted to..." *His chest rises and falls with a jerky breath.* "I know we've never—I mean..." *A minute passes and then two. The soft noises of bugs buzzing and small animals rustling the underbrush soothe my nerve endings. Still, I wait. Then...* "I once told you that I'd never come to your aid," *Regis murmurs.* "That I wouldn't help you even if Ophelia ordered it. I ... I didn't mean that. I said it in anger. I said it because you're—"

"I know, Regis," I say, stopping him from saying the reason for his animosity. There's no need when we're both well aware of it.

"I'm sorry." The apology comes unexpectedly. "And thank you ... for coming for me. For killing for me."

And because I don't know what else to say to a man who's hated me for the last seven years, a man that I've trained with, sparred with, beaten, and been beaten by, I do the only thing I can think to do.

I punch him.

"What the fuck!" Regis stumbles under the blow. "I was fucking apologizing. Why did you punch me?" He comes out of the shadows, rubbing his jaw and glaring as he does.

I shrug. "Just making sure you were real and not a mirage," I answer lightly, pivoting back toward the path. "Now, hurry your ass up or I'll leave you in my dust like I always do."

"Gods, you're annoying," Regis mutters.

My steps are lighter. "Yeah, but now that you've apologized, this means we're friends so you'll just have to put up with it."

"Fuck no, we're not friends!" His objection echoes into the night.

I snort. "Oh, we're definitely friends," I say. "You're the only one I know who will stab me in the chest rather than my back."

"What?"

Glancing back at his befuddled expression, I laugh at his creased brows and twisted lips. "A true friend will make sure you know who's betraying you," I tell him before turning back to the path before us. "They'll stab you in the chest rather than the back."

Regis grumbles about throwing me off a cliff, but I hear the telltale sound of his footsteps following after me a moment later. The smile that comes to my lips can't be contained. Turning my face to the night sky and glittering gems of the sea of stars overhead, I release a slow breath.

Maybe we don't need to be rivals. Maybe we really can be

friends. Though I'd never admit it to him now, I've always hoped for as much. My first real friend. Not my father. Not just a comrade, but an honest-to-Gods friend.

Even killers need someone to pull them back from the edge of darkness now and then. If Regis can be that for me, then I'll always come for him.

CHAPTER 40
KIERA

Present Day...

Drip. Drip. Drip.

I wrinkle my nose and bat at whatever the annoying thing is tickling my nose. Something wet hits my knuckles and my eyes shoot open to see a haggard, but very much awake Regis leaning over me, flicking water on my face.

I blink. His face stretches as he offers me a wan smile. "Morning, Kay."

"Regis!" My body is already moving, bounding out of the chair and tackling him to the bed before I give myself conscious consent to move.

I plow into him with all of the subtlety of a runaway carriage through a glass shop. He grunts as I wrap my arms around him and squeeze, tears burning at the back of my eyes as I do.

"Yeah, I'm happy to be alive, too," he wheezes. Regis lifts his arms and meets my embrace. Burrowing my face into his chest, I bite down on my lower lip to keep from making a sound as my throat convulses. I snap my eyes shut and refuse to let the floodgates open.

We stay like that for several long moments, the two of us wrapped around each other, taking in the sound of his beating heart and his even breathing. *Alive, Regis is alive.* I never thought I'd be so grateful for something so damned ordinary, but I am.

Finally, Regis presses his palms against my shoulders and pushes me back. "Kiera, before you say anything else, I want you to know that I'm fucking sorry—so damned sorry about what happened with Ophelia."

"You knew about my debt to Ophelia," I state, discreetly turning to the side and wiping the side of my face with the flat of my palm as I check the door. It's still shut and there's no sound of anyone coming up the stairs outside.

"I didn't know that she ... I didn't know that the brimstone made you a blood servant."

Though I've already decided to forgive Regis, I pivot to face him and cross my arms over my chest. "And you think that makes what you did okay?" I ask, arching a brow.

Regis dips his head. "No, you're right. I'll—I'll make it up to you." He heaves a great breath. "Fuck, Kay, I'll—"

"Two weeks," I say, cutting him off as I hold up two fingers. He lifts up and looks at me with a frown.

"Two weeks what?" he replies.

I offer him a smug smile. "Two weeks without bathing," I tell him. "And you have to sleep outside—in the woods with the bugs."

Blue eyes widen. "Kiera..." I press my lips together as they begin to tremble. "Two weeks?" Regis' expression is full of what can only be described as a blend of horror and repulsion.

I nod. "If you want me to forgive you, that's what it will take."

Regis begins to look a little green, his face paler than it had been when he'd been sleeping, as he contemplates my offer. "What about setting up a camp?" he asks. "Can I—"

"Nope." I grin. "Full elements. No cover. No pallet. Just you and the dirt and the creepy crawlers."

His gasp is music to my ears. "You're a fucking monster."

I shrug, the epitome of nonchalance. "You can always turn me down."

"*Fuck.*" Regis shoves a hand over the top of his head, scratching at the dry and unkempt dreads that are half smashed into the back of his skull from how long he's been lying on it. "No," he finally says, meeting my gaze. "I can't. If that's all it'll take for you to forgive me, then I'll do it."

He holds his hand out as we'd seen so often when merchants made their deals. "Are you sure you can handle it?" I ask, amused by the curl of his upper lip and the sallow look he gives me.

The comment, itself, is nothing but a part of the game. The two of us had been through far worse than sleeping outside without bathing. Part of the Underworld training had been that exact challenge. We'd been unleashed upon a forest with nothing but the clothes on our backs, and for two weeks we'd had to fight and claw our way through survival.

Any shelter built had to be from our own hands and what the forest could provide. Any food we ate, we had to catch ourselves. A few of the trainees had died. One of them had been mauled by a bear and her body was deemed irretrievable. And though we'd been half starved and full of fresh cuts and injuries by the end of our days in the woods, both Regis and I had made it out alive.

I've never been entirely sure where his initial disgust over bugs and dirt stemmed from. I suspect he's always been cleaner than most people, but that exercise had taken him to his limits and no matter how many people he's killed, how many bodies he's moved, and how many times he's returned covered in muck and filth—he's never gotten used to it.

Yet, even as I think that, he takes a step towards me and bumps his hand against my abdomen with meaning. "*Take. My. Hand. Kiera.*" Each word is full of meaning.

I laugh and do as he demands. "Your punishment can't be imminent, unfortunately," I say, dropping my amusement as we establish the mended bond between us. "What the fuck happened with the Underworld and who attacked you?"

Dropping my hand, Regis takes a seat on the edge of the bed, planting both hands against the mattress. "Carcel."

Shock stabs my gut. "Carcel betrayed the Underworld?"

His responding nod doesn't lessen my dismay. There's only one question that comes to mind.

"*Why?*"

Dishwater blue eyes lift to meet mine. "I don't know," he admits. "But Madam Brione's shop isn't safe anymore. She was away when it happened—I sent the crow to deliver notes to her and you after I managed to escape ... I hope she didn't return. If she did, despite my warning, then she's probably dead."

"When *what* happened, Regis?" I lower to the chair next to the bed and lean forward. My skirts bunch against my butt and I scoot forward, annoyed that I hadn't thought to change before falling asleep in here.

"Carcel came to the shop with some men I didn't recognize," Regis says. "I thought they must have been new recruits—Carcel's Ophelia's son, after all. He's almost as good as you or I. It never even occurred to me that he'd try to..."

Regis pauses as if something has occurred to him.

Reaching down to the hem of the tunic I dressed him in after staring at him in the dark stained clothes he'd been brought in for too long, he lifts it and looks down at the hollowed ridges of his stomach. A fresh scar marks a diagonal line across several of his abs before curving upward towards his breastbone as if someone had tried to first gut him and then changed their mind and decided to carve out his heart instead.

"How long have I been out?" he asks. "This looks months old."

"A few days," I admit. "I had a healer check you out and she sped up the process. You were out of the hard part after the first day, but she said you'd stay asleep awhile yet."

The scar disappears from view as he drops the overly large tunic back into place. "I should be dead," he mutters hoarsely. "Carcel tried to kill me."

"Did he say why?"

Regis scowls. "He didn't have to." His eyes darken. "That little shit's always been jealous of both of us. I figured when he took over Ophelia's position, he'd boot the two of us, but I never thought he'd do this." He gestures to his now covered stomach.

I stare at the light cloth as if I can see past the fabric to the puckered and raised scar beyond. Everyone in the Underworld is capable of violence, but the one thing the Underworld drummed into us was that active Guild members were never to be the target.

Carcel, whether he realizes it or not, has broken a cardinal rule and I would bet every goddamn denza in Anatol that Ophelia is in the dark about it. If she's not ... well, then there's only one other explanation. Carcel might be a lot of things, not the least of which being a backstabbing bitch, but I can't imagine him killing his own mother.

That is, if he even could.

"There's more to it than revenge or jealousy," I say.

Regis blows out a breath. "Of course," he agrees. "Carcel first came and asked after Madam Brione. When I told him she wasn't there, he began asking me questions about you and about the men—the Mortal Gods—you'd brought with you last time. He kept asking if you'd responded to any of my communications. He thought I was lying when I told him that you hadn't."

I will not feel guilty.

"One of the men he'd brought with him started going through the shop and another even went upstairs and went through the room you'd used when you were staying there."

"What did they look like?" I ask. "The men he brought?"

Regis' brows pinch down as if he's thinking back. "I—it's hard to remember." He grits the words out as if they're shameful. "I do know that they were weird though."

I tilt my head. "Weird how?"

"I'm not entirely sure," he confesses. "It was like ... there wasn't anything wrong with the way they looked or even anything they said—well, actually, they didn't say anything."

"None of them?"

He shakes his head. "They never talked," he says, tone growing more confident. "Maybe that was it. It was like they were puppets, they followed Carcel's commands, but their eyes were all..." He frowns and then waves a hand in front of his face. "Like there was no one home, you know? I think one stared straight at me and when I met his eyes, there was just ... nothing in them. It almost looked like..." Regis pauses, his words drifting off as he tucks his head down, a deep frown marring his features. "No." He shakes his head again, harder this time. "There's no way."

"What?" I demand, reaching forward and grabbing him

by the shoulders. "Regis, if the Underworld is compromised, then so am I. We all are." Me. The Darkhavens. Him. Carcel knows everything and if he wanted to, he could take all of our secrets straight to the Gods. I'm shocked he hasn't already. "What did you notice about them?"

When Regis lifts his head again, his eyes are glassy. His nostrils flare and he starts to tremble. "Their eyes..." His voice is barely above a whisper and I lean closer. "They were the eyes of dead men."

CHAPTER 41
RUEN

When I was young, there was a horrible epidemic that spanned across the eastern part of Anatol. The infected were locked away in their homes with large red Xs painted over their front doors to warn others away from the affliction. During that time, my mother and I traveled between smaller villages in the back of a wagon along with a poor merchant in exchange for errands and mending. We saw the devastation, witnessed the families of the infected sobbing over burning huts and left in the cold if they were well and their loved ones slowly died of the disease.

My mother had likely paid the merchant in more than simple errands and mending. She'd likely given him more than I'd ever have wanted her to. Despite that, I don't begrudge her for doing what she did. I simply wish I'd been stronger so that she wouldn't have been forced to make those choices. Perhaps that's why I don't judge Kiera for what she's had to do for survival even if I can't and won't offer the same grace to myself.

Now, as I stare into the eyes of the man who came for me

at age ten, I see the same horror as I did then. The only difference is that he *is* the disease, the devastation wrought upon the land and all of its people—all of the Gods are. They have no loved ones who will mourn them; I certainly won't.

"Well?" Azai arches a brow, his upper lip curling back as he awaits a response to his demand.

"I can't give you what I don't know," I say coolly.

The snarl he unleashes is a sound that belongs in the throat of an animal and not a man—Divine or not. My back slams against the stone wall in the next instant and his hot breath fans across my face as he holds me off the floor.

"*Then. You. Will. Find. Out.*" Each word is clipped and full of rage.

I tilt my head down, picking a spot on his forehead to stare at as I angle my chin in just the right way to crack my neck. Then I straighten back up and return his angry glare with a slow, apathetic blink.

"No."

"No?" His hands slip and my feet touch the floor again.

"Correct." I reach up and circle his wrists with my fingers, squeezing harder and harder until I feel the creaking of his bones under my grasp. Azai releases me. "I won't be your spy, *Father*." I spit the last word at him.

"You think to deny me?" He gapes at me as if he truly cannot believe that anyone would do such a thing. I know that it's likely the only reason I managed to get him to release me. I also know that it's likely a poor idea to provoke him further.

Therefore, it's to my own surprise as well as his that I do so. "What are you going to do?" I ask. "Punish me? Who are you going to kill? My mother? Wait, you already did that. Scar me? Oh, yes, you've done that too." I bare my teeth at him in a feral smile and shove up the sleeve of my tunic, brandishing the scars there for him to see. "And I've got more where those came from so that won't do you any good."

Azai's shoulders swell as he sucks in a breath. Never once does he look at the scars on my arm. I lower it again and let my sleeve fall back into place as I stare back at him.

"I don't know why you're so obsessed with a girl who is no more than another bastard child of the Gods." My words may sound casual, but my insides riot with nothing but fury.

"My reasons are not to be questioned by you," Azai snaps.

"I'm not questioning them," I reply. "But I can't help you." *I won't help him.*

"You are making a mistake, boy." Azai's words are cold, despite his anger.

I straighten my tunic and brush off a piece of invisible lint just to feel as if I'm showing him I don't care.

"Master Ru—" I don't move at the sound of a familiar almost breathy male voice, not even when it, along with the footsteps I hadn't heard approaching, cuts off abruptly. "I'm so sorry, my Lord."

I know without looking that Niall is bowing to Azai, likely straining his back to get as low as he possibly can without falling to his knees. All it would take is one flick of Azai's fingers, though, and that's exactly what this boy, this human, would do. I refuse to look at him lest any interest in the Terra that Kiera considers her friend results in punishment from Azai.

Thankfully, Azai merely ignores Niall and steps closer to me. "There will come a time, *Son,*" he emphasizes that hated word, "when you realize that the choices you make will define you. I hope that you will see that any power you think you wield is bestowed by *me.* You would not be without me and should you continue to defy and fight me, you will cease to be any further."

He lifts a hand and when I would step back, I find that I can't. His fingers grip the sides of my throat and I'm forced to look into eyes the color of beaten gold. "You breathe because I allow it," Azai states. "Right now, you are drunk on the thought that you are protected. That is an illusion. If I wanted to, I could kill you right here and now."

Breath ragged, I bare my teeth at him. "Then why don't you?" I growl.

His lips curve into a bemused smile. Azai's hand on my neck eases back before dropping away completely. *It is not time.* It takes a moment for me to realize that those words weren't spoken aloud. I was staring at his mouth, but his lips never moved.

"Get me information about the girl by the end of the week, Ruen," Azai says, taking a step back. "Or suffer the consequences."

As the God of Strength prowls away, I distantly hear the sound of Niall's panting breaths. I close my eyes. Suffer the consequences? Every step I've ever taken is a consequence made by his choices.

No matter what I do, there will be consequences. In my words and in my silence.

Reopening my eyes, I cast my attention back to Niall and frown at what I see. Dressed not in his usual Terra attire, Niall is covered in a thin layer of dust over what looks to be a robe similar to those of the librarians.

"What—"

Niall jerks his head up as if realizing we're finally alone. He looks one way and then another before he leaps forward and latches on to my arms. Never before has this human acted with such impudence that I'm stunned silent as he drags me down the hall and into a quieter alcove just out of the way of anyone who might pass through the corridor.

"Master Ruen," he says, eyes searching around the corner, "I've found something."

He turns to me and then from his robes, he produces a small leather-bound book. "I know you ordered me to stop searching—please don't punish me—but I—"

I hold my hand up, cutting him off. "I won't punish you," I promise him. "What did you find?"

Eyes similar to that of a pup, wide, brown, and trusting gaze up at me. "The records of Mortal Gods' deaths over the last thirty years."

CHAPTER 42
KIERA

They were the eyes of dead men.

Regis' words echo through my head as I leave him in Kalix's room.

Things are not right. If Regis believes that the men following Carcel are dead then I believe him. The two of us have seen more than enough dead bodies, open unseeing eyes gazing into a world no one living can ever know.

We know what death looks like.

That can only mean that Carcel is manipulated by a God. Who it is, I don't know, but what I do know is that none of us are safe in the Academy anymore.

I need the Darkhavens.

Racing through the corridors, passing by classrooms and the training arena, I'm sweating by the time I come across the Mortal Gods' courtyard. It, too, is empty with its fountain gurgling merrily. I grit my teeth and turn, hoping that I'll at least find Ruen in the library. My feet fly over stone, the skirts of my dress thrust against my calves as I run. No more dresses. I really need to burn them whenever I see them. Rounding the next corner, I slam head first into a wide chest and am saved from falling by twin hands that grip my upper arms.

"Kiera!" Ruen's face appears in front of me and relief floods my bones.

"Ruen!" I grip him right back, dimly aware of just how good it feels to have him so near after all that Regis revealed.

"I have to tell you something."

I blink, frowning when I realize that my voice was overlayed by his own.

"Me first, it's important," I say.

Ruen glances back and then nudges me to the side. "My information is important as well."

"I—"

He places a palm over my mouth, the heat of it stealing past my defenses. Ruen doesn't appear to notice as he glances back over his shoulder and then shakes his head. "Not here," he says.

Unwilling to wait any longer than necessary or waste time arguing, I concede and grab his wrist, pulling his hand away from my face as I drag him with me. I peer into a nearby classroom and check to ensure that it's empty before hauling him inside and locking the door.

"Regis is awake." The words fly out of my mouth before I can stop them.

"That's good," Ruen says. "But I—"

"He told me what happened," I continue, chest heaving as I try and fail to slow my heart rate. "Carcel—Ophelia's son—attacked him. Regis doesn't know why but Ruen..." I force myself to stop and take a breath before I tell him the next part. "He brought dead men."

Ruen frowns, two vertical lines appearing between his brows. "Dead men?"

I nod vigorously. "He says that the men Carcel brought

weren't any he recognized. He said when he looked at their eyes, that they weren't there—like they were just puppets following a command. That can only mean he's working with someone with Divinity. A God."

"It could be a God or it could be the child of one," Ruen considers.

"You think a Mortal God could have that kind of ability?"

He nods. "It's possible. Many abilities of God children aren't present in their sires, but—" Ruen stops and shakes his head. "Never mind, that's something we'll have to figure out later. I also have something to share with you."

"What is it?"

Ruen slips a hand beneath his tunic and pulls out a small leather-bound book that's worn at the edges. "*This*." He hands it over.

Flipping open the front cover, I examine the neatly printed handwritten notes. The contents of the book are simply names and dates. Some of them have locations, but none of it makes sense to me. I leaf through the pages, noting more and more names and the dates growing closer together.

"What is this?" I ask finally.

"It's a ledger of the deaths of Mortal Gods over the last thirty years," he admits. "Not the official one, of course, but the person who found the information wrote everything down. Look." Leaning over me, Ruen takes the book and flips to one of the later pages. "The dates of death come more often than they did in the beginning."

"What does that mean?"

"There are coincidences, Kiera," Ruen says, shutting the book, "and there are causes." He taps the book with a finger. "These deaths have a cause and every one of them happened after these Mortal Gods were sent to Ortus."

Ortus. The first Mortal Gods Academy to ever exist and the place of the Gods' rising—according to what Caedmon had told us before. The distant memory of those sand and rock shores with my father all those years ago lingers in the back of my mind, coming closer and closer to the forefront. The jagged spikes of black stone jutting up from the small island off the coast is burned into my consciousness.

A shiver steals over me and I lower my lashes in response as if I can cut off the image. Of course, it doesn't work. I should have known better. Closing my eyes only seems to bring the mirage of the Academy's outline closer. The tall skeletal towers of ore that are the first Academy gleam under a sun that appears duller simply because it's in the presence of something insidious. Sweat beads on the back of my neck and the taste of dry fear coats my throat.

"Kiera." Ruen's hand comes down on my shoulder, disrupting the memory and pulling me back to reality. My eyes pop open and I'm met with the dark burning blue flames that are his irises. "Are you okay?"

I jerk my head in a nod even though I'm not entirely sure why I reacted so viscerally. "I'm fine," I say, hoping the words aren't a lie. "I think we need to leave the Academy."

Fine lines bracket Ruen's lips, but he doesn't immediately refute my words. That, in itself, is telling. "Where would we go?" he asks.

I consider it. We could go to the Hinterlands—it's truly the only place known that the Gods wouldn't go to. As far as I'm aware, no one truly knows why the Gods never went into the dark woods that make up the ancient forest, but I'm grateful for the fact now. It gives us at least somewhere as a safe haven while we figure out the rest.

I open my mouth to make the suggestion when the sharp toll of the Academy's bell tower chimes. The sound reverberates through the empty classroom, echoing through the windows on the far side and slipping through the cracks in the door as if it's a living thing. A beat passes and then the sound of doors opening in the corridor beyond reaches us. Students talking. Footsteps approaching and passing by.

Midnight eyes meet my own. "The arena," he states flatly.

My breath catches in my throat.

The Gods have already made their decision.

CHAPTER 43
THEOS

Sweat slicks over my spine as the stands of the arena fill, bodies crushing together, the scent of dread mixed with excitement. The Gods have called us all here for a reason and as those of the academies fear them, they, too, also worship their sires.

Not everyone, though. Not my brothers or me. Not Kiera.

I turn my head, seeking her out amongst the crowd, but I don't yet see her.

"There are no Terra." Kalix's low voice is nearly drowned out by the chattering of classmates and Lower Gods, but I hear it.

"What are you talking about?" I glance his way and then gesture to the front of the arena, the head Terra, Dauphine and Hael, are both present. Their dull features are prominent in the sea of Divine Beings and Divine offspring that surround them where they're both positioned on either side of the U-shaped ring of the stands.

I lift my arm and gesture towards them. "Look, there they..." I drift off, though, because another pass around the area reveals that, other than the two head Terra, there are no servant Terra in the vicinity. None standing alongside their Mortal God wards. None with offerings of extra cushions or drinks. Just those two, their backs ramrod straight and their faces drawn and pale as if they aren't servants but sentinels standing guard before prisoners being led to the gallows. I lower my arm back to my side.

"We have not been summoned here for battle."

I'm not so sure he's right about that, but in terms of Academy normalcy, I doubt that today is a day for the sands to be drenched in Mortal God upon Mortal God bloodshed. Battle, however, can have different meanings.

The sight of a familiar head of silver hair being led by an equally familiar head of dark hair through the throngs of people gives me a modicum of comfort. The sight of Kiera's face with dark circles mimicking the shade of bruises beneath her eyes and the jut of her chin, forced up and forward as if she's trying to maintain a careful facade of calm destroys my relief. My lingering rage towards her abates, though not gone, I can tamp it down and compartmentalize it now that we're faced with a monster none of us truly knows how to handle.

Put swords in our hands and give us an opponent and we can take it down. But this? This collection of dire circumstances with Gods and their presence constantly watching us as we struggle and try to hide away secrets that will get us killed should they be revealed ... this is too much. They've brought us here for something, and though I don't believe all Gods are truly cruel, too many of them are complicit in the cruelties of their brethren. Even—as much as I hate to admit it—Caedmon.

Ruen and Kiera join us where we usually sit. Neither of them say anything. Kalix and I shuffle and allow them to take their places to our left with Kiera on the inside and Ruen guarding her other side. Trained though she might be, the protective instinct we feel toward her will not abate and it's more natural to take up positions as knights might around a Queen of old. An action we can't seem to help nor, does it appear, that any of us want to change.

I scan the arena and the stands further as the students settle into their seats and the patience of the Gods begins to wane. In a sudden rush, silence descends upon the crowds as Tryphone takes a step towards the lip of the Gods' balcony and lifts a hand out, palm up and facing the rest of us. Dolos hovers to his side, the shroud of darkness that converges upon his unseen body rippling in what I have always assumed are visual representations of his emotions.

What is he feeling now? I wonder. Fear for the God King or anticipation?

My stomach churns with unease and I lean my head to the side before crossing my arms over my chest. Turning my body the slightest degree, the heat of the body next to me—Kiera's—permeates the fabric of my clothes and delves into my flesh.

The God King's power surges out, pressing into not just me, but those surrounding our little party as well. The sensation of weight upon our shoulders is felt in mass waves. Grinding my jaw, I remain steadfast in my determination to keep my head up and my eyes forward.

In my periphery, there are plenty of students who gag and cry out. Some even slump over where they sit, passing out at the heaviness of his presence and power.

What the fuck is this? I want to demand. *A ploy to remind us who's in charge?*

Without shifting my head, I continue my perusal of the arena. I see several familiar Gods situated in their usual positions, but when I come upon Caedmon's usual seat, it remains empty. I scowl. "Where's Caedmon?"

Kiera shifts next to me, the action drawing her heat away. I grit my teeth and force my arms to remain locked in place, refusing to allow them to bring her closer again.

"I don't see him either." It takes me a moment to realize that it's Ruen who's answered me.

This is—My thought is disrupted as Tryphone begins to speak.

"Welcome, children." Tryphone needs no added Divinity to reach the highest of the stands. Even from as far back as we're sitting, the sound of his deep voice reverberates as if he's merely a few feet away.

"We've gathered you here today," the God King continues, "to bless you, our glorious blood."

The softness with which he speaks is unsettling. Kiera bumps into me and I glance down. Her face has me releasing my arms from their position and reaching for her. All of the color has drained from her cheeks and her eyes are glassy, her pupils dilated until only the thinnest ring of gray color is still visible. Her whole body goes rigid, and her throat bobs as if she's fighting back the urge to throw up.

"Kiera?" She doesn't seem to hear me, swaying a little in her chair before going rigid once more. Lines of pain strain around her eyes and mouth. Ruen's head snaps to the side and Kalix leans around me.

"Where's Maeryn?" Her question confuses me, but the way she says it—with swallowing breaths and stilted syllables—concerns me.

"Kiera, do you need healing?" Is that why she's asking for Maeryn? She doesn't answer. I put my hand on her arm. There's no reaction. Her breathing is shallow and uneven.

My eyes flick up to meet Ruen's for a brief moment, but his expression tells me he's just as confused as I am.

"We are so proud of the Academy of Riviere," Tryphone's

voice cuts through whatever we try to say to her next, his volume growing as if he knows we're not paying attention to him. I have to bite back a snarl of annoyance.

Cupping my hand against Kiera's cheek, I turn her head towards me. Her gaze is unfocused. "We need to get her out of here," I say.

"We can't leave," this from Kalix.

Whirling in my seat with a few choice curses on the tip of my tongue, the moment I spot his hard features, I know he's not saying as much to piss me off. I follow the direction of his eyes. The Gods are watching us.

Not as if they are scanning the crowd and peering at each section of students with the false pride in Tryphone's tone. No. They're watching *us*.

Tryphone. His Queen, Danai. Azai. My upper lip curls back at that last one. My father's interminable gaze remains unflinching. I can't tell if Dolos is as well, his dark swath of physical oppression keeping me from seeing past the barrier, but I have no doubt if the God King is fixated on us then so is he.

"Dead men..." Kiera's whisper has me looking back at her. "Dead men," she repeats. She tries to get up, but just as quickly slumps back into her seat as if she has no energy.

"Dead men?" I look at Ruen, but he simply shakes his head.

"Not here," he says, lowering his voice even as he wraps his arm around her shoulders.

"Run ... trapped ... darkness..." Kiera's voice is unsteady, but at least it's quiet, barely loud enough for us to hear. "Truth ... taboo."

She's breaking down and though I can understand the stress of what's been going on getting to anyone, now is not the fucking time.

"What caused this?" I ask, directing the question to Ruen as he gazes down at her with furrowed brows.

Indigo eyes meet mine and the world begins to blur. I don't move as he weaves his illusion, around and around, like cloth curtains separating us from the real world, hiding what's happening—both the conversation and Kiera's shaking—from prying eyes and those of the Gods.

"The Gods are sending students to Ortus Academy," he admits once he's comfortable that we're not going to be overheard here. Sweat beads break out on his upper lip and his brow. Dimly, I recognize that it's likely Tryphone's power pressing down that's making him work twice as hard to keep up the illusion. It's time to talk fast.

"Why would that make her like this?" I nod down to the woman between us. She's not screaming or crying, but Kiera's head is somewhere far away. I don't want to admit it, but she reminds me of ... me. In that dark room before my brothers had found me.

"There's more to it," Ruen says. "She talked with Regis and we think that the son of the Underworld is working with a God. They probably know her secret and about all of our connections with her. We were hoping to leave before they called us, but it just happened and—"

"Enough."

As if he simply put his hand through the surface of a pool of water and snatched us from the depths, Kalix's voice cuts through the illusion. In an instant, it's all gone. I blink as chatter rises up. Others are standing, talking animatedly as they leave their seats and begin streaming towards the exits.

"What..." I look around. "What's going on?" My gaze falls on Kalix, on the hard set of his grinding jaw.

At my side, Ruen uses his hold on Kiera to get her to her feet. Her lashes flutter against her pale cheeks and when she lifts them again, her pupils are back to normal. She frowns and then looks at him first before turning to me and then Kalix.

"What ... happened?" Her voice is thready, as if she's just woken from a long deep sleep.

Fuck me, but I recognize that tone. Closing my eyes, I shove back the awful memories of that dark room and the following weeks, months, and years after I'd been freed. Dark places. Weight on my chest. Unable to breathe.

Ruen and Kiera step out onto the stairs and I take a moment to shake my head before following them.

Kalix is the one that finally answers both of our questions. "The Academies of Riviere and Perditia are being summoned," he announces as people spill around our bodies, ignoring the way we're all stock still amongst them. Cool green eyes turn to lock each of us with his stare. His pupils are dangerously slitted. Just like a snake's. "We're all going to Ortus Academy."

CHAPTER 44
KIERA

To know yourself well is to know your worst enemy because only you can decide what will make you suffer the most.

And I know. I know it all.

The board we've been playing upon has been uneven and murky thus far, but now I see it in crystal clarity. Jagged sharpness has opened my eyes.

The Darkhavens hover around me, ushering me this way and then that. I don't pay attention to the movements of my body as my mind transcends the physical. Somehow, beyond the reins of my consciousness, I find that I trust them implicitly. With my body, with my soul, and my life. I close my eyes and just breathe for several long seconds. Those seconds turn into minutes, into hours, into eternity, but when I reopen them, I know that only a small amount of time has passed.

Panting. Sweating. My skin feels as if it's crawling. I'm out of breath. We're out of time.

Ara? I reach out with my mind, seeking something familiar. *Ara, are you there? Answer me.*

Nothing comes back. I try again and still ... nothing.

When panic seizes my chest, I reach out and latch on to Ophelia's training, but it all ... just ... slips ... away.

"—iera? Did you hear me?" Hands cup the sides of my face. I don't recognize where we are, but we're no longer in the arena, no longer outside. It's too dark here. Too closed in.

The face before me is familiar. So, too, is the voice those words are spoken with. Sunburnt eyes the color of liquid gold bore into me. "Kiera?" His hands are cool upon my skin. I have to warn him. I have to warn them all. We need to get out of here. We have to leave. The Gods ... oh dear fucking Divinity. We're in so much danger.

The pieces have clicked into place. The missing Mortal Gods. The book with the names crossed out. Caedmon ... I understand now why he wouldn't—couldn't—tell me the truth. I shut my eyes and wish I could shut out the whole world.

Be careful what you wish for, isn't that what people say? I pushed and I hunted and now, I know the truth. It's as if I had a shroud over my head for so long, fighting my way through the world, squinting to recognize faces distorted by fabric. Tears burn at the back of my eyes.

I was a fucking fool. I thought I was so strong simply because I knew how to use a blade. I assumed that because I'd suffered that there wasn't anything worse. There always is.

"Do you understand what we're telling you, *Dea*?" Theos' voice is back and I open my eyes, fixing my attention on him for a beat and then glancing over his shoulder to the two shadow-like men hovering behind him.

"What?" The word is a croak and it sounds nothing like me.

Theos' brow furrows. "We have to get ready," he tells me. "The Gods are sending us all to Ortus—Ortus Academy." *No.* Reaching up, my nails sink into the backs of his hands on my face. "Fuck!" He releases me and when he yanks himself back I see that there are streaks of blood on his skin.

Stumbling back, away from him, I bump into something. It slams into the back of my legs and sends me careening to the floor. Ha. Some assassin I am. Pathetic. I don't even bother to get up off the floor. I just lie back and let the tears trail from the corners of my eyes to my temples and into my hair. We're all fucked. Every single one of us. Not just the Darkhavens and me, but the entire race of Mortal Gods.

"What's wrong with her?" Kalix demands, hard anger in his tone.

Warm hands touch my face and hands, feeling for … what? A physical wound to explain this breakdown? Nothing physical could ever have ripped me apart this badly. The moment we'd walked into that damned arena, I'd felt the pressure of Tryphone's abilities. At first, it had hovered at the fringes and then it had burrowed, deeper and deeper still, until it had reached the darkest parts of my mind.

His power had wrapped me in chains, in claw-like tendrils that had refused to let go even when I'd fought against their hold. He'd trapped me in my own fucking head, held me in place just so I could feel him penetrate my innermost core. My lips curve, though, as I remember what I'd done next.

Block after block had been thrown in his way. Barriers made of shadows and webs. Walls of brimstone and darkness. Maeryn—oh, how I wondered if she could help me. She's a healer, after all. Just the thought of her had given me all that I needed though. Healers took what was before them and used it to their advantage. They aren't fighters, so their best offense is defense. Instead of blocking Tryphone, I'd taken down each boundary, each wall. Then I went after him. The link had been opened and just as he was able to get into me, I was able to get into him.

Sickness churns in my gut at the cold recollection. So many years and pain and despair, but above all was the constant desire, the yearning for dominance. For power. He'd deflected, of course, but not before I'd taken the last clue I needed to find the truth.

Dark midnight eyes appear over me. "Kiera?"

Parting my lips, I stare back into Ruen's face even as more wetness runs down my temples and I just breathe. I'm not crying because of the ache still lingering in my head. I don't even know why the tears won't stop. Flashes of Tryphone's memories—dark, horrid places full of the putrid stench of death and decay, pale faces with sunken eyes, glistening blood shining off ribcages that had been ripped open and bared. Skeletal frames leached of all life. Young ones shriveled into ancient husks.

"Kiera, what happened in the arena?" Ruen's calm demeanor helps me to get my racing thoughts under control.

"Tryphone," I say, voice cracking. "He tried ... to get into my mind." I have to command my body to do things that I would normally do on instinct. *Swallow. Salivate. Lick lips. Talk.* "I took his ... instead."

Kalix's grinning features appear just over Ruen's shoulder. "Next time, kill him, little Thief," he says.

I shake my head as I feel the coolness of the floor on my cheek. I can't kill him. Caedmon was wrong. I cannot kill the unkillable, but now ... if I don't ... we're all doomed.

"You took his mind?" Ruen's face is the focus once more. "What did you find? Do you know where the others went? Are they going to Ortus?"

I close my eyes and swallow back the bile that threatens to storm up my throat from the images of those faces. Malachi and Enid. "They're dead," I hear myself say.

"*What?*" Theos. Poor Theos. He recommended Enid for

advancement and though he'd never admit it, if he knew ... that the Gods only choose the most powerful of their offspring, he'd blame himself. Enid was powerful. So was Malachi. Now ... they're dust and bones.

The swallowing is compulsive now, more and more rioting happening in my stomach even with the cool floor pressing into me. Ruen tries to sit me up and I struggle against him. He doesn't stop, and finally, I just let him do what he will—lifting my body and carrying me to a lounge. I'm sapped of strength, all of my energy having been taken up by Tryphone's underhanded attempt at slipping past my defenses.

"The taboo the Gods have broken is ... filicide," I say.

Ruen jerks against me as if his body recoils at the last word. "The Gods are killing their own children?"

An almost hysterical laugh bubbles up out of me. "Killing them? No." I shake my head. If *only* they were merely killing their own children. Try as I might, the memories from Tryphone's mind creep past my defenses. It's like trying to cover my eyes with my hands to hide his thoughts. Useless. They're already inside me.

I reach out and find Ruen's hand with mine. He feels like fire against the ice of my skin, but I clutch on to him anyway. I need the physical touch to ground me, remind me that I'm not in my head anymore and neither is Tryphone. "They're *consuming* them."

The Gods are dying and they're using the Divinity of their children to replenish their life sources. Draining every last drop of power from the strongest and brightest students of the Academies to keep them young and powerful forever. Disgust is a pitted weight in my soul. In a flash, I recall the night that Ruen helped me to leave the Academy to meet up with Regis—the very night that he'd discovered my secret.

The image of the tarp covered wagon ambling out of the gate we'd used to get past the walls and the shriveled branches comes to the forefront of my mind. Staring at Ruen's hand, so strong beneath mine does the trick.

That branch had looked like a hand ... no, it had *been* a hand with leathery gray skin sucked dry of life and blood and muscle, only left to cling to decaying bones.

"They're ... consuming us?" Shock is a rippling wave through the room as Ruen chokes out his question almost as if he can't understand my words.

I bite down hard on my lower lip until all I taste is blood. It fills my mouth with its deep rusty flavor. Old metalwork and ash on my tongue.

"There's more," I say even though I don't want to.

"*Fuck,*" Theos breathes.

I force my eyes to leave the tanned knuckles of Ruen's fist to meet Theos' horrified gaze. Then Kalix's. Then ... back to Ruen. If only my heart were as cold and distant as I once pretended it was. Then maybe the tragedy of my next words wouldn't be such a dagger in my chest.

"Caedmon is dead."

About the Author

Lucinda Dark, also known as USA Today Bestselling Author, Lucy Smoke, for her contemporary novels, has a master's degree in English and is a self-proclaimed creative chihuahua. She enjoys feeding her wanderlust, cover addiction, as well as her face.

When she's not on a never-ending quest to find the perfect milkshake, she lives and works in the southern United States with her beloved fur-baby, Hiro, and her own found family.

Want to be kept up to date? Think about joining the author's group or signing up for their newsletter below.

Facebook Group (Reader Mafia)
Newsletter (www.lucysmoke.com)

ALSO BY LUCINDA DARK

Fantasy Series:

Mortal Gods Series

A Sword of Shadow & Deceit

A Reign of Storm & Madness

The Blood of Gods & Monsters

TBD

Awakened Fates Series (completed)

Crown of Blood and Glass

Dawn of Fate and Valor

Wings of Sunfire and Darkness

Twisted Fae Series (completed)

Court of Crimson

Court of Frost

Court of Midnight

Barbie: The Vampire Hunter Series (completed)

Rest in Pieces

Dead Girl Walking

Ashes to Ashes

Sky Cities Series (Dystopian)

Heart of Tartarus

Shadow of Deception

Sword of Damage

Dogs of War (Coming Soon)

Contemporary Series:

Gods of Hazelwood: Icarus Duet (completed)

Burn With Me

Fall With Me

Sick Boys Series (completed)

Forbidden Deviant Games (prequel)

Pretty Little Savage

Stone Cold Queen

Natural Born Killers

Wicked Dark Heathens

Bloody Cruel Psycho

Bloody Cruel Monster

Vengeful Rotten Casualties

Sinister Arrangment Duet (completed)

Wicked Angel

Cruel Master

Iris Boys Series (completed)

Now or Never

Power & Choice

Leap of Faith

Cross my Heart

Forever & Always

Iris Boys Series Boxset

The *Break* Series (completed)

Break Volume 1

Break Volume 2

Break Series Collection

Contemporary Standalones:

Poisoned Paradise

Expressionate

Wild Hearts

Made in the USA
Middletown, DE
18 July 2025